BAD MEN
WILL COME

BAD MEN WILL COME

A NOVEL OF CAIN CITY

Jonathan Fredrick

MYSTERIOUSPRESS.COM

OPEN ROAD

INTEGRATED MEDIA

NEW YORK

Copyright © 2021 by Jonathan Fredrick

ISBN: 978-1-5040-7559-6

This edition published in 2023 by MysteriousPress.com/Open Road Integrated Media, Inc.
180 Maiden Lane
New York, NY 10038
www.openroadmedia.com

For Chandra, and for Charlie

BAD MEN
WILL COME

CHAPTER ONE
THE BLUES FOR REAL

The house was right where Rosalind said it would be, at the end of this crumbling old road that ran out behind the Kmart. There were four houses in total, prefabricated ruins from the twentieth century that'd been abandoned for decades. At one time, there'd been more than thirty homes on the street. Scant traces of them now—piles of rubble, a couple of cement foundations still intact, the carcass of a pickup truck propped on cinder blocks in the middle of an empty lot, an outdoor basketball hoop tipped on its side. The Kmart was a relic, too, though somehow, miraculously, it was still in operation, its customers shuffling in and out like stragglers from a zombie horde.

Eric Pippen studied the houses, all in a cluster where the road dead-ended. Thick vines snaked up the aluminum siding, weaved in and out of broken windows as if they were attempting to drag the structures down to where the earth could swallow them whole, put the decrepit things out of their misery. The third house in had tree branches jutting obscenely through the shingles of the slumped roof. The grass in the yards was knee-high, as were the weeds that stalked up from the giant cracks in the sidewalks and road. A dense wood pressed against the back of the dwellings like a great wave of foliage, ready to crash and wash it all away.

The structures reminded Pippen of the weary old-timers down at The Terraces who had long ago given up and now did nothing but rock away on their stoops, watching their tiny corner of the world slide by, dispassionately marking the comings and goings in the lives of others, each labored breath a gentle tug toward that final one. Nobody to care when that came.

These houses could blow away in the wind or burn to the ground or get whisked away by magic and no one would even notice, Pippen thought.

The last house standing was situated on a little rise and faced the road head-on. This was the one Rosalind had told him about. It was different from the others, in that it had a door and a few windows that hadn't been broken. Any missing windows were boarded up. A walking path that led to the front steps had been stamped down through the weeds.

Rosalind had sworn that it'd be easy-peasy, no sweat at all, because nobody thinks to fuck with the Stenders, so they were lax when it came to security, but Pippen worried the whole scenario was too good to be true—the wishful thinking of a girl who didn't have much going for her but wishful thoughts, and pipe dreams, and him. He pictured her now, sitting on the futon in the little apartment they were squatting, fingers crossed as she waited for word the job was done.

"How you know all this?" he'd asked her the other night in bed, after she let him do to her all the things she typically refused. She was pressing him about doing the very thing he and his boys were now fixing to do.

"I told you—my daddy was a Stender," Rosalind said.

"That don't make no sense. If your daddy was one of 'em, why you trying to rob they ass?"

Rosalind explained for what seemed like the hundredth time that her father was meaner than a snake, a man who used to knock her mother from one end of the house to the other purely for sport, and when he was shot dead by some private investigator, the Stenders didn't throw two nickels her or her mama's way. Just left them to suffer on their own.

"They wouldn't have cared if we up and died of starvation. Probably preferred it so we wouldn't weigh on their conscience no more."

Her mama didn't starve to death, in the end. She OD'd on fentanyl while driving her Cutlass Supreme. Slow-rolled off the berm of the road and into a pond, whereupon she drowned.

"Still," said Pippen, "there's a reason nobody messes with them Stenders. I ain't looking to catch my death, know what I'm sayin'. Shit, them Klansmen probably tag my black ass as soon as I step out the car in the West End. I ain't 'bout to get foolish."

"Don't you see, Pip? That's what makes this so perfect. They won't never see you coming. This is our chance. Think about all the things we can do with that money. We can get our baby's mouth fixed, finally. And we can get up out this god-awful town. For good. Go anywhere we wanna go. Never look back."

"New Orleans," Pippen murmured. "My Grams would go on and on about how my people came from there. Talked about how we used to be cultured, how our last name meant something down there. I always wanted to go to New Orleans. Hear the blues for real."

Rosalind nestled deeper into the crook of his arm, stroked his bare chest. "Me, you, and Jalen, we can go anywhere you wanna go. New Orleans. Wherever. We can be whoever we want to be. The three of us. That's all that matters."

Pippen shook his head dismissively and asked her what he was supposed to tell Rodney and Kevon.

"Tell them what you got to tell them, Pip. Shit, they gonna be in the money too. They can do whatever they want with it. That'd be enough to convince me."

"You know Nico finds out we did something like this, he'll kill us hisself."

"Now you just talking scared, Pip. Like a coward. That ain't you. How Nico gonna find out anyhow?"

Rosalind explained again how the house she was talking about was used kind of like a weigh station. How money and product got dropped there before being cut up and sent off in all directions. How she knew all this because her daddy used to drag her along with him sometimes when he delivered or picked up packages from there. How she'd seen the stacks of money, big stacks, and bags full of drugs. How last Tuesday when she was up to the Kmart to steal toilet paper from the women's bathroom and purchase a balm for Jalen's cough, some jars of baby food, she saw the same old woman she'd seen in that house when she was little, picking through the aisles. The woman who banded the cash, bagged the drugs. Rosalind had watched the woman walk out of the store and down the old road to that house.

"Yeah, but you talkin' like eight years ago," Pippen said. "How you even know it's still the same thing?"

"It's the same. She was exactly the same as I remembered."

The baby started crying in the next room and Rosalind got up and went to go stick a boob in his mouth. Jalen could breastfeed all right, despite his gnarled lip, and that was a blessing because Pippen saw how stupid-expensive formula was. He lay there and listened to the baby's screams come to an abrupt halt when he latched onto that nipple. Then he heard the soft, greedy sucking sounds and wondered how he'd gotten himself into this mess in the first place, and how he'd ever get out of it, but already he knew there weren't but one answer. Knew before she'd even started arguing him into it.

Pippen felt as though his entire life had been largely predestined. When he took the time to look back on it he saw there wasn't much choice to the path he took, and if he didn't do this thing Rosalind was leaning on him to do, his life would likely trudge, now and forever, on its current course. An everyday hustle just to scrape by, one false move away from becoming one of those panhandling zombies on the corners who they themselves tormented. And, always, one step from prison. He and Rosalind didn't have insurance. Doctor said Jalen's lip was gonna cost him six thousand dollars, minimum, out of pocket. Where else was he going to find that kind of dough? *Heist like this, with this kind of fortuitous timing, presents itself but once in a lifetime.*

Kevon came trotting around the corner of the Kmart toward where they were idling in Rodney's uncle's Lincoln Continental. In exchange for some weed and a full tank of gas, his uncle lent Rodney the car whenever he needed it. Long as there were no dings to the vehicle, he didn't care where Rodney took it, or what he got up to.

Kevon held on to his pants to keep them from falling as he ran. His knock-kneed legs loped sideways with each stride, his big feet flopping like he was wearing clown shoes, and he nearly tripped over himself.

Rodney said, "Look at this goofy mug, man." He lowered the driver's side window. When Kevon reached the car he was ashen-faced and puffing for air.

"You out of shape, man," Rodney told him.

Kevon grabbed the lip of the window and bent forward to catch his wind. He scratched furiously at the back of his neck.

"I think something bit me in those weeds back there."

"What's good?" Pippen asked impatiently. "You see inside?"

Kevon leaned over to see past Rodney and address Pippen. "Most of the windows boarded up, but I got a good look in one of 'em out back. Didn't see nobody in there 'cept that old lady you was talking about."

"What she doing?"

"Couldn't tell. Her back was to me. But she was sitting at this table, kinda hunched over, messin' about with something in front of her."

Pippen stared down the length of the deserted road for a minute, scrutinizing the crumbling house at the end of it. For all his flash and big talk, for all the time he'd spent on street corners moving product, or pulling the occasional stickup, Pippen had never squeezed the trigger on another human being. He realized then and there, as he sat trying to decide if the house on the knoll portended the beginning of a new life or the end of this one, the hard front he put on, the bluster, it was all a charade. Posturing. One big full-of-shit bluff.

From seven years old when he became a lookout for one of Nico's crews, to the first time he made a run, or joined a crew himself; or at sixteen, when he got put in charge of his own corner, people thought he'd been chomping at the bit to get into the game from the start. To be a little gangster. But truth was, he'd been doing the opposite. His efforts had not been made to dive headlong into the game. To the contrary, they'd been made to stay *out front* of the game. To outrun it. And not by a step or two, but by so great a distance that he'd never hear the footsteps creeping on him from behind, never let it draw close enough to look him in the eye, much less catch him. That'd been his plan all along. To outfox the game. To move on it before it moved on him. *How foolish,* he thought now, in this moment of clarity. *Who did you think you were? You can't bluff the game.*

"We doing this or what?" Rodney asked.

Pippen gestured for Kevon to get in the car. "Yeah, let's get this motherfucker."

Kevon hopped in the back seat. Rodney slid the Lincoln into gear and steered them onto the craggy road. Chunks of asphalt crunched beneath the tires as they rolled cautiously toward the dead end. They pulled to a stop in front, left the motor running while Pippen and Rodney eyed the house through the windshield, looking for movement. There was none. Rodney cut the engine.

"Wear these," said Pippen. He reached into a plastic bag on the floor, pulled out knit ski masks and tossed one to both of them. They put them on and fixed them over their faces. Rodney dug a Ruger Security-9 out from the console and Pippen slid a silver .32 ACP with a black grip from his waistband. He looked around to Kevon, who was flipping the safety off on his .22 pistol.

The three of them got out of the car, shut the doors quietly, and walked up the knoll. Nothing moved but the tall grass swaying in the soft wind coming down off the hills that boxed in the city. Maybe Rosalind was right, Pippen thought as they climbed the rot-softened wood stairs to the porch. Maybe this was going to be the easiest score he'd ever have. Maybe his fortunes were about to change.

The knob on the front door turned. He swung it open, and the three of them strolled in as casually as if they were entering their own homes. The old lady was sitting at a long wooden table in the middle of the room, bopping her head along to a song playing in her earbuds. Pippen's grandma used to listen to Tina Turner and he recognized the melody she was humming as "Proud Mary." There was no other furniture in the room, save for the standing lamp with a naked bulb next to the table and an old refrigerator that no longer had doors on it.

Laid out on the table was a scale and what had to be upward of five pounds of unchopped methamphetamine. There was a stack of empty plastic baggies in front of her, along with a small pile that she'd already measured and filled. The old lady didn't startle. She calmly set the baggie she was working on aside, removed the earbuds, placed her hands facedown on the table, and looked up at the intruders.

The way the light bulb shaded the woman's features, Pippen thought she looked like a witch or a demon or something. Her eye sockets and cheeks were hollow caverns. Her waxy, reptilian skin stretched taut over her skull as though somebody was yanking hard on the back of her hair. The hair itself was rust-colored and sprouted out in wild tangles that framed her head like a lion's mane. There was no meat to her. The arms jutting out from her T-shirt looked like the sticks you'd put on a snowman.

With a quick switch of her eyes the woman sized up the three men and snorted in disbelief. Their skin was exposed through the holes of their masks, and she saw that the intruders were Black. The idea of three Black boys strutting in here to rob them tickled her to near laughter, and she would've done just that were it not for the guns in their hands. The old lady sucked air in through the gaps in her teeth and narrowed her eyes. She let out a growl, low and phlegmy. "If you jungle-bunnies know what's good for you, you'd better turn your peckerwood asses around and run on out of here as fast and as far as them skinny little legs can take ya."

For a second nobody did anything. Then Pippen said, "Where's the money?"

The old lady puffed. "If it was up your ass, you'd know."

Rodney stepped forward, leveled his 9-millimeter at her head. "Where's the money?" he repeated.

"Jumbo," the woman called out.

Something creaked in the corner of the room behind them. All eyes followed the sound. A fat man with a long goatee and hairy belly bulging out of the bottom of his shirt sat sleeping in a folding chair. His head nestled back into the crook of the wall. Across his lap was a riot shotgun, the kind without the shoulder stock. The man stirred, but his eyes remained shut. The old lady said again, louder, "Jumbo!"

The fat man twitched and groaned, then sat forward and worked his eyes open. When the room came into focus the first thing he saw was the business end of a shotgun aimed square between his eyes.

"Hey, Jumbo," Rodney said.

Reflexively, Jumbo reached for the weapon that had, moments before, been on his lap. He came up empty, clawing at his own thighs. It was then, in the last second of his life, that he realized he was about to be murdered with his own gun. Rodney pulled the trigger. The boom sent a shockwave through the house. The fat man jacked back. His head assumed the same general position it had been in a few seconds ago, lodged in the crook of the wall, but where there once was a face was now a bloody mess of flesh and membrane that dribbled down over the beard and onto the hairy belly.

Rodney pumped the shotgun, cocked its hammer, and walked over to the old lady. He didn't have to speak a word.

"Beneath them floorboards, that's where it is," she said without hesitation.

"Where?" asked Pippen.

The shotgun blast had rattled the woman's brain and she had her hands cupped over her ears. "Huh?" she shouted. "Whaa?"

"Which floorboards?"

She shook a bony finger in the direction of Jumbo. "Under him you fucking twats!"

Rodney pushed Jumbo and the chair over. Pippen and Kevon each took hold of an ankle and dragged his big body clear of the corner. Rodney tossed the chair aside. There was a sizable knothole in the middle of one of the floorboards. Rodney stuck a finger into the hole and tugged on it. A three-by-two-foot section of floor sprung loose, revealing a cinder-blocked compartment with a heavy-duty black garbage bag inside. Rodney lifted the bag out, felt its considerable weight, and set it on the ground. He peeled open the cinched top, peered in, then held it wide for Pippen and Kevon to have a look. In the bag were stacks of cash, used bills banded together by denomination: tens, fives, twenties, fifties, hundreds. The bag was stuffed full.

Pippen and Kevon squatted down and started sifting through the stacks, trying to estimate the size of the score, and how much each of them stood to make.

Kevon counted out ten bundles of hundreds, saw that there was at least a dozen more, and looked to Pippen in disbelief. "This more than you thought would be here?"

"Yeah. Lot more."

Rodney stood apart from them. He stepped quietly to the old lady. She didn't move a muscle as he approached. She knew, by the way he moved and by the hardness in his eyes, that her mortal time in this realm had come to its end.

"Not in the face," she said, and she twisted around.

CHAPTER TWO
THIS LITTLE BLOOD OF MINE

Ephraim Rivers coughed himself awake. An alarm trilled out from the phone on the bedside table; he didn't know how long it had been going. He'd tried, time and again, to set the sound of the alarm to soft wind chimes, but the thing always defaulted to the factory setting that woke you up like the house was on fire. Ephraim wondered whether or not it was him that had malfunctioned, not the phone. He pawed at the device to turn it off and ended up knocking it to the floor.

"Fuck me," he mumbled. Another day. He threw the covers off, sat up and rubbed the fog out of his eyes. Then he got the phone off the carpet and fiddled with it until the alarm ceased, mercifully. The time on the touch screen read 2:52 p.m. Ephraim stood stiffly and walked into the adjoining bathroom. He stuck his head under the cold water of the faucet for a solid minute before toweling the excess off his hair, brushing his teeth, and getting dressed.

On his way out he peered into the living room where his father was napping on the recliner. A replay from an old

Cincinnati Reds game was playing on the TV, the volume turned too low to make out any of the commentary from the announcers. Just mumbled noise accompanied by the ticking of a grandfather clock. Tony Perez hit a double into the gap, scoring Pete Rose. His father's tubes had fallen out of his nose and hung down over his gaping mouth. Ephraim inserted the prongs into his father's nostrils without waking him, checked the oxygen tank to make sure the levels were right, and he left the house.

Three fifteen on the dot, Ephraim pulled his truck into the parking lot of his son's elementary school and parked. He joined the parents waiting by the side entrance for their kids to come out and soon enough the mass exodus commenced. Though it was only the fourth week of school Ephraim recognized some of the kids from Caleb's class streaming out of the building. He scanned the various faces and looked for Caleb's blue rain jacket amongst the throng. When he spotted Caleb the first thing that went through Ephraim's mind was how much the boy looked nothing like him. His high cheeks, wide bovine eyes, full mouth, all from his mother. Caleb's long and stringy body even favored the men from her side. If it weren't for the bristly brown hair and dueling cowlicks that replicated his own head, Ephraim may have felt compelled to question the parentage.

Ephraim noticed that Caleb wasn't alone. He was being accompanied by his teacher, Mrs. Dinwiddle, a callous-looking woman who nonetheless spoke in a soft and practiced manner. The close-mouthed smile she wore, corners downturned, alerted Ephraim to the fact that something not good had happened during the day, again. He approached son and teacher with a countenance that mimicked hers.

"Hey, bud," he said, putting a little faux pep in his voice. Caleb averted his gaze, took an interest in his toes. He was wringing his hands one over the other incessantly, his latest compulsive tic. His pallor didn't look right either, Ephraim thought. His face looked bloodless.

Mrs. Dinwiddle greeted Ephraim pleasantly and asked if he could come to her classroom in order for her to speak with him for a moment. Ephraim winced and started to make up a reason to put her off, but the teacher preempted him before he was able to string two syllables together. "Shouldn't take but a minute," she said definitively, and made for the doors.

"Okay."

Ephraim followed the teacher into the school and down the hallway. It was lined with artwork from the kids and two large banners. One read, *We Are The Blue Streaks* and was punctuated with a bunch of exclamation marks in the shapes of lightning bolts, while the other banner urged students to *Make Every Day Count* and was peppered with colorful numbers. The inside of the building seemed miniature compared to his memories of the place, but the smell was exactly the same.

Ephraim glanced over at Caleb to try to glean exactly what it was he was walking into, but Caleb scuffled along, eyes fastened to the floor. In the classroom, Mrs. Dinwiddle invited Ephraim to sit at one of the student tables, while she crossed her legs at the ankle and leaned back against her desktop. He squeezed into one of the small chairs. Caleb stayed in the hallway.

"You know, I really think Caleb is a neat kid with a lot going for him," Mrs. Dinwiddle began. "His creativity is one of the highlights of my day, it truly is. For our creative writing lesson, he wrote this story about a duck that keeps waddling into unlucky situations with all these monsters that want to steal his brain. Trolls and dragons and witches, all these fun characters. It was hysterical. And that essay he wrote about his grandmother being his guardian angel was so sweet. He also jots these little things at the bottom of the work he turns in. On one, he wrote 'Classified,' which I thought was funny. Last week he wrote something . . . Oh, what was it?" She squished her face up, trying to elicit the memory. "'This assignment is sponsored by Value City Furniture.' That's what it was. I got such a kick out of that."

"He does come at things from a different angle. Has that got to do with whatever happened today?" asked Ephraim.

"No, it doesn't. I just wanted you to know that there are some positives mixed in with everything that's been going on." Mrs. Dinwiddle pressed a hand over her sternum, took a deep breath and let it out heavily before she resumed speaking. Ephraim thought it a tad dramatic. "We had to clear out the class again, for safety reasons, because Caleb stood up on his table and began shouting . . . unpleasant things."

"What kind of unpleasantness we talking?"

"It was a lot. One of the things he said was that he was going to travel to the North Pole so the Abominable Snowman could murder him. Do you have any insight into why he would say something like that?"

Ephraim ran his hand down over his face and beard. "No. I mean, there's that animated movie about the Abominable Snowman. He's watched that a few times, but I don't know how that leads to"—Ephraim nearly laughed at the thought of it—"to being murdered by it."

"When I tried to coax him down, he started tossing the supplies from the baskets on the table up in the air. Glue and staplers and markers. Then he shouted, 'Nazis kill babies.' He repeated that a few times." She gave Ephraim a look that said an explanation for this one was required.

"I mean, he's interested in World War Two. He knows Nazis were the biggest bad guys ever, that kind of thing." Ephraim shook his head. "I assume you couldn't get him down; that's why you—"

"Cleared the room. Yes. Like I said, I truly think Caleb is a unique child. He has more depth than your average eight-year-old, especially when it comes to the boys."

"Nine," Ephraim said.

"What?"

"Today's his birthday. He's nine now."

"Oh, I didn't know. I wish I would have . . . we would have sung to him."

"Doesn't sound like it would have been the best day for it."

"No. Maybe tomorrow." Mrs. Dinwiddle placed her hand over her sternum again and made a disconcerted face. Ephraim wondered if she didn't need some Alka-Seltzer.

"What did you do? Ephraim asked. "Put him in that room?"

"Our sensory calm room, yes. He spent the rest of the day there. Has his behavior at home gotten worse, or has anything changed? Anything that indicated something like this was coming?"

Ephraim didn't want to be forthcoming about the severity of his situation with Caleb. How the littlest thing could set his son off, cause him to become verbally abusive, or violent, or both. How Caleb would have these rages that devolved into ceaseless crying jags and screams and slamming doors and curses. How the other day he'd called Ephraim a dick-faced bitch, which, even in a moment so fraught with pain, Ephraim found to be quite humorous.

How during these fits, Caleb would dig his fingernails into his arms until he broke the skin. How the sight of his own blood was the only thing that seemed to calm him, snap him back into the world.

Once, when Ephraim was trying to pin Caleb's arms down to keep him from hurting himself, Caleb got a hand free and clawed at his father's face. Caught him clean from his temple down to his jawline, left four gashes deep enough to where blood was dripping. It looked as though Ephraim had been attacked by an animal. So that's what he told people. That he'd happened upon a wolf and her pups in the woods out back of his house. Told 'em it was the damnedest thing, an impromptu fight with a wolf. Made the details outlandish to ward off any deeper inquiry.

Ephraim didn't much feel like sharing these aspects of his son's behavior with anyone, much less Mrs. Dinwiddle, so instead he offered a watered-down version of the truth. Said Caleb had been edgier since he and his mother had gotten into a car accident a little over a year ago.

Mrs. Dinwiddle crossed her arms over her chest in a protective gesture. Her voice turned solemn. "Yes, I did hear about that."

"Yeah, so, Ashlee, his mother, she was having a hard time gettin' along after the wreck. She was having some mental health problems, just some difficulty with the day-to-day parts of life. So she left—ohh, what—'bout eight months ago now."

"I'm very sorry."

Ephraim shirked the sympathy. "Is what it is. I'm not trying to dredge it up. I'm just trying to give you a full picture, I guess. Anyway, we started seeing some things around then, but just at home, really. Acting out, having some issues, that's when the tics and stuff started. Pulling his hair out, that kind of thing. But he seemed to keep it together in public. Till now, at least."

"She's not currently a part of his life."

"Not really." Ephraim glanced at the door and wondered if Caleb could hear everything they were saying out in the hall. Figured he could.

"It's my understanding that Caleb wasn't harmed in the accident."

"No. His mom had a couple broken bones, but he was fine. Walked away without a scratch. They checked him for a concussion and everything." Ephraim sighed, shook his head. "I dunno. He's always been a sweet boy. And sharp, like the stuff you're saying he writes on his homework, always been like that. But lately it's like a Jekyll-and-Hyde-type thing. Like he's always liked school, but now it's everything I can do just to get him to walk into the building."

"That's what has me concerned, Mr. Rivers. Caleb's never gotten into an ounce of trouble before this year." Mrs. Dinwiddle detailed how Caleb's schoolwork had regressed. His writing had gotten messy, almost like when a child first starts to draw letters. Half the time, he flat out refused to do his math lessons. "Have you seen a doctor?" Mrs. Dinwiddle asked. "Or a psychologist?"

"Oh yeah. Yeah. Over the summer. They put him on"— Ephraim looked to the paneled ceiling as though it might assist him in remembering the name of the drug—"Lexapro. Which just made him worse. More erratic. So they weaned him off it and tried the other one—whatzit called?—Zoloft, thinking maybe it was just a bad reaction, but it didn't take either. Same thing. You know how doctors are. Think there's a pill for everything. One of them said they thought it was delayed psychological trauma or something."

Mrs. Dinwiddle's expression turned thoughtful. "You know, we had a student a couple of years ago, a little girl, who had a similar situation. She was completely fine, then all of a sudden her behavior became very volatile. Had to be taken out of school. It took some time, but I'm pretty sure they figured out that she had gotten some virus that caused her brain to swell or some such thing—brought on by strep throat, or something simple like that her body had an adverse reaction to."

"I've never heard of anything like that."

"Nor had I before then, but you know, there are all kinds of things out there we don't know about, aren't there?"

"Is that little girl okay? Is she back in school now?"

"She is. Though not here at Jarvis Hayes. I don't think her parents wanted her to carry the stigma of being the girl who went crazy."

Ephraim nodded. "I mean, I guess I can call his doctor. I'm open to anything. That'd be a thing to get checked out anyway."

"I think that would be a prudent thing to do, Mr. Rivers. Just to rule out any underlying illness that could be causing the behavioral swings." Mrs. Dinwiddle's face pinched in consternation. "Because as it stands, we've come to an impasse with Caleb. If things remain as they have, we're going to have to do something different."

Ephraim felt suddenly uncomfortable in the small chair, felt his butt going numb, and shifted his weight. "Do what different?"

"In a situation like this, we have to think about what's best for the whole classroom. And what's best for Caleb as well. He can't spend the whole school year in the sensory calm room. So if things don't take a turn for the better soon, we're really not going to have much of a choice but to look for alternate methods of education for him."

Now we're getting to it, Ephraim thought. *Here's where she was steering me all along. To how they are gonna pass him off.* "Alternate?" he said politely. "What's that mean?"

The small man, who by nature was restless and jittery, stood stock-still in the middle of the room. He surveyed its contents: a long wooden table; the scale atop it, along with the tool used to crush the drugs; two metal chairs, one of which was turned over; a doorless refrigerator; a tall lamp in the corner; a couple of spent shotgun shells; and two murdered Stenders. One of the dead, Jumbo Harless, was sprawled out on the floor, meaty face shot to bits. His fat body had smooshed under its own weight and spread out beneath him like a puddle. The other dead, Maid Marion, was still seated in her chair, head pitched forward between her legs, back half of her skull caved in, her scrawny arms suspended at her sides. Shards of bone and flesh and blood clung to her stringy hair. There was no meth on the table, or anywhere else it may have been stashed if they'd found themselves in a pinch. Nor was the money in the compartment beneath the floorboards.

Despite the death of his confederates, Momo Morrison couldn't help but feel a certain elation at the prospect of hunting down whoever dared to cross the Stenders in such brazen fashion. It'd been a while since anything had come along to quicken his heart rate, but he could feel the organ thumping hard against his rib cage now, the violence coursing through his bloodstream. His mouth drew back into a deranged grin, revealing a set of gray teeth that resembled sawblades. When he was a kid people teased that he had a mouthful of canines, like a dog. Or gator teeth. They didn't say that shit now that he was an adult, not even behind his back.

When Momo's two henchmen came in from outside, they couldn't tell if he was in high spirits or verging on furious. So they stood to either side of him, each a head or more taller than he, and waited in deference for their boss to speak.

"What's what?" Momo asked evenly.

The older and burlier of the two lackeys was called Buddy The Face. He got that name because in his day he was known to be something of a lady-killer. This was before he accidentally lit his hair full of pomade aflame and sizzled his skull into a melt of scars and craters. Buddy also wore a piratical eyepatch over his left socket, a permanent reminder of the one and only time he'd been bettered in a fight. The aggregate of those events rendered the once-sincere nickname cruelly ironic.

Buddy The Face said, "Somebody tramped through the weeds out back and peeped in through that window there." He pointed to the one he meant.

"One person?" Momo tocked his head back and forth, weighing the likelihood. "You think a single person pulled this heist?"

"Couldn't say for certain." Buddy The Face picked up one of the spent shells, held it up. "It's likely they turned Jumbo's very own shotgun on him. Now, I don't put no feat of stupidity past Jumbo, but all the same, I'd venture it'd be a hard thing for someone to pull off all by their lonesome."

Verbals, the younger and taller of the two men, moved over to where Jumbo lay on the floorboards. He stopped short of the ring of blood that had pooled around Jumbo's head, and squatted down to examine the fat man. Flecks of flesh and brain matter floated throughout the fluid. "Jesus," Verbals said in a hoarse whisper. He had a crushed voice box, so everything he muttered came out froggy. "Whoever done it maimed Jumbo good. Tore his face clean off."

Momo said, "Fuck Jumbo. Big dummy. Surprised he stayed alive this long. You know what that fat fucker said to me one time when we was kids?" Momo paused in case anybody wished to prompt him with a *What, Momo?* Neither of them did, so he went on. "We was about twelve, thirteen at the time, kicking rocks or something. I don't know what the fuck we was doing. Middle of whatever it was, Jumbo eyes me up and down, and for no reason at all proceeds to tellin' me that I have a face that only two cousins could have made. You believe that?"

The two henchmen again stayed mum, knowing better than to involve themselves unnecessarily in any of Momo's bombast. Momo kept a running tally in his mind of every insult, every slight he'd ever felt, both real and perceived, and Buddy The Face and Verbals had no doubt that each and every party responsible would one chosen day receive a reprisal tenfold. Hell, they'd been the ones to dole out half of these punishments. Which is all to say, they didn't much care to be added to the dubious list.

"Now, I got some pretty good-looking cousins," Momo continued. "Y'all know Clover Holley, right? So at first, I took it as a compliment. Thought, shit, I'd be so lucky to look like a couple of my cousins. But then Jumbo made clear that's not how he meant it. Not in the least. Made me feel downright dumb. So I kicked his fuckin' fat teeth down his fuckin' fat throat." Momo started laughing. "Took him three shits to get all those teeth out, swear to God. You ever seen teeth in shit? Looks like corn kernels do when they come out. Jumbo got them nice falsies out of the deal, but he always talked with that lisp after that; had that little whistle on his S's. They never did figure how to get that bridge right." Again, Buddy The Face and Verbals kept quiet. "Verbals, peel back his lips, see if he still has them pearly whites in his head."

"Ain't no lips to pull back, Momo."

"Just as well."

Verbals next went over to Maid Marion, got on a knee and bent sideways to get a look at her face beneath the canopy of blood-crusted hair. The way her head hung it had already purpled and started to bloat. Blood and foam oozed from her lips.

"Goddamn," Verbals said. "Maid Marion. How old was she anyhow?"

"Seventy-some, had to be," Buddy The Face said. "I remember her from when I was a kid. Thought she was old as hell then. Gotta give that to her. She put together a good long run."

"This ain't no way for her to go out."

"Yep," Momo agreed. "If we was all made of her stuff we'd have us a goddamned kingdom."

"We'll be needing to get word to their people right quick," Buddy said. "And your uncle."

Momo sighed. "I reckon so. We'll find them a nice spot to lay out in The Trees. Give 'em a proper sendoff."

"Even Jumbo?"

"Even Jumbo, the dummy."

Verbals was still on his haunches, gazing fixedly upon Maid Marion. "Think of all the things she's seen and done." With the backs of his fingers, he gently brushed her swollen cheek. "Who would do such a thing?" he muttered.

"Well." Momo walked over to the window the voyeur had peered through and looked to the bare curtain rod above. "Give me a boost, will ya Buddy, and we'll just find out."

Buddy The Face came over and squatted and cupped his hands. Momo stepped into them and Buddy hoisted him up. Momo braced against the wall and unscrewed the finial on the end of the rod. He hopped down and examined the hidden camera inside the finial, pleased to see it was still recording.

CHAPTER THREE
THE CUCKOO KID

In the truck Ephraim told Caleb to strap his seat belt on, which got them off on the wrong foot from the jump.

"Like I don't know to buckle my seat belt," Caleb snapped. "Like I'm stupid and gonna forget to do it. That of *all* things is something you never need to remind me to do."

"How come you ain't done it then?"

"Can you just shut up?"

Ephraim reached over and grabbed Caleb's shirt by the collar, balled it in his fist. "Don't talk to me like that, son."

"Let go of me." Caleb's eyes got wide and his neck jutted forward to where the veins were popping out and his face started shaking. "Let go of me," he screamed. "Let go of me or I'll jump out of this car."

Ephraim released his shirt. "Buckle, now."

"Fine. Don't talk to me for the rest of the day."

"Gladly."

"I said don't talk to me."

Ephraim gripped the wheel tightly and didn't respond. For his part, Caleb made a frustrated noise that split the difference between a sob and a snarl, but then he acquiesced, pulled the belt across and clicked it in. The two of them stayed silent the rest of the drive to the diner. It was on the edge of town, just off Interstate 64. The bell on the door jingled when they entered. Lucia, the waitress, looked up from the table she was serving and gave them a beaming smile and the place's customary "Welcome to Harold's" greeting.

They sat in their usual booth by the window. Ephraim looked out at the cars and trucks rumbling by on the two-lane highway and at the hills beyond where the colors were changing in the leaves of the trees. Caleb stared dead-eyed at the menu, even though he ordered the same food every time they came there. Ephraim broke the wordless standoff.

"Listen, you're not in trouble—"

"I don't want to talk about it."

"Let me finish."

Caleb raised his voice. "I said I don't want to talk about it."

"Fine, you don't have to talk about nothing, but you're gonna damn well listen."

"Why would I ever listen to you? You don't know anything."

"You're making it real hard to be nice to you right now."

"*You* be nice and I'll be nice. You're the one being rude."

Ephraim gnashed his teeth together to keep from screaming, and balled his fists beneath the table to keep from reaching across the booth and grabbing his kid's head and shaking it until something like common sense magically appeared in there, till Caleb could be reasoned with like a normal human being. If, in fact, he would ever be normal again. Could ever be reasoned with.

Ephraim waited a full minute for the tension in his body to relax, for him to no longer feel like punching a wall. He spoke to his son in a calm and deliberate manner. "Please, Caleb. It's important. I just need to talk to you for two minutes about school. Then we can be done. We can talk about anything else, or we can sit here like two doorknobs and not talk to each other for the rest of the day, okay?"

"I don't want to talk to you for the rest of my life."

"Fine, we don't have to talk for the rest of our lives."

Caleb warned him. "If you say one word about school, I swear to God I'll scream."

"Caleb—"

"I'll scream." Caleb bobbled his head back and forth maniacally. "Do you want me to scream? Cuz it'll be your fault for making me do it."

Ephraim leaned forward. "You scream, son, and I'll drag you out of here by the scruff of your neck in front of all these people. I don't give a shit. You wanna try me? Try me."

There weren't but six other patrons in the diner, but the idea of being embarrassed in front of strangers was still enough to quell Caleb for the time being. "Fine. You have one minute. That's all you get."

"I'm sorry—"

"You are sorry."

"I'm trying to apologize here. Can you let me do that at least? I'm sorry I cursed at you."

"Why? It's not the first time."

"No, it's not. But we shouldn't speak like that to anyone, especially the people we love, and I'm sorry."

"I don't love you."

"Well, you don't have to if you don't want. I still love you."

"You've got like thirty seconds left."

Keep cool, Ephraim told himself. *Don't let the goddamned kid bait you into murdering him in a diner.* He worked to keep his tone as flat and neutral as possible. "I know you heard everything your teacher said to me in that classroom, so you know how serious this has gotten. She's not playing, Caleb. I know you're having a hard time right now. I get that."

"No, you don't."

"I get it as much as I can, okay? Look here, if you don't keep it together, they're gonna pull you out of Mrs. Din-widdle's and put you in a special class—"

"What kind of special class?"

"I don't know, but generally, any class with the word *special* attached to it ain't great. They're gonna put you in something like that, or they're gonna get you an aide to go around everywhere with you looking over your shoulder. Or they may just kick you out and make us do homeschool. Then I'd have to hire a teacher to come to the house. And I'm telling you right now, I can't afford to hire no teacher. So I don't care what you have to do. Please, I'm begging you, please, just try to keep it together for the six hours you're in school every day. Just white-knuckle it if you have to. Do your work as best you can. After that, you can come home and do whatever. Go out in the woods and scream or punch a tree or do whatever you need to do. Just please, I'm asking you to try your best to keep it together from 8:30 a.m. until 3:20."

"I already do that," Caleb protested. "Do you think I want to act this way? Do you think I want to be the cuckoo kid?"

"No. Who would?"

"Exactly. That's what I'm telling you. I can't help it. It just happens."

"So you'll try?"

"Time's up."

"Just tell me you'll try."

"Whatever, I'll try. Time's up."

"Okay." Ephraim raised his palms in surrender and leaned back in his seat. "Let's have a good meal, okay? Here comes Lucia."

The cherry-cheeked waitress approached their booth with her pencil poised over her notepad. The diner's female employees were made to wear old-timey uniforms that consisted of a short-sleeved white blouse and a brown and yellow striped apron/skirt combo. They also wore cheap paper hats with the Harold's logo on it. Lucia wore her hair with a twisted braid up front, while the rest was pulled back into a mess of curls that kept the thin cap perched just so atop her head.

"Well, I'll be," Lucia exclaimed, smiling brightly. "If it ain't the most handsome young man in all of Cain City come right here to my booth just to make my day."

When Caleb didn't respond, Ephraim said, "I don't think she's talking to me, pal."

"I know," Caleb said. "You're not young or handsome."

"Hey, thirty-two ain't that long in the tooth. Some might even say I'm in the middle of my prime. Can you back me up on that please, Lucia?"

Lucia guffawed. "Um, no. I want to know who this *some* is, and what are you paying them?"

"Okay, so you two are a team now. Noted."

"How you doing today, Caleb?" Lucia asked.

"Fine."

"Just fine?"

"Good."

"You have a good day at school?"

"Yeah."

"What can we get for you today? Denver omelet?"

Caleb shook his head sternly.

"Biscuits and gravy?"

"Nuh-uh."

"Corned beef and hash?"

"No. You know what I get."

"I do?" Lucia tapped the pencil against her chin thoughtfully. Then she feigned as though it came to her all at once. "Patty melt, no onions, double order of hash browns covered in cheese. Oh, and extra pickles."

"No!" Caleb giggled. "No pickles."

"Are you remembering right? I'm sure you always get lots of pickles."

"Pickles are gross."

Lucia pretended to scribble on her pad. "Jarfuls of pickles."

"Yuck."

"Okay then, if you insist, I'll hold the pickles. Your loss. Apple juice?"

"Apple juice."

"What about you, old-timer, same thing?"

"Correct me if I'm wrong," Ephraim said, "but aren't you older than me by a year or three?"

"You wanna eat, you better hush your mouth."

Ephraim ordered his usual and passed her the menu. Lucia handed Caleb a package of crayons from a pocket in her apron so that he could draw on the paper mat, then went to put in the order with Harold, the proprietor and cook. Ephraim watched her go. He didn't want Caleb to catch him gawking at Lucia like a creeper, but she had about seven handfuls of ass that bounced like a drumbeat with every step, and he couldn't help himself. In fact, most of his time in the diner was spent resisting the urge to stare at her. But the more he tried to fight it, the more compelled he felt to steal one glance, then two, three—of her hooded brown eyes, the full curve of her lips, the dimple in her chin, the freckles dotting her cheeks, the smooth hue of her butterscotch skin, the thick contours of her legs, bare from the hemline of the apron on down. The sense memories these images conjured were intoxicants of smells and tastes and touch that wended beyond language.

The woman was plump in all the right places and, some might say, a few of the wrong ones. But Ephraim wasn't to be counted among those people. For him, looking at Lucia was comparable to gazing into a bright light; upon closing your eyes, its image scorched into the back of your eyelids like an incandescent photo negative. Ephraim didn't know if it was Lucia that made the world plain, or if it was the plain world that accentuated her brilliance. The answer didn't matter. Either way, she had occupied a space in his mind and his body that had long been vacant. He couldn't believe his luck, if he was being honest. She was above his station. Above most anybody's station. Yet some man had decided to cheat on her, and here she was, Ephraim thought, this enchanted being working in a shitty highway diner in Cain City of all places, disguised as a waitress.

Lucia slid their order across the window and crossed the restaurant to wait on another table that'd just come in. Ephraim told Caleb he'd be right back and got up like he was going to the bathroom.

He timed it to where he walked behind her just as she was wrapping up the drink orders and telling the table to take their time figuring out what they wanted to eat. He gently squeezed her elbow and nudged her toward the corridor that led to the bathrooms.

"Can I speak with you for a second?" he whispered.

Under her breath she protested, "Ephraim, I'm working," but she allowed herself to be guided into the shadows of the corridor where none of the patrons could see them. She stood with her back pressed against the cold tiles. He put his hand against the wall by her head and leaned in toward her.

"How come you ain't been returning my calls?" he asked, keeping his voice low.

"Because I'm not gonna be that kind of girl."

"What kind of girl?"

"You know what kind of girl."

"How long you gonna make me do this dog and pony show?" he asked.

She cocked an eyebrow as if to say *Long as I want*. Then she peered over his arm-bar to make sure no one was watching them. "I gotta get back to work. Harold catches me back here talking to you again he'll have a conniption."

"Answer me, then."

"Let me go." She whacked his arm with her notepad. "You trying to get me fired?"

"How they gonna fire you? You told me yourself Harold's been trying to find a new waitress for a month, cain't find nobody worth a damn."

"What a way to gain job security." Lucia looked at Ephraim, shook her head, and huffed. "Look, you wanna string somebody along, why don't you throw some of that two-dollar charm at one of those women work out there with you? I'm sure they'd be happy to oblige."

Ephraim cracked a grin. "You know them women out there're rougher than cobs. Gives me the willies just thinking about it. 'Sides"—he hooked a finger inside her apron and tugged her close—"you're the only woman I want."

"It don't take a rocket scientist to know what you want. You ain't got no game."

34

"You just told me I had two bucks' worth."

"Pshh. In change, maybe."

Ephraim leaned in for a kiss, but Lucia turned her head. The poof of her ponytail smacked his face and he caught a whiff of whatever product she put in there to make it shiny. A sharp, chemical smell with an overlay of vanilla. He tried to veil the irritation rising within him.

"What do you think I come in here five times a week for? Harold's five-star cooking?"

"'Cause Caleb loves eating here. That's what you told me."

"I know, but—that's not— Jesus, this is not my day." Ephraim filled his cheeks with air and blew out a sigh of discontent. "You had a good time the other night, right?"

Lucia's face ruckled. "What good time?" She moved to duck under his arm, but he blocked her and she stood back up, eyelids fluttering with anger. "Will you let me go, please? My table needs sodas."

"They can wait."

"They've been waiting."

"Do me a favor?"

"A favor? Look at this boy asking for a favor. I can't wait to hear this. Go on."

"Come out to the plant again tonight," said Ephraim.

"Was it a figment of my imagination, or did we just have a whole conversation about how that's not gonna happen?"

"I can't stop thinking about you. I need to see you before this weekend. I crave you."

Lucia put her fist to her mouth to stifle a laugh. "You crave me?"

"I'm obsessed with you."

"Oh, you're doublin' down?"

Ephraim tilted his head down, brushed his lips against hers. She allowed it, and let him linger for a moment before placing her hands solidly on his chest and pushing him back to arm's length and holding him there.

"Come out tonight," Ephraim said. "Please."

"I'm supposed to watch my nephew."

Ephraim inched toward her. "Get out of it."

Lucia *tsk*ed. "Like it's that easy."

He moved to kiss her again. This time she didn't turn away. He pecked her lips gently, hesitantly, and when she didn't resist he sank his tongue into her mouth. She tasted like the peppermints they gave away at the register, the ones that went chalky on your tongue. Pulling back, he said, "Say you'll come."

"Maybe."

He reached down to the hemline of her skirt and ran the backs of his fingers along the inside of her thigh, where there was a mist of sweat from where she'd been on her feet all day, moving, working.

"Come. Please . . . Please . . ." Between the *pleases*, Ephraim peppered her with kisses on the nape of her neck, on her freckles, her earlobe, beneath her jaw. "Please."

Lucia palmed his face and shoved it away. "I said maybe."

"Full of maybes. I'll take it."

"I don't see as you having much choice in the matter."

"Hey, can you do me one more favor?"

"Good lord."

"Will you wear your uniform when you come?"

From around the corner Harold bellowed for all the diner to hear, "Luciaaa! Order's up."

"Ope, gotta go." She pushed Ephraim's arm aside and stepped out from him.

He grabbed her wrist to stop her leaving. "One last thing."

"Let go of me. What?"

"It's Caleb's birthday. Can you bring him a piece of pie or something after dinner, maybe throw a candle on there?"

"His birthday? Why didn't you tell me?"

"He's been having a rough go. I didn't know if he'd even want to celebrate it."

"Jesus." Lucia smacked her lips. "Of course he would. He's a kid. I'll bring him something. What kind of pie's he like?"

CHAPTER FOUR
KENTUCKY TILT

The patty melt and hash browns in his stomach put some life back in Caleb's eyes and infused some color into his cheeks. Ephraim sopped the last bite of his pancakes in some syrup and forked it into his mouth.

"Feel better?" Ephraim asked. This meal had become the last thing Caleb could be counted on to eat. The other staples of his diet—peanut butter sandwiches, pancakes, spaghetti, macaroni and cheese—he'd dropped them all, one after the other, refused to touch them ever again.

"Yeah, I guess," Caleb replied.

"Maybe you just needed food."

"Yeah, maybe."

"Did you eat your lunch at school?"

"Some of it."

"Why not all of it?"

"Didn't have time. Lunch ends too fast."

"We talked about this, bud. You gotta eat your lunch to get you through the day. What'd you do, just eat the Z-bar?"

Caleb huffed out some air. "I guess. Can we go home now?"

"Hold your horses." Ephraim reached into the pocket of his coat and pulled out a small wrapped gift. He forced a smile and handed it across the table. "You didn't think I forgot that it was your birthday, did you?"

"Kind of."

"Glad you think so highly of me, bud. Open it."

Caleb ripped off the paper. The gift was a video game called *Call To War*. Ephraim had purchased it from Walmart that morning when he'd gotten off work. Caleb scrutinized both the front and back of the cover for a while without saying anything.

"That's the game you were talkin' about wanting, right?" Ephraim asked.

"Yeah, it's just—this is *Call To War 5*, and the new one is *Call To War 7*."

"Oh, I didn't know. That's the only one I saw on the shelf there, so I thought it was the newest version."

"It's probably sold out. It's okay."

"We can take it back, buddy. It's no big deal."

"No." Caleb shook his head vehemently. "It's okay. I promise. I'll play it. Thank you."

"You're welcome. If you change your mind, let me know and we'll exchange it. It won't hurt my feelings, I promise."

"I don't want to."

"Okay."

Lucia came out from the kitchen with two other waitresses in tow and a piece of coconut cream pie topped with a tiny wax candle. The trio sang "Happy Birthday" to Caleb, who flushed with happiness at the gesture.

"Lucia is nice," he said on the ride home. "I like her."

"Yeah, that was sweet, huh?"

"Do you like her?"

"Yeah, she's a nice lady."

Caleb laid his head back against the headrest and squinted to make his eyes go out of focus and he gazed out his window at the blur of trees on the hillsides and beyond them the stars that dappled the evening sky.

"I mean, it's okay if you like, *like her*, like her," Caleb said. "I don't expect you to wait for Mom to come back or anything."

Ephraim glanced over, noticed that Caleb's hands were calm in his lap. "Well, thanks for your permission."

"So you do?"

"I like her a little."

Caleb smiled at the trees. "I knew it. I knew you weren't in that bathroom the whole time."

"It ain't nothing yet, really. I just enjoy talking to her."

Caleb thought about that for a second. "Dad?"

"Yeah."

"Is it unnatural?"

"Is what unnatural?"

"You know, that you're white and she's not."

"Unnatural?" Ephraim snorted. "Who the hell told you that?"

"I dunno. Kids in school say things sometimes."

"Like what?"

Caleb shrugged. "I dunno. Stuff about other people."

"Jesus Christ, in third grade?"

"Yeah, and other grades too."

Ephraim shook his head, annoyed. "Listen, you're gonna hear plenty of that kind of garbage. 'Specially around here. Your classmates probably heard it from their stupid parents, who probably grew up hearing that same stuff and never learnt no better. Or if they did know better at some point, they've just gone along with it for so long, one day they start believing it, too, like osmosis. Then it's hard for them to turn it around because to do that, they'd have to admit that they've been wrong their whole lives, and their parents were wrong. And their grandparents were wrong. And that's hard to do. That make sense?"

"What's osmosis?"

"Like it just seeps into people without them knowing it. People that say crap like that, they just need to prop themselves up, feel like they're better than somebody else. But you and me, we know better, and we're not gonna pay talk like that any mind. Got it? People are people. Good or bad's got nothing to do with what people look like. It's about how they show themselves."

Caleb nodded. "I didn't mean to make you mad."

"I'm not mad. But so we're clear, I ever hear anything ignorant like that come out of your mouth hole, I'll beat the living snot out of you myself. We clear?"

"Crystal."

They drove a little longer before Ephraim asked, "Is that what you're doing? Waiting for Mom to come home?"

"I dunno. Not anymore, I guess. Not if you aren't. You think she remembers today's my birthday?"

"Of course she does. How could she forget? Day you were born was the greatest day of our lives."

"Even Mom's?"

"Especially Mom's. Plus, you know what you did? Soon as the doctor smacked your bottom and got you crying, he laid you there on your mom's chest. She was overcome with tears, you know, happy tears."

"And I pooped on her."

"That you did. Big old dookie right there on her chest. She didn't even care, probably would have left it on there if the nurses didn't clean her off. Couldn't forget a thing like that even if you tried."

"I've heard that story a thousand times."

"Well, a good poop story always holds up on repeat telling."

"You think she'll call me at least?" Caleb asked.

"I know she will. Looky here." Ephraim pointed to something dark and coiled in the middle of the road in front of them. The serpent's eyes shone brightly in the glare of the Ranger's headlamps.

Caleb sat forward. "That a snake?" he asked.

"Yeah." Ephraim turned the wheel slightly so that the truck rolled directly over the snake without hitting it. Caleb twisted to look out the back window and watched the snake uncoil and slide across the road.

"What kind was it?"

"Don't know. Rattler probably. Didn't look too friendly."

Their family home was in an unincorporated town called Buffalo in the next county over from Cain. It was situated on a hillside off State Route 75. One main road ran up the high slope and two little lanes shot off from that. Each of the lanes held three houses, split-level jobs that were built into the hill. The grade was so steep, it looked like there was nothing preventing the dwellings from toppling one right over the other on down the hill and onto the road, but in fifty years of weather not one of them had budged. Theirs was the last house on the higher lane, called Marvel Heights. So they had a couple of neighbors beside and below them, and wilderness the rest of the way around.

Darrell Rivers was gently rocking back and forth on the porch swing when Ephraim turned onto Marvel Heights, pulled the Ranger up the gravel driveway and under the carport, and cut the ignition. Darrell stood feebly with the aid of his walker, and when Caleb climbed out of the truck he began singing "Happy Birthday." Despite the lung disease, the old man had maintained a deep, resonant voice he'd honed over decades of singing in the church choir, and he liked to put it to good use when given the opportunity.

Ephraim and Caleb stepped onto the porch and waited for Darrell to finish the song. "Thanks, Grandpa," Caleb said when it was over.

"You're welcome, young man," Darrell wheezed. The singing had taken the air out of him. "How was your day today?"

"Fine."

"Yeah? You get into any trouble?"

"Not too bad."

Darrell looked to Ephraim, who gave a shrug and grimace meant to convey that wasn't exactly the truth. Darrell patted Caleb's shoulder.

"Well, why don't we go inside? Might just be a present in there waiting for you."

Caleb leapt into the air like he'd been zapped with a cattle prod. "What is it?! What is it?! What is it?!"

"Calm down. Go on and take a look."

Caleb flung open the screen door and bounded into the house. Ephraim caught the door before it slapped shut and held it for his father to shuffle through.

"What'd he do now?" Darrell asked.

"More crazy shit. I'll tell you about it later."

"Nothing a good ass-whoopin' wouldn't take care of."

"Not helpful, Dad."

"I'm just sayin'."

"What you're saying makes things worse. You've seen for yourself."

"You turned out all right."

"So you say. You take your meds today?"

Darrell groaned. "Why is that the goddamn first thing you always ask me?"

"I don't know, Dad, maybe 'cause I don't want to deal with you dying today."

"You want to know what's killing me, it's those pills."

"You take them or not? Yes or no?"

"Yes, I took them, goddammit. I gotta take a pill for everything. Take a pill for my heart, pill for my blood, pill for my bones, pill for my lungs, pill for my dick. I don't see none of 'em doing nothing."

"Now you're exaggerating. You don't take a pill for your dick."

"If I had the chance to use it, you better believe I'd have to take a goddamned pill for it," crabbed Darrell. "Only reason I take any of 'em is 'cause I wouldn't hear the end of it from you."

"Well, you're welcome for me keeping you alive." A cry of joy emanated from the interior of the house. Ephraim cast a leery eye on his father. "What'd you get him?"

"You'll see for your own damn self in about twenty seconds, won't you?"

Darrell halted the walker, squeezed a fist against his sternum and cleared his throat. This turned into a coughing fit. You could hear the gunk rattling around in his chest, some of which he regurgitated into his mouth. He made a noise of complaint and hocked the bile over the railing of the porch, wiped his mouth on the back of his wrist.

"You all right?"

"Never get old," Darrell groused.

"I'll take it into consideration. You know, you can still make your way around a note, Pop. Despite it all."

Darrell scoffed. "Despite it all? Still sing a million times better than you, even on half a lung." He crept forward on his walker. "You remember that song you sang in church when you were ten?"

"I wasn't ten. I was thirteen. Right when the voice starts crackin'."

"Thirteen? Lord have mercy, who thought that was a good idea?"

"You, if I recall."

"Not me. Must have been your mother. I looked out over that congregation, people was plugging their ears with their fingers, tucking their heads down like turtles, cringing like this." He squished his features together to demonstrate the face he meant to convey.

"Yep, I was there," said Ephraim.

"Sounded like a calf in distress."

"That's what I was going for. So I'd never have to do it again."

Darrell laughed, causing him to choke and start coughing again, though this time less violently. Once recovered, he said, "Well, you succeeded. Got your musical abilities from your mother, God rest her eternal soul. Angel in every other way, but a voice to make the birds fly south."

Ephraim noted how his dad's recollection of his mother grew more revisionist with each passing year. Never in his whole life had he heard him refer to her as an angel. He didn't remark on it now. No point. Maggie Rae Rivers had been a wonderful mother to him, the gentlest soul he'd ever known, the safest arms he'd ever been wrapped in. But the overwhelming memory he had of his parents from childhood was of them screaming at each other all hours of the night, all manner of nasty words he'd come to reuse in his own marriage.

As a boy he'd ask his mother why he never got any brothers or sisters to play with. She'd say simply, "It just never worked out that way." But now when he thought on it, Ephraim reckoned she didn't want to anchor herself to his father any more than she already had. The more children, the harder it would be to cut bait and run. But she never did leave, never made a break, as Ashlee had. No, his mother stayed to the end. Diagnosed with pancreatic cancer and three weeks later gone.

They entered the house to find Caleb at the window in the living room, peering through a telescope into the evening sky. Darrell had already affixed it on the Big Dipper.

"Where'd you get that from?" Ephraim asked his father.

"Still have some tricks up my sleeve. Had it delivered from the Amazon."

"The jungle?"

"Smartass. Off the computer."

"With whose money?"

"Mine, tightwad," Darrell said, perturbed. Then, off a skeptical look from Ephraim, he qualified his answer. "Don't worry, it wasn't that much. We'll survive the next recession."

Caleb was giddy about the gift. He beckoned them to come over for a look at the constellations, but Ephraim said to give him a minute—he had to make a phone call—and he went down the hall to his bedroom and shut the door. He took his phone from his pocket and sat on the edge of the bed.

Ashlee was the first name in his contacts, but he had multiple numbers from all the different phones she'd had in the past year. He scrolled down to the last number she'd supplied him with and tapped it. He had no idea if it would work or not, or if she'd pick up the phone if it did, but the line connected and started ringing, so that was a good sign. It trilled five, six times. In his mind, he started to formulate the message he would leave, the neutral tone he'd try to strike, but at the eighth ring she went ahead and answered.

"Hello, Ephraim," she said. Her voice was soft and resigned, half-dazed like maybe she was on something. The familiar Kentucky tilt made his chest tighten. The vestiges of a whole life together contained in the way she spoke two words.

"Hey, Ash. How you doing? You still down there in Florida?"

"Why?"

"What do you mean, why? 'Cause last time I talked to you, that's where you were. In Florida. Don't freak out, I'm not right outside your door or nothing."

"Yeah, I'm still in Florida. I was beginning to think I was never going to hear from you again."

"I think you got that backwards, sweetheart—"

"Don't call me that."

"—'cause I'm right here where I've always been, and I've still got the same number. Both cell phone and landline. Been the same for about a decade now."

"Okay, you can stop. You've made your point."

Ephraim shook his head in frustration. There was an interval of silence. He pictured her on the other end of that line, the sullen expression. There had always been something delicate about her face, brittle, as though tapping it in the right spot would make the whole thing go to pieces.

"You back with that guy?" he asked.

"What? No. Why are you asking me that?"

"Just wonderin', you know. You haven't withdrawn any money lately."

"If you don't want me to have access to that account, cut me off then."

"Did I say anything about that? I don't want you to be fucking destitute, Ashlee."

"I'm not destitute."

"I didn't say that you were. I said I don't want you to be."

"Not like you put much in there. And I'm not back with Jamie. If you must know, I got a job."

"Doing what?"

"You don't have to sound so shocked. Cleaning office buildings overnight. Now I know what it's like to be a stinkin' vampire like you."

"Gets old fast, don't it?"

"It ain't that bad. Solitary, so it suits me. I'm the only white woman works for 'em. All the Latinas think I'm loco or something."

"Huh."

"They don't know the half of it, do they?"

"I'm not taking that bait."

Ashlee sighed wearily. "Ephraim, you call me for a reason?"

"You think to ask us how we're doing, or does that not even cross your mind anymore?" The line went silent. "You still there?"

"Do you want me to hang up?"

"No, I'm sorry. Don't hang up. That's not why I called."

"Good, 'cause I'm not in the mood for a scolding."

"You know what day it is?"

"Wednesday," she ventured.

"It's Caleb's birthday, Ash."

"Oh."

"Yeah. Listen, he was asking about you. I think it'd really make his day if you gave him a call, you know, wished him happy birthday, talked to him for a little bit." She didn't say anything, but her breathing became audible over the line. Thick breaths in and out, then a loud bang like the phone dropping, and then nothing, empty air. "Ash? Ash, you there?"

"I'm here," she said, her voice sedate. "What am I supposed to say?"

"I don't know. You can muster up a little interest, can't you? Tell him you miss him."

"Nine years old," Ashlee whispered. She suddenly sounded like she might be crying. "Crazy."

"Yeah, loco."

"He still having fits?"

Ephraim squeezed the phone and clamped his mouth tight. This is what Ashlee called any behavior one might deem extraneous or outside the realm of normal. Fits. Fits of melancholy, fits of destruction, or anger. Fits of agony, or fatigue. Fits of excitement, or one step beyond that, za-niness. This was how she classified her own manic behaviors. Little fits.

"He's fine," Ephraim said.

"Okay, give him the phone."

Ephraim told her to call him back on the landline a couple of minutes after they hung up so it would look like she hadn't been prompted. Before they got off, she said, "It hurts too much."

"What does?"

"Wondering about y'all. Worrying how things are going. I do better if I can just put everything out of my mind. It's just easier."

"I'm sure it is," Ephraim said. "I reckon everybody'd be better off if they could blank it all out, but that's not really the way the world works, is it, Ash?"

She muttered something he couldn't understand and hung up on him. Ephraim walked back into the living room, watched his dad and son looking through the telescope, talking about the man on the moon, and waited for the phone to ring. Five minutes later, it did. Caleb stiffened up and looked at his father.

"Answer it," Ephraim said. "If it's a telemarketer tell them to take us off their list."

Caleb ran to the side table and snatched the phone off its cradle. "Area code says 850," he said. "Where's that?"

"Florida. Answer it."

Caleb hit the talk button and held the phone to his ear. "Hello," he said shyly. Ephraim listened to his son's end of the conversation, which consisted mostly of monosyllabic answers to what Ephraim guessed were generic questions about his birthday and school and whatnot. Caleb told her about his gifts, the video game and telescope, and at the end of it said, "You too."

Caleb held the cordless phone away from his body and stared at it with a glum expression.

"How'd that go?" Ephraim asked, though he could tell something about it had upset him.

"Fine," Caleb responded. He reset the phone on the cradle and kept looking at it and started wringing his hands.

"Why don't you play your new video game?" Ephraim told him.

"Yeah."

CHAPTER FIVE
DAMN FINE MARGARITAS

The Cut was a nightclub located on the main avenue in downtown Cain City. The place didn't open until ten, after most of the surrounding businesses were closed. A fine-dining joint operated out of the old hotel on the other end of the block, and there was a bar next door to the hotel, but that was it. Nothing closer. So after dark, The Cut effectively dictated all the foot traffic in that section of downtown.

Just before 11:00 p.m., Buddy The Face parked a conversion van across the street from the club. He and Momo Morrison got out and approached two bouncers standing guard at the entrance. The security men were both well over six feet, girthy, unsmiling, and nearly indistinguishable from one another, save one was a little darker hued. The other was an inch or two shorter and had a pair of eyes so close-set they looked in danger of knocking together. Each man took a keen measure of Buddy, who equaled them in size and, with his disfigured head and eyepatch, resembled a cartoon villain. They didn't pay much attention to the diminutive Momo.

"You boys lost?" the taller one asked.

"No, sir," Momo replied, real chipper. "Buddy here loves to cut a rug. Don't ya, Buddy?"

"I'm a dancing machine," Buddy deadpanned.

"And he loves black pussy."

The bouncer cocked his head and took note of Momo for the first time. "Come again, little man?"

"Black pussy," Momo repeated, louder. "The sticky pink? C'mon, y'all know what I'm talking about."

In unison, both bouncers took a threatening step forward. The taller one scowled down at Momo. "You serious right now, twerpy little motherfucker? Look here, you fools best get to steppin', you know what's good for you."

Momo leaned back from the waist and held his hands up in mock surrender. "Whoa whoa now fellas, we seem to be misunderstanding each other."

"You speak English, don't you? Get the fuck outta here before we do a tire change on your fucking arms and legs."

The close-eyed guard reached his hand beneath his jacket. Buddy shook his head slowly back and forth to warn him off that action. Momo lowered his hands to his sides. His mouth split into a madman grin that showed off his serrated teeth. "Y'all talking about rearranging body parts? Jee-zus, that's morbid. Let's all settle down and try a different tack, shall we? Here's what we're gonna do. One of you is gonna mosey on in there and tell Nico Blakes that his old pal Momo is out here trying to see him. We're simply looking for an audience with the man. Now, if he wants me to fuck off, which I doubt, then that's what we'll do. We'll scootchie right on outta here, everybody's night continues without incident. Course if that happens, it'll make Momo a little pissy, and Nico knows what happens when Momo gets pissy."

"Ain't no Nico here," the tall bouncer said.

"Oh, I hope for your sake he is, friend. And if he isn't, I think you better just go ahead and get whoever's in charge to give him a ring, convey my message. He ain't here, I'll bet he'll come on down in a right jiffy." Momo snapped his fingers. "Like that." He could tell the bouncers didn't know what to make of the situation. They stood there gawking at each other like two mutes who'd never learned sign language. "Go on and deliver my message now," Momo prodded. "We ain't gonna wait out here all night."

The tall one nodded for Close-Eyes to go inside, then directed Momo and Buddy to raise their arms. They obliged, and he wanded them to check for weapons. They were clean. Close-Eyes opened the door. Purple lights and trap music escaped out into the night air, and he disappeared inside. The door shut and took the noise with it.

The tall bouncer eyed them warily. "Y'all who I think y'all are?"

"Suppose that depends on who you think we are," Momo answered.

"Y'all part of them supremist motherfuckers down there on the West End. Like the Klan and shit. The ones everyone so scared of."

"Klan?" Momo cut a jagged smile. "Naw, we don't fly under that banner, friend. The Kluxers, they some silly fuckers, ain't they? Got silly names. Like to call themselves . . . what's one, Buddy?"

"Grand Dragons."

"Grand Dragons," Momo echoed. "Or Imperial Wizard, or Exalted Cyclops. I look like a wizard to you?"

The bouncer took the question earnestly and considered Momo for a moment. "Not to me you don't."

"Naw, not me. Besides, what is it I'd be called in the Klan, Buddy?"

"A Night Hawk."

"See now, that's plain silliness. Night Hawk. Like they wrestlers or superheroes or something. Naw, the Klan is just for show. They like to trade on that old name, make a lot of noise, gas each other up like they gonna take over the world one day. Us, we don't make no noise. Don't operate under no illusions. We just look after our own, that's all. West End folks. You can respect that, I'm sure. Far as people being afraid of us, well, in that case, we probably are exactly who you think we are."

Close-Eyes came back out. "Nico says to please enjoy a drink at the bar, on the house, and he'll be with you in a moment."

"Looky there, Fat Mac." Momo slapped the tall bouncer on the shoulder. "A little communication and we avoided a big dustup over nothing. And you'll never know just how close you came."

Music pulsed inside the club, colored lights flashing to the beat. Immediately upon entering there was a square bar top, a section of tables next to it, and beyond that, a large dance floor and a raised platform for a DJ booth. A giant disco ball hung down from the ceiling, refracting and bending the lights. The walls were lined with booths that stretched the length of the long, rectangular room. The crowd in the place was modest, as the night was young.

Momo and Buddy The Face took seats at the bar and ordered a margarita rocks and two fingers of whiskey, respectively. A pretty young black girl with a shiny afro and clothes that hid absolutely nothing delivered the drinks. They were only a few sips in when Junior Brown, Nico Blakes's right-hand man, politely tapped Momo on the shoulder.

"Follow me," Junior told him.

"What's that?" Momo said, yelling over the music.

Junior beckoned him with a finger. Momo grabbed the margarita and slid off his stool. Buddy followed suit, but Junior raised a hand to stop him. "Not you, big man. Just Momo."

Momo gave Buddy a wink and signaled for him to comply. Buddy settled back onto his stool and turned his lone eye toward the dance floor where four women were dancing with each other like they wanted to be watched.

Junior Brown delivered Momo to a circular booth in the far corner of the club, where Nico Blakes sat alone, hands intertwined on the table in front of him. Nico gestured for Momo to take the chair opposite.

Momo raised his glass in salute, said, "Y'all make a damn good margarita," and plopped into the seat. Junior Brown retreated to the mouth of a passageway that led to the unseen parts of the club and positioned himself against a wall where he could casually keep watch over the booth.

Nico Blakes's yellow, rheumy eyes fixed on Momo and didn't come off him. Many a person had been freaked by those eyes because they never gave anything away, never got bigger or narrowed, never betrayed an emotion of any kind. This, coupled with the fact that his corneas were muddy, nearly black, created the illusion that his pupils never dilated or shrank. Rumor had it his own grandmother, before she passed when he was twelve, had speculated that Nico had either sold his soul to the Devil, or worse, was just a flat psychopath. None of these superstitions fazed Momo. Quite the opposite, they imbued in him a feeling of kinship. Though Momo knew the tall tales were nonsense, part of him wished they were true. Part of him wished the Nico Blakes of lore was as wicked as advertised, as wicked as he was.

Momo gazed benevolently into those storied black eyes now. There were no speakers in the back corner of the club, so the music wasn't as grating and you didn't have to scream to be heard.

"Never thought I'd see the day you'd darken these doors," Nico said coolly.

Momo snorted. "Darken these doors! That's funny. Pun intended, right? Darken these doors." Momo shook his head and laughed, a loud, honking laugh that went on for a protracted length of time. Nico's expression didn't crack. He observed the spectacle dispassionately and waited for it to be over. When Momo's cackling ebbed, he sighed contentedly and took a long gander over his surroundings. "You know this place used to be a country and western bar called Do-Si-Dos?"

"I'm waiting," Nico said.

"Yeah, what for?"

"For you to come 'round to telling me what you're doing here. You ain't one to bring good tidings, Momo, and I know this ain't the kind of place caters to your *desires*. So."

Momo leaned forward conspiratorially. "You mean 'cause the only pussy on the menu in here is the dark cola?" He sat back and puckered his face as if the mere thought were distasteful.

"There's that, and the fact that we don't get many ladyboys in here."

Momo cocked one of his flimsy eyebrows. "Now that's a missed opportunity if you ask me. This place could use some more catnip. Bit of glitz. Couldn't hurt none." Momo's face lit up like he'd just thought of something bright. "This reminds me of a joke. How do you fit four queers on a barstool?" Momo pricked an expectant ear toward Nico, who didn't answer, so Momo provided the obvious punchline. "You turn it over."

"You'd know."

The smile ran off Momo's face and hid somewhere. He sat back in the chair and slowly ran his tongue over his teeth. "You're not making this a whole lot of fun, Nico. I'd think that you'd be a little more hospitable to me under the circumstances."

"What circumstances are those, Momo? Besides you steppin' in here like you ain't got a fear in the world. Like there won't be repercussions. Asking for an audience with me like you're owed such a thing. Unless you're defecting or something. Crossing the invisible line from west to east. That what's happening?"

"Defecting?" Momo chuckled. "To the *darky* side. That'll be the day. Now you're being funny."

"Okay, then. Let's put the shoe on the other foot, Momo, for argument's sake. I pay a visit to one of your people's joints down there on the West End, you think I'm gonna be treated . . . hospitably?"

"Now, any regular old Afro-American walks in, wellll . . ." Momo blew the wind out of his lungs. "I can't speak to that. But you?" He closed one eye and pointed a finger at Nico as if he were taking aim. Clucked his tongue. "You walk in, you'll be treated like royalty. I'd make sure of it." He slurped down his drink and cracked an ice cube between his teeth. "Hell, I already owe you a drink. Of which I'll say again, damn fine margarita. And I'm something of a margarita connoisseur. Much better than Do-Si-Dos was. You're gonna have to give me your recipe."

"Look here, Momo. I got things to do, so whatever this thing is, let's get it through."

"Okay, that's the way you want it, we can skip the light fandango." Momo leaned back relaxed-like in his chair, its two front legs coming off the ground. He waved a hand to indicate the club and the world at large. "You know, we got people all over this town, workin' people from all walks of life, walkin' around here invisible. Unseen. We're everywhere, like an all-seeing eye. We can find out anything we want to find out. About you. About whoever we want. You think because you know I like to bang a tranny or two, you know something about me? Okay. Let me tell you what we know about you. We know what cable package you have, NFL Ticket, Disney Plus, yadda yadda yadda. We know how much your water bill is, your telephone company, who installed the alarm system at your house. We know where your ladies sleep, all three of 'em. Your baby son. What's his name, Tevin?" Nico offered no confirmation or denial, so Momo continued. "We also know where that nephew you look after goes to school, know the name of his home-room teacher, where you like to park to pick him up when school lets out. We know exactly when your license needs to be renewed at the DMV. We know everything, Nico. So yeah, I apologize if I seem a little cocky, but then again, I ain't too sorry about it."

Nico Blakes's fingers were still laced together on the table in front of him. He hadn't shifted in his seat, nor changed his expression, but his demeanor had become focused, coiled, and Momo perceived the difference. He cocked his head, quizzically, and considered his counterpart.

"You seem tight, Nico. Maybe you oughtta let the cornrows out, relax a little."

A viperous look skimmed across Nico's face. Blink and you would have missed it. But Momo didn't blink, and he didn't miss a thing. He turned his palms up, real smug-like, and set the front legs of his chair down, as if daring Nico to make a move.

The next words Nico spoke came out slow and measured. "Day comes, I think it might be a little harder to take me down than you think."

Momo snickered. "I'm not threatening you with all this talk, mind. You asked me why I'm not too afeared walking in here, so I'm telling you the truth. Straight up. Now, I know you could signal your boy Junior over there and he could cut me down right now, easy as pie. But that'd be pretty fucking stupid. And you may be many things, Nico, but stupid ain't one of 'em."

Nico's yellow eyes flicked to Junior, who raised up off the wall in alarm. A small hand gesture from Nico kept him back. "My patience is running real thin, Momo."

"All right, then. No more fun." Momo scratched at the fuzz on his chin and went ponderous for a moment. "I guess I'm here to see if you know why I'm here."

"Fuck does that mean?"

Momo narrowed his eyes to assess Nico's reaction, to suss out any hint of betrayal or deception, and came to the conclusion that Nico was playing it straight and was none the wiser to the day's events. "You ain't looking to expand into the meth trade, are you, Nico?"

"Naw, y'all can keep that ditch drug for your veins."

"See, earlier today"—Momo tipped his glass back and slid the last of the margarita into his throat; he made a satisfied sound, set the cup down, and continued—"somebody robbed one of our safe houses, took a bunch of money, bunch of product, shot two of our people dead. Shot one right in the face. Other was to the back of an old lady's head. Real nasty cleanup job."

"Okay. What's that got to do with me?"

"Happy you asked. I'll show you." Momo gestured to a pocket on his Carhartt jacket as if to ask permission, then reached in and fished out a phone. He fiddled with it for a second, then passed it across the table to Nico. "We got the whole fracas on video."

Nico took the phone and stared at it for a beat.

"Just hit play," Momo prompted him. "The little triangle there."

Nico tapped the screen. The video came to life with a wide angle of a large room, black-and-white footage, shot from a high on a wall. There was a lady sitting at a table with her back to the camera. With her movements and the scale next to her, what she was doing was obvious to Nico. Beyond her was a door, and in the corner was a fat guy dozing in a chair with a shotgun across his lap.

Nico watched as three masked men entered through the door and pointed their guns at the woman. There were words exchanged, but no audio on the recording. Then all three men, as if choreographed, whipped their heads around to see the sleeping man in the corner. The tallest of the intruders quickly strode over, snatched the shotgun, and when the fat man woke, blew his face off.

Nico glanced over the phone at Momo, who knew which spot he must have been at in the video. "Oh, keep watching the show," Momo said.

Nico did, through the killing of the woman to the ransacking of the drugs and the money from the trick door beneath the dead man. He watched it all the way to the point where the three masked men pulled said masks off their heads, revealing a crystal-clear view of their identities. The video stopped there on a freeze-frame. Nico too was frozen, staring at the image in disbelief.

"So you see," Momo said. "This here visit I'm paying to you is what you might call a courtesy. Honor amongst the wicked, if you will. Somebody without a head level as mine might have just said to themselves, out of hand, 'Self, you know these three boys work for Nico Blakes. And Nico Blakes, he runs a pretty tight ship over there on the East

End. Nobody does nothing without old Nico giving 'em the okay.' Therefore, by that hypothesis, Nico Blakes must've told these boys to do what it is that you just seen them do with your own two eyes. Heinous, really. But Momo didn't jump to that conclusion. No, sir. Momo thought on it real hard, and Momo said, 'Nico Blakes ain't never done nothing this foolish. Seems out of character. So why don't we just go over yonder and liaison with him, give him a chance to explain this here fucking calamity.'"

"I ain't have nothing to do with this," Nico said, staring coldly at Momo.

"You know something, Blakes? I believe you, I do. I's leaning that way before I even wandered in here, but you've convinced me fully of your innocence. However, as I'm sure you understand, you still bear some responsibility. Now, I've been tasked with the job. I got to find these boys, and I got to kill 'em. You know how it goes. Decision come down from on high. I had nothing to do with it." For emphasis, Momo made a show of dusting his hands off.

Nico placed the phone on the table and, with one finger, slid it back across to Momo.

"Technology's crazy, huh?" Momo said, pocketing the phone. "Now, I know these are the boys usually run your shit down there on Spring Street, but lo and behold, they ain't there. So time to take your medicine, Blakes. I need three names. I need where to find them. And I need this before I walk out of this bar. Better yet, why don't you just give those boys a call, find out where they are for me?"

Nico didn't speak for a while. Momo was content to let him stew. He didn't mind uneasy silence. Enjoyed it, even.

"You expect me to just let you walk out of here and kill three of my employees?"

"Yep."

"Why would I do that?"

"Self-preservation."

Nico ran a hand over his face, spoke through clenched teeth: "So you sayin', I step out the way on this, that's the end of it. No beef between us and you?"

"Now that you say it out loud"—Momo's jaw dropped slack and he tilted his head, thoughtful-like, as if he hadn't played out all possible angles before coming there—"I'll be damned if that doesn't sound like one hell of a deal. I'd take that deal. You take that deal? I'd take that deal."

Nico squeezed his fists to where his knuckles went white, and he resisted the sudden, overwhelming urge to commit a homicide. "I need some time to think on this."

Momo frowned diplomatically. "Naw . . . you don't. Look here, I understand it's no easy thing to give up your people, but it'll be a breeze, really. All you got to do is open your mouth and speak the words. *Voila.* They go away, other hoodrats sprout up in their place, and that's that. Life goes on. All in all, it's a small pittance compared to what it could be. What it *will* be, this don't get resolved."

"Okay." Nico nodded malevolently. "Okay." He leaned forward and spoke low, so that Momo had to move closer to hear. "Something of this nature, somebody's got to pay the piper. I get that, Momo. But I'm not in this for anything collateral, you understand me? You'll get your names. Anything beyond, anybody else gets hurt, you and me gonna have an issue. Personally."

Momo's wormy lips stretched back over his sharp gray teeth. "You promise?"

"Step across that line, you fucking devil, and you'll find out."

"Devil?" Momo sat back and feigned offense. "You know, whenever anybody talks about devils, it reminds me of something somebody said about me one time. They said, scrawny as I was, difficult as I was to look at, I must have been one of God's afterthoughts. Said I must have been made from spare parts left over from where he made everybody else. Person that said it, I don't think he meant it nice, but I kind of liked the idea of me being God's own Frankenstein monster."

"What'd you do to him?" Nico asked.

"Who, the person said that to me? I loved him. He was my daddy. I got him back eventually. He got the cancer, was on his last leg in the hospital. Body wrecked, you know, shrinking to nothing. But I didn't think he deserved to die of natural causes."

"What'd you do? Put a pillow over your own father?"

"Oh, no. No, no, no. What I did, I injected him with a syringe full of liquid fentanyl. Stuck it straight in his heart. You should have seen his eyes when that thing exploded. Nearly popped out they sockets. You ain't never seen nothing like it, I'm telling ya. It was like a movie."

Nico had no response for that. Instead, he restated his terms. "I'll give you the names. I'll even try to see where they've ducked to. But it ends with those three."

Momo pretended to mull over the conditions, then threw up his hands. "Fair enough. But we got one last stipulation. Non-negotiable. Three hundred and ninety thousand dollars, that's a lot of money. Five pounds a lot of methamphetamine. We got to recover our goods. We don't, you're on the hook."

"How you suppose I pay that shit? Installments?"

"Not my problem." Momo clapped his hands once, hard, and rubbed them together. "Whattaya say we give those boys a call?"

CHAPTER SIX
THE WAY OF DUST

What Mrs. Dinwiddle had said at their after-school meeting, the thing about the little girl who caught some virus that made her go nuts, kept banging in Ephraim's consciousness. While his son played his new video game and his father flipped the channels between the news and an old John Wayne movie, he got on his phone and typed *virus that makes kids go crazy* into the browser's search bar. The first article that came up was some study about delirium in children, but the next seven items below that all had to do with a syndrome called PANDAS or PANS. He clicked on the first link and skimmed the article. At the bottom there was a list of common symptoms. After reading the first four, Ephraim sat forward. A shot of adrenaline zipped through his body.

- *obsessive behaviors*
- *panic attacks*
- *emotional and developmental regressions*
- *tics or unusual movement*

The list went on, over twenty categorized symptoms in all.

- *hyperactivity*
- *trouble sleeping*
- *depression or suicidal thoughts*

Caleb displayed all but two of the symptoms on the full list. "How have I never heard of this shit?" Ephraim muttered. He read the article again, more thoroughly, and then a handful of other ones about the syndrome. There was one that dealt with the link between strep throat and PANDAS. The massive amount of information overwhelmed him, and caused him to reflect back on some recent incidents.

One evening a few weeks before, Ephraim had turned the corner to the kitchen to find Caleb gently pushing the sharp tip of a steak knife into the soft flesh at the top of his belly. Ephraim snatched the knife away, but not before Caleb had broken the skin. Blood dribbling down his stomach.

"What are you doing?!" Ephraim had yelled.

Caleb swore up and down he had no idea how the knife had even gotten into his hands, swore he didn't want to hurt himself. Claimed he didn't know what he was doing. He'd sunk to his knees, sobbing, screaming, "I don't know what's wrong with me! I don't know what's wrong with me!" over and over. When Ephraim tried to comfort him, Caleb smacked his hands away. He refused to be touched. Then he made a break for it, tried to run out of the house. Ephraim caught him before he reached the front door. He bear-hugged Caleb from behind, pinned his arms to his sides, and sat down on the floor with his son in his lap. This prevented him from being hit or kicked or clawed again. He was helpless against a reverse headbutt to the face, but luckily Caleb never thought of it. Ephraim stayed vigilant nonetheless.

Just let me go somewhere and die, Caleb had pleaded. Ephraim didn't respond, didn't want to give the idea air to breathe. He just held him tightly to his chest and shushed him like a baby. Eventually the screaming stopped, the flailing stopped, Caleb's breathing calmed, and Ephraim gently released him. Caleb was dull-eyed after these outbursts, nearly catatonic, unable to speak more than a few words. Ephraim laid his son in bed that night, waited for him to fall asleep, then hid all the knives in the house.

Caleb had even started wetting the bed again, something he hadn't done since he was four. Another symptom box checked. Every time it happened, Caleb tried to conceal it, covering his soiled mattress with a towel, saying he was sweaty, or that he'd gotten up for water in the middle of the night and spilled it.

All the web articles claimed these symptoms emerged suddenly and overwhelmingly, over a period of a few days, but Ephraim didn't remember it happening like that. The development had seemed more gradual to him. A symptom appeared, and then another, and then another, one at a time until finally they all fused into a united, combustible front with the common goal of wreaking havoc upon his son.

The slower escalation Caleb presented gave Ephraim a jolt of hope that maybe his son didn't have this particular disorder. Every source iterated how medically complicated and hard to treat it was. There was no clear way to diagnose the condition, and the underlying cause was likely a multitude of illnesses, bacteria, and genetic predispositions. The combination served to hijack the immune system and make the brain swell, hence the volatile behavior. Maybe whatever was going on with Caleb was simpler, easier to explain, easier to eradicate from the body. But to Ephraim's dismay, the more he read, the more things seemed to match up.

The websites he browsed were informative, but they didn't go much beyond the general, so he turned where everyone does to get their answers, Facebook. His wife, Ashlee, had suffered from many self-diagnosed (and self-medicated) afflictions of the mind: PTSD, migraines, seasonal affective disorder, insomnia, and the twin pillars of all modern scourges, anxiety and depression. She belonged to at least one Facebook support group for each of these illnesses, so Ephraim figured one must exist for PANS or PANDAS. He had an old Facebook page that he'd posted about three things on and abandoned years ago, but his passwords were the same for everything, so he logged on easily enough and started pecking around. It didn't take long to ferret out a support group called the PANS/PANDAS Awareness Collective. He began scrolling through the posts.

Many of them were parents reporting on what medications their kids were taking, which combinations worked for them, which ones didn't. Other posts read like testimonials, warnings, confessionals, pleas for help. Some were more akin to horror stories. Of children who had to be fed through tubes because they refused to eat. Of children who could no longer function in society. Parents having to quit their jobs to look after their kid full time. Parents who just wanted to know there was someone out there who had experienced what they were experiencing. Parents begging for someone to tell them everything was going to be okay, that their child would someday heal. Some commenters on these posts gave hope, or relayed their successful journeys back to health. Others who had battled the illness for years with no discernable progress, not so much.

Most of the contributors to the forum had kids that were still in the thick of the malady. Ephraim figured those with children who had recovered probably no longer trolled the boards. They probably quit the group as fast as they could and did their best to banish the ordeal from their minds. Placed the whole experience in a box labelled THE PAST, stocked it away, and prayed it stayed there. At least that's how Ephraim rationalized the lopsidedness of the content, which consisted, from his vantage, primarily of pain and suffering. There wasn't much on there to give one confidence.

Nonetheless, he couldn't stop reading. Stories of doctors who were skeptical the sickness was real. Doctors who flat out denied its existence. Whole hospitals that refused to diagnose anything other than a psychiatric disorder. Doctors who actively dissuaded patients from seeking out specialists in the field, insisting they were quacks who were merely fleecing desperate parents because, apparently, insurance companies didn't cover the syndrome. All treatment costs were out of pocket and generally ran into the tens of thousands.

One post had a video link that he watched. It was a eulogy for a thirteen-year-old boy who'd committed suicide. Another video was this mother who confessed to how much she resented her sick child for ruining her life. She talked about how her husband had recently moved out and she had no idea how to keep going, how she was struggling to find a reason to do so. The post elicited lots of supportive comments. People saying they felt similarly, or had in the past. That the woman was stronger than she knew. Encouraging words about how things would get better. That there was nowhere to go but up. Whenever Ephraim heard someone spouting platitudes like "things couldn't get any worse," he always thought, *Just you wait. Things can always get worse.*

Ephraim scrolled through post after post like this until his eyes felt like they were bleeding and all the stories blurred into a giant knot in his stomach.

Ephraim decided to join the group. He typed out a message: *Hello, I'm new here. My son has a lot of these symptoms. Most actually. Calling doctor tomorrow. What tests should I have them run to see if he has this illness? Any help would be greatly appreciated. Thank you in advance.*

He hit "send" and closed the Facebook window.

"Lost again," Darrell groused from his chair. He clicked back to the John Wayne movie.

"Lost what again?"

"Stupid lotto."

"That's a hell of a losing streak you got going there."

"I'll say. It's lasted a lifetime."

Ephraim looked at the grandfather clock. It was 9:00 p.m., past time to get Caleb off the PlayStation. His phone was nearly out of battery, so he plugged it into the charger, then went and got Caleb moving. Ephraim had to chaperone him through his bedtime routine: going to the bathroom, washing hands, brushing teeth, changing into pajamas. Left on his own, Caleb could no longer be trusted to complete these straightforward tasks. He might squeeze all of the toothpaste out of the tube or, during his showers, pour all the shampoo out of the bottle. Prior to his behavior going sideways, Ephraim would tuck him in tightly along the edges of his body, like a burrito, and lie next to him, sometimes until they both drifted off. But now there were times Caleb complained if his father brushed against him accidentally, much less touched him. The simplest affection, such as a kiss goodnight, was out of the question.

Caleb's mother had painted and decorated his bedroom. Planets hung from the ceiling, shelves crammed with books and toys and *Star Wars* action figures, a huge basket of stuffed animals at the foot of the bed, a desk that had a globe and artwork and a large glass jar of seashells collected from their vacation a couple of years ago to Emerald Isle. The beige walls were covered with posters from his favorite movies, his favorite characters. *Star Wars* again, Harry Potter, *Jumanji*. Ephraim wished he'd had a room that cool when he was a kid. The only thing that'd been on his walls were the inserts to CD covers he'd cut out and Scotch-taped up.

He sat at the edge of the bed, toward the bottom, careful not to encroach upon the invisible bubble of space that would irritate his son.

"Hey, bud. Have you had a sore throat, or anything like that lately?" Ephraim asked.

"No."

"You remember having a sore throat at all in the last few months?"

"Nu-uh. Why?"

"Just wonderin'. Can you tell me what it feels like? When you start feeling bad?"

Caleb groaned. "Do we have to talk about this?"

"I'd like to, yeah."

Caleb huffed petulantly and smacked his hands on the covers. "You wouldn't understand."

"Try me."

Caleb winced as though he were afraid to give voice to his thoughts. He drew his knees up to his chest and spoke so softly Ephraim had to lean in to hear the words. "It feels like it's too hard to live sometimes. Like all I want to do is go away."

Ephraim didn't say anything for a minute. When he did, he spoke tenderly. "You mean like you want to die?"

Caleb nodded. "Kind of."

Ephraim tried to breathe, but the air stuck in his throat. He reached for his son, wanting to comfort him, rub his back, stroke his hair, anything, but Caleb shirked from his touch, mumbled "No," and Ephraim dropped the hand back into his lap.

"Was it talking to your mom? Did that upset you?"

"No, it was fine."

"It wasn't anything she said or anything, was it?"

Caleb shook his head. "I pretty much always feel that way. I just don't tell you."

"I'm so sorry you're going through this, buddy. If I could take all your pain away and put it in me, I would do that. I'd do it in a heartbeat."

"I know. Thanks."

"We're going to figure it out, okay? I'm going to call your doctor tomorrow and get them to run some tests. We're gonna do whatever it takes. I'm not going to quit until we get you better. I promise. I just need you to hang in there for me. 'Cause I don't want you to die, buddy. Okay? If you die, I wouldn't want to live anymore. That's how much I love you."

"I love you too."

"This stuff you're feeling, one day, it'll be better. I promise. And the good thing is, you love to write, right? Your teacher was telling me today about that great story you wrote about a funny duck. I brought it home with me."

"Did you read it?"

"Not yet, but I will. Better yet, you can read it to me. But the good thing is, all this stuff you're feeling, you're gonna be able to use all that for your stories. That's what makes stories great is all that experience. The highs, the lows, everything. You can put it all in there. And you're gonna be the toughest kid, having gotten through all of this, toughest kid in the world, I promise you. Just hang in there for me. Think you can do that?"

"Okay," Caleb said, not at all convincing. "Dad?"

"Yeah, buddy?"

"What happens to you when you die?"

"Well." Ephraim scratched at his beard. "That's a big question, isn't it?"

"I guess so."

Ephraim took a moment to formulate an answer. He bumbled through some things about how nobody really knows and how a lot of people believe you go to heaven or hell, like the Bible says, depending on the choices you made in life. And he explained the flip side, how some folks don't believe there's anything after; that when you die, that's that. You're just gone. "Really it's up to you to make up your own mind about it," he told his son.

"Yeah, but what do you believe?"

"I guess I'm just kinda waiting my turn to find out who's right," Ephraim hedged.

"But if there's nothing after, then you won't be able to find out, will you? You'll just be dead."

"You got a point there. I don't know, Caleb. I'd like to think there's some kind of reason for everything, you know. Something beyond what we can comprehend by ourselves. Whether it's God or something else. But this isn't stuff you need to be worrying about right now. You got plenty of time to figure it all out."

Caleb gave him a funny look, like he had some thoughts on the subject, but was reticent to share them now.

"Why, what do you think happens?" Ephraim asked.

Caleb lifted his shoulders and dropped them.

Ephraim, sensing his son's dissatisfaction, tried to think of something a little more stirring to say. "You know, since I was your age, I always had this idea that—you know what a soul is?"

"The thing that floats out of your body when you die."

"Right, sort of like that. They say your soul is kind of like this magical invisible spirit that makes you *you*. It's probably silly, but I always had this picture in my head that when you die, before you go wherever it is you go, your soul gets one last chance to sort of travel around and visit the people you love one last time. Wherever they are, you get to kind of look in on them, spend a moment to say goodbye in your own way, or whatever. It's probably silly."

"It doesn't sound silly to me," Caleb said.

"No?"

"No. But then what happens?"

"Then we go find out who's right."

"About heaven and hell?"

"Yep. The last great mystery."

"I hope I get to visit you before I float away."

"I don't think that's the way it works, bud, because you're gonna be an old man, and by that time I'll be long gone. But I'll tell you what. Whenever that is, wherever that is, I'll be waiting for you."

"But maybe not. Not if you just go away."

"I guess we'll have to wait and see."

Caleb yawned, his mouth opening so wide it looked unhinged, like a snake's mouth. "Can I go to bed now?"

"Sure," Ephraim said. "Is it all right if I give you a kiss?"

"Mmm . . . not tonight. Maybe tomorrow. Sorry."

"It's okay. If it bothers you, it bothers you. You don't

have to be sorry." Ephraim patted his son's arm and stood from the bed. "I love you, buddy."

"I love you too. I'm sorry I'm mean to you sometimes."

"I'm sorry I'm mean sometimes too. Listen, I'm off to work. Grandpa will be here if you need him."

Caleb rolled over to face the wall. At the doorway Ephraim flipped the light off and stood there with his hand on the knob, looking back into the bedroom. "Happy birthday," he whispered. "See you in the morning."

From the darkness came no reply.

The procession of cars rumbled up the dirt road that switchbacked along the face of the mountain. The road came to an end in the middle of a gorge about a half mile below the peak. They parked them in a line that stretched a couple hundred yards back down the road. Engines were cut, headlights extinguished, and the people stepped out of their cars and into the black night. No one spoke. After the doors of some eighty-odd cars clunked shut the only sounds were those of the natural world and of scuffling footsteps as the people fell into line behind Fenton Teague, the longtime leader of the Stenders.

Teague was not an imposing man. Smallness ran in his family, as did a cunning nature, sadism, and a prodigious talent for violence. He'd inherited a surplus of all these genetic traits. Not a man or woman among them would claim to be meaner than Teague, nor smarter, and no one with two brain cells to rub together would dare cross him. If they did, odds were they'd end up feeding worms somewhere on that very mountain. Perhaps a family member or two would accompany them for good measure.

Teague had a taut, weather-beaten face that looked as if it had been whittled from hickory, a bust come to life. His body was lean and ropy, eyes thin slits of intensity. If you were to see him on the street, most likely you wouldn't think twice about it. But if someone happened to plant the seed in your brain that he was the head honcho in a white separatist organization that dominated all vice, from drugs to prostitutes to gambling, in a territory that spanned from the West End of Cain City to a large swath of eastern Kentucky and southern Ohio, but also had tendrils in a good number of legitimate businesses and local unions, then you'd probably give him another look-see, and upon closer inspection, you'd likely say, "Yeah, that sounds about right."

Behind Teague they funneled through a gap in the gorge wall and then trekked the half mile up through the forest toward the summit of the mountain. Only scant traces of moonlight slipped through the foliage of the trees to guide their way. A difficult climb over steep terrain, but the path to the burial ground was well trod by every individual present and no one stumbled or complained.

They arrived at a small glade that abutted a twenty-foot-high escarpment, at the top of which was the mountain's peak. This was the place. Two graves had been dug at the foot of the bluff. Fenton Teague walked between them and stood next to the dirt piles at their heads. He placed his hands flat against the cold face of the rock wall and gazed upward through a gap in the treetops where the waning moon hung like a silver ornament, as if God himself had hung it for the occasion. Teague closed his eyes and inhaled the sweet loam of the freshly dug earth, and turned to face the congregants.

Those bringing up the rear of the column crammed into the clearing and fanned out among the surrounding trees. Eight men had been tasked with lugging the caskets to the top of the mountain, Momo Morrison, Buddy The Face, and Verbals among them. They set the two boxes down at the foot of the gravesite, then stepped back and blended in with the crowd. Teague signaled for the bonfires to be lit. Matchsticks were struck and tossed into metal barrels situated throughout the glade. With a deep *whoosh* each can lit to flames. The faces of the crowd came aglow in the hot orange firelight.

The bonfires cast Teague's long, distorted shadow over the rock wall behind him. He took his time gazing out over his flock. Among them he saw electricians, mechanics, truckers, cooks, construction workers, state employees, receptionists, firefighters, railroad conductors. People from all walks. All beholden to him. Awaiting his words.

Teague motioned toward the bodies lying in the caskets. The violence inflicted upon them made it to where the corpses were unfit to be viewed, and both of the deceased were wrapped head to toe in gauze, like mummies. It was easy enough to discern who was who because Jumbo's body was about four times the size of Maid Marion's.

"Jeremiah Harless," Teague called out, the words rumbling like peals of thunder.

The crowd repeated after him. "Jeremiah Harless."

"Marion Fudd."

"Marion Fudd."

"These names will never be forgotten. They will be spoken here, on this day, and every day forward until we ourselves have gone the way of dust. And when they are spoken, it will be with the reverence they have earned, both on this day and all their days that came before. Jeremiah Harless—Jumbo—and Maid Marion were our people, and they died for us. We are one with them, and they are one with us, now and forever. Jeremiah Harless."

"Jeremiah Harless," the chorus exclaimed, louder this time.

"Marion Fudd."

"Marion Fudd!"

"Tonight, their bones, like many that have come before and as ours will come after, will become a permanent part of this mountain. The rot of their body will nourish its soil, become twined with the roots of the trees to be pulled, ever so slowly, into the depths of the earth, into the heart of the world. Because we are the earth. And the earth is us. May they rest in peace knowing that they served their purpose in this life, which is the highest praise I could bestow upon a person. To serve a purpose, to play your part in this society. Our society. When the time comes for you to gather in my honor, and my name is spoken in such a manner, I will be content." Here, Teague paused for a moment and stared into the depths of the graves. When he lifted his head and resumed, his tone, while still reverent, was tinged with anger. "None of us knows when our last day has dawned. This is a fact of our existence. A fact that we accept. It's the thing that makes this life precious, knowing it will end, and the mystery of what comes after. But nobody's end should come the senseless way in which Jumbo's and Maid Marion's came today. Nobody's."

The audience murmured their approval. One person hollered, "Damn right!"

"So before we celebrate the lives of our departed friends in our tradition, I make a vow to you here and now that their murderers will be brought to heel. And they will be made to suffer tenfold!"

The throng hooted. A palpable frenzy buzzed from one person to another across the gathering. Teague raised his arms for quiet. The giant shadow on the wall behind him loomed like a vengeful spirit pantomiming the gesture. Everyone hushed immediately, as if they'd fallen under some kind of sorcery.

"You've all probably heard the rumors of what happened. That Maid Marion and Jumbo were killed by three colored boys. This is true. It is also true that they stole half a million dollars' worth of money and goods. So let this be a reminder!" Teague's voice quivered with rage now. "We cannot lower our guards. We cannot rest on our laurels. Because there will always be those who wish to damage us. Who wish to conquer us. To snatch away what we have built, what we have earned. But hear this now! No one, and I mean no one, will ever conquer us. Least of all those savages." Here Teague pointed to the east, and there was no mistaking whom he meant. "For these egregious acts, we do not rest until our vengeance on these animals has been satisfied. Jeremiah Harless!"

"Jeremiah Harless!"

"Marion Fudd!"

"Marion Fudd!"

Teague gestured to Momo Morrison, who was standing at the front of the pack. "My nephew has names. Hear them, spread them, and find them. This is everyone's job. Momo."

Momo stepped forward and turned to face the members. "Eric Pippen," he shouted. "Twenty years old. Kevon Thompson, nineteen years old. Rodney Slash, twenty years old. You find them, don't try nothing silly. You tell me where they are. You tell Buddy where they are. We'll take it from there."

Momo ceded the floor back to his uncle and rejoined the audience. Teague pontificated some more about the lives Jumbo and Maid Marion lived and the lives they lost.

Momo watched him droll on, bored, only partly listening. He considered his uncle half country preacher and half politician, forced to endlessly pander to this mob, work that seemed to Momo like no fun at all. Done speaking, Teague stepped aside from the makeshift pulpit. An old woman with flowing white hair and a flowing white gown and a face craggy as a salt flat took his place. Alongside her was a long-limbed man toting a banjo and another with a violin. The two men struck up a bluegrass melody and the woman launched into a murder ballad, composed that day in tribute to the deceased.

> *Jumbo Harless was a West End son*
> *Caught off guard with his own damn gun*
> *They shot him in the face and they stole his life*
> *We'll treat those bastards and their own in kind*
> *So you rest in peace, Jumbo Harless*
> *You rest in peace, Jumbo Harless*
> *Yes you rest in peace, Jumbo Harless*
> *When we see you next, you'll be with the prophet.*

From a side of the crowd came a wailing loud enough to drown out the banjo. Momo looked over to see Jumbo's mother making a mad dash for her son's casket. She threw herself atop the body and started clawing at the mummy wrappings. The music ceased. A couple of men tried to pull her off the corpse, but Jumbo's mother was nearly as big as Jumbo and she refused to let go, so it took them a minute. Finally they dragged her back, but not before she'd wrangled two handfuls of bloodied gauze. Her body went limp in the men's arms. They plopped her on the ground, and she sat there cross-legged, rocking back and forth and pressing the dirty bandages to her cheeks.

The players took up their instruments again. The

next stanza extolled the virtues of Maid Marion. As the old woman sang of six children and a life of uncommon devotion, Teague made his way around the semicircle of mourners to where Momo stood.

"How's it coming, nephew?" The music was loud enough that no one else was privy to their words.

"Well, I'll tell ya," Momo clucked. "I'm 'bout still outta goddamned breath from carting fuckin' Jumbo all the way up this goddamn mountain."

"One day, you'll be carted up this mountain."

"Yeah, well, I expect it'll be a whole lot easier of a job. Besides, didn't nobody tell you? I ain't never dying."

Teague's lips curled into the faintest of smiles. "You'll be the first, huh?"

"That's me, uncle. The first eternal."

"I meant with the hunt, Momo. How goes it with the hunt?"

"Now we got the word out, matter of time. They'll turn up. They're too young to make a play like this without doing something stupid."

As if on cue, a bony man with hunched shoulders approached them from across the clearing. He removed his ball cap as a sign of respect.

"Mr. Teague, Momo," the man said. His name was Jerry Perky. "I believe I might know where them boys we're looking for are."

"Go on," Teague said.

Jerry scratched at his receding hairline. "You know I got some girls working the Sundown Courts, not the one down there by the Pizza Hut. The one just off the interstate."

"You talking about Tracy and Janice?" Momo asked.

"Yeah, and D'Ann."

"What about 'em?"

"Last time I checked in with D'Ann, she told me they

was holed up with three black fellas in a room down there. Been down there all afternoon. Said they brought a big party and lots of money, so they might be indisposed for a while. When they say they're having a party, that means them boys brought their own drugs."

"What kind of drugs?"

"Meth, I believe." Jerry tilted his head back to think. "Yeah, I believe they said it was meth."

Teague said, "You just now thought to tell us this, Jerry?"

"I didn't know who we was—who we was after," Jerry stammered. "It ain't that out of the ordinary to get black johns now and again. Wasn't till just now when you said there was three of 'em and how old they were that I put it together."

"Call those girls right now, see if the johns are still there. If they are, you tell them to do whatever they have to do to keep them there."

Jerry nodded and pulled out his phone. He tapped some buttons and bounced impatiently on his heels while it rang. A film of sweat broke out over his high forehead.

"They might not pick up," Jerry explained, "if they're, you know, indisposed."

But somebody did pick up. Jerry was so relieved he nearly shouted. "Hey, D'Ann, you still got them black fellas down there at the Sundown?" Jerry stuck a finger in his other ear so that he could listen, then looked at Teague with an expression of relief and gave a thumbs-up. He gave the girls their marching orders and ended the call.

Momo grabbed Jerry Perky by his lapel and said, "You're coming with me."

He rounded up Buddy The Face and Verbals, and down the mountain they went, off to go kill some Black folks.

CHAPTER SEVEN
BULLFROG SERENADE

The Bismark Carbon plant was located just outside Cain City's western limit, on a large swath of land that jutted up against the Big Sandy River, a tributary that fed into the nearby Ohio. Nothing else was around it. Come around a bend on State Route 52 and suddenly this behemoth of steel and industry was upon you, its nine-story hearths and hundred-and-fifty-foot-tall silos looming oppressively over the nightscape. Tall stacks billowed clean white puffs of steam into the shroud of black above, and with the whole facility awash in artificial light from Kliegs and LEDs, the plant looked at once like a lodestar from the future and a remnant from the past.

Ephraim steered the Ranger through the main gate and then past the brine tank and the water treatment center, to the parking lot designated for employees. When he stepped out, sharp winds coming down off the hills and into the river valley swirled about him, creating miniature cyclones of dust and debris that flew into his eyes. Ephraim slung his duffel over his shoulder, shielded his face, and cut through the maintenance shop to get to the change room, located in the next building over. The two repairmen who worked the overnight shift, Bo Wayne and Don

Sparks, were in there, drinking coffee and loading gear into tool chests that were attached to the utility bicycles they used to rove around the plant. The bikes were these three-wheeled jobs equipped with a cart welded between the two back tires.

Sparks was a surly old bat who didn't even acknowledge Ephraim coming in, but Bo Wayne glanced up and said, "Them little piggies are huffin' and puffin' out there, ain't they?"

"Sure are," Ephraim replied. "That coffee spiked?"

"Does the Pope shit in the woods?"

"If he has to, I reckon he does."

Ephraim went out the other side of the shop, braced against the wind, and walked the twenty yards to the building that housed the change room. A couple years prior they'd replaced the good old-fashioned time clock with a bone-density scanner. Ephraim stuck his finger on the panel, waited for it to beep, and moved on.

Bismark had been constructed in the fifties, and in the intervening years a total of zero alterations had been made to the change room. A pungent bleachy smell failed to offset the decades of grime and scum that had accumulated in the grouting and on the tiles. Ephraim's locker was three rows down. He turned onto his row and found Billy Horseman standing there with his hands on his hips, waist-down naked.

"Put that heinous thing away," Ephraim said. Billy was uncut and his foreskin was roughly the same length as his actual penis, hanging down like the deflated neck of a balloon. On a dare he'd once tied it into a knot and tried to piss. Turned out to be more painful than he'd imagined.

"Shh," Billy put a finger to his lips. "Listen."

"I'm serious Billy, you swing that thing in my face I'm gonna punch you in the nuts."

"Listen," Billy said again, voice low. He perked an ear. "Play along, okay?"

"With what?"

From across the room somebody boomed, "Fuckin' Horseman!"

Billy scrambled to get the rest of his uniform off the hanger, sat down on the bench and started casually dressing. Ephraim opened his locker and started unbuttoning his flannel. Lou Manns came barreling around the corner like a hot ball of fury and nearly knocked Ephraim over.

"Whoa, now," Ephraim exclaimed, regaining his footing.

"What seems to be the problem, Lou?" Billy said, calmly standing on the other side of Ephraim, buttoning his pants.

Lou, red-faced and nearly spuming at the mouth, thrust his hard hat out in front of him. Somebody had filled it with spray foam. "You trying to tell me it wasn't you pulled this shit?"

"I don't know what you're talking about, Lou. I didn't fill your goddamned hat with spray foam if that's what you're insinuating. Why would I do such a thing?" Billy turned incredulous. "Frankly, I'm insulted you would automatically come to such a conclusion."

"Let me ask you something, Horseman."

"You have my permission, Lou. Ask away."

"Do you think I'm a fucking idjit?"

"Well, Lou, I would have never volunteered my opinion on the subject, but since you are eliciting me for it— yes, I do."

Lou Manns brandished his hard hat as a weapon. Raising it above his head, he made for Billy. Ephraim shoved his palms into Lou's chest and held him back.

"Bring it on, big fella," Billy taunted him, raising his fists and feinting like a boxer.

Lou maneuvered to get around Ephraim's block, but it wasn't a full-hearted effort, and Ephraim kept him at bay with minimal exertion.

"Easy now, Lou," Ephraim said. "When did this happen?"

"Just now!" Lou yelled, already winded from the outburst. "I went to take a shit and when I came back my helmet was full of fuckin' foam."

Billy asked, "You sure it didn't come out of your ears?"

"Goddammit, Billy," Ephraim spat. "Shut your yap for a second." He turned to Lou, who looked as if something may, in fact, be on the precipice of coming out of his ears. "So this just happened?"

"Right," Lou said.

"See," Billy crowed. "Couldn't have been me. I've been sitting here talking to Ephraim for least ten minutes. Ain't that right, Ephraim?"

Ephraim said, "Don't put me in the middle of this thing."

"If it takes you longer than ten minutes to drop a turd, Lou, maybe you should see a doctor."

Lou cocked the hard hat back and hurled it at Billy, who ducked it with ease. The hat banged off the lockers.

"That's one way to treat your protective equipment," Billy said.

"Like I can ever use it again," Lou fumed.

Ephraim raised his hands, signaling for everyone to calm down. "Look here, fellas, I'm about tired of playing peacemaker here. If y'all wanna tussle, can you wait for me to get my shit out of my locker please? I will just say, Lou, Billy is telling the truth. Me and him have been sitting here talking for a good handful of minutes, and he didn't get up and go anywhere or anything like that while I was talking to him. So unless he messed with your helmet a while before that, I don't know what to tell you."

Lou fixed an odious glare on Billy, but addressed Ephraim. "He didn't say nothing to you about doing this?"

"Not a word. And you know well as I do it ain't like Billy to not gloat about this type of thing."

Lou grimaced, unconvinced. He poked a finger at Billy. "I find out this was you, Horseman, me and you are gonna have it out once and for all."

"You know where to find me, ya old fart."

Lou clenched his teeth and made a weary growl that quivered his cheeks, gave the side of the lockers a little kick that hurt his toe, threw a couple curses together, and slunk off in a snit. Ephraim sat beside Billy on the bench, then peered around the corner to make certain Lou wasn't coming back for a second helping.

Billy said, "That was fun, right? Totally worth it."

"You're gonna get me in trouble."

"Nah." Billy waved a dismissive hand. "You worry too much. These fuckin' old-timers don't have no sense of humor. 'Sides, I had to get Lou before they can me."

"What are you talking about?" Ephraim said, leaning over to tie his boots. "Before who cans you?"

"You ain't heard the rumors?"

"What rumors?"

"They're shutting down one of the lines."

"You shitting me?" Ephraim sat up. "Says who?"

"Little birdie on my shoulder. Fuck you been? Everybody's heard it. Ask around if you don't believe me."

Ephraim ran a hand through his hair and fretted over the implications of such a thing being true. "Which line?" he asked.

"That I don't know. Might not be us."

Ephraim shook his head. "Who you kidding? We're two of the youngest operators in this place."

"Tell me about it. We're surrounded by the infirm." Billy hiked an eyebrow and tapped his pointer finger against his temple. "If you know what I'm saying."

"Yeah, I picked it up."

Billy finished getting dressed while Ephraim sat there being gloomy. Billy grabbed his sack lunch, closed his locker and stood. "Welp," he said with a shrug, as though he'd already come to terms with his demise. "C'mon, maybe they'll tell us what's what in the meeting."

The overnight supervisor, Trent Napier, was a dopey-looking fellow with a prodigious belly no ordinary set of pants could rein in. When seated, the belly made it hard for Napier to reach the table without a little extra heave forward. He did that now, scooped up the paperwork that detailed the output for the previous sixteen hours, and, in his uniquely drab and nasally voice, recited the numbers for every baker operator and activator operator coming on shift. Ephraim operated the two D-line activators, which were located at the south end of the plant, so his briefing always came last.

"Feed rate's looking good on D, averaging"—Napier scanned the printout—"ninety pounds per minute. Discharge rate is solid, spitting out at roughly forty-six pounds. Temps are good on all the hearths. Zach said evening shift was getting some clunkers in the grizzly bars down at the bottom there, Ephraim, so do a couple checks on those throughout the night. Make sure nothing's getting jammed up." He asked the eight men sitting around the table if they had any questions.

Billy raised his hand. "Got one right here, Chief."

"Go ahead, Horseman."

"A lot of talk going around about possible layoffs, but no word's come down official yet. Can you tell us what gives there?"

Napier pursed his lips, put his elbows on his paunch, and leaned into his clasped hands. "I don't know how that got out."

"So it's true?" Lou Manns jumped in. "They're shutting down one of the lines?"

Napier winced as though fielding such a question physically pained him. "Yes, that's true. We weren't going to announce it until the end of the week, but somehow you already know."

"Which line?" Ephraim asked.

"I've not been told which line, just that there is going to be a shutdown of one of them."

"So how's it gonna work? Is everybody from that line gonna get laid off, or are they gonna base it off of seniority or what?"

"I really can't speculate. You're not supposed to know this. I'm not supposed to be talking about it." Napier wiggled miserably in his seat, which groaned with its own form of misery. "These are not my decisions, you understand. If it were up to me, we'd never lay anybody off, and I know Mr. Crawford feels that way too. What I do know is this is happening for multiple reasons. It's not just one or two things. But finding the quality of coal we need is hard to come by lately, as the mining industry keeps taking hits. On top of that, the demand for a number of our products has waned in recent months. So we're getting pinched on both ends. Hopefully this whole stall-out blows over, things pick up soon, and the layoffs will only be temporary, as they were when this happened four years ago. But in the meantime—"

"That layoff lasted for over a year," said Billy.

"Yes, it did," Napier acknowledged.

"So that's what we're looking at? Least a year?"

"I'd say so."

"So we better start searching for something else, huh Trent?"

Napier exhaled, his nose wheezing. "I'll tell you what I know when I know it."

Ephraim and Billy exited the administration building and trekked across the defunct railroad tracks that bisected the plant. The wind was still whipping up dust, but they had their hard hats and safety goggles on now, so they didn't worry about shit blowing in their eyes. They took the path that split between the A-line hearth and the B-line silo and eventually came to the bake quarters, where Billy worked.

"So," Billy said, speaking for the first time since they'd left the meeting. "We're fucked."

Ephraim nodded in agreement. "Seems like it."

"You see Napier? I thought that goof-nut was about to cry. He's not too bad a guy I don't guess, as company men go."

"I don't guess."

Ephraim said "Adios" and continued on his way to the D-line station. Its activator, the nine-story hearth, and its silo were the last major structures on the southern end of the plant. Beyond them was a back access road; the coalfield, where giant stores of coal were kept and replenished daily; and a spare lot where large replacement parts were kept. Past that was nothing but river and wilderness.

The D-line station was a single-story cinder-block

building located at the base of the activator, nondescript in every way, save for a giant mural of the American flag that'd been painted on the wall by the door. Ephraim scanned his key card and waited for the buzzer to sound and the door to click open. When neither of these things happened, he looked and saw that the door wasn't completely shut. The lock bolt was a little worn and sometimes failed to catch in the jamb. You had to give it a little extra oomph to make sure it latched, and whoever had been in there last, presumably Zach on the evening shift, had failed to do so. Ephraim went in and pulled the door fully shut behind him.

There wasn't much to the station. A short hallway with a utility closet, bathroom, and small conference room to one side, a break room and the operator's office to the other. Ephraim walked down the short hall to the office. He checked the control panels on the computer. Everything looked to be running proper, so next he grabbed a black sample bag from the dispenser on the wall and went back out of the building. First thing he did was make sure there were no clunkers jamming up the exit mouth of the hearth. There weren't; the activated carbon was coming out unimpeded. Ephraim couldn't see any evidence of there having been a problem either. He suspected Zach and some of the other operators reported stuff like that just to seem like they were doing something. Those were the types of guys that managed to keep their jobs, Ephraim thought. The cheats and embellishers.

From the hearth he made the hundred-yard slog over to the packaging warehouse, where he unscrewed a sample basin from the pipe that connected it to the transporters. Every ten minutes, an automated system took a small cut of the activated carbon and diverted it to the basin. Three times a shift this sample was to be collected and labeled in order to be shipped to the lab and inspected.

Ephraim poured the sample cuts into the plastic bag, tied it off, and headed back to D-Station.

In the office he removed his hard hat and safety glasses, printed up the product label, and applied it to the sample. Then he checked the monitors again. Everything was the same.

Ephraim sat down in the swivel and settled in for the long night ahead. Other than keeping an eye on the control panels, collecting the remaining samples, checking the hearth a time or two more, and filling out the standard paperwork at the end of the shift, long as things went smooth, he'd have fuck-all responsibility for most of the night.

He was a man at his post, nothing more, nothing less. There was merit to showing up day in, day out, doing your job well and without complaint. But there was nothing honorable about being laid off; of this, he was certain.

They were able to text on their phones, or make a call, but the company didn't allow Wi-Fi access outside of the admin building, so Ephraim kept a selection of books stashed in a desk drawer to alleviate the hours of boredom. He pulled one out now. Usually he went for thrillers or books that had a little snot to them, a little attitude, but some yahoo at the library recommended *A Confederacy of Dunces*, and he'd been slogging through it for a month. The book was clever enough, had even made him laugh aloud a time or two, but if there was a story somewhere in there Ephraim didn't know what it was. He'd gotten most of the way through a chapter when somebody thumped on the outside door.

Ephraim checked the time: 11:30 p.m. Lucia's shift at the diner ended half an hour ago. Possibly it was her, though he didn't think she'd actually come. He hopped up and walked briskly down the hallway, hoping he was wrong and that she'd found somebody to look after her nephew.

Whoever was doing the thumping kept at it, and Ephraim hurried down the hall, calling out, "Hold your horses." The power of the wind bearing against the door made him have to push hard to open it. Billy Horseman was on the other side, leg reared back to kick it again.

Billy set his foot down. "Took you long enough. What you doing in there, rubbing one out or something?"

"Oh, I don't know, Billy. Working."

"Yeah, right. Whatcha reading?"

"*Confederacy of Dunces*."

"Still."

"Yeah, still."

"Look here, got something for you." Billy's hands were clasped over an object of some sort that he was hiding down by his side. He looked very pleased with himself, which made Ephraim skeptical on reflex. Billy brought his hands forward like he was making an offering and revealed the thing that was in them. A big-ass bullfrog. Its neck pulsed steadily, its ogling eyeballs rolling around as if it were simply taking in the scenery, like nothing at all was amiss.

"Fuck you doing with a bullfrog?" Ephraim asked.

"I'm gonna tell you what I'm doing with it. I'm gonna *throw it* into one of the hearths and see what happens."

"Not in my activator you're not."

"Says you."

"Yeah, says me."

"Why not?"

"Cuz if I open one of the hearths, the temperature's gonna fluctuate, and my luck some jackass supervisor will notice, and then they're gonna ask me about it, and I'll have to say, 'Fuckin' Billy talked me into murdering a bullfrog and you know how persuasive he is. There was nothing to be done.' And I'm not dealing with that bull-shit today."

Billy looked at Ephraim as though it must be pleasant to be so simple. "We're probably getting fired any day now as it is, man."

"Yeah, all right," Ephraim conceded. "Let's go."

They climbed the stairs up to the fourth rung of the ac-tivator, high enough to where opening a hearth wouldn't cause too much temperature variance. They didn't have to worry about being seen because nobody came around at night, and Trent Napier was lazy as hell; he never checked on them. Also, everybody that worked at Bismark knew there were only three security cameras on the property. One at the gate, one on the admin building, and one di-rected toward the parking lot, so no worries there.

Each level of the hearth had a stove-like hatch that could be used to observe the interior of the furnace. It was rarely opened and as Ephraim pulled the lever the squeal of metal on metal grated their ears. The hinges were cor-roded, but finally he felt the lever release. He turned to Bil-ly and had to yell to be heard over the din of the machinery.

"When I open it, throw it right in. Don't dawdle."

Billy bobbed his head excitedly. "Yeah, yeah. Open it."

Ephraim yanked the hatch open, and only then, when it saw the shimmer of heat and the magma-colored glow in-side the oven, did the frog catch on that shit was about to get real. Its body rapidly inflated and contracted and it emitted deep-throated croaks of alarm. Billy tossed it in.

The frog landed amongst the hot coals on the conveyor belt, took one hop, and its whole body exploded. For once

Billy was speechless. He clapped his hands to the sides of his head as if he were in shock. His mouth fell open and he pointed toward the space where, a second ago, a frog had existed. The whole thing had just disintegrated, nothing left.

"Holy shit," Billy said in wonderment. "Now we know."

"Know what? What fifteen hundred degrees does to a frog?"

"Yep. I bet not too many people have seen such a thing."

Ephraim shut the hatch and shoved the lever over to seal it. Everything up there was black and dirty from coal dust and Ephraim's palms were black from touching the lever. He wiped them on his uniform.

"I feel kinda bad about that," Billy said sheepishly, as though he were trying guilt on for size, see how it felt. "Maybe I should say some words."

"Sure. Little late for regrets, though, don't you think?"

"You're right." Billy nodded. "What's done is done. Hey, I got a joint." He fished a spliff from his pocket and held it out for Ephraim to inspect. The roll was packed fat with weed.

Ephraim shrugged. "Why not."

Billy couldn't get the joint sparked in the wind, so Ephraim cupped his hands to help shield the flame, and Billy got it lit. They set their hard hats on the grated floor and rested their elbows on the south-facing rail, passed the smoke between them, and looked out over the river valley. The wind blew heavy through the trees and they could hear it whistling over the noise of the machinery. The moon hung fat in the sky and reflected off the river in a million tiny glints. Far off on the horizon they could see cracks of lightning, but no accompanying thunder reached their ears. Ephraim looked at the moon and thought about his son and the telescope he'd gotten for his birthday. Maybe Caleb had found some joy in that today, at least.

"Y'all got a bunch of kids," Ephraim said. Though Billy was a couple years younger, he married into a gaggle of step-kids whose ages ranged from preteen to low twenties, and he'd sired three of his own that were around Caleb's age.

"You're telling me. Sheila's like a damn baby mill. I give her a hug and somehow nine months later a baby comes out."

"I don't think that's the way that works. Maybe you should check paternity."

"Oh, I'm not that lucky," Billy said. "They're mine."

"How is Sheila?"

"Moody as hell. I could lasso that moon right there and she'd find something to complain about how I did it. You did it correct, I'm telling ya. One and done, get rid of the lady. That's the way to go."

"I don't know if I'd say all that."

"I got a theory about women."

"This should be good."

"Hear me out, I think I'm right about this. What I think happens is, women, you know how most of 'em don't ever fart in front of you? They hold all their farts in, see, and what happens is, it comes out as *drama*."

Ephraim chuckled. "That's a theory, all right."

"Tell me I'm wrong."

"What number y'all up to now?"

"Number of what?"

"Kids."

"Seven by last count. Though now you say it, I'm not sure that last one's mine. Got a funny look to him."

"Then he's yours for sure."

"Yeah, probably."

"You ever heard of a thing called PANS or PANDAS?"

"You mean like the animal?"

"No. It's an illness."

"No, I ain't never heard of that one. What is it?"

"I dunno." Ephraim flicked the ash off the end of the joint and took a long drag. He blew a thick column of smoke from his nostrils and passed it to Billy. "It's no good. Has something to do with your brain swelling up, making you go psycho, basically."

"You think that's what Caleb's got?"

"Maybe. I dunno. I typed his symptoms into Google and a bunch of shit on that popped up. Whatever it is, he's getting worse. I gotta call the doctor tomorrow."

"Sorry to hear that, buddy. But you shouldn't be looking that shit up on Google. Talk about making you go crazy."

"Yeah."

Ephraim told Billy about Caleb climbing on top of his table at school that day, and how he screamed about Nazis killing babies and wanting the abominable snowman to murder him.

Billy hit the joint and thought about that. "Well," he said, "he's not wrong. Nazis did kill babies."

"That they did."

The two men smoked the rest of the joint without conversation. When it was cashed Billy flicked the roach over the side of the railing and they watched the dying ember arc down and vanish.

"Say, whatchoo gonna do when they fire us?" Billy asked.

"Scrounge around for some odd jobs I suppose, like last time. Try to get something under the table. I dunno. I gotta make some cash somehow. You?"

"Oh, I already know what I'm gonna do. I'm gonna hock makeup and beauty products."

Ephraim snorted.

"You laugh now, but just you wait. There's a fortune to be made. Sheila buys that stuff all the time off the internet, and you know who she buys it from?"

"People that sell it on the internet."

"A bunch of fat moms who all look alike. I've not seen one man selling that stuff. Not one. That there's what you call a gap in the market. I'll bet women would love to be told how beautiful they are by a man, and how beautiful they're gonna be. Every woman wants to be made to feel like a million bucks. It's gonna be a gold mine, I'm telling you. You should do it too. After a while, you get other people to sell it under you—they're like your disciples— and you get a cut of their profit. It's a win for everybody."

"That's called a pyramid scheme."

"Damn right. I'm gonna climb to the top of the beauty and wellness pyramid. Get me a YouTube channel and everything. Do makeup tutorials. It'll blow up, you watch. You ever get a gander of me in eyeliner, you better watch out. You might feel a tingle in places that make you uncomfortable with your worldview."

Ephraim squinted his eyes and pretended to scrutinize Billy's mug as if he were giving it an imaginary makeover. Billy twisted his body away, then whipped his head back over his shoulder with his lips puckered and cheeks vacuum-sucked in.

"Seductive as you are at present, I don't know that I could get past, you know"—Ephraim gestured to everything above Billy's neck—"how butt-ugly you are."

"Could be a problem," Billy admitted. "Maybe I'll just be a rapper. What was that one redneck rapper's name?

Bubba Sparxxx? That's what I'll do. I'll be the next Bubba Sparxxx."

Ephraim was about done. "You ready to get back to it?"

"If I must. Hey, you think Bubba Sparxxx is any relation to Don?"

"Eh, I'd say there's plenty of people with the surname Sparks."

"I'm gonna ask him."

The two men descended the four flights of stairs. Before going their separate directions, Billy dug into his pocket and asked if Ephraim needed a little pick-me-up to get through the night.

"Naw, I'm good."

"Suit yourself," said Billy, popping the pill into his mouth.

Since he was already out, Ephraim considered walking back over to packaging and collecting his test sample, but it wasn't time yet, and he didn't want to cut corners, even if he was likely to be laid off. He scanned his key card, went into the station, and checked the controls to see if there'd been any temperature variation on the fourth-level hearth. The monitor registered a forty-degree flux, probably from the increase in draft and oxygen. That'd bounce back in a jiff, with nobody being none the wiser.

There came another bang at the door. Ephraim knew it wasn't a supervisor because they all had card access. He walked to the front, fully expecting to see Billy again, probably with another bullfrog or some other devised mischief. But this time the knocker wasn't Billy. This time, it was Lucia.

She stood with her arms crossed, making a face like she was already ruing the decision to come there. She had her hip jutted out to sprinkle some sass over the tableau.

But this stance belied the fact that (a) she'd shown up in the first place. Bismark Carbon was no hop, skip, and a jump from anywhere. Top of that, she'd had to walk damn near half a mile in the wind to get here from the access road. And (b), she'd granted his request and was still wearing her uniform from the diner, minus the paper hat.

"I thought you were gonna text me," Ephraim said.

"I did text you. You didn't respond, and I wasn't gonna sit alone on that creepy-ass road waiting for a horror movie to break out."

"Sorry, I didn't get it. Service out here is terrible."

"Yeah, no shit."

"It's good to see you, though. Great to see you, actually."

She cocked her head dubiously. "Uh-huh."

Ephraim leaned against the doorframe. His eyes skimmed her top to bottom and he flashed a wide smile. "Well. You gonna give us a twirl?"

"Don't push it," Lucia warned, but it didn't have much teeth to it.

"You say so," Ephraim said, dialing the smile down a few notches. "It's getting cold. You thinking about coming in, or you gonna stay out here getting windblown a bit longer?"

CHPATER EIGHT

FAT TIMES IN CAIN CITY

The Sundown Courts Motel was laid out in three separate buildings, each three stories tall, that formed a hard U-shape around a dingy courtyard. The courtyard boasted a pool that looked more like a lagoon at this point—pond scum germinated out from the corners, and there were a few tables and lawn chairs scattered around. In its heyday the Sundown had been the premier motor lodge off the I-64 pass, but sometime around the Clinton presidency it fell into a state of disrepair and stayed that way. From then on it was the type of place that rented rooms by the hour, or half hour if necessary. Whatever it had to do to stay in business. If junkies or the similarly downtrodden could scrape together five hundred bucks, a room could be had for the month. Occasionally it would lure in some weary travelers from the interstate, but often they'd get a look at the rooms, or the riffraff, and move on down the road.

There were only a handful of cars parked in the lot when Verbals pulled the minivan headfirst into a spot by the courtyard. Jerry Perky pulled his Chrysler LeBaron in next to it, clambered out, and moseyed into the office. A minute later, he emerged with a key card and motioned for the others to come on. Momo, Buddy The Face, and

Verbals got out of the van and followed Jerry around the pool, where a plump middle-aged man and woman were reclined on the lounge chairs, nursing wine coolers. The couple watched the serious-looking men with the detached curiosity of drunkards.

"Get in your room," Buddy barked at them. The pair didn't protest. They walrus-rolled out of the chairs, collected their mini-cooler, and scurried away, the man repeatedly nudging the woman to move faster, she slapping his hand away.

Jerry Perky pointed out the third-floor room on the far building where the prostitutes were holed up, number 327. With Momo leading the way, they ascended the stairwell and strode down the corridor. Each man drew his gun. Buddy also had an extendable steel baton that he snapped out to its full length. The curtains to the room were closed. The TV was on inside; it sounded like an action movie was playing. Jerry slipped the key card in and out of the slot, a tiny light flashed green, and the door clicked. Momo stepped to the fore, turned down the handle, and went in, Buddy and Verbals direct on his tail, Jerry bringing up the rear.

The blue glow of the television illuminated the otherwise-darkened room. Momo quickly parsed the visual information in front of him. Two empty pizza boxes on the dresser next to the TV. Clothes strewn about. In the near bed one of the black boys lay beneath the floral-patterned comforter pulled up to his chin, sleeping. Another, on the far bed, was *in flagrante* with two of the girls. The one called D'Ann was attending to him orally while the one named Tracy suckled his neck. All of them stark naked.

The third girl, Janice, was perched on a stool back by

the vanity sink, snorting meth off the counter. She won the superlative for best dressed, seeing as she was the only one wearing a stitch of clothing: a cutoff white tank and a pair of long fuzzy socks, nothing in between. She threw her head back after hitting the meth and was the first to notice the intruders. She smiled brightly and waved at them with both hands, fingers twinkling, as though four killers entering a room made for a nice addition to the party.

Pippen was oblivious to their presence. His eyes were on the ceiling as he mouthed noises of pleasure that sounded vaguely like the moans of a deaf seal. He had a handful of D'Ann's lemon-bleached hair and was forcing her down to where she was gagging on him. Momo squatted down to admire their naked forms at eye level. He lingered for a moment, enjoying the show, before standing and motioning for Buddy The Face to position himself on the far side of the bed. As Buddy crossed the room he briefly blocked the glow from the TV. Pippen felt the shadow wipe across his face. As he looked to see who it was, Verbals threw on the lights.

Pippen squinted against the sudden brightness and shielded his eyes. It took about half a second for his brain to compute how much trouble he was in. Four figures, all white, all brandishing guns. The little one in front had a teeny upturned nose and far-set eyes that made him look downright amphibian. Two tall men flanked him, and on the other end of the bed was some muscled-up, Frankenstein-looking mug wearing an eyepatch. He'd never seen these men with his own eyes, but he'd heard enough of the stories—the myths—to know, instantly, whom he was dealing with. Stenders. Dread mainlined into his veins.

Tracy, ever the professional, had yet to stop sucking on Pippen's neck. He shoved her clean off the bed, threw D'Ann's head off his cock, and scrambled for the .32 ACP on the nightstand. Buddy The Face brought the baton down hard on Pippen's outstretched hand. His metacarpals crunched beneath the blow, his fingers bending backward around the rod. Pippen yelped in pain. He retracted his arm and jerked into a sitting position. Buddy swept the baton across the nightstand, knocking a bottle of Crown Royale and the .32 to the floor. The liquor glugged from the mouth of the bottle.

"Hand me that, will you, darlin'?" Momo said to Tracy, who was already down there, Pippen having shoved her from the bed. She grabbed the bottle of Crown and offered it up.

"The gun, darlin'," Momo said.

"Oh." She dropped the liquor like a sack, picked up the silver .32 and handed it to him. Verbals helped her to her feet. Momo examined the weapon for a moment, tested its heft, felt to see how well it fit in his hand, then tucked it into his waistband.

The hubbub stirred Kevon. He came to groggily, peeling his eyes open to find the barrel-hole of a Smith & Wesson 500 leveled at his face. He bolted upright, knocking the back of his head against the headboard, and thrust his hands into the air. Verbals yanked the covers off him, saw that he was in boxers and didn't have any guns.

"It wasn't me!" Kevon shouted.

This got Momo and his cronies laughing. "It wasn't me? Ain't that a song? '*It wasn't me.*'" Momo screwed up his face trying to remember, hummed a few bars, then started singing it. "'*Saw me fuckin' in the ocean. IT WASN'T ME. Caught me hittin' on her mama. Duh duh duh-duh.*' Who sang that shit?" he asked. Nobody buzzed in with the answer. "C'mon, who sang that shit?" He searched the faces in the room, got blank stares in return.

"Never heard of it," Buddy The Face growled. "Sounds awful."

"I might not be doing it justice." Momo waved his pistol at Pippen and Kevon. "You two gotta know."

D'Ann, who was still lying on her stomach atop the bed, rolled over, swung her feet to the floor, and sat forward with her elbows on her knees. She wiped her mouth on the back of her wrist and mumbled, "They probably wasn't even born when that song came out."

"You drowsy from dick or what, girl? Speak up."

D'Ann raised her voice. "I said that song is old as shit. These fools probably wudn't even born yet."

"Goddamn, you don't have to yell. You know who sang it?"

"Shaggy."

"Shaggy? Naw, I thought that was what's his name? Caribbean dude . . . Akon."

"Wudn't no Akon. Some other fella sings the one part you was butchering, but it was Shaggy's song."

"Huh," Momo shrugged. "Learn something new."

"We still gonna get paid or what?" D'Ann snapped. She made a show of rubbing a crick out of her neck. "This was a long-ass day."

Momo deferred that question to Jerry Perky, who said, "Course you are, D. Y'all are all getting a big fat bonus for this here."

"Good. Can we leave now?"

"Hold on for a second, sweetheart," Momo said. "We got to get to the bottom of some murderin' and thievin' 'fore you light outta here." He turned his attention back to Pippen, who'd tucked his maimed hand into his armpit and had his good hand hiding his genitals. "Why you being shy? We done seen that flagpole." Momo tilted his head to scam a look through Pippen's drawn legs. "My, my, my-y-y-y. Anybody got a good blade on 'em? I like to slice that thing off, balls and all. Get it taxidermied. Mount it on the wall. I'd make it my centerpiece. Present it to my houseguests at parties like, 'Have you seen my African cock?'

"'Ooh,' they'll say. 'I've only seen ones with such width and girth on the internet. Did you get it from the Congo? Or perhaps the Dominican?'

"'Guess again,' I'll say.

"'The *black* market?' they'll ask.

"'No, no, no, you'll never believe it, but I bagged this beauty myself right down here in Cain City. At the Sundown Courts of all places.'

"'You're kidding,' they'll say.

"And I'll say, 'Do I look like a kidder? I tracked him for a full day and into the night, snuck right up on him. He never even saw me coming.'"

"Fuck you," Pippen spat.

"You offerin'?" Momo smiled. "How long you been going at it with these girls? Four, five hours?"

"Seven," said D'Ann.

"Seven?!" Momo exclaimed. He dropped his jaw open in mock awe, started pacing at the foot of the bed. "My God, tires me out just thinking about it. Seven. I'm surprised you ain't fucked out by now. Behold, behold, the stamina of youth. Enjoy that shit while it lasts. Now," he flicked his gun at Pippen, narrowed his eyes on him. "Which one are you, Rodney Slash . . . Kevon Thompson . . . or Eric Pippen? I'm guessing . . . Eric Pippen. Am I right?"

"Yeah."

"Man, I'm good. And that makes you"—Momo twirled his finger and landed it on Kevon—"Thompson. Right again, ain't I? I'm on a roll. That means we're missing one Rodney Slash. Where, oh where, is Rodney Slash? Hmm? . . . Anybody?" Momo's gaze flicked back and forth between the two of them. "You seen him? How 'bout you? He a magician, vanish into thin air? He under the bed, what?" Kevon seemed incapable of articulating anything more than an infantile sob at this point, which left the onus on Pippen, who wasn't faring much better.

"I—I don't—" Pippen stuttered.

"Careful what you say now, 'cause this is on the record." Momo gestured with a sweeping hand to everyone in the room. "Got a bunch of witnesses. Everything that comes out of your mouth *can* and *will* be used against you in these here Sundown Courts." After a beat with nobody saying anything, Momo said, "Tell you what. We'll put a pin in it. You two gather your wits about you and we'll circle back. You." He tapped D'Ann on the shoulder with the barrel of his Colt 9. She jerked away from him. "No need to get skittish. These mooks stole a big bag of my money and a bunch of our methamphetamine to boot. Now, have you seen that money or that methamphetamine?"

"They each had a thick wad of cash and a bunch of crystal baggies stuffed in their pockets, but I ain't seen nothing more than that."

"Was it good stuff?"

"Was what good stuff?"

"The meth, dummy."

"Oh. It hit clean enough I reckon. Wudn't too stepped on."

"Yeah," Tracy concurred. "I thought it was a pretty sweet fix."

"Sweet fix. Sounds like our stuff!" Momo exalted. He fixated on Pippen, exaggerating an air of impatience.

"Times up, Eric. I'ma ask this once. Where's the money, where's the drugs?"

"I don't know what you're talking about," Pippen said feebly. "We ain't stole shit."

Momo nodded at Buddy. He cracked Pippen across the shins with the baton. Pippen screamed and curled into a ball, holding his legs, and writhed back and forth.

"That was nothing. That was the rip of a Band-Aid. You open your mouth with another lie, I *will* lop that pecker off. You understand me, shitbird? I'll slice that pecker clean, and I will rip your fuckin' head off your neck and let D'Ann here stuff it right down your goddamn lying throat. Show you how it feels. Oh, quit your hollerin' and let me know that you understand the words that are coming out of my mouth." Pippen bit his lip and bobbed his head vigorously up and down. "Good. Now, where's your third man? Rodney."

"I dunno," Pippen croaked.

Momo signaled for Buddy to take another whack.

"I was fucking, man!" Pippen cried. "You saw me. I was fucking. I don't know where he went. Swear to God."

Momo cuffed Kevon alongside his head. "What about you, sleepyhead?"

Kevon was so petrified he could barely form words. "I . . . was . . . sleep."

Momo looked to Tracy, who claimed ignorance, then to D'Ann.

"I didn't see," she said. "Had my mouth full."

"Jesus Christ, he had to go somewhere. What do I have to do, call in the K-9 unit?"

A delicate voice squeaked out from behind Buddy The Face. "He might've went down to the vending machine." Buddy stepped aside, revealing Janice, the tiny, malnourished-looking thing that'd waved to them when they came in. She had raw, knobby knees; greasy black hair; and stretch marks spiderwebbing out from her belly button. But her face was soft, unblemished, young. If she was eighteen, she was *just* eighteen. Through all the ruckus she'd maintained a tranquil smile, as though the sun were shining and the flowers were blooming, and a little gunplay amongst the wicked was all in good fun. She sniffed to clear the meth drip from the back of her throat and said, "I saw him counting out quarters a little bit ago."

"When was this?"

She scrunched her shoulders. "I dunno. Not long 'fore you guys showed up."

Momo sent Verbals and Jerry out to find Slash and told the girls they were free to leave. Quick as they could, they hurried into their clothes and gathered their belongings. As they did, Momo saw there were still a few pieces of sausage pizza left in one of the boxes on the dresser and helped himself to a slice. When the women left he started back on Pippen.

"You like white women, huh?"

Pippen didn't respond. Momo waved his gun at him, talked while he was chewing the pizza. "I'll bet you're the one knocked up Lil Mike Mike's girl, ain'tcha?"

"I don't know no Mike Mike."

"No, you wouldn't know Lil Mike Mike 'cause Lil Mike Mike's dead. But I bet you know his daughter. What's her name, Buddy? The one that had the little tar baby."

"Rosalind."

"That's right. Rosalind. Pretty little thing, ain't she? But trouble. Bet she gives you fits. Huh, boy? She give you fits?" Momo craned his neck down to make eye contact with Pippen, who looked as if he was in some kind of trance, gazing at everybody's navel. "Yeah, you know what I'm talking about.

She always was trouble, Rosalind, ever since she was a little thing. Go from zero to cunt in about point-six seconds. But you know that, don't you? You know Rosalind real well."

"Never heard of her."

Momo polished off the pizza, wiped his greasy hands off on his jeans, and sighed. "See now, I told you I'd had 'bout enough of the lying." He took a step closer and aimed the Colt at Pippen's head.

Pippen raised his arms in a defensive position. "No, wait," he pleaded. "Please. I got a kid."

"Yeah, I know that, dipshit. Did you not hear what the fuck I was just saying?" Momo pressed the muzzle of the gun hard into Pippen's forehead. Pippen squeezed his eyes shut, started breathing thickly in and out, then opened them and glared defiantly up the length of the barrel.

The bravado amused Momo. He appreciated a man who could muster a little swagger when facing the end. "Last chance," he told Pippen. "Lightning round. Your boy, Rodney, he's who pulled the trigger on our friends today, isn't he?" Pippen didn't say anything. "Isn't he?" Momo jabbed Pippen's forehead with the barrel of the gun.

"Yes."

"Where's our product and our money?"

"He's got it."

Momo rammed Pippen's head back against the wall. "Where's our shit?"

"He's got it. I just told you, motherfucker."

"You find my shoes under your mother's bed?"

"What?"

"You called me a motherfucker. Did you find my shoes under your mother's bed?"

"My mom's been dead since I was five years old."

"Sorry for your loss, but you're fixing to meet her right quick, you don't tell me where your buddy is *right now.*"

Pippen grit his teeth. "Even if I knew, which I don't, no fucking way I'm telling you."

"Now that, I believe." Momo removed the gun from Pippen's head and waved it toward Kevon, who was quietly weeping on the other bed. Snot dripping out of his nose. "What do you think? You think he'll give up the goose? Huh? I do."

Pippen glanced over, saw Kevon blubbering all over himself, his eyes squeezed shut, hands steepled in prayer, and realized in that instant that there was no way out, Kevon would give them everything, and they were going to die. Pippen played the last card he could think of.

"If Nico Blakes finds out about this, you in for a world of pain."

"Nico Blakes?" Delight flashed in Momo's eyes. "Ooh-wee, I was wondering when you was gonna invoke that name. That's a lot of hiss, boy. But see, what you are is a snake with no venom. Nico Blakes. Who do you think gave y'all up?" Momo watched the meaning of those words dawn on Pippen. He jammed the muzzle back into his forehead.

"Wait," Pippen blurted. "What if Nico's the one who told us to do it? Told us to take that place?"

"You talking hypothetically? 'Cause you know what I said about fibbin'."

"Yeah, yeah. Just what if, you know? What if he did send us?"

"Then I'd say nice try, little puppy. But Nico Blakes ain't stupid enough to break on us, after all these years, for some piddly stash-house loot. Naw, I reckon if Nico were to ever make a move, he'd go big. Try to take us out all at once. But he don't strike me as the suicidal type. He strike you that way?"

"No," Pippen admitted.

"Naw. I believe *you*, however, are just stupid enough to try and pull off some such nonsense. How 'bout one last chance, Eric? Bonus round. Your girl Rosalind is how y'all knew about the stash house, right? She told you where to go?"

Pippen again squeezed his eyes shut, and this time he kept them that way. "No," he said.

Momo feigned disappointment. "Goddamn. Now that's just aggravating. What did I just say about lying?"

Pippen said, "Don't hurt—"

But that was as far as he got. Momo pulled the trigger, robbing him of his last words. The shot wasn't loud. Kevon had expected more noise, like the shotgun had made that morning. Something that jangled your brain, set your ears to ringing. But this sounded more like a pop-gun, a firecracker. All the same, the back of Pippen's head came apart in chunks, and his brain splatted against the wall. For a moment, improbably, his head stayed suspended above his neck, eyes going crossed, but then his chin fell to his chest and lolled there. Kevon vomited all over himself.

Momo admired the gore as though it were a piece of fine art hanging in a gallery. A pus-like substance oozed from the edges of the bullet hole between Pippen's eyes. Momo bent at the waist to get a better look and stared at it, mesmerized. The pus was gray and yellow and thick like batter.

"You see this?" Momo said in amazement. "The kid literally had shit for brains."

The muzzle flash had singed the skin around the entry wound, and an odor of burnt flesh wafted faintly through the air.

"What do you think he was about to say?" Momo wondered aloud. Then, as if a spell had been lifted, he shrugged, said, "Oh, well, we'll never know," and whirled around to face Kevon. "Your turn to play."

"I didn't know anyone was gonna get shot," Kevon said.

"There, there, now. Course you didn't. You were just along for the ride, am I right? Thought you'd score you some easy money, have some fat times in Cain City, and that'd be that."

Kevon snorted up some snot. "Yeah."

Momo struck a regretful tone. "But things didn't end up working out that way, did they?"

Kevon shook his head. He had cried himself breathless and now he was hyperventilating. Momo waited for the panic to pass.

"You don't want to die today, do you?" he asked tenderly.
"No."

"No, I didn't think so. Answer me a few questions, and we'll get you cleaned of that mess and get you on your way. How'd that be?"

"Good," Kevon sniveled.

"Yeah. Nico Blakes didn't have nothing to do with this, did he?"

"Nuh-uh."

"It was Rosalind led you to it, wasn't it?"

Kevon nodded.

"See, you're doing better than Eric already. Now. Where's. Our. Shit?"

Kevon's whole body began shaking. His arm trembled as he lifted it and pointed to an area behind Momo and Buddy. Momo turned. All that was back there was the TV atop the dresser, a lamp, and a thin door that adjoined the neighboring room. Nothing else. Buddy started flinging the dresser drawers open.

"No, no, not in there," Kevon said, the words coming out sloppy and wet. "In the next room."

From the other side of the wall came a loud thump, like something heavy had been knocked over. Momo and Buddy raised their weapons, stood stock-still, and listened. Kevon whimpered like a puppy left out in the cold.

"Shut up," Momo told him. Kevon obeyed.

For a moment, there was nothing. Pure quiet. Then a series of rapid footfalls hurtled across the floor of the neighboring room, heading in the direction of the exit. Momo and Buddy unleashed a volley of bullets into the wall, firing in slanting patterns to cover both high and low. They didn't stop until their clips were empty. Again, they listened.

The outside door of the next room burst open. Whoever it was started running down the corridor. Buddy rushed across the room. He extracted the used clip, pocketed it, plugged in a full one, and flung open the door. The fleeing man was sprinting away fast, was already near the stairs at the end of the corridor. Buddy hastily took aim and popped off a few rounds, but the bullets missed their mark. The man made the stairs and dropped out of sight. Buddy gave chase.

Momo looked back at Kevon, who, rocking back and forth with his hands over his ears, didn't seem like he was going to be much of a problem. He went over to the adjoining door, unbolted the lock and swung it open. The door on the other side was already ajar. Momo stepped into the room. No one home. The lamp from the dresser was sideways on the floor, base cracked in half, shade torn, its light shining askew on the wall. Feathers floated through the air from where their slugs had hit the pillows. On the bed was a backpack. Momo ripped it open. Inside, by his estimate, was the bulk of the meth that'd been stolen. Outside, gunshots sounded. Momo paid them no mind. He turned the motel room out—beds, drawers, closet, bathroom cabinets, toilet tank. The money wasn't there.

Another exchange of gunfire outside, this time a farther distance away. Momo went back into the other room. "Look at me," he said to Kevon. "I said look at me, you fucking dimwit." Kevon raised his wet eyes. "The money was in that room?"

Kevon nodded.

"How much was there?"

"I dunno," Kevon said. "Like three hundred and some thousand."

And with that, Momo removed the .32 from his waistband, put it to one side of Kevon's head, his Colt 9 to the other, and fired both weapons.

CHAPTER NINE
PLAY GANGSTERS

What Rodney doesn't get is why Pippen is all the time trying to front hard, trying to play gangster. Even on the day they make the biggest score of their lives, the first thing Pippen says in the car afterward is, "Now that we got this money, what's the first thing you gonna buy?"

"I'm getting me a souped street racer," Kevon says. "Like something out of *Fast and Furious* and shit. Like the black CCX."

"All right, all right." Pippen looks at Rodney. "What about you?"

Rodney doesn't know where this line of questioning is leading, but he knows it can't be good, so he says, "I'm not buying shit. I'ma sit on it until no one even remembers that house got took. Until no one would blink twice at me throwing around a little scratch. And so are you."

Pippen smacks his lips in disappointment. "That ain't the game, Rodney. Damn. You about as much fun as a wet fart, man."

"Yeah, Rodney," Kevon says, giggling, "Why you being lame? What about you, Pip. Whatchoo gonna get?"

"My first purchase? A bunch of fine-ass pussy that don't talk back. That do exactly what it's told to do." He looks at

Rodney as he says this, but Rodney purposefully keeps his eyes fixed on the road ahead. "In fact," Pippen continues, "that's exactly what I think we should do. Why shouldn't we celebrate? Why shouldn't you get that car, Kevon? You can afford it. You earned it. And why shouldn't we all go and fuck some bomb-ass pussy right now?"

"We gotta be smart with this," Rodney cautions. "Lay low. Last thing we need to do is start flaunting shit, making it obvious." Even as he's speaking, he knows it's a done deal. Whenever Pippen gets some flight of fancy in his head, he won't be satisfied until it's done. There's always been an imbalance of power to their dynamic. Because Pippen has been under Nico's wing since he was a gup. Because he's always basked under the cover those wings provided. And because Rodney is a member of Pippen's crew, not vice versa.

"You right, you right," Pippen says. "We need to lay low. So that's exactly what we're gonna be doing. We just gonna be doing it in style, know what I'm saying." And that's how they ended up at the strip club, Lady G's, and from there to the Sundown Courts.

When Rodney thinks about it, he knows that this is who Pippen is, who he's always been. People fear Pippen because he's quick to flash his gun, quick to fuck with customers, because he talks mad shit that puffs up his own legend. But Pippen only pulls his gun in situations where he knows he won't have to use it. He only fucks with customers who present weak, like preppy students or junkies. And he only talks big game around gullible types, younger kids, girls, other dumbass bangers, who are prone to buy his bogus hustle. But Pippen would never dream of doing any of this stuff if he didn't have Nico's backing, and Rodney to provide the necessary muscle. *When the juice is real, you don't have to front*, Rodney thinks. *It's just there.*

Rodney doesn't want to be part of it anymore. Not Pippen, not Nico Blakes, not peddling poison on the corners for chump change, not what's going on in room 327, none of it. He doesn't even want the pizza they ordered because cheese inflames his guts. He's fantasizing about just jacking the money himself and bouncing. Never looking back. He could do it too. He's got the keys to the Lincoln. The money is stashed up in 329, all by its lonesome. It's not like anyone would come after him. Pippen and Kevon wouldn't squeal. Who would they tell? They'd be implicating themselves. And they wouldn't have the ability to track him down. He'd be a ghost. They'd never hear from him again.

Rodney doesn't have anything anchoring him here; not a new baby like Pippen, no siblings to look after like Kevon. His brother's in prison for at least a twenty-piece. He has no idea where his mom is, hasn't seen her since, what— April? May? Dad is dead. He is free. The possibilities swim through his mind. Where would he go? What would he do? *Anywhere*, he thinks. Someplace it never snowed. And be anybody. Be a maintenance man or a fucking barista. It didn't matter. As long as it was different than this it would suit him just fine.

Even as he's running this scenario through his head, Rodney knows he won't make the play. For better or worse, he's not wired for treachery. No, he'll see it through, even with Pippen acting a fool, he'll see it through, face up to whatever he has to, if it comes to that. He thumbs the quarters in the vending machine and hits the button for some SUNCHIPS. They get caught in the hook of the dispenser and Rodney shakes the machine, tries kicking it a few times, but the chips don't budge. Shit is good and stuck. *Screw it,* he thinks, *I'll just go grab some of the money, run out and get something.* Pippen and Kevon won't even know he left.

He turns the corner to head back to the rooms, and that's when he sees the backs of the four men ascending the stairs in front of him. Sees the guns at their sides. Rodney waits until they're two flights up before he follows in their wake. At the third-floor landing he peers over the top step and watches them enter the room. He waits for a minute. Then, Ruger out, safety off, Rodney moves quickly, silently, down the corridor, hugging the wall the whole way. At room 329 he inserts the key card into the mechanism. It clicks, almost inaudibly, and he slips in, careful to ease the latch bolt into the catch of the door.

The duffel bag with the money is sitting out on the bed, along with the backpack of meth, the fat man's riot shotgun from that morning, and Kevon's .22 pistol. He tosses the pistol into the duffel, straps it across his shoulder, and picks up the shotgun. Just then he hears a hollow *thwop* next door, followed by Pippen's scream. The voices through the wall are muffled. He puts his ear to the wall. Still can't hear what's being said. Whoever's talking isn't doing so very loudly, or they're facing the other direction. Then one of the hookers pipes up. She's plenty loud. She says she hasn't seen any money or meth other than what they brought in their pockets.

Then he hears someone asking about him. Asking by name. Rodney wonders how they know his name, how they found them so fast. Then it comes to him. Those white-trash hookers. *Fucking Pippen, man.* Rodney thinks about what to do. If he bursts into the room, he could tag one, maybe two of them before they dispatched him. And then what? They kill him, they'll kill Kevon and Pippen too.

No, the only thing to do is run. Hope Pippen and Kevon can find a way to stay alive long enough for him to reach Nico, tell him what's happened, lie about the robbery if need be, the killings. Fight that battle another day. But he can't risk calling Nico from this room, being heard. He has to get some distance.

Rodney makes for the door, is about to go out, when he hears people exiting the next room. He puts an eye to the peephole and sees two of the armed men float by. Their images are distorted in the fisheye aperture, but one of them, whose voice is croaky, says, "Should we split up, Jerry, or stay together?"

The one called Jerry responds, but the men are already past the door, and Rodney can't make out the words.

Fuck. They're looking for him. *But there's only two of them in the room now,* he thinks. *I can take two.* He moves to the adjoining door and slowly unlatches the bolt, then pulls the door open a fraction to make sure the other side is still shut. It is. He opens the door all the way, secures it against the wall.

The adjoining doors are thin and now he can hear what's going on more clearly. Kevon is crying. Someone tells the hookers to leave. Rodney checks the safety on the shotgun to make sure it's ready, then waits for the hookers to clear out. He braces to ram through the door, but first he cups his ear to it one last time to try to get a sense of where the two men are located in the room. That's when the single shot pops off.

Kevon wailing and throwing up and heaving, and Rodney knows that he waited too long. Pippen is dead. Then a gentle, encouraging voice asks Kevon about Rosalind, about the money. For a moment, nothing; the room goes quiet. Rodney presses his ear tight against the door.

Suddenly there's a succession of loud whams that jolt Rodney back from the wall. He realizes it's drawers being slammed open and shut. And just above the din he hears Kevon say, "No, no, not in there. In the next room."

Rodney's eyes pop wide. He turns to run, but the barrel of the shotgun knocks into the lamp on the dresser, sends it crashing to the floor. The bullets come.

The sound is cacophonous, like a tornado bearing down, like the thunder of a thousand storms. Rodney throws himself to the floor, begins army-crawling to the exit as the wall turns to grist, the room around him shatters. At the door he stretches for the handle and bullets rip a line just above his hand. He flattens on the ground, covers his head with his arms. As suddenly as the gunfire began, it ends. The concussions echo in Rodney's ears. His head is vibrating. He doesn't think. He lunges for the door, and then he's out, in the corridor, running. So fast his feet feel as if they're not even touching the ground. At the stairwell he leaps. Shots from behind ring out. He feels the bullets cut the air beside his head, hears them smack against the concrete.

Rodney drops onto the half-landing between floors, bounces off the railing, and nearly tumbles over it. Quickly, he regains his balance and continues down the stairs, flying, escaping. On the second floor he makes the turn and sees, at the bottom of the well, the two men who'd been sent to find him. Rodney stops on a dime, and, as they begin shooting, dives backward into the corridor. Bullets rip into the wall above him.

Rodney scampers to his knees, crouches low, and takes a quick look around the corner. Two more rounds whap into the wall, spitting plaster into his face and eyes. Rodney bends the shotgun around the corner and squeezes off a few blind shots. Then he's on his feet again, sprinting down the corridor in the opposite direction, the bag of money bouncing against his hip, slowing him down. Above him he hears the thunderous footfalls of someone matching him stride for stride. Rodney realizes he must sound like that too, stops, and tucks himself into a doorframe.

Seconds later, a little farther down the corridor, the footfalls above him cease. A man with a bald head and eyepatch leans out over the third-floor railing. Rodney points the shotgun in his direction, and the man ducks back. From the corner of his eye, Rodney sees movement at the end of the hall. He swings the shotgun in that direction and fires, sending the two goons down there scrambling for cover. Rodney turns the gun back toward the upper balcony where the bald man is now dangling out from the railing, taking aim. Rodney pumps one round at him, then another, and the man ratchets up out of sight before he's able to get a bead.

Rodney takes off again. He makes it around the next corner and puts his back against the wall. No footsteps above. No noise at all, save for the crickets residing in the surrounding thicket of the motel. Rodney risks another look-see around the corner, spots one man at the far end of the corridor, slinking his way. He does some quick accounting. One shooter on the floor above, one on this level. Two unaccounted for. There had been a second man on this level. Where'd he disappear to? *Down probably,* he thinks. *To pin me in.*

Rodney knows he doesn't have much time, literally seconds. He moves or he dies. He's on the short side of the building and there's a stairwell just at the other end, no more than fifty feet away, but the man upstairs could be positioned above it, waiting for him. Rodney takes a tepid step forward, stretches his neck to peer over the railing. Between this and the next building over is a strip of grass with some bushes and some barren flower beds. Rodney backs up to the wall, takes another peek around the corner. A shot rings out, whizzes past his face. Rodney ducks back. The man in the corridor is close, too close.

Rodney tosses the shotgun over the railing into the plants, adjusts the duffel to where it's tight on his back, not swinging into his side, then dashes for the railing. He vaults over, falls through the air, and lands in the flower bed. The soil is soft with dew and mulch, and Rodney rolls with the fall and comes swiftly to his feet. He moves to retrieve the shotgun, but bullets thud into the ground next to him. He pulls the Ruger from his waistband, spins, and sprays bullets at the man firing on him from the second-floor balcony. This stops him shooting long enough for Rodney to take refuge beneath the first-floor portico.

He sneaks a look around the corner and doesn't see anyone in the lower corridor. To his left is the courtyard and pool. To the right, the short hallway, and beyond that, a back parking lot and then woods. In front of him is the side building. That's a no-go. Too exposed. If Rodney can make it to the woods, then he can work his way through the trees back around to the Lincoln. But there are two guns minimum in that direction, itching to mow him down. No, he needs to go back down the long corridor to get to the far side of this building. That route, though farther, holds the better odds of getting to the woods without getting shot to death. But from where he stands it looks miles away. Impossibly far away.

For a moment, he stands there paralyzed—then he thinks, *Fuck it. Get it over with*. Rodney unzips the duffel and pulls out Kevon's .22 to go along with the Ruger, then zips it back up and turns the corner. He runs, but it's not a sprint. It's controlled, quiet. He stays tight to the wall, ready to shoot anything that moves. Every few steps he checks behind him to make sure no one's creeping up on his tail, scans above to make sure no one's setting up to snipe him from the balcony. Nothing. To his surprise, Rodney reaches the end of the corridor without incident. He peeks around the edge of the building, sees no one lurking, no one lying in wait. All he has to do is cross the small open area between buildings, then get through the parking lot and into the woods. That gives him a chance.

A chance he never gets.

As he makes his break, gunfire erupts. It comes from everywhere. A fusillade from all directions, in front, above, and behind. It sounds like the grand finale on the Fourth of July. For a brief moment that's what Rodney thinks of: colorful fireworks bursting overhead. He dives beneath the stone stairwell and peers through the slats of the steps. Bullets skip off the cement, ricochet off the stairs, slap into the wall. Rodney focuses, gets his bearings. Someone's shooting straight down from the balcony. Another is advancing down the corridor he just came from. A third man is perched behind the next building, the very spot Rodney was trying to reach. If the shooters had been patient for a few more seconds, Rodney would have walked smack into a bullet.

The scent of nitroglycerin soaks the air. Rodney waits for a lull in the gunfire. It comes when the gunman from above shoots out his clip. Rodney throws a couple potshots at the shooter who's posted behind the building, forcing the man to dip behind the wall. Then Rodney takes his chance. He runs full tilt toward that location, both the Ruger and the .22 aimed out front of him. The shooting recommences. Bullets kick up the ground all around him. The gunner from the balcony. Rodney feels a couple *thwop*s into the duffel bag on his back. The shooter from the corridor. The hits nearly knock him over, but the thick stacks of money inside the duffel absorb the blows, and he keeps his feet. He gets clear of the line of fire from both balcony and corridor, and the shooting ceases.

When the man behind the building pokes his head out to see what's what, Rodney is five feet from him. He blasts away with both guns. A bullet tags the man's wrist, knocking the pistol from his hand. Another round hits him in the upper-right chest and sends him staggering backward behind the building. Rodney rounds the corner and sees it's one of the men he glimpsed through the peephole, the one called Jerry. He calmly pops four more bullets into Jerry's chest. A fifth shot rips his jaw off his face. Jerry topples onto his back and lies there, fish-flopping, as Rodney leaps over him and runs, flees, down the rear corridor toward the front parking lot. He can see the Lincoln. It's parked straight ahead. He's almost there, he thinks, almost out of this.

As he draws closer to his escape, closer to the sanctuary of the vehicle, Rodney tucks the .22 into the back of his pants and fishes the car keys from his pocket, presses the unlock button. The Lincoln emits a tiny *beep-beep*, and the headlights flash. Rodney doesn't stop or even slow down at the edge of the building. He darts across the lot to where the Lincoln is parked, swings the driver's side door open, tosses his Ruger into the passenger seat. He goes to lift the strap of the duffel over his head, and that extra second is what does it.

A bullet pierces the driver's side window and plugs into his gut.

Rodney feels the weight of the slug hit him, but not the pain. Not yet. The momentum of it sends him sprawling across the front seat. He gets the duffel off his back and shoves it into the floor space on the passenger side, then somehow manages to insert the key into the ignition and start the car. He hunches down and slams the gearshift into drive. The Lincoln lurches from its parking spot. Bullets rain down on the vehicle, pinging off the metal, shattering the windshield and side windows. Bits of glass embed in Rodney's face and neck and hands, but he doesn't feel it, doesn't stop. He punches the gas.

The tires spin out. Another bullet comes through the window, punctures Rodney's shoulder, and causes him to swerve smack into the side of another parked car, a Chrysler LeBaron, which happens to be packed full of hookers. Through the blown windshield Rodney sees the women gawking at him, each wearing her own distinct expression. The blonde looks straight-up pissed, her mouth flapping mutely behind the window like she's giving him the business. Another's face is contorted in agony, like maybe her leg got smashed in the collision, while the young one with the greasy hair smiles serenely, leans forward, waves at him like she's sad to see him go.

Rodney reverses the car, spins the wheels, and accelerates around the LeBaron. The Lincoln roars out of the lot, tires squealing as it peels onto the byroad, fishtails, then regains purchase on the pavement. Rodney floors it, makes for the interstate, then thinks better of it. The Lincoln doesn't have the giddyup it once did, and they'll be expecting him to take the highway. If they catch up to him, he'll be boxed in with nowhere to turn.

He heads toward the on-ramp but doesn't merge. Instead he hooks a left onto a back road that winds through some woods. He looks in the rearview, sees nothing but black road. No lights. *I've lost them,* he thinks. *I made it.* Then he remembers that he was gut-shot and looks down. His shirt is soaked with dark blood, glugging out with each rhythmic pump of his heart. All at once the pain comes. And the fear. When Rodney checks the rearview again, he sees a pair of high beams burning through the darkness. Their glare catches the mirror just right, reflects into his eyes, and renders him temporarily sightless. He blinks away the floaters swirling across his retinas, stomps down on the gas and barrels forward. He glances once again in the rearview and sees the bright headlamps of his pursuer's car extinguish, leaving nothing behind him but overwhelming darkness.

Rodney's never driven much outside of Cain City proper, and he's used to city streets and avenues, not the sharp curves and sudden dips of country roads. He takes a bend too fast and nearly careens off the berm and into a double-wide that sits in the hollow below. Rodney corrects the wheel and jerks back into the center of the road. In his high beams, he sees a gravel offshoot up ahead. He takes it.

CHAPTER TEN
BLEEDING MAN

Lucia took care to leave her panties in the car. She straddled Ephraim on the swivel chair, skirt bunched up above her hips, blouse unbuttoned. Her bra was tugged haphazardly beneath her breasts, propping them high and full. She knew what to do to take care of herself early. Before this she'd been the one in the chair, and she'd leaned back and pushed his head between her legs, shifting ever so slightly to steer his tongue where it needed to hit. That got her most of the way there, and as her legs started to quake she took him by the hair and pulled his body atop hers and whispered, "Fuck me now," guiding him into her, deep and hard, and she cupped his face and kissed his mouth and she exploded.

So now she made it all about him. They'd slept together enough times for her to know the sequence of moves needed to bring him to the finish. First she volleyed slowly up and down, squeezing the walls of her pussy around his thickness. When he started to moan she switched tactics, sitting all the way down and rocking back and forth, clenching on the rise of each thrust.

"Holy shit," Ephraim panted. And that's when she started talking.

"Yeah, baby?"

"Yeah."

She took his hands, placed them on her breasts and crushed them. "Cum for me, baby," she cooed, kicking it into another gear. "That pussy feel good?"

Ephraim grunted in the affirmative. She braced against his chest and grinded faster, harder. She knew her own pleasure was his biggest turn-on, so even though she was mostly numb by this point, his girth inside her felt good, satisfying, and she focused on it pressing fully against her circumference. "You feel so good," she moaned. "You fit so perfect inside of me." His whole body tensed beneath her and he started to shake. "Cum, baby, fill me up. Fill me up."

"Inside?"

This was part of their ritual. He needed to hear her consent. Needed to believe she wanted his load inside of her, and only inside of her, like it was the only place he was allowed to finish, nowhere else. "Yes," she encouraged. "Cum, baby. Cum in me."

He obliged. With a choked gasp and a violent shudder, he poured himself into her. Small twitches followed, little aftershocks of pleasure. She glided smoothly back and forth on his slicked shaft, milking the last shivers out of him. When she stopped moving they sat there for a moment looking at each other, him still pulsing, enveloped beneath the weight of her, chest heaving up and down.

"You're fucking amazing," Ephraim said. He realized this was about as generic as you could get under the circumstances, but the sentiment was truthful and the best his hollowed-out mind could articulate in the moment.

She leaned down, ran her full, soft lips across his rough ones and said, "You'll do I guess, for now anyway."

Ephraim smiled. "Till something better comes along?"

"Till something better comes along."

"That could be, what? Days, weeks, months? Just trying to get an idea of how long I've got."

"Sure. Years even. There's no telling when Mr. Perfect will walk into the diner and sweep me off my feet."

"I'll take it."

He reached for a box of tissues on the desk, snagged a few and handed them to her. She lifted off him and caught the dribble of his blast on the paper.

"Better not forget to take your pill tonight," he said. It was meant for a laugh, but the happy look slid off her face and was replaced by a hardness that caused a sharp drop in room temperature. Ephraim knew instantly that he'd miscalculated the moment, and he had to eat crow—and fast—before the clay set. "I'm kidding. Hundred percent didn't mean anything by it. Terrible joke."

"Like I'd want one of your babies," she said. This stung him. He had confided to Lucia the difficulties he'd had with Caleb, how frustrating and exhausting it was sometimes to be his parent. Whether she'd meant it that way or not, her remark held an undercurrent of putting the blame for those hardships on him, or at least on his DNA.

"I swear I didn't mean anything by it," he said.

"You must think awful high of yourself if you think I'm trying to trap you for a lifetime."

"It'd just be eighteen years," he teased. Her face flushed livid. She threw him a quick, savage look that would make any mortal man tremble. "I'm kidding, I don't think that. Not at all. Hey, I'm sorry, really. Look, you just, I don't know, make me feel some kind of way. Off-balance or something. And I always end up saying the wrong shit."

"I don't try to make you feel that way. I don't think I do anything to make you feel that way."

"I know you don't. It's me. I go dumb around you. My mind turns to putty."

"I'll say." She finished cleaning off her thighs and threw the wad of tissue away, then straightened her skirt, fixed her bra, and buttoned her blouse. Ephraim watched her. He loved the way she stretched the fabric of her uniform to the limit of its capabilities.

"Why are you doing this with me?" he asked her.

Lucia finished smoothing the wrinkles from her skirt before regarding him. When she did, the corners of Ephraim's mouth curled into a sheepish, apologetic smile. Straight away she saw the uncertainty behind his question, the earnestness of it. This diffidence beneath the gruff exterior made him seem boyish and vulnerable, and immediately the aggravation she'd felt at his crass humor evaporated. She grabbed a paper cup and poured water from the cooler and drank it down, then refilled it.

"You want a real answer?" she asked.

"I want the truth."

"You can't handle the truth."

Ephraim was fairly certain he knew the reasons she was seeing him. Lucia had had a procession of deadbeat boyfriends, the last of whom had tried to strangle her when she broke it off, left finger-shaped bruises wrapped around her neck. Another had been a low-level drug dealer. Her ex-husband had gotten a friend of hers pregnant while they were still married. So Ephraim was the beneficiary of Lucia's misfortunes with men, her wary perspective on the species. Compared to her exes, Ephraim looked like a goddamn fairy tale. In reality, he was merely the best of a bad-to-mediocre lot.

He feared her realizing this one day, when she'd figure out there was a large world over the horizon, a world that could be easily had by someone like her, with her wattage. A thousand better paths to choose from, all of which led away from him. In a way he was already protecting himself from this eventuality. Not letting her too far behind the curtain. Regardless, like any good masochist, he couldn't help but question her on the subject.

"You can tell me," he said. "I'm a big boy."

Lucia stepped toward him, a bemused smirk on her face. She finger-tapped her lips as though she were trying to decide the most delightful way to fuck with him.

"That tough to come up with an answer?" he said.

"Mmm." She handed him the paper cup and he drank from it. "I like your eyes. They're sad, pretty eyes. And I like your voice." She feigned further contemplation.

"The list end there?"

"Pretty much." She reached down and stroked his face with the backs of her fingers. "No, I like how strong your arms feel when they're around me. I like that you're tough on the outside, soft within."

"I'm not that soft."

"Yes, you are. You're tender. And you're decent. A decent man. You'd be surprised how rare that is. And I like my reflection in your eyes. The way you see me. I like the way you make me feel."

"How's that?"

"Perfect," she whispered. "You make me feel like I'm perfect just as I am."

"You are." He grabbed the back of the hand she had resting on his face. It was warm and soft, and he squeezed it and kissed her palm. Tears brewed in his eyes. He blinked them away.

"And you're handsome enough," she said. "If I squint."

This buoyed him a little and he laughed. "Let's never get your eyes checked then. The blinder, the better."

"Okay. I'll go blind for you," she said.

"I've already lost all my senses for you, so that should make us square."

Her countenance darkened. "When I'm with you is not the problem, Ephraim. It's when I'm not with you that's the problem. It doesn't feel real then. It feels like a fling."

"It's not."

"I need you to prove it. I want to be with you, but for real. Anytime I tell anyone about what I'm doing with you, they tell me I'm being played. That I'm being used."

"Don't listen to them. It's not true."

"How do I know? I'm too old to waste my time."

"You're thirty-four."

She raised an eyebrow.

"I understand," he said. "It's just—"

"See there? No. No more 'it's *just*' anything. I already know what you're going to say. You have to take care of your son who is having problems, your dad who is sick. And you're still technically married. I've heard it, I get it. These things don't scare me. I'm still here. But I won't wait around forever."

"I know."

"Okay." She leaned down and kissed him softly. "I've got to go."

Ephraim put his work jacket over her shoulders and walked her out of the building and back to where her car, this little Mitsubishi Galant she shared with her sister, was parked on the access road at the rear of the plant. The wind was raging now and he put his arm around her to keep her from blowing over.

"So gallant," she teased. They walked the gravel lane that went past the large silo, the coal dump, and the spare-parts lot. There weren't many lights in that section of the grounds and the giant heaps of coal silhouetted against the night sky loomed on all sides like the rubble of a destroyed city.

"This place is creepy at night," she said.

Ephraim looked around. "I guess it is."

"What is that pipe?" Lucia pointed up ahead to a huge red pipe that measured a hundred and twenty feet long and ten feet high.

"That's a replacement baker tube," Ephraim said. Lucia looked at him like he was speaking Kurdish, so he elucidated further. "It's used to heat the coal before it goes into the baker activator. Which is that structure there." He twisted around and gestured to a giant round edifice that stood eight stories high. "Gets the impurities out of the coal so we can extract the carbon."

"I'll pretend like I understand everything you just said."

"Oh, it's quite fascinating," he said facetiously. "I can explain the whole process to you. You'll be riveted."

The Mitsubishi was parked by some trees just past the spare-parts lot, angled in where it was hard to see if you weren't looking for it. Lucia handed Ephraim his jacket back and climbed behind the wheel.

"Listen," Ephraim said, holding her door open. He worked his thoughts over and how he wanted to phrase them. "So you're aware, Caleb, he knows about us."

"You told him?"

"No. I mean, I did, but he kind of figured things out on his own. More perceptive than I gave him credit for, I guess."

"And how does he feel about that?"

"I mean, I think he's good with it. He likes you a whole lot, so I think he's good."

"Well, I do bring him pie."

"That's true."

Satisfaction came into Lucia's face. "That's a step."

"Yeah."

"Will I see you at the diner tomorrow?"

"Reckon so. I'm likely to be hungry."

"Maybe you'll order something different."

"Wouldn't count on it."

Ephraim leaned into the car and kissed her and shut the door. He watched the small sedan navigate the bumpy road out of there. Its taillights flickered through the trees of the woods and receded to nothing, and she was gone. Ephraim walked back into the main plant and detoured over to packaging where he retrieved another sample of the carbon. Back at the D-line station he put the sample through a series of tests to make sure it met the specification guidelines for the product, 12x40 ZBFs, which, as always, it did. He recorded the measurements on the paperwork, bagged the remainder of the sample for the lab, and the bulk of his work for the night was done. Ephraim checked the monitors, saw that all was well with the furnaces, then went back to reading *A Confederacy of Dunces*. He was starting to believe the fucker at the library who recommended the book did so simply because *Confederacy* was in the title and he thought Ephraim was a hick.

Ephraim tossed the book back in the drawer and sifted through for another, narrowed it down to a Stephen King yarn about the JFK assassination, or one called *Crapalachia* that he'd picked up on a whim because he'd flipped to a random page and it seemed funny. *Crapalachia* was written by a guy from West Virginia, so he went with that, and wasn't ten words in when a loud bang came from the front of the station. And then another. And then another.

The first thought through Ephraim's head was *Fucking Billy*, but the noises were too loud to be someone pounding on the door, or even kicking it. The next thing in his mind was Lucia, fear that something had happened to her. He hustled into the hallway. There he saw the source of the disturbance and relaxed. The faulty latch bolt wasn't catching in the strike and the door was being flung shut by the wind. It whopped against the frame, floated open, and whopped again.

Ephraim tried to remember if he'd pulled the door tight when he'd come back from collecting the sample, couldn't visualize having done so, and reckoned he'd forgotten. Still high, he thought, admonishing himself. On pussy and weed. Some kind of way.

He checked outside to make sure Billy wasn't pulling some prank, but the wind was gusting fiercely, and nobody was out there. A cache of PVC piping had come untethered from a tarp and was being lifted into the air and flung about. A couple of them rolled past Ephraim like they were racing the hundred-meter dash and he watched them go. Dust whipped into his face, and he retreated into the station, figuring even Billy wasn't fool enough to pull something in that kind of weather. This time when he shut the door he tested it to make sure it was latched. As Ephraim turned to go back to the office something wet squeaked underfoot. He looked down and saw the blood.

That it was blood was unmistakable, but there were different shades to it. Evidence suggested it was the product of multiple wounds, differing in their severity. Some of the blood was dark crimson, almost brown. It had fallen in thick splats that looked similar to tobacco juice. Mixed in with that were smaller, more compact droplets that shone bright red in the fluorescent tube lighting. Both types formed a trail that led down the short hallway and through the near door on the left, the break room. Ephraim's first inclination was that a hurt animal must have sought shelter, wandered in somehow, but he was quickly disabused of that notion when he caught sight of a shoe print stamped in the liquid.

"Hello?" Ephraim called out, alarmed now. "Billy? You in here?"

He got no response. He moved forward, following the tracks, careful not to step on them, careful not to make a sound. The shoe prints were much larger than his own, meaning they were definitely not Billy's. The breakroom was pitch-black. Ephraim reached in and felt for the wall switch, then flipped it on. The room was empty. He checked behind the door, under the table, nothing. But as he went to turn the lights back off, what he saw stopped him cold. On the wall beneath the switch were smears of dark blood. Beside them, plain as day, was a bright-red handprint, reminiscent of a child's early artwork. But no child had a hand that large, fingers that long.

On the floor beneath the stains a large pool had coalesced, indicative of someone having stood there for some duration. Ephraim went through his pockets looking for his phone, then remembered he left it in the office. He rushed into the hallway. And that's where the bleeding man was waiting for him.

Before Ephraim had the chance to react or throw his arms up in defense, the man slammed his forearm into Ephraim's windpipe and drove him back against the wall, hard. Ephraim's air duct was cut off. His face immediately swelled with a rush of blood and his eyes ballooned from their sockets. He swatted at his attacker's arms, a futile effort that got him nowhere. The much taller man possessed an animal strength and he had Ephraim pinned solid, helpless. He pressed a pistol against Ephraim's temple, cocked the hammer.

"Whoa, whoa," Ephraim protested. He stopped resisting and raised his hands in submission.

"Don't try a fuckin' thing," the man growled. His breath was hot and rank, and his words were a little slurred. He let off the pressure just enough to allow Ephraim to speak.

"I won't," he croaked. "I won't."

The man jammed his forearm deeper into Ephraim's throat, causing him to gag, then pushed off of it to put some space between the two of them. Ephraim bent forward, clutched his knees, and coughed for air. It took him a minute to breathe normally. He hocked up some gunk, then glanced up to find himself eye to eye with the muzzle of a Ruger Security-9. He also got his first good look at the person behind it.

His attacker was black and young, with a smooth face contorted now with an anguish that only came from severe pain. Ephraim assumed the visible injuries on the man's body, one in the stomach, another in the right arm, were the sources of his distress. Gunshots, had to be. Bright blood was still leaking steadily from the man's shoulder, while the lower half of his shirt and jeans were soaked through from the wound in his gut. The left side of the man's chest and sleeve were the only parts of his clothing not tie-dyed in crimson. The man wobbled backward until he contacted the wall, and he braced himself against it. With each of his steps you could hear the blood squish in his shoes. But whatever discomfort he was in didn't prevent him from keeping the pistol steadily trained on Ephraim's head.

Slowly, Ephraim lifted his hands out to his sides. He stayed partly bent to make sure his body language didn't convey anything that could be misconstrued as aggression or threat.

"You're hurt," Ephraim said.

"What gave me away, motherfucker?" The man lowered the pistol and clutched at his stomach in agony.

"You need help," Ephraim said. "I'll call an ambulance."

"No, no ambulances."

"You gotta get some help, buddy. I don't know much trouble you're in, but I know those holes in you don't look too good."

The man raised the handgun. "No ambulances," he said firmly.

Ephraim stretched his hands wider and bowed his head further down. "Gotcha. No ambulances."

"And no cops."

"Okay."

The man lifted his hand off his belly, looked at the dark blood that coated it and grimaced. "Fuck. You got a first-aid kit or something?"

"Should have. In that supply closet there." Ephraim pointed to the door just a few feet away from where the man was standing.

"Get it," the man ordered. The closet was toward the back of the building, not the front, and there was a security exit back at the far end of the hallway there. If Ephraim could reach it, an alarm would trigger. The man must have sensed these thoughts flashing through Ephraim's mind because he added, "Don't try nothing funny."

"Nope."

Ephraim took a few cautious steps toward the closet, hands still in the air, and the man told him to hurry his ass up. Ephraim opened the door and started digging through the shelves. They were stocked mostly with cleaning supplies, stationery, reams of paper for the printer. The door to the closet was made of hollow metal, decently thick, and Ephraim figured it would shield him for long enough to break for the exit, if he could get behind it. He peered out and saw that the man had slid down the wall and was now sitting on the floor with his legs splayed open. But, somehow, his eyes and his gun were still on Ephraim.

He found a bottle of hydrogen peroxide and the first-aid kit tucked in behind an industrial-size bucket of soap and took the items back to the hurt man. He knelt and set them on the ground next to him.

"Open it," the man said.

Ephraim flicked the latch and lifted the kit's lid. The man rummaged through the bandages, plasters, gauzes, and Q-tips, but abruptly, his hand went limp. His head lolled sideways and his eyes went vacant, glassy, for a few seconds. Just as fast as he'd gone, he snapped back to the present and glared at Ephraim. His mouth was dry and pasty at the corners and he licked his lips as though probing for saliva. The man pointed a finger in the direction of the office. From where they were they could see into the corner of the room where a watercooler sat.

"I need some water."

"Sure, we got water. Just in the office there."

The man made a motion with the gun as if he were granting permission. Ephraim turned to go.

"Hey," the man snapped. "No funny business."

"I understand."

Ephraim went into the office. At the cooler he twisted ever so slightly to see if he was still within the man's sights. He was. He filled the paper cup slowly and played out his options in his head. None of them was super, seeing as one false move was likely to get him killed. Trying to get the gun was too risky. If he kept doing what the man said, chances were he'd be able to wait him out until he died, but there was no guarantee he *would* die. If Ephraim could retrieve his cell phone, maybe he'd find an opportunity to sneak a call to 911. If not, his only hope for outside help was to find a way to get to the office landline, but this guy would shoot him a dozen times before he'd allow that to happen. The thought dampened the appeal of that option.

Ephraim cut his eyes sideways, saw that the cell was sitting right on the corner of the desk by the door, and decided that was the best of his bad choices. He'd snag it on his way out, slip it into his pocket, and bide his time until he was able to sneak a call. He finished filling the cup, turned to leave, and found that the bleeding man had dragged himself across the hall and was sitting propped in the doorframe. He braced his elbow against his leg to keep the pistol trained stably in his right hand. In the left he held Ephraim's cell phone, waggled it around.

"You look like you might be thinking funny thoughts," he said.

"No. I wouldn't do that."

"Uh-huh." The man tucked the phone beneath his crotch. Ephraim walked over and handed him the water cup. The man gulped it down fast, too fast, and choked most of the water up.

"Fuck," he groaned, then tossed the cup aside. His head swung loose on his neck like he was missing a vertebra.

"Look buddy, let me call somebody for you. You need help."

"I'll be fine. I just need to rest here for a second. Get rejuvenated. I'm already feeling better. No cops."

"Yeah, no cops."

"No cops," the man repeated. His breathing was labored now; a wet gurgle accompanied every breath he took. "You don't want them to know I'm here. For your own good. Cops'd be like leaving bread crumbs. They'll hunt us both down."

"Who is 'they'? Did you get shot by the police?"

The man's bloodshot eyes popped wide. "Ha!" he chortled. The laugh sent white-hot pain through his midsection and he doubled over. It took a moment for him to recover. When he did, he sat up and said, "Cops. I wish it was the damn cops. Look here, I need you to do something for me."

"You want me to get the kit?"

"What? No, fuck the kit." The man was struggling to breathe now, struggling to speak. "Look," he rasped, "if I tell you something, then you got to promise me you ain't gonna tell nobody else. Got it? If I tell you this, we're partners. You'll get a little somethin' somethin', if you catch my meaning. But if you screw me, I'll fuckin' kill you."

"Okay."

The man held up a finger as if to ward off death and clawed at his chest, gasping, trying to get some air past his throat. "I took some money," he said. "But I hid it, see. I hid it, ain't too far from here. There was this little cave by these rocks."

"Okay."

"If you go get me that money, and take me to Dayton, I'll give you half."

"Half the money?" Ephraim asked.

"Did I stutter? Yeah, half. I'll give you half. It's your lucky day."

"Half what? How much money we talkin'?"

"Do we have a deal?"

Ephraim glanced at the man's gun, still aimed in his general direction. "Okay, yeah. Deal." The man set the Ruger down and extended his bloody hand. Ephraim shook it.

"Three hundred and ninety thousand dollars," the man said. Ephraim gulped hard, and this reaction brought a faint smile to the man's lips. "Told ya. Your lucky day. All profits for you."

"And you hid it in a cave by some rocks?"

"I hid it by some rocks, in the rocks, by a cave. You know." The man flit his hand around weakly. "There were some trees, woods and shit. I hid it there after I drove my car into a ditch, some fucking ditch."

"Like a creek bed or something?"

"What?" The man's eyelids fluttered, and for a moment his eyes showed all white before rolling back into place.

"Like a creek bed, or an irrigation ditch, or what?" Ephraim pressed him.

"Yeah, like that."

"Is the car near the cave?"

"Close. It's close. But's it far out there, man. Far out."

"Near here?"

"Yeah. There was this big field. Huge. It was weird. Real flat. Hilly, but flat too. I didn't see that ditch coming. The cave was through some trees, by the rocks."

"Next to the field?"

"Yeah." The shot man's eyelids drooped and his head teetered forward. Ephraim shook him by the shoulders and he momentarily snapped back to life.

"Which way did you come from?" Ephraim urged. "Hey, which way did you come from?"

The man didn't answer. His eyes rolled into the back of his head and his chin dropped to his chest. There was scarcely any breath going in and out of him now. Ephraim reached across his body and grabbed the Ruger, then poked the man with it a couple times. He didn't stir. Ephraim pressed the muzzle of the gun into the hole in the man's stomach. That did it. The man jolted straight, gulped in a big suck of air and winced in pain. His eyes pinged around his sockets like he didn't know what planet he was on, but then they locked on the gun in Ephraim's hand.

"Fuck you doing?" the man said. He reached behind him and produced a pistol, then cocked the hammer and aimed it at Ephraim.

"Whoa, whoa," said Ephraim. "Whoa. Here, have it back."

He laid the gun flat in his palm and offered it over, but the man waved him off and set the pistol in his lap. "Doesn't matter. We partners, right?"

"Right, yeah. But you gotta tell me which way you came from."

The man thought about it. He looked confused. "South. No, wait. Had to be north, right? I think . . . Hold up. I just need to rest for a minute."

"Wait, wait, wait," begged Ephraim. "Wait, how'd you get here? Through the woods?"

"No. The tracks. Found the railroad tracks."

South, Ephraim thought. *Had to be south.*

"I had a cat once, liked to jump out front of cars and eat tigers before it went swimming in the sink," the man said deliriously.

"What?"

"Tiger sharks. In the ocean." The man's head flopped to one side and then came back. "I'm Rodney," he said.

"I'm Ephraim."

"Ephraim? Fuck kind a name is that?"

"Biblical."

"You religious?"

"No."

"Too bad. We could use that good juju 'bout now. I'm

gonna close my eyes for a second, Ephraim. It's your lucky day. No cops, remember. They'll kill us both. Fuck up our luck."

"Got it."

Rodney shut his eyes and slumped against the side of the desk. His breathing lapsed into a staccato of gurgles that grew slow and irregular, and then stopped altogether. His body went slack.

"Rodney," Ephraim said. "Rodney . . . Rodney." He stuck the gun into the hole in Rodney's stomach again. This time he didn't flinch. Ephraim felt for a pulse, put his hand in front of Rodney's mouth to see if he could feel any air coming out.

But none would ever come again.

Ephraim sat back against the wall, let out a deep, abluting breath, and for a solid minute he stared at the dead man. A weariness overcame him. He did not want to move, but he mustered the resolve to reach between Rodney's legs and pull the cell phone out from under him. He pressed the emergency button, dialed 911 on the keypad, and went to tap *connect*, but something inside of him stopped his thumb from completing the command his brain had given him.

Ephraim stared at the phone, then at the pistol in his other hand, then at the lifeless body lying before him. Rodney. Ephraim saw now that he was just a boy. A boy covered in blood, a boy full of bullets. The blood was everywhere. All over the tile, the doorframe, the walls, the desk, Ephraim's uniform. But Ephraim couldn't help but remember the rush of words that came out of the dead boy's mouth not two minutes ago: *cops, kill, ditch, car, field, rocks, cave . . . Money*. That's the one that echoed in his ears. *Money*. Three hundred and ninety thousand dollars' worth, to be exact. Not nothing.

Don't do it, you dumb fucker.

Ephraim clicked off the call screen, put the phone away. He rifled through Rodney's pockets and found a wallet and two key cards labelled *Sundown Courts Motel*. The wallet was one of those Velcro jobs that little kids have. It was old and worn, with Lightning McQueen on it. Inside was a driver's license and sixty-seven dollars. Ephraim stuffed the money into his pocket. He read the name on the license, Rodney D. Slash, and the stats, six foot three inches tall, two hundred and five pounds, eyes brown, hair black, twenty years old. Ephraim slid the license back into the wallet, refolded it, and jammed it into the pocket from whence it came.

He wiped the guns off on the clean square of Rodney's shirt and packed them away in the drawer where he kept the books. Then he went to the supply closet and collected the industrial bottle of soap, the mop and bucket, and a pack of paper hand towels meant for the bathroom. He also got the bottle of hydrogen peroxide from the hallway. Then he went into the bathroom, made sure there was no blood visible on his skin. There wasn't. It was just on his shirt and pants.

He put his work jacket on and took the bucket outside and set it under the spigot on the side of the building. While it filled he walked over to where the tarp that held the piping had come undone. Ephraim untied the rest of it and bunched the tarp under his arm, then retrieved the bucket of water and went back inside, making sure the door was latched shut behind him. The time on his phone read 1:53 a.m. Five hours till his shift ended.

He got to work.

CHAPTER ELEVEN
THE YIN YANG TWINS

Willis Hively awoke on the first ring. In a single fluid motion he reached over and silenced the call, swung his feet to the floor, and unplugged the phone from the charger cable. If it looked practiced, it was because he'd done it hundreds of times. He knew who was calling before his brain had the time to form a thought. The ringtone, the kind that sounded like an old landline, had been designated for one contact: police dispatch.

The clock on the screen read 2:16 a.m. He'd been asleep for exactly one hour and fifteen minutes. Before that he'd been at Kyova Hospital, waiting for a witness who'd overdosed to wake up from a coma so that he could find out who'd sold her the heroin laced with an ungodly amount of fentanyl. Twenty-three people had OD'd off one rotten batch, fifteen had died, and eight were in a coma. The woman Hively was there for, Michelle Harmon, had briefly woken up. She'd been lucid and talking. The nurses, per instruction, immediately called Hively. He had stood up from dinner with his family and rushed over, but Harmon stroked out before he arrived. He'd sat outside her room until midnight, when the doctor informed him that the patient's brain activity had decreased dramatically, and it wasn't likely she'd wake up anytime soon, if ever again. He came home, reheated the Chicken Alfredo his wife had made, ate it, and crashed.

Now Hively took the phone into the bathroom so as not to wake Rachel. He shut the door and flipped on the lights.

"Hively," he answered, keeping his voice low.

"Sir," a male voice chirped. "You're needed at a Code 12 crime scene at the Sundown Courts Motel. Location is 84 Woodmere Drive off I-64."

"Code 12? This isn't about the OD at the hospital?"

"No, sir."

"You know this isn't my night. I'm not on call."

"I'm aware of that, sir. You've been specifically requested for the investigation by Captain Hale."

"The hell I have."

"The captain believes you might be *acquainted* with some of the victims, sir."

"Victims, plural?"

"Yes, sir. Three victims accounted for so far. Two African-American males, late teens to early twenties. One Caucasian male, between forty and fifty. All gunshot fatalities."

"What do you mean, so far?"

"From what I understand, it's quite the scene. Possible it could still be active in another location. Detective Sturges is already en route." The dispatcher conveyed the rest of the information to which he'd been made privy. It wasn't much. There were six witnesses at the scene, but he didn't yet know the identities of the deceased. Hively confirmed that he was on his way. He hung up the phone, set it on the sink basin, and looked at himself in the mirror. Eyes puffy and bloodshot. Though he'd always been in shape, he could see traces of bulk starting to creep into his mid-section and chest. Hively clapped his hands to his cheeks and pulled the skin down to where you could see the membranes under his eyelids, then splashed some water on his face, threw in some mouthwash, ran a brush over his hair, and went back into the bedroom where he dressed quietly in the dark. The rustling stirred his wife. She rolled over and cracked an eye.

"What is it?" she asked.

"Bodies."

"Oh, no."

"Yeah. Go back to sleep. Don't worry about it. Dead people can't kill me."

Rachel flung the covers off and sat up. "I'll make coffee."

"No, got back to sleep. I'm awake, I'm good."

"You sure?"

"Yeah."

She flopped back down and pulled the covers to her chin. Hively walked over and gave her a peck on her cheek. "Kiss the girls for me. Tell Brae not to sweat this spelling test. She's got it. Just remind her there are three types of *there*'s."

"K," she said, already drifting back into slumber. "Careful."

"Always. Three *there*'s."

"Three *there*'s. Got it."

Some twenty minutes later Hively and his partner, Clyde Sturges, stood amid the carnage of room 327. The detectives were a study in contrast, so wholly different from one another in both appearance and personality that within the force, the partners were referred to with blatant irony as The Yin Yang Twins. Hively, lean, fit, and Black, cut an impressive figure. Even at two in the morning he was dressed impeccably in a suit and tie, mustache and the patch on his chin trimmed neat, not a follicle out of place. With him you weren't quite certain if the clothes made the man or the man made the clothes.

Sturges, on the other hand, was perpetually rumpled, as though he'd slept not only in his clothes, but possibly outdoors, under a bridge or in some bushes, and had also probably forgotten to brush his teeth. He was squat and dumpy, stooped at the shoulders. He rocked a comb-over that only served to accentuate his baldness, and had a chin that was indistinguishable from his neck. These characteristics, combined with the bumpkin accent he'd retained from his backwoods upbringing, and a slow, clopping gait that made people think he had either a peg leg or a permanent case of gout, had long ago earned him the nickname, The Slug.

Before they'd partnered, other cops in the department went out of their way to avoid working with The Slug, the thinking being that his insipid appearance and languid speech patterns were harbingers of laziness and stupidity. Sturges was aware of his reputation, but it didn't bother him much. He preferred working solo. And outside of Hively, he held no great esteem for any of his colleagues. In his opinion the majority of those employed by the Cain City Police Department were, on the whole, knuckle-dragging fucktards. At their best, they topped out at adequate, and at their worst, they did more to induce crime than to solve it.

But a while back he and Hively had been forced to collaborate on a murder and corruption case that involved some of Cain City's high-end players. That case had gone sideways, but Hively had found Sturges to be a thorough, if leisurely paced, investigator, and more than competent.

The rumors of his fecklessness had done him a disservice, and increasingly the two found themselves requesting the support of the other on their cases. Before long their captain, Bruce Hale, who preferred salt-and-pepper detective teams ("a foot in each door," he liked to say), told them it was time to make a choice, either end their affair or get married, so they made the union official.

Their opposing styles proved complementary. Where Hively was hard charging, always in action, stalwartly applying pressure to suspects, witnesses, and superiors, Sturges was calm and methodical, a cool head, as it were, a person able to see things from a remove. In addition to that, he didn't mind the grunt work of the job, the relentless paper trail, data entry, research. Most important, at least to Hively's mind, Sturges didn't mind taking a back seat to him, following his lead or taking his orders. This, even though Hively, at age thirty-three, was twenty-plus years his junior. So, incongruous as they were, the setup worked, and the city bore the fruit. Most high-profile cases, such as a midnight slaughter in a motel, now got tossed their way.

Sturges did a full spin in the middle of the motel room, gawking at the 360-degree massacre that lay before them. "When I heard Sundown Courts, I figured it must be another overdose or something." He gestured first to Pippen, who was still sitting upright, head lolled forward, with lumps of brain glommed onto the wall behind him, streams of blood having sluiced from his ears, nose, and mouth; then to what was left of Kevon, whose body had teetered sideways to where his shoulders and what was left of his head dangled off the bed. "What do you think took the top of his skull off like that?"

"Bullets, I reckon."

Sturges bent to inspect the injury closer. The trauma had caused Kevon's eyes to skew lopsided. One now rested about two inches lower than the other. His head was missing most everything above the eyebrows. Sections of skull, chunks of hair from his flattop still attached, were lying on the floor, mixing it up with what looked and smelled like vomit. Some spinal fluid seeped out of the decimated brainpan and dripped down into the medley.

"Jesus." Sturges recoiled as if the man's gray matter were infectious. He clasped one hand over his mouth and flapped the other around as if to shoo away the sight. He turned to Hively. "Hale said you might know these guys."

Hively nodded. "Seen 'em around. They run a corner on Spring Street for Nico Blakes."

"Blakes? Shit the bed. That doesn't do us any favors, he's involved."

"That one there is Kevon Thompson. And this one is Eric Pippen."

"Yeah. Wallets were in a drawer over in the room next door. Cell phones were over there too. Locked, though."

"iPhones?"

"One of them. Other two are burners."

"You try holding their fingers up to the touch screen?"

"Yeah, didn't work."

Hively pointed to the pool of vomit and innards between the beds. "This part of the scene or from one of ours?"

"This muck here is evidence. The sick outside the door is courtesy of our first responder. Lady patrol officer. One of the new ones. Mounts, I think her name is. Becca Mounts."

"She interview any witnesses?"

"Yeah, she recovered enough after she lost her lunch to get some preliminary statements. Enough to get the shape of the thing at least." Sturges studied the blood spatter that circled Kevon's body and mimed the angles from which the shots must have come for him to arrive at such a gruesome end. "It's like that goddamn emoji they have on your phone that says your mind is blown. Plain overkill if you ask me. Who'd do such a thing?"

"Somebody with a gun or two."

"You're sassy tonight."

"I'm tired. What'd the wits say?"

"Far as I've gathered, the fun started in here. Four men, white men, mind, enter with guns. Bang-bang, these two meet their maker. For whatever reason, the party involved rented two rooms, this one and the one next door." Sturges hiked a thumb toward the adjoining wall that was pocked full of bullet holes. Beams of light from the next room filtered in through the cylindricals like tiny searchlights. "Our shooters must have been alerted to this fact somehow, because all of a sudden they strafe the wall with everything they've got. From there, the whole melee spills out into the corridor. Four against one, from what I understand. They chase this one guy all over tarnation, shooting up the joint. We got shells on all three levels of the motel, the courtyard, between buildings, and the parking lot, coming from at least six different weapons. Anyhow, as our running man flees, he tags one of the gunmen. You see the body on your way in, over there on the backside of the motel?"

"No, I came straight up."

"Well, he somehow manages to get to a car and lights outta here. Not before ramming another vehicle, from what I understand. The three gunmen that are left hop into two different cars, give chase. And poof, they all disappear into the night. That's that. For now."

Hively had been frisking the room as Sturges related these events, looking through drawers, sifting through the pockets of the clothes scattered about. He came out of the bathroom holding a small garbage pail with a loose latex glove. "Did anybody see this? There's a half dozen condoms in here."

"Makes sense. Couple in a room on the first floor was watching the whole thing. Saw a bunch of girls go out of the room shortly after the gunmen went in. You wanna start with them or the motel owner?"

Hively thought about it. "Show me the third vic."

They stepped over the puddle of vomit outside the doorway, went down the stairwell and around to the back of the adjacent building. All along the route, techs were tagging physical evidence. There were so many bullet casings on the ground it was like playing hopscotch to get around them. The sheer volume of spent cartridges and blood would keep the techs busy until the sun rose and cut a line across the sky and fell again. At one point they'd run out of markers and have to make a run to the station for more.

A female patrol officer was standing guard over the area where the third victim lay while a police photographer snapped pictures of the scene. Hively asked the photog to step aside and squatted down to examine the body. He had to be careful not to step on the teeth that littered the sidewalk from where the man's jaw had been blasted off his face.

"We got a name on this one?" Hively asked.

"No ID on him," Sturges said.

The patrol officer cleared her throat and spoke. "I know who he is, sir. Name's Jerry Perky. He's a lowlife, runs some girls here at the motel. Prostitutes," she clarified.

"You Mounts?" Hively asked.

"Yes, sir."

Mounts was a short, compact woman with stern, furrowed features and ramrod-straight posture. Her brown hair was shorn on one side with the rest of it slicked back into a tight knot. The way she spoke was very formal. Hively asked her if she'd been in the military.

"Yes, sir. Army."

"Where'd you serve?"

"Germany."

"How do you know Mr. Perky here?"

"I've been night patrol in this area for the last three months, sir. In that time, I've responded to three calls at this location. All of which involved disputes between various men and a couple of the women who I believe worked for Mr. Perky. He showed up in all three instances."

"This your first murder?"

"First one quite like this, sir."

"These women who worked for him, you know who they are?"

"I know the ones who were involved in disputes."

"Good. You know where to find them?"

"I have their last-known addresses."

"We're gonna need to speak with them as soon as possible. Track them down and bring them in."

"Yes, sir. There's one other thing, Detective. The tech found this." Mounts handed a small plastic evidence bag over to Hively. Inside was a key card for the motel. "It was in his shirt pocket. They wanted me to wait and turn it over to you when you got here."

Hively flipped the bag over, examined both sides of the card. There was no room number.

"Was this guy a guest at the motel?"

"If he was, he wasn't registered," replied Mounts.

Hively stood from his squat and stretched his back

out. "Sturges," he said, "whattaya say we have a go at the owner now?"

Members of the press were crowding the A-frame barricades that spanned the entrance to the parking lot. As Hively and Sturges trekked past them on their way to the motel office, the reporters cajoled them for a statement. The detectives ignored their hollers, but then a sharp whistle turned Hively's head. He noticed Ernie Ciccone, the crime reporter for the *Cain City Herald*, standing apart from the rest of the throng. Hively stopped walking and signaled for the patrolmen manning the barriers to let Ciccone through.

"Not this asshat," griped Sturges.

"Bear with me," said Hively. "We can use him."

The reporter ducked under the tape and strutted over, much to the dismay of the assembled journalists, who voiced their protests. Sturges waved his hands up and down to settle the disgruntled horde.

"Quit your moaning. You'll get your statement in due time."

Ciccone, a chinless little fellow with squint eyes, more hair sprouting from his ears than his head, and a beak that hooked off his face like an upended question mark, was no one's favorite human. The man didn't seem to have hobbies or interests outside of his vocation. He hovered at the edge of every crime scene like a scavenger biding its time, waiting to swoop in on the scraps. He had a way with the printed word, but the manner with which he wrote about crime was tinged with the salacious. Murder, in particular, he treated more like a fetish than any great tragedy. The ramifications of such horrors, the impact on families, communities, were inconsequential to him, tacked on at the end of his articles, if at all, to appease his editor. The murder was the thing.

But Ciccone had been on the beat for going on three decades, so for better or worse, he was more tapped into the criminal enterprises in town than half the cops were, had watched them morph and grow, die, and flourish again. He understood the lineage of Cain City crime from the roots up. Plus, it was too late in the night for anything he wrote to make the morning papers, so Hively figured it couldn't hurt to fish around a little.

As he approached, Ciccone said, "If it ain't my favorite interracial couple."

"That nose of yours ever give you neck problems?" Sturges cracked.

"That's rich coming from you, Slug. But since you ask, no. None whatsoever. It does, however, allow me to smell your bullshit from a mile away, so don't try to feed me any of it." Ciccone clapped his hands in anticipation. "What do you have for me, Detectives? Word on the line is we got a real bloodbath on our hands. That true?"

"That's pretty much the sum of it," admitted Sturges.

Ciccone's slit eyes sparked to life, and his body did this little twitch of excitement. "How many you got toes-up over there?"

"Three," said Hively. He got straight to the point. "Me and you are gonna play a little word association."

"Ooh," Ciccone said, puckering his lips. "I like games."

"Jerry Perky."

Ciccone looked back and forth between the detectives like an expectant puppy awaiting its next treat. His expression gave way to disappointment. "That it? Jerry Perky? Who is he?"

"I'm asking you."

"Never heard of him. I know a Dale Perky got busted for armed robbery of a check-cashing place couple years back. And a Shalaine Perky got ten years at Mounds-ville on a manslaughter bid, stabbed her boyfriend in the throat, claimed self-defense." Ciccone pointed to his head. "But I don't recall any Jerry Perky in the catalogue."

Sturges said, "They related? The other two?"

"Cousins, I think."

"Where'd they live in town?"

"Where else? West End."

Sturges stole a quick glance at Hively. Ciccone caught it.

"What am I missing here?" Ciccone asked. "This have something to do with that batch of overdoses on Saturday?"

"No connection that we know of," said Hively. "You hearing anything about that?"

"Nothing you haven't already read. But, bunch of bodies in a short period of time. Usually these things aren't coincidental."

"C'mon, Ciccone," said Sturges. "This is Cain City. You know as well as anybody, butterfly flaps it wings on one end of town, don't mean it causes a triple homicide on the other."

"Holy hell, you know something big's going on when The Slug starts spitting chaos theory at you."

"Oh, I'm full of surprises," Sturges said.

"You're full of something. Of that, I have no doubt. All right, Detectives, how 'bout telling me who this Jerry Perky fella is? He one of the three you've got on the slab?"

"Yeah." Hively tapered his mouth shut and he chewed his lip while he thought for a second. "We need to find out if those Perkys have another cousin. Tell you what, Ernie. Whatever you find on this, you pass it to me before you write it up. In return, the information we get, I'll feed it to you before it breaks. Exclusive to you. But you gotta keep that name under your hat until we release it. Deal?"

"You got it." The false grin of a ventriloquist dummy spread across Ciccone's face. "Pleasure doing business with you fellas."

He rejoined the pool of reporters outside the perimeter while Hively and Sturges continued into the motel office.

"You thinkin' what I'm thinkin'?" said Sturges. "Two of Blakes's crew dead. If this Perky turns out to be a Stender—"

Hively finished the sentence. "It means the truce is over."

Sturges whistled. "If that's the case, this little brouha-ha here could just be the Archduke Ferdinand of the whole shebang."

CHAPTER TWELVE
THERE'S A MAN WITH A GUN OVER THERE

The office of the Sundown Courts was a cramped, airless affair with a thick pane of safety glass dividing the business side from the customer's, and was hardly big enough for the desk and one chair it housed. The owner, an old curmudgeon named Merle Frickie, had a fluff of dove-white hair, a beard that matched, and a face like a crustacean—eyes bulgy and wide-set and with no lids to speak of. He sat in the chair, arms crossed in the defiant stance of a child, and scowled at the standing detectives. Hively had played nice with Frickie to this point, but the old man was being cagey, giving answers that were intentionally opaque, and he was starting to lose patience.

"We kept the cameras up," the old man explained, "to create the illusion, you know, that we had some kind of security apparatus in place, act as a deterrent, but them things crapped out years ago. We were past warranty on 'em, so wasn't much incentive to get 'em fixed."

"And you say you didn't see any of the gunmen?" Sturges asked, real friendly-like, ingratiating. "Didn't see the cars fleeing the scene?"

"No, sir. I heard the shots and crawled my ass under this here desk fast as you can say dagnabbit. Didn't even peek my head out until I heard the police sirens coming up the way."

"Didn't sneak a look, even when you heard the cars tearing out of here?"

"That's when you catch a stray right between the eyes." Frickie jabbed a finger into the middle of his forehead. "When curiosity gets the best of you."

"How long did the whole thing last?" Hively asked.

"Shoo." Frickie let out a whistle that trailed off like a bomb's descent. "Good little skirmish, that was. Went full-on for a long while. Thought it weren't never gonna end. Damn near gave me flashbacks to the Tet." The old man mimicked having an M-16 in his hands, bracing for action. "There I was, mortar fire on my right, machine-gun fire on my left, knife in my teeth, gooks all around me." Frickie chortled at his own big joke and looked to the detectives to validate his humor. Sturges gave a half grin to placate the old man, then picked up the motel's logbook and started perusing its pages.

Hively said, "Can't imagine the types of clientele that frequent this place are too good for business in the long run."

Frickie wiggled his features around until they looked sufficiently aggrieved. "Not sure what you're insinuating, Detective. I have a motel that has rooms to rent, and if people want to rent them, I'm not likely to run 'em off by asking what they're about to get up to in there. Long as they don't trash the joint, they're fine by me."

"So you turn a blind eye to the junkies, hookers, gang-bangers?"

"Look here, business is business. I'm in no position to police no one's morals. If I turned people away 'cause

I thought they were on hard times, I wouldn't *have* a clientele. Hell, I sympathize with them. I've seen hard times. Me and my brother been running this place for forty-three years."

"Uh-huh. So you know there are ordinances in Cain City against renting rooms by the hour or half day, anything like that?"

"I know the law, thank you very much."

"So we poke around, we're not gonna find any improprieties?"

"No, sir. We keep things above board here at the Sundown."

"No exceptions?"

"None whatsoever."

"Then why"—Hively pulled the plastic evidence bag with the key card out of his inside jacket pocket, dangled it in front of the man's face—"was this found in the possession of the man who's lying dead out there behind your motel right now? Shot to death. Last I checked, it was illegal to rent a room to someone without checking them in with some form of ID. And he wasn't registered in your logs as a guest. No description of a vehicle, nothing like that. So I'm stumped. Where'd the key come from?"

Frickie lifted his shoulders to where they nearly touched his earlobes and dropped them. "Beats me."

"You know what room this key opens?"

The old man folded his top lip over his bottom one and sighed dully, his mouth flapping like a horse's. "Ain't got the foggiest. But I'm sure you're gonna tell me."

"327. Isn't that something? A key to a room that was already rented, where two people were slaughtered. How do you think he got a hold of that key? Magic?"

Frickie blinked his big eyes once, fat and slow like a gator, then shot forward in his chair like a flashbulb had gone off in his head. "You know we give two key cards when there's multiple people in a room. I suppose somebody could have passed one of them to whoever that man is that bit the dust out there." Frickie sat back and nodded his head contentedly, as though the mystery had been solved.

Hively said, "If that were the case, it'd mean one of the victims passed a key to the persons who turned around and killed him. Doesn't make a lot of sense."

"What does anymore?" Frickie said.

Sturges set the logbook down on the desk and spun it around to where the old man could read it. "We got reports that at least three vehicles were involved in the shootout. Now, far as I can see, you've got the make and model written down for everybody who checks in here going back weeks. Here's tonight's entry for room 327 right here." He pointed the scribbles on the book. "Black Lincoln sedan. License plate 5HM-069. The other four cars that you have written down for tonight are all still in the lot."

Frickie crossed his arms. "You got a point to make?"

"Just that you seem like a pretty thorough fella, write down every car that comes through this place. On previous nights, you've even written down some makes and models of cars in the margins here." Sturges pointed to one such entry that had a question mark behind it. "I'm assuming that means a suspicious car, or a car that wasn't registered. There's a couple more like that in here, with the question mark. Yet, conspicuously, two vehicles involved in a triple homicide don't rate a mention."

"You people." Frickie sniffed. "You'll make up whatever story fits your theories, won't you? Answer's right there in front of you. I write down the make and model of every person that checks into the motel. For liability purposes. I don't write down every car that comes in the lot. Hell, you know, people are in and out. That'd be impossible. I don't know what I even meant by that question mark. When was that, two weeks ago? I have no idea what it means."

"Okay, but tonight was a slow night," said Hively. "We're talking about two cars out of seven. You didn't notice the two cars that came into your lot that weren't registered with the motel?"

"You guys can drill down on me all you want. I didn't see what I didn't see."

Hively looked out through the Plexiglas to the front windows of the office. The anterior parking lot and the driveway in from the road were in plain view. "Hard to miss. Weren't they parked right there?"

The old man groaned. "All right, look here. I'll be straight with you."

"Don't start now."

"Come again?"

"Nothing, go ahead."

"Maybe I fell asleep some, okay. Is that okay with you fellas? Is that permitted? A catnap on the overnight shift, for Chrissakes. Like life isn't hard enough, and then I have to deal with this shit."

Hively cut a malevolent grin. "Let's try this one on for size, Mr. Frickie. That man that's dead on your pavement. His name was Jerry Perky. How well do you know him?"

"Who, the dead fella? Not in the slightest."

"That's funny, because our officers have responded to multiple distress calls to this motel that he's been involved in."

"I tend not to get too social with the customers. You understand. Better off not to open that door, lest you find yourself entwined in all sorts of personal dramas. I'm no concierge. You want that you can go on down to the Marriott in town."

"Maybe your brother would know him."

"Doubt it. J. D.'s 'bout as observant as an Easter Christian. Legally blind in two eyes to boot. You know what, though? Last I checked I'm a victim in all this. You seen the amount of damage they done to us out there? Not to mention I coulda just as easily been shot right along with the rest of them. So why does it feel like I'm being interrogated like I'm the perp in this situation? Huh? Like I did something wrong?"

"Maybe because you're feeding us so much bullshit we're about choke on it," said Hively.

"Excuse me?"

"Would you like me to repeat myself?"

"I think I just might, jackass," Frickie said. "You got something to say to me, buck, you go right ahead and say it."

Sturges cut in to salvage whatever goodwill they might have left, in case they needed to question the motel owner again. "No, I think that'll be all for now, Mr. Frickie. Thank you for your time. Sorry about your shop here."

Between interviews, Hively and Sturges sat out by the scummy pool and compared notes. Hively kept a pet rock in his pocket at all times, for stress, for luck. It was smooth and edgeless and he worked it over as he thought out loud.

"If Jerry Perky were just some lowlife pimp, Frickie wouldn't have a problem dishing the dirt, covering his own ass best he could. No reason not to. So he's got to be in league with our shooters."

"Or the man's just trying to find a way to keep his business from going under because of a triple homicide." The look Sturges got from Hively caused him to raise his hands in mock innocence. "Just playing devil's advocate. But you didn't exactly lube him up real well before you started sticking it to him."

"That's because if I fuck you, Sturges, you're gonna feel it."

"Ooh, my ass just puckered a little."

Hively kept his train of thought rolling. "Let's make sure a patrol car is posted here day and night for the next few days, nice and visible right out in front of the office. If it's business he cares about, let's disrupt it for a while. See if that squeezes anything to the surface."

At that moment, Becca Mounts escorted the couple with a room on the first floor over to where Hively and Sturges were conferencing. The detectives rose to greet them, everybody shook hands, and Hively pulled some deck chairs over so that they could sit. Leland and Nancy Turnball were their names. They were one of those middle-aged couples that had probably been together since they were twelve, and as the decades stacked up, each started to look more like the other. Both were gibbous at the waist and penguin shaped, each had a little waddle to their gait, their hair was similarly peppered and coiffed. Both also wore Hawaiian shirts, khaki shorts, and Teva sandals. Though to be fair, her shirt was purple beneath the flowers, and his was red. Other than that, the only characteristics you could say distinguished one from the other was his mustache was slightly thicker than hers, and she wore bifocals.

The Turnballs recounted the story they'd earlier laid out for Officer Mounts, all the same facts aligning where they should. The couple hailed from up north, a pint-size town in West Virginia's panhandle called Weirton, were on their way to a family reunion in Nashville and decided to break their trip up over two days, make a pit stop somewhere in the middle.

"Coulda pulled off anywhere from here to there," the husband said nervously. Though the night air was cool, he was sweating heavily. He wiped his hand across his brow and flicked the moisture off his fingers. "Passed dozens of other places where we could have stopped. Course, that would be our fortune to select the one motel where a full-scale nightmare was about to take place."

"Did you get a decent look at any of the four men?" Hively asked.

"I didn't," the husband said, a little too quickly, glancing at the wife. To this point, Mrs. Turnball hadn't said much. She'd paid as much attention to her cuticles as she had the detectives, behaving almost as if the whole thing had happened years ago. But now she stared at her husband with contempt, as if he'd violated some heretofore agreed-upon version of events.

"Ma'am?"

"Well." Mrs. Turnball set aside whatever indignation she was feeling toward her spouse, raised some knuckles to her mouth, and daintily cleared her throat. "We were having our nightcap right in those chairs there when I saw the men coming our way. Well, the one man in front was all I saw at first. We hadn't seen much foot traffic to that point, though we'd heard some"—she paused to find the right word—"*carnal* noises from the room where it all happened. Leland had wondered aloud if they were the only other ones staying here, if we had the run of the place. Quaint thought now. Anyhow, my chair was facing the parking lot and I heard a car, saw the headlights swoop in, so I looked over thinking I would be friendly, say hello. Not that we were hoping for company or anything. It was just another person, you know. But immediately I saw the gun in that first man's hand, just brazenly out in the open, and I said to Leland, I said, 'There's a man with a gun over there.' That's when I saw the rest of them, too, filing in behind."

"And that's when one of them spoke to you?"

Mr. Turnball answered that one. "Yes. He told us to get

out of there, so we didn't hesitate or look twice or anything like that. We just went straight back to our room."

"Did either of you notice any characteristics on any of them that could be easy to identify? Anything you can think of. Short, tall, the timbre of the man who spoke's voice."

Again, the wife shot a look at her husband.

"Tell them," he said. "They're trying to catch these people, dear."

Nancy Turnball shook her head rapidly, like she was trying to rattle the information out of her brain before she had to speak it aloud. She squeezed her eyes shut, took a deep, calming breath, and opened them again as though she'd hoped to find herself in some faraway place.

"What is it that you saw, ma'am?" Hively prompted her.

Her next words were for her husband. "I just want the record to show that my position in all this is we just needed to keep our traps shut, act like we barely saw or heard anything, didn't smell anything. Nothing. Just admit we heard some shots and then skip to my Lou on outta here."

"But there's more to it than that," Sturges said.

Mrs. Turnball squished her face together and she chewed her lip. "The man I saw was tall, lanky. He was wearing a ball cap."

"That's it?"

"No. The one who spoke to us, he was the biggest one, burly, but that's not all. He had no hair, and there was something wrong with his head."

"Scars?" said Hively.

"I don't know. I just remember thinking, 'That's an odd-looking head.' Could have been scars, I suppose."

Sturges groaned. "Shiiiiiit."

Mrs. Turnball looked anxiously back and forth between the detectives. "What? What does that mean?"

"He didn't happen to have a patch over one eye, did he?" Hively asked.

"I don't—I didn't see one."

"Yes," Leland Turnball said. "Yes, he did. I saw it. Who is he?"

"He, uh—" Hively almost laughed at the question. "He's somebody we've had run-ins with before. Him and his associates. If it's who we're thinking."

"Oh, God." Mrs. Turnball pressed her palms against her eyes, then quickly released them as if struck with fear. "Are we in danger? Do we have to stay here?"

Hively explained that as long as they had their contact information, he didn't see why they couldn't continue on to their reunion.

"Is there anything else you can tell us?" he asked. "Anything at all. Doesn't matter how small you think it might be. The cars they were driving, a snatch of something you might have heard, anything about the girls that came out of the room before things popped off?"

Mr. Turnball squirmed in his seat, wriggled his mustache. "There is one other thing."

"Oh, God," Mrs. Turnball whinnied again.

"I—um—after I heard the gunfire, I videoed some of it from our room. Out the window. I don't know if you can see anything on it."

"I told him not to do that," Mrs. Turnball said. "I told him he was asking for trouble."

"I think we better have a look at it," Hively said.

The husband handed them his phone. The detectives watched the full duration of the video twice through. When it was done, Willis Hively looked up from the screen and said, "Yeah, I think the faster you guys leave town, the better."

CHAPTER THIRTEEN
BODY MOVIN'

The first thing Ephraim did was deadbolt the door, which was against company policy, but hey. Then he laid the tarp out, rolled Rodney Slash's body onto it, and wrapped him up. Next he set to work cleaning up the blood. He attacked the job methodically, first scrubbing the walls, and mopping the floors. Then he filled up buckets of water and poured them over the trails left outside the station to disperse them. It was rare for anyone to come to that area of the plant late at night, and fortunately for him, no one did.

After Ephraim rinsed the mop in the outdoor spigot and wrung it out, he put the cleaning supplies back in the supply closet, took a bag of trash filled with bloody hand towels out to a nearby dumpster, and buried it beneath the other garbage. He knew the trash would be collected later that morning, so the timing worked out favorably.

When Ephraim got done with all this it was 4:30 a.m. All that was left to do was figure out how to dispose of a dead body. *There's a task you don't come across every day,* he thought. One way to do it would be to drag the tarp to the lift at the center of the activator, ride it to the top, and stuff the body into the hearth. A human body probably wouldn't combust the same way the toad's had, but you never knew. There were no security cameras surveilling the area he'd need to cover to get there, and it would be unusual for anyone to venture to the south end of the plant in the early morning. One danger was the guys from the maintenance shop. If a repair was needed, they could be lurking around, but that was it. The only other person he'd need to account for was Billy, who at this hour was more likely than not sleeping in his station.

As Ephraim worked through all this in his head, he thought to himself, *Who the hell are you, a fucking psycho now?* But he didn't have time to stop and fret over it. Concerns for another day.

One problem he foresaw with the hearth route was the possibility that some of the bones would survive the ovens. Ephraim could wait at the bottom, sift through all the carbon that came out on the conveyor, but there was no guarantee he'd spot everything, or that a chunk of bone wouldn't get lodged in the grizzly bars. Also, it took two to three hours for whatever went into the top of the hearth to work its way down, and his shift ended at 7:00. So that option had to be nixed.

The only other solutions Ephraim could think of were to dispatch the body somewhere in the plant, which was plum stupid, or find a way to get the body off the premises. That would buy him time, give him the chance to put some distance between the body and Bismark Carbon.

Risky for sure, and probably more difficult to pull off, but also maybe the only way to get clean of the whole thing. If a corpse were recovered here, or a bone, it was a matter of time before an inquiry led straight to D-Station, and to him. But if the body was never found, no one would have any reason to presume it had ever been there.

Despite Ephraim having scrubbed it silly, the break room still had a faint stain on the drywall. He was sure nobody would see the mark and think, "That looks like somebody stood there for a while, bleeding to death," not without a reason to suspect such a thing. And as of now, there was absolutely no cause for foul play to enter someone's mind. Anybody who noticed the stain at all would most likely assume it came from a spilled drink or maybe water damage, if they even thought twice about it.

But how to get the body out?

Ephraim washed up, checked his uniform to make sure there was no visible blood. There were some specks here and there, but mostly it was on his shirt, so he put his jacket on, then his goggles and hard hat. He grabbed a plastic bag and walked to packaging to collect the third and final sample of his shift. The wind had died down and now the air was crisp and still. The sky had purpled with the oncoming sunrise, and a sliver of orange glowed weakly over the river valley to the east. Nervous adrenaline coursed through Ephraim's body and he tried to slow his breathing down the same way he'd taught his son to do when he became agitated—in through the nose, out through the mouth.

Ephraim retrieved the cut sample, but instead of heading back to D-Station, he trudged over to the maintenance shop. There he found Don Sparks and Bo Wayne sitting at a foldout table, Wayne with his forehead resting on his arms, and Sparks staring slack-jawed at the wall clock, quite literally watching the seconds tick by until the shift was over. When Ephraim came in, Sparks's eyes casually slid from the clock to him. No other parts of his body moved.

"You fuck something up?" Sparks asked. Every word he spoke sounded like a gripe or a precursor to one.

Ephraim had a precooked smile prepared for the occasion, and he busted it out. "No. Don't worry, you don't have to work none."

Sparks squinted at him with suspicion. "Fuck you up to?"

Ephraim took a couple of casual steps toward the maintenance bikes. "You hear the news?"

"Yeah, we heard. Fuckin' management, huh? What a shitshow. You gonna start looking for something else?"

"Reckon I'll have to. In the meantime, I've always wanted to take one of these babies for a spin." Ephraim took hold of the handlebars on one of the bikes and without waiting for permission began hustling it toward the exit. Sparks finally moved more than his eyes. He tried to stand up too fast and his old legs buckled. He grabbed his knees for support and gingerly straightened.

"Don't get up on account of me," Ephraim said. "I'll show myself out."

"What in the god-dern you think you're doing?" Sparks asked.

"Making my escape—what's it look like?"

"That's my bike!"

At this, Bo Wayne finally lifted his head from the table. "Jesus. Can you two keep it down? I'm trying to sleep over here."

"Don't worry, Don," Ephraim said. He threw his leg over the seat, got his feet on the pedals and started pumping. "I'll have her back before midnight."

Sparks hollered after him: "Your little ass better swing a hard U, or I swear to God I'll file a complaint. Go on and test me."

Ephraim made it to the service door and gave a happy little wave as he pedaled out of the shop.

"You little prick," Sparks spat. He wiped his mouth on his forearm. "All those tools better still be in that chest when you get back, or else."

"How much you think I can get for that Hitachi drill?" Ephraim called over his shoulder.

"That ain't a bit funny," Sparks hollered.

There were two routes to choose from to get back to D-Station. He decided on the faster of the two, riding out through the parking lot and down the main drive along the edge of the plant. He'd be caught on camera there, but Bo Wayne and Don Sparks had witnessed him take the bike anyway. Could be good to have witnesses, he reckoned, if anybody came around asking why he'd done it. As he rode away, he could hear the two men bickering.

"Did you see that?! He took my bike!"

"Who cares? What do you think he's going to do, sell it for parts?"

"That's not the point. These young guys have no respect!"

"Well, they've learned from the best."

Their bickering voices disintegrated in the fresh air of dawn. Cycling through the plant, humming with energy, Ephraim felt momentarily euphoric, imagining this was how gamblers and bank robbers felt after a big score. He found this reaction within himself inexplicable, given what had transpired over the past three hours, and given what he was fixing to do. Nevertheless, it was there, floating on the breeze that cut past his cheeks as he rode, so he breathed in the sensation while it lasted. Outside of packaging he passed Lou Manns, toting his little plastic sample bag. Manns gave Ephraim a funny look. Ephraim doffed his hard hat and kept pumping.

He didn't see anybody else. Ephraim parked the bike outside the door of the station. Inside he took hold of the tarp's edge and dragged the body over the tiled floor, careful not to tilt it so far that blood would run out. He hefted the body on top of the toolbox on the back of the bike's cart, fixed it diagonally across so that the tarp wouldn't get caught in the wheels, and secured it with some shock cords. The additional weight on the back made it hard to get the pedals going, but once he did, he was able to chug along pretty smoothly. He rode out down the access road, past the silo, the coalfields, and the spare-parts lot. In the secluded area where Lucia had parked her car, he untethered the body and pulled it into the brush behind some trees.

When his shift ended at 7:00 a.m., Ephraim did what he always did. He filled out his paperwork, turned it in, and patiently shot the shit with Billy in the showers. The only variance in his routine was he didn't put his work shirt in the dirty bin to be laundered. He tossed in the rest of his uniform, but the shirt had blood on it and he kept it back, quickly removing it at his locker and stuffing it, along with the two pistols he'd taken off the dead man, into his duffel.

After the shower, Ephraim dressed hurriedly and left. Billy caught up with him in the parking lot. "You're moving purposeful, aren't you? Got somewhere to be?"

"Naw. Caleb had a rough day yesterday. Just want to get home, make sure everything's good, you know."

"I gotcha," Billy said. "See you tonight, brother. You know, unless we get canned."

"Yeah."

Ephraim fiddled around with his phone and waited for Billy to leave the parking lot first. He didn't want Billy to see him turning the opposite way from home when he pulled out. Once he was gone, Ephraim drove the short distance to the southern end of the plant, crossed over the railroad tracks and turned onto the access road. The trucks bringing in the coal wouldn't start arriving until around

8:30, so the road was clear. He rolled down the gravel lane to where the body was stashed, pulled it from the brush, and wrestled it onto the bed of his truck. Luckily, he had a bed cover back there. He fastened it into place, slammed the tailgate shut, and drove back out the access road.

The whole thing went off easier than Ephraim had imagined it would, and he hoped that was a portent of things to come. He came out onto the state road and turned for home. Having a corpse in the back of his truck made Ephraim hyper-aware of his surroundings, and a bit paranoid, as he wound his way out to Buffalo township. He pictured the body sliding with the curves of the road, banging against the sides; pictured the tailgate falling open and the tarp tumbling onto the road, coming undone, the body rolling out, and the car behind him running over it.

Ephraim checked his rearview incessantly and scanned the faces in the oncoming cars to see if any of them were Black and therefore possibly looking for Rodney. These thoughts and actions were irrational, he knew, but it didn't stop him from doing them. At one point, a state trooper came up behind the truck. Ephraim eased off the gas to reduce his speed and prayed to God that he didn't have a tail light out. He racked his brain to try and remember whether or not he'd updated his tags earlier that summer when they'd come in the mail, or if he'd promptly set the stickers aside and forgotten about them. He'd been known to neglect such things. But when he made the sharp turn onto Marvel Heights, the trooper zipped right on past.

Ephraim pulled into his carport and saw his father sitting on the porch swing.

"Everything all right?" he asked, getting out of the truck. "Where's Caleb?"

Darrell staggered to his feet and threw up his arms. "I don't know what happened. I asked him what he wanted for breakfast and he wouldn't answer me, so I started giving him some options, you know, cereal, Pop-Tarts, waffles, and he went full Exorcist on me again, just started screamin' and hollerin'."

"Okay." Ephraim sighed, trudging up the steps.

"Gird your loins. This one's a doozy. He won't get dressed or nothing. Said there's no way on God's green earth he's going to school."

"Did you yell at him?"

"No, I just said, you know, it's not that hard to sit down and eat some goddamn breakfast."

"All right. I'll handle it."

"What was I supposed to do?"

"Nothing. I said I'd handle it."

Ephraim went in and to the back of the house where he found Caleb on the floor of his room, kicking his pillow into the air. As soon as Caleb noticed his father he shrieked at him to get out.

"I can't do that, buddy. We gotta get you ready. We're gonna be late for school and you still gotta eat something."

"I'm not going to school!"

Ephraim took a step toward his son. Caleb tried to crawl under his bed to get away. He made it halfway before Ephraim got a hold of his waist and tugged him back, but Caleb grabbed the slats beneath the bed and wouldn't let go. He kicked his legs wildly. Ephraim blocked the kicks with his arms, though one of the blows caught him pretty solidly in the ribs. He laid across Caleb's legs, clamped down on them.

"Let go of me!" Caleb yelled.

Ephraim yanked the boy hard and got him to let loose of the slats. Caleb slid out from under the bed, screaming bloody murder and still kicking, swinging his fists with the ferocity of the rabid. His pupils were dilated out to large black saucers, wide-open apertures, and the ligaments in his neck stretched taut and bulged. As the two of them struggled, the thought crossed Ephraim's mind, not for the first time, that his son might be possessed. That maybe they did need an exorcist. He worked to keep Caleb's legs detained with one hand while catching his flailing arms with the other, saying, "Stop it. Stop it, Caleb."

"You're trying to kill me!"

"No, I'm not."

Ephraim flattened himself atop his son and bear-hugged him tightly, pinning down his extremities. Keeping him clamped, Ephraim rolled around to a sitting position behind Caleb, bracing his back against the bed.

"Let me go!" Caleb howled. He began to gasp. "I can't . . . I can't . . ."

"You're okay," Ephraim assured him. "I'm not hurting you. Breathe. See, I'm not hurting you. It's okay, it's okay. Shh. I'm here for you. Shh. Breathe." Ephraim modeled what he meant, inhaling and exhaling nice and slow. Caleb fought against his father's restraints, bucking his head back numerous times before giving in, letting his body go slack. Caleb's heart thumped heavily against his chest and his breathing was still panicked, but Ephraim could feel him easing up.

"See," Ephraim coached. "There, just like that. That feels better, right. Breathe. Breathe." He kept whispering things like that in Caleb's ear, telling him he loved him, telling him everything was going to be all right—things he was no longer sure of being true himself. Eventually

Caleb's chest quit heaving and his pulse relaxed. Ephraim made sure the calm was going to hold before speaking again. "We have to go to school, bud."

"No," Caleb whined. "Nooooo."

"I know it's tough. I know it is, but that's your job. That's how you have to look at it. Remember what we talked about last night. Just hang in there. I promise you, we're gonna figure out what's going on with you, and we're gonna get you better."

"I don't want to feel like this anymore."

"I know. I know you don't. And I don't want you to. I'm gonna call the doctor as soon as they open this morning, and we're gonna get this thing going. We're gonna figure it out, okay? But until we do, if we can't go to school, then we'll need to go to the hospital again. And if we do that, so you know, they're gonna make me admit you this time. That means I won't be able to stay with you like I did last time. They'd keep you there for as long as they feel it necessary. I don't want that for you. I don't want to be separated. Do you want that?"

Caleb shook his head, no.

"Then I need you to help me out, okay? I need you to work with me."

"Okay."

"Now, I'll lay some clothes out for you. You put them on and go ahead and brush your teeth and comb your hair in the bathroom. Then come get some breakfast. Deal?"

Caleb whimpered a meek objection, but Ephraim got to his feet and started sifting through the dresser, pulling out items and arranging them on the bed. The boy followed suit. He stood, mopily, removed his pajamas, and slowly started dressing. Ephraim left him to it.

The laundry room was off the kitchen. Ephraim took his duffel in there, got his work shirt out, poured some stain remover over the blood splotches, and threw it in the washer. Then he went out to the kitchen and poured a bowl of Cheerios for himself and one for Caleb. He held off putting milk in Caleb's bowl so that the cereal wouldn't get soggy.

As Ephraim ate, he opened the map feature on his phone, typed "Bismark Carbon" into the location bar, and brought up a satellite view. When looked at from outer space the plant appeared as a mere sliver of steel and manufacturing, an industrial blip on a canvas of green forest. He zoomed in and navigated the map south from there, tracing along the railroad tracks, keeping an eye out for tiny roads that cut into the forest or led to nearby open ground. There were at least a dozen vast fields within a couple-mile radius south of the plant, mostly farmland. He zoomed in and out on the images of these spaces, searching for signs of a rock formation or quarry, anything in the topography that matched the description the dead man in the bed of his truck had given him. Nothing seemed to fit the bill.

He finished his cereal and went to check on Caleb, who was brushing his teeth.

"What?" Caleb snapped, blowing bubbles of foam toothpaste into the air.

"Nothing," Ephraim said. "Just checking on you."

"I'm brushing my teeth like you said."

"I see that. Finish up. We gotta get going."

Next he went into the living room where his dad had taken his post in the recliner to watch the morning news on full volume. Darrell noticed Ephraim in the doorway and turned the volume down a couple notches.

"He okay?" Darrell asked.

"Define 'okay.'"

"Will you look at this?" Darrell stabbed at the TV with the remote.

"What is it?"

"Some kind of shootout at that old motel down there off the interstate. Three people dead. What's this world come to? I swear, from the time you can think a thought, you're forced to listen to people 'round here spouting off about heaven and hell and the criteria needed to get into each of 'em. But you ask me, the people who wrote the Bible, they were just writing what they saw, 'cause it can all be found right here on earth. All of it. You wanna see hell, turn on the goddamn evening news."

"This is the morning news."

"What?"

"This is the morning news."

"It's all the same."

On the screen was a female reporter with bright-red hair teased-out beauty-queen style, and high-arching eyebrows that made her look as though she were in a perpetual state of shock. She was positioned on the ground-level corridor and gesturing over her shoulder to an area that comprised a courtyard with a couple of tables and umbrellas, a greenish-looking pool, and beyond that the back section of the salmon-colored motel. The sun was peeking up over the corner of the building, its rays shimmering off the murky water of the pool. There were no other people visible in the shot, and if there wasn't police tape strewn across every walkway and X'ing out a couple doors on the top floor, the scene would be downright tranquil.

Darrell was still making his points about the divine and the secular being one and the same. "It's all right there. What you see when you look at the world says more about you than it says about the world. I've always said that, so I don't know what that says about me, 'cause when I look at the world all I see is pure shit."

Ephraim shushed him. "I want to listen to this."

"What?"

"I wanna listen to this."

"The police have remained tight-lipped thus far," the reporter was saying, "amid fears that the perpetrators of this crime are still on the loose and are obviously armed and very dangerous." The reporter held a finger to her ear and listened for a few seconds before continuing. "I'm being told now, Tim, that the police do know the identities of the victims, though those names have yet to be released to the public. Also, they may have an indication as to who the participants in these murders might be, based on interviews with eyewitnesses and because they are familiar, I'm told, with the deceased."

"Wow," the anchor exclaimed. "So, this is an extraordinary example of an investigation unfolding in real time, Jessica. Right before our very eyes."

"Indeed it is, Tim."

The anchor then informed viewers that a video of the incident, purportedly taken by a guest of the motel, had been obtained by Channel 3 News, and he warned that the images they were about to broadcast were graphic and disturbing.

The report cut to handheld footage you could tell was shot on a phone. For a few seconds, nothing happened. But then there was the unmistakable *pop-pop-pop* of gunfire, followed by an all-out fusillade. On the second-floor corridor, a figure in a white T-shirt and dark pants sprinted like mad from right to left. He was carrying a shotgun in one hand and had some sort of large bag strapped to his back.

Ephraim fixated on the television, unable to blink, hardly able to breathe. The shooting ceased, and another person emerged from the shadows on the third floor and began running in the same direction as the man on the floor below. The figures were too far away to make out their features, but Ephraim knew, beyond a shadow of a doubt, that he was watching Rodney Slash, when he was very much alive, not eight hours ago in fact, being chased by a pack of killers on the morning news.

Ephraim felt the odd sensation of knowing how the story ends. The video continued through Rodney trading shots with the man on the balcony above, then leaping over the railing and fleeing. After he disappeared around the corner of the motel, figures on both the ground level and the third floor unleashed a barrage of bullets in the direction where Rodney turned out of sight.

The video froze there.

The anchor asked anyone with information about the shootout to call the police hotline, which they posted at the bottom of the screen, and with that they segued into their next story, something about an effort to curb the high rate of obesity and heart disease in the Tri-State area. Darrell lowered the volume and slammed the remote down against the upholstered armrest. His voice shuddered with anger.

"You see where twenty-three people OD'd in a two-hour timespan the other day?" he asked.

"No, I didn't see that."

"You live under a rock, son. This was just day 'fore yesterday. Now today, *this* idiocy."

"Dad?" Ephraim said. "You ever hear of any caves down where you grew up? South of the plant there?"

CHAPTER FOURTEEN
LEFT FROM PURPLE

Willis Hively held the transmitter end of the telephone away from his mouth and stifled a yawn so that the man on the other end of the line, his captain, wouldn't hear. He pinched the bridge of his nose with a thumb and forefinger and rubbed the itch out of his bloodshot eyes, then gulped down his third cup of coffee. Quickly he realized three cups was nowhere near sufficient on this morning.

The station wasn't humming yet; it'd be an hour until the day shift supplanted the overnight crew. Clyde Sturges strolled down the row of empty bullpen desks, a little piece of stationery thrust out front of him as though he were in possession of a winning lotto ticket. He slapped the paper down on Hively's desk with a giddy look of satisfaction. Hively gave the sheet a once-over. Scrawled on it were three ten-digit numbers, all starting with local area codes.

Hively cupped his hand over the phone's mouthpiece. "What's this?"

"We broke the passcode on one of the three burners."

"Already?" Hively took his hand off the phone and spoke into it. "Yes, sir. We can pick him up today if that's what you want . . . No, we can do it . . . Yes, sir . . . Got it.

Look, we got a lead on something here with the Sundown case . . . Yeah, I'll let you know if it goes anywhere." Hively dropped the phone on its cradle and let out a big sigh that he punctuated with a curse.

"What was that all about?" Sturges asked.

"Michelle Harmon just died."

"Harmon? The OD that woke up?"

"Briefly, yeah."

"Jesus. What's that make?"

"Sixteen down. That leaves seven still in a coma."

"Jesus. Did none of these fools get Narcanned?"

"I think they all did. Some multiple times. That junk must have been pure poison. If none of the ones left come out of it . . ." Hively trailed off. He didn't have to finish the thought. They both knew if they couldn't get an ID on the seller, chances were they'd never figure out where the batch of heroin came from, which made it that much more likely to happen again.

Sturges said, "Well, it's early, but this fucking day is on pace to break the world record for the worst of my career."

"Yeah," Hively agreed.

"Somebody's gotta know something."

"Somebody always knows something. Whether they tell us or not is a different matter. Hale's feeling some top-down heat. Wants us to roust the Hinkle kid."

"That little wannabe cocksucker from the Southside?"

"That's the one. Says he's dealt with him before, we shake him down a little bit he'll buckle under scrutiny. Says he's a weasel, but he's pretty in the know about who's doing what in town, even if he doesn't know what he knows, that kind of thing."

"You tell him we have other matters to attend to. Can't somebody else do that shit?"

"I told him. He's gonna distribute all our other cases to different detectives. He thinks the overdoses and the murders might be connected somehow. Murders being payback for the overdoses."

"Who put that in his head, Ernie Ciccone?"

"Probably."

"How would that even work exactly? These boys from the East End sell some tainted junk kills a bunch of people on the West End, so the Stenders get pissed and kill them in retaliation? Doesn't make a lick of sense. These guys don't cross streams. Besides, you ever know either of them to cut their product with Fen?"

"No."

"What's Hale think? We're gonna clear nineteen murders in one fell swoop?"

"I know. But the Sundown and the overdoses are the biggest two things we got going, so for better or worse, they're all ours."

"You know something," Sturges complained. "I think I liked it better when everybody around here thought I didn't know my left from purple."

"Verdict's still out on that one, Clyde. How'd the lab boys crack the phone so quick?"

"Fuck if I know? They went on about some mumbo jumbo about UV lighting or some shit. Long story short, the security screen had stacks of fingerprints on three of the digits. One, four, and seven."

"Down the first column."

Sturges tapped his nose to indicate that Hively was spot-on. "Nothing gets past you, boy genius. Like a fox. Anyhow, they knew from the type of phone it was likely a six-digit code, so they tried a bunch of combinations using those three digits, and presto. Took 'em all of three minutes to land on it. Get this." Sturges stabbed his finger down onto the paper with the numbers. "I don't know if the burner was only two days old, or if it had its call log erased or what, but it only had these three numbers stored. Mostly incoming, though it looks like the calls were returned a couple times. These other numbers are all from disposables, too—I checked—but this top one here, take a guess how many times it tried to call our phone here last night."

Hively looked at his partner impatiently.

"I'll spare you the suspense. Thirty-three. Every fifteen minutes or so. Calls didn't stop coming until the story of the shootout hit the news this morning."

"They must have needed to speak with our vics pretty badly," said Hively.

"Must have."

"Let's call it and see if it's still up."

Sturges wagged his finger. "I thought you might say that." He produced a plastic evidence bag from behind his back as if he were performing the prestige of a magic trick and set it on the desk. "Voilà."

In the bag was the burner from the motel. Hively slid a drawer open and fished out a plastic glove, snapped it on, and removed the phone from the bag. "What's the security code?"

"One-four-seven, seven-four-one."

"Isn't that your passcode?"

"How'd you know? Now I'm going to have to change all of them."

Hively punched in the digits and the phone's screen brightened to life. He checked the call log and saw the list of incoming calls from the number in question.

"How much you wanna bet it's a girlfriend?" said Sturges. "Only a woman would be that relentless, calling over and over again."

Hively didn't buy that line of thinking. Dealers used disposable phones primarily for business purposes. They wouldn't want a bunch of females blowing them up, expending their minutes. No, Hively's hunch was that someone knew the Spring Street boys had jumped headfirst into the shit and had tried to warn them.

"Only one way to find out," Hively said. He punched in the number with a gloved finger and put it on speaker. The call connected and began to ring.

Sturges leaned in to hear better. "Tenner says it's a girl."

"Bet."

Someone picked up on the third ring, but whoever it was didn't say a word. They just sat there with the line open like dead air on a radio station. The detectives didn't want to squander the opportunity to speak with this person, whoever they were. If the call got cut, the next thing the person would do is break the phone into pieces and toss them through a sewer grate.

So Hively said, "Who's this?"

For another couple seconds, nothing. Then a low, thick voice parroted, "Who's this?"

Sturges had no idea who the voice belonged to, but those two uttered syllables were plenty enough for Hively to know exactly who the owner was.

"Not who you were expecting, I'd imagine."

"Oh, I don't know about that, Little Willie," the man said. "I doubt you have the slightest idea on my expectations."

Blakes, Hively mouthed to Sturges. Then to Nico, he said, "You wouldn't have been thinking one of your boys from Spring Street was calling in, would you? The one who's presumably still alive anyway."

The line again fell silent for a moment before Nico responded. "Which one is it?"

"Who's gonna get promoted, get their own crew down there now? I'm sure you got some teenagers lined up for the job."

"Who's still alive?" said Nico, his voice sounding clenched. Hively could practically feel the vise grip Blakes must have had on the phone.

"You tell me what they did to piss off the Stenders, and I'll tell you which one of your boys made it out. Or is it something *you* did to piss off the Stenders? Is this the first salvo in a new beef?"

"Whatever's going on, it ain't have nothing to do with me."

"Funny then how you called them about forty times last night."

"Always good catching up, Little Willie. Be seeing you 'round the way."

"Wait, Nico," Hively snapped. "Give me something to go on here. Do you know who cancelled your boys? What'd they do? What set this off?"

After a hesitation, Nico replied. "Who made it out?"

Hively hesitated, then told him. "Slash." Stillness from the other end. No response. "You haven't heard from him?"

"No. Whatever trouble them boys got into, they brought it on they own selves."

"But you knew about it. Tried to warn them?"

"Now, if I did that, it'd make me a part of this thing, wouldn't it? And I ain't got no part to play. Far as I know, it ends with them."

"You mean when they're all dead? When they get Rodney too? Did they sell that bad batch of heroin?"

"Happy hunting, Little Willie."

The call disconnected. Sturges looked down at Hively with a keen expression. "Little Willie?"

"Blakes and I came up together in the Terrace. Same year in school."

"You never told me that."

"Never came up."

"You guys close?"

"Back then? Close enough."

"So what do you think?"

What Hively thought was this: Nico Blakes would never cross the Stenders unprovoked. It'd start an all-out war between the two factions. And while there was no doubt Nico would put up a hell of a fight, for a while at least, in the end he'd lose, and he knew he would lose. Given the Stenders' numbers and reach across the tri-state, any aggression against them was suicide, be it by one quick hit or a thousand cuts. If they wanted you gone, you were sure to get gone, one way or the other. Hell, even as they spoke Hively was sure the Stenders still had police officers on the pad. This despite a wide-sweeping anti-corruption initiative that had gone into effect the previous year.

So that left two scenarios in play. One, the Spring Street crew moved against the Stenders without Blakes's knowledge, and whatever they did got them killed. But Nico had to have known they were set to get their tickets punched. What other reason could there be for all the calls? The logical explanation is he had to be trying to warn them. But that didn't jibe with what Blakes had just asserted, that he played no part in it. Hively suspected, if this was how it went down, what really occurred was Nico traded their lives to avoid the conflict between the East and West Ends.

The second, worst-case scenario, was this: A wobbly truce between the two sides had held firm for decades, but what if the Stenders were finally making their long-feared play for the East's territory? Maybe they were riding the wave of white nationalism that had reared its malformed head across the country in recent years, and decided it was time to take control of not only the West End, but all of Cain City. If an operation such as this were already in motion, the police would be powerless to stop it. Nothing less than a bloodbath would ensue.

Hively thought—or rather, hoped—that the first scenario was more likely, more logical. But they were still missing too many pieces of the puzzle to make sense of anything that had transpired in the last twelve hours.

All that is what went through Hively's head. But what he said was, "I think you owe me a tenner."

"Oh, you thought that was for real?" Sturges asked, contriving to sound innocent.

Hively held out his palm. Sturges fished two fives out of his wallet and grudgingly handed them over.

Hively pocketed the cash and said, "Let's call the other numbers."

The second number they tried was the pizza joint Kevon Thompson had ordered delivery from, his name being on the ticket. But the third was answered by a young woman. "Pip?" she said, drowsy, like the call had woken her.

"With whom am I speaking?" Hively asked.

The unfamiliar voice knocked the fog out of her brain. "What . . . who?" she stammered. "Wait, who is this? Where's Eric?"

Hively identified himself and asked her to do the same.

"Not until—what's going on?" There was a growing frenzy to her words. A baby began to fuss in the background.

Hively said, "We're investigating a crime, and we need to know who you are and what you spoke to him about last night."

"What kind of crime?" she said haltingly. "Why do you have Eric's phone?"

"Ma'am, can you please tell me your name and your relationship to Mr. Pippen?"

The baby was full-on crying now and the woman shushed it repeatedly.

"I'm . . . is he in trouble?"

"Can you tell us where you are, please, so we can come speak to you?"

"Is he dead? Is he dead?" The baby, as if sensing the moment, shut up. Sturges pantomimed a knife across the throat to signal how he thought Hively should answer the question, which was to lie to the woman, string her along until they got the information they needed. Hively didn't do that.

"Yes, ma'am," he said. "He was killed last night."

"Oh God, oh, God!" the woman bawled. In the background the baby started up again.

"Are you in a relationship with Mr. Pippen?" Hively asked. There was a thud, like the phone had been dropped. This was followed by a muted scream, a loud crack, and the line went dead. "Fuck."

Sturges clucked his tongue. "I mean, you are really shitting the bed this morning. We should use these calls to train future generations of lawmen what *not* to do."

"Shut up." Hively redialed the woman's number. It rang and it rang. He tried twice more, only to achieve the same result. Next, he hit up Nico's burner again. On that one, he received the ever-enduring automated message: *The number you have called is no longer in service. If you'd like to make a call, please hang up and try again.*

CHAPTER FIFTEEN
CATTLE VALLEY

As it turned out, Darrell did remember some caves he and his friends used to explore back when they were teenagers—three or four caverns tucked into the bluffs that overlooked the old McDowell cattle farm, now the Mercer farm, an expansive piece of property that snaked along the valley floor to the sum of fifteen hundred acres. Problem for Ephraim was, his father's memories were sixty-plus years old, and he couldn't recall exactly where they were or how to get to them. It was possible they no longer existed at all. Decades ago, the mountaintop adjacent to the farm had been strip-mined down to its last coal lump.

"They dynamited the hell out of that mountain," Darrell recalled. "Took least a couple hundred feet off the top. Changed the whole landscape over there." His tone turned wistful. "Yep, we had the run of the place back then. Knew every inch of those hills. Wasn't like now. In those days kids was given some freedom, allowed to roam. Ol' Bobby Jenks—you know Bobby, worked over at DK Steel in Ironton."

"Yeah."

"He got bit by a rattlesnake down near one of those caves. You should have seen this sucker, big ol' thing, thick as my fist. I mean this snake just kept coming." Darrell thrust his fist out, miming the snake's strikes. "Got him two or three times on the calf before Bobby even knew what was happening. 'Fore long whole leg was swelled up. We had to carry him outta there, two of us. Took forever. I swear, we thought Bobby was gonna die. He just kept muttering, 'Oh my God, oh my God, oh my God,' all the way down the mountain. I don't know that we ever went back after that." Darrell squinted up toward the ceiling for a moment, conjuring in his mind these far-gone images of youth, pleasant now, the harrowing bits dulled by the passage of time. He refocused his eyes on Ephraim. "Why do you wanna know about all that?"

"No reason." Ephraim shrugged. "Guys just shooting the shit at work. I don't think they were talking about the same ones you're talking about, though."

"Mercer's got flooded this last spring. Saw it on the news. Mining company never did reclamate the land when they left out of there, not the way they should've anyhow, and those bad rains we had sluiced right down that old valley fill. From what was told, it loosed some of that old slush, brought it down there with it. Just slid right on top of everything, ruined a bunch of their pasture. It was on the news. You didn't see it?"

"No."

"They was trying to sue the old mining company or some such thing, but it'd been out of business for years. Wudn't nobody left to sue."

"Huh."

Caleb slunk into the room, backpack on, mumbling something about being ready to go. He said it in a baby voice, another weird thing that'd come out of nowhere recently, this baby babble you could hardly understand. Annoyed the shit out of Ephraim, but he was too keyed up and impatient to get going to get on him about it. Instead, he prodded Caleb out the door and packed him into the Ranger. Before Ephraim got in he went over to the shed beside the house and came back with some gloves, a shovel, and an old pair of Bushnell binoculars. He stuck the gloves in his back pocket, slid the shovel inside the bed of the truck to keep the dead man company, and handed Caleb the binoculars as he climbed behind the wheel.

"What are these for?" Caleb asked.

"To look through."

"I know that. Why you bringing 'em?"

"Nunya."

"Nunya?"

"Yeah. Nunya business. See what you can see while we're driving."

Looking off the roadside through the binoculars made Caleb dizzy, so he put them down. He didn't want the radio on either, and they took most of the drive in silence. When they neared the school, Caleb, again with the baby mumbo, asked, "Did you call the doctor?"

"Can you talk in a regular voice, please?"

"This is my regular voice."

"Okay." Ephraim sighed.

"What?"

"Nothing. I can't call the doctor till they're open."

Caleb didn't say anything for a minute. Instead, he set to running the zipper of his backpack open and shut a couple dozen times.

"Can you stop that?" Ephraim asked, but Caleb kept at it. Ephraim put his hand over his son's and squeezed it and Caleb stopped.

"Do you think I've got what mom has?" he said. His voice was back to normal.

"You mean bipolar?"

Caleb nodded.

"I don't know, bud. The doctors didn't think so before, but that doesn't mean it isn't related in some way."

"I don't want to be like her."

"You're not gonna be. Even if that's what it is, it won't necessarily be like that. You're your own person; that stuff comes out differently in everybody. She never would do much about her issues until somebody forced her to. But listen, she's not—it's a complicated thing. Those memories you have of your mother, the bad ones, that's not who she was, not really. A lot of the time she was great. She just never could hang on to it for long, you know what I'm saying?"

"Like me?"

"No, not like you. Whatever's going on with you, we're gonna catch it early and get it sorted out. Okay?"

"If you say so."

"I do say so." Ephraim pulled the truck up to the front of the school. They were fifteen minutes late and no one was outside. "Do I need to come in, or do you need a note, or what?"

"No, they'll just give me a tardy."

"Okay. Let's just get through today," Ephraim said encouragingly. "Whatever you gotta do, just, you know, white-knuckle it and get through so we can figure this out. One day at a time, okay?"

Caleb looked at him dully, then pushed open the door and slid out.

"Hey," Ephraim said. "Can I tell you something?"

"I already know," Caleb grumbled. "Have a good day, I love you, blaa blaa blaa."

Ephraim repeated his son's words verbatim, including the blaa blaa blaas, and watched him mope into the school. As soon as he was in and the big doors swung shut, Ephraim got back onto his phone and looked up the phone number for Caleb's doctor. The time wasn't yet 9:00 a.m., and his call went to a voice mail giving the clinic's hours of operation and advising to call 911 in the case of an emergency. Ephraim ended the call. He opened an internet browser, typed the name of the farm in the search bar and found their website. A quick skim of the site yielded a little information. The Mercers' primary interest was cattle, but they also farmed hay and alfalfa or soybean and corn, depending on the year. The site also had links to social media accounts and it took only a little digging to figure out they'd finished harvesting their crop in late September, weeks ago. They'd even uploaded some pictures of combines doing their collecting.

He exited the browser and brought up the Maps application. The satellite imaging showed that the old strip mine was about a mile and a half southeast of Bismark Carbon. Down the mountain from that was the vast expanse of the valley and the Mercer farm. The depiction of the land wasn't current. The trees were green and lush, whereas the foliage outside now had begun to color with the change of season. There was no evidence of a recent landslide his father had mentioned. Zooming in, he saw that there was a sediment pond at the bottom of the fill. A dry creek bed or an irrigation ditch fed into the pond from the pasture. He tried to get a closer look at the woods that surrounded the fill, see if there were any rock ledges visible between trees, but the image was too pixilated to make anything out.

There were multiple access roads that led to different areas of the property. A couple of these lanes were so narrow as to be nearly invisible, but if you enlarged the image enough, you could piece together sections of the roads slithering beneath the canopy of trees. Rodney Slash could have come from any one of them, but one lane in particular exited the woods not far from the railroad tracks, roughly a mile south from the plant. If this was indeed the area where Rodney had crashed, Ephraim thought this road was his best bet for finding the vehicle. And if he could find the vehicle, the money had to be close by.

"You better hope so you fuckin' ass-clown," Ephraim mumbled to himself.

A knock on the window startled him. He looked up from his phone. A fat security officer was bent forward, peering into the truck. "You got business in the school, sir? This is a bus lane. You can't be idling here."

Ephraim gave a conciliatory wave and said, "Just dropped my kid off."

The guard said that was fine, but he needed to move his vehicle. Ephraim put the truck in gear and got on down the road.

Bismark Carbon looked different in the raw light of day, a gloomy, man-made blight, ugly and oppressive. Gone was the ethereal quality the facilities gave off in the nighttime. One would be excused for thinking it a different location altogether. The rust showed. The incongruity between the manufactured steel and the natural world showed.

As he drove past the plant, his heart doubled its tempo. Ephraim took some deep breaths in through his nose, out through his mouth, and once the factory receded in his rearview, so did the panic.

"Fuck was that?" he muttered, clutching his chest. But he knew the answer. Knew it was the proximity to the events of the previous night. The matter-of-fact violence he'd seen on the TV, perpetrated by men who placed no worth on human life. Men who were likely at that very moment searching for the same thing he was after. Money. All that killing for a little coin, he thought. For rectangles of paper printed with numbers that meant nothing in the abstract, but in the real world dictated the course of one's existence.

Another factor to consider, of course, was the dead man in the bed of the truck. That on its own was enough to shake a person—at least, a person with all their faculties in order. Ephraim wasn't sure that was him anymore. He shoved these crowded thoughts out of his mind. He'd made his choices. Now was no time for self-analysis.

He came to Greasy Ridge Road and turned onto it. Forest rose up on either side of the blacktop. A couple hundred yards in he came to the train crossing and slowed going over the tracks. Not fifty yards beyond them was his destination, the single-lane gravel road he'd spotted on Google Maps. Ephraim didn't turn in. He wanted to drive past the house and facilities first to see if there was any action on the property. Big as the place was, it seemed like a family-run operation, so he hoped there wouldn't be a large presence to account for, especially with the harvest complete.

Greasy Ridge Road wound through the trees and sloped up and down with the uneven land. A half mile on, the woods to his right gave way to a great sweep of pristine lawn. Ephraim slowed the truck. The house was one of those multi-tiered jobs with a wraparound porch and a sizable wing extending out from its left side, culminating in a two-story portico supported by giant columns. It sat at the end of a long drive that was lined with dogwoods and weeping willows that lent an antebellum flavor to the whole tableau.

Near the house, the driveway forked around the left wing of the building and led, after some distance, to a parking area and a large pole barn. The barn looked to be nearly as long as the house. Across from the barn was a stable and beyond that were a couple of grain bins. The only indication of anyone being on the property was a lone SUV parked in the circular roundabout out front. No cars in the parking area by the barn, no machinery whirring in the distance. No dogs barking, or horses braying. More important, there was no sign of any police presence. If the dead man's car was there and it had been discovered, surely there would have been.

The next turnoff, Ephraim flipped a U and took another pass by the house. Nothing had changed. The place was quiet as a midnight mouse. Ephraim checked his rearview to make sure there were no cars coming up from behind, no one to see him make the turn into the woods. There weren't, so he steered onto the gravel lane.

The road took a steep dip into a basin and flattened out. The woods were dense all around and the lane was nearly grown over. Scrub pushing in from the berm brushed the sides of the truck. Deep ruts pocked the gravel and made the driving slow going. By the condition of the lane, Ephraim figured it was seldom, if ever, used. Steering deeper into the holler, an acute feeling of claustrophobia washed over him, an unsettling notion that the wilderness might, at any time, choose to swallow him whole. Disappear him forever.

A moment later, he rounded a curve, the woods opened up, and Ephraim came to the edge of the clearing. He cut the engine and gazed out over the land. The satellite imaging he'd seen didn't do the scope of the thing justice. The mountains looming on the far side were near a half mile away, maybe more. Between here and there were rolling hills that stretched a good two hundred acres to his left. Far off that way he could see the roof of one of the grain bins peeking just above the treetops. To his right the pasture extended as far as the eye could see, eventually hooking with the shape of the mountain and dropping out of sight. Maybe twenty yards in front of him a wire fence spanned the length of the farm. A gravel path laid out in front of it.

Ephraim stayed like that for a spell, perfectly still, hyper-aware of the crickets chirping, the katydids whirring, the leaves of the trees swaying with the intermittent breeze. The imperceptible spin of the earth on its axis. He half expected a swarm of police to jump out from the thicket, find the corpse in the bed of the Ranger, and toss him in prison for the remainder of his days. But that didn't happen. Nothing at all happened.

Ephraim looked at the time on his dash—9:17—and got his phone out to try the doctor again, but there was no service this deep into the valley. He made a mental note to try calling again as soon as he got back on the main road, then grabbed the binoculars and got out of the truck. He crossed over the gravel path, stood at the fence, and pointed the scopes east toward the estate. The binoculars were old; his dad had used them years back when he still hunted, and the glass was dusty and difficult to see through. Ephraim unscrewed the lenses and the eyepieces and blew hard into each of them to stir the dust loose. Then he spit on his shirtsleeve and rubbed each side of the lenses until they were well enough clean, twisted them back in, and looked again.

The land slanted off the mountain and ran on a soft grade down to an irrigation ditch that bisected the pasture. On the near side of the chasm, the terrain evened out. A couple of plank bridges situated at either end of the range linked the two sections of land. Toward the facilities a bunch of cows were clumped together, grazing. Further up the valley a triumvirate of vultures circled high over the trees, looking for dead things. He watched the country that way for a good while and saw nothing else of interest. No sign of Rodney's wrecked vehicle.

He turned around and glassed the mountains. The hillsides were packed with trees—tall pines, hemlocks, oaks—all thick with autumnal leaves. At the far end of the field where the mountain turned was the valley fill where, indeed, a landslide had occurred. Rock and debris littered the face of the slope from the summit on down.

Ephraim grabbed hold of a fence post, scaled the wire, and hopped down on the other side. He walked a good fifty yards into the soft plain, knelt on the turf at the top of a rise. From that vantage he could see farther each way, but the sediment pond at the bottom of the valley fill was still obscured by the hills. And still no hint of Rodney's car. Ephraim stood in the middle of the bucolic scene and wondered what to do. He trekked back through the field, hopped the fence, leaned against the grille of his truck, and chewed things over in his mind. He gazed one way down the lane, toward the grain bin, and then the other, over the western plain—all the while trying to put himself into the mind of a man with a bullet in his gut who was being chased by a bunch of killers.

From the Sundown Motel you'd have to bypass the interstate in favor of Route 52, hoping to lose them. Middle of the night, unfamiliar roads, you make a hard turn onto a dark, almost-nothing road, and then . . .

"What do you do?" Ephraim muttered.

Again, he looked in both directions, then shoved off the truck and walked down the lane to try to see how far it went. Gravel crunched lightly underfoot. After a good distance, there was a bend around the edge of the wood. What Ephraim saw there stopped him moving and set his heart racing. *Calm your ass,* he thought.

He raised the binoculars. Up ahead the path dead-ended at a metal gate that was attached to the wire fence. More accurately, it was a field gate that *used* to be attached to the wire fence. Something had busted through it. There were a couple of cows chewing on grass down there, lazy-eyeing the gash in the fence as though it may be some sort of ruse, an optical illusion of freedom, and they stood there deliberating the first step into the great unknown.

Ephraim went back and got his truck and rolled it nice and slow down the lane to keep the tires from grinding too loudly on the gravel. At the ingress he got out and had a look. Whatever came through had bowled it right over, taken the gate off its hinges.

Tamped into the soil where the gravel changed to pasture was a set of tire tracks so neat it was as if they were laid out purposefully to be followed. Ephraim knelt down and examined the impressions the tires had made, the pattern of the tread, then walked back to the Ranger and looked at his own tires. Similar enough, he reckoned.

Ephraim got into the truck and slowly eased her off the lip and into the field. He kept his wheels within the grooves of the tracks. They led him first along the perimeter of the farm to where the land crooked right with the shape of the mountain and then sloped steeply down. For no discernable reason, the tracks veered sharply to the left, out into the plain. Ephraim did his best to follow the erratic path the car had cut. He ascended a large knoll and came up onto the plain. To the right, the bottom of the valley fill became visible and he saw where the rubble from the flood had spilled down from the mountain, leveled the pond, and ruined a large section of pasture beyond that.

The tracks then swerved to the right over a small embankment. Coming over top of it, the section of the valley floor that had been previously obscured came into view. The irrigation trench that fissured the lowland and ran the length of the farm stretched out in front of him.

And there, sticking out from the middle of the trench, was the ass-end of a Lincoln Continental.

CHAPTER SIXTEEN
A GOD IN DISGUISE

After Rosalind hung up on the police, she immediately began to hyperventilate. She ran out of the bedroom so she wouldn't scare Jalen and hurled the disposable phone against the wall, shattering it to pieces. Her mouth opened to scream, but the sound came out funny, strangled and high pitched, like an early-warning alarm somewhere off in the distance. She sank to her knees, pressed her face against the plywood floor, and slapped the ground until her palms stung with pain. Her cries took root then, deep inside her, and emerged in a thick, guttural wail. Rosalind covered her head with her arms and convulsed with sobs.

At some point during all this Jalen had climbed out of his crib, toddled over next to her and plopped himself down. He reached for his mother now and patted her between the shoulders in the same gentle manner that she used when trying to get him to burp.

Rosalind lifted her head and did her best to twist her mottled face into some semblance of happiness.

"How did you get here?" she asked.

Jalen's cherubic face lit up and he slapped his uncoordinated baby hands together as if climbing out of his crib had been some great feat of acrobatics. In a sense, it was.

For the eleven-month-old it was a marked leap in cognition. This was the first time he'd successfully scaled the bars. He'd only begun to walk a couple of weeks before.

Jalen didn't have on any clothes, just a fat diaper ballooned with piss. That, coupled with his round belly and his jelly-rolled arms and legs, made him look like a pocket-size sumo wrestler. Rosalind stood gingerly and walked toward Jalen's room.

"C'mon," she beckoned. The boy rolled onto his stomach, worked his feet under him, and padded after his mother. Rosalind got a diaper from the box that lay on the floor and noted there were only three remaining.

"We're going to go on a trip," she cooed as she tore off the dirty diaper and strapped the fresh one over his chubby legs. "We're going to go far, far away. Yes we are. Far, far away from here." She pulled his shirt over his head and smooshed her nose into his. "And we are never, ever gonna come back."

Rosalind thought about where they would go—or rather, where they *could* go. Nowhere in Cain City, that was for certain. There wasn't a place in town where they wouldn't suss her out. She admonished herself for not thinking this far ahead. For not planning on this eventuality. *But you wouldn't let it come into your mind, would you?* she told herself. *Wouldn't put that possibility into the universe for fear it'd come true. Stupid girl. It came true anyway, and now look at you.*

Rosalind had two hundred dollars to her name. That'd be enough to get her a bus ticket to Knoxville. An older cousin lived there, Amanda. Amanda was six years her senior, the daughter of her Aunt Janie, one of her mother's sisters, and the closest thing Rosalind ever had to a sibling. Every time her parents wanted to go out and party, which was frequently, Amanda had babysat her, and Rosalind had fond memories of those days. Amanda had treated Rosalind like her very own doll baby, dressing her up, making over her face, warning her off boys. Six straight years they'd counted the clock down on New Year's Eve together, just the two of them, dancing along to whatever cheesy pop songs were being performed, toasting the ball drop with apple juice.

Amanda, who, the minute she turned eighteen, fled Cain City like somebody had lit the streets on fire, never to return. They hadn't spoken in years, but they kept in touch via Facebook and Insta. Wrote comments on each other's posts. When Jalen had been born, Rosalind had been embarrassed of his facial deformity, didn't post a picture of him for months. When she finally braved it, Amanda was the first to comment: *I have never been more in love. He's perfect. I wish I could snuggle that beautiful baby right this instant! Congrats!*

The words had made Rosalind cry tears of joy then, and she still welled with emotion whenever she thought of them. They'd also given Rosalind permission to think of Jalen in those terms, beautiful, perfect, and to love him fully.

Well, Rosalind thought, *she'll get the chance to cuddle you now. 'Cause that's where we're going. Knoxville.* Amanda lived with some doofy-looking guy who worked in an IT department or some such thing. *But she will take us in, for a little bit at least, and that's all we need.*

Rosalind got Jalen dressed, then dumped the plastic drawers full of his clothes into a laundry sack. She stuffed the two remaining diapers and some toys in there as well, and the blanket Jalen slept with, the stuffed giraffe. She packed her own things and their toiletries into plastic grocery bags and took a last look around to make sure there was nothing else she should take.

"Are you ready?" she said to Jalen. He tugged at her pant leg and made a sucking *mwah mwah* sound that indicated hunger. "Okay," Rosalind said. "Okay." She set the bags by the door, scooped Jalen up, and sat down on the futon. She flipped him sideways in her lap, lifted her shirt and brushed her nipple against his lips until he latched on. His new baby teeth felt like sharp little razors when he clamped down, but soon he found his rhythm, and the pressure eased. Rosalind watched him suckle for a while, his big, trusting eyes locked on hers, his tiny jaw working, and she listened to the comforting repetition of his gulps. She had been up most of the night worrying over Pippen, and now, sitting still, exhaustion crept into her. She battled to keep her eyelids open, but before too long gravity won out. She rested her head against the back of the futon and in no time at all she drifted away.

She couldn't have been dozing for long—Jalen was still gorging on the same boob—when she sensed a change in the room, a drop in air pressure, and opened her eyes. Three men hovered in a semicircle above her. Of course she recognized them straight away. They'd been colleagues of her dead father. So she knew what kind of men they were and what they were here for, and she knew there was no getting around it. She couldn't escape if she tried; they had her hemmed in. Fear prevented her from moving anyhow, save for her chin. It began to quiver.

Momo Morrison grimaced down at the baby. "Ugly-looking thing, idn't it? What's wrong with his lip?" Rosalind struggled to find her voice. Momo snapped his fingers in front of her face. "You deaf? I said—"

"It's cleft."

"Can you fix it?"

"Costs money."

Momo clucked his tongue. "I imagine it would. Guess it don't matter no how."

Rosalind cradled Jalen tightly to her. "Don't you touch my son. He's done nothing to nobody."

Momo hiked a thumb toward the door. "Saw where you got some bags packed. You two going somewhere?"

Rosalind swallowed. "Just the laundromat. I got some laundry to do."

"Uh-huh. Kind of seems like we might have caught you just before you lit out for the territories."

"No."

"Uh-huh." Momo squatted down to look closely at the boy. Jalen took notice of the motion next to his head and blithely shifted his eyes to see what had moved. Momo jutted his tongue out through the split in his teeth and shook his head in mock bafflement. "What do you think your daddy'd have to say about you giving birth to such an abomination?"

"My daddy never put two good words together for me. I figure this wouldn't be no different."

"Fair enough. He did always say you came out the pussy a spiteful little thing. Tell me this then, what do you reckon he'd say about you sending your three black boyfriends to rob his friends and kill them dead?"

"Oh, God," Rosalind croaked. "Oh, God, please."

"God don't have nothing to do with it. What's happening here is taking place on a purely human plane." Momo tilted forward to where the tip of his nose nearly touched hers. His mouth split into a hideous grin. She smelled his rot breath. It took the baby scent right out of her nose, and that, as much as anything, was why she started crying. "But if you're prone to that line of belief," Momo said, twirling his hand around, "thinking there's some God up there with grand designs, making decisions at his own whimsy, then he must have decided to send me here, now, to this very moment. So maybe I'm the reaper come to hand-deliver you one way or the other, to the maker or to the devil. Or maybe"—Momo rose and did a slow three-sixty turn to display himself—"I'm a god in disguise, your personal deity."

"You're a fucking psycho is what you are."

Momo laughed. "Don't bode well for you either way."

"No," she pleaded. "Please, Momo. I just told them I'd seen a bunch of money in that house once a long time ago. I swear it. I didn't know what they was gonna do."

"Uh-huh. Tell me something. You let all three of them black boys fuck you rotten, or was it just the one?"

"What? No. Just Pip. Eric."

"So what's this here little feller's name, Eric Junior?"

"Jalen."

Momo reached a hand toward the baby. Rosalind wrenched Jalen away from his grasp. "Don't you touch him!"

"Look here," Momo said calmly, "you can give us the baby nice and peaceful like, or we can just take it from you. Either way, Rosie, you're gonna answer for what you've done."

"No." Rosalind shook her head furiously back and forth.

"Yes." Momo mocked her, bobbing his head up and down in the same manic fashion.

Rosalind looked down at Jalen. He'd come off the nipple and his head was lolling around, lips puckered, eagerly searching for his food source. She helped him latch back on, then forced herself to stop crying. "Promise me you won't hurt him."

"Don't you fret none. Verbals won't hurt him, will ya Verbals? Verbals got a soft spot for little ones, even those with a little extra pigment."

"I won't hurt him, Rosie," Verbals assured her. "I swear it."

Momo surveyed the apartment. Half the walls were stripped to studs; the flooring had been ripped up. Water stains blotted the ceiling. "You just wanted to get a little money, didn't you?" he said. "Wanted to get out of this shithole. And there was one place you knew of, thought it'd be simple as pie. You'd say the words and wish for it, and that money'd be hand-delivered right to your door. All you had to do was flap your gums."

"I didn't think anybody'd get hurt," Rosalind whispered.

"Come now?"

She cleared her throat. "I just thought it'd be that old woman in there. I thought she'd just hand the loot over and that'd be that."

"Course you did." Momo tsked. "That'd be that. I know how it is. How could you have imagined you'd set off a chain of events that'd lead to so much blood, to so many people getting their heads blown off? You could have never seen that coming."

"Right. That's what I'm sayin'."

Momo squatted down again. "But you should have, Rosie. You knew your daddy, and you know me. And you know that somebody crosses us, we cain't spare them no quarter. So hand that baby on over before you make this worse than it has to be, and let's get on with it, huh."

"Can I finish feeding him?" Rosalind pleaded. "Please? I don't know when he'll eat again and he stopped taking a bottle."

"No."

Rosalind looked down at her son. His golden-brown eyes and thick lashes. The dimple in his chin and soft curls around his ears. One of his eyelids was crusty around the edges. She gently pulled him off of her, dabbed the milk from his lips with her shirt, kissed his soft cheek, and inhaled his scent for what she knew would be the last time.

Verbals reached down and she let him take the child from her arms. He carried Jalen into the bedroom, and Rosalind watched them go. Then she steeled herself and turned to face Momo.

"Do your fucking worst," she spat.

Momo scoffed. "Sweetie, I don't need an invitation. Now put that sloppy boob away. You're making me thirsty."

Rosalind had forgotten her breast was even exposed. She adjusted her T-shirt, and when next she looked up, Buddy The Face coldcocked her. A handful of teeth came spilling out of her mouth and blood poured down her front like somebody had turned on the spigot. Momo grabbed a fistful of her hair and yanked her head up, slapped her face until her eyes stopped dancing in their sockets.

"You . . . you killed Pip," Rosalind sputted wetly.

"Yes, I did," Momo said, his face creasing with solemnity. He jabbed two fingers into her forehead. "I shot him right between the eyes. Weirdest-looking brains I ever did see. You should probably know, when we found him and his buddies up there at the motel, they was with a bunch of whores. White girls like you."

Rosalind thrashed and kicked, but Momo still had a hold of her hair and she couldn't get the leverage to make any of the blows count for anything. He punched her in the stomach to settle her down.

"Fuck you, Momo," Rosalind moaned. "Fuck all y'all. Fucking ingrates. I pray to God you get the ends you deserve. I pray that all the pain and death you've doled out comes back doubly on your heads."

"There you go calling down the Lord again." With his free hand, Momo wrapped his fingers around her throat and squeezed. Rosalind's eyes bugged from their sockets, the blood vessels popping, turning the whites of her sclerae red. "You know who I did not kill, Rosie? I did not kill Rodney Slash. Which is bad for you 'cause he's got my money. And I want my money. So 'bout now'd be the time you tell me where he is. *Comprende*? You see how this works?"

Momo loosened his grip so that Rosalind could speak. "I swear," she panted. "Oh God, I swear, I don't . . . I don't know where he is. I didn't even know he was alive."

"That's unfortunate." Momo held out the palm of his free hand and Buddy brought forth a switchblade, set it there. Momo flicked the blade out in front of her eyes. "All this biblical talk has proved inspirational. What do you say we go for a pound of flesh? How'd that be?" Momo drew the knife along her trembling jaw and down her neck to her breasts where he traced out a figure-eight. "Think I could get a pound out of these titties? They look awfully weighty, all plumped with milk as they are. What do you think?" He stuck the point of the blade into the middle of one of them and leaned forward just enough to pierce her skin. "One more try. Where's. Rodney. Slash?"

With no answer to give, Rosalind took the opportunity to summon up one last bit of vitriol. "A pound of flesh comes from Shakespeare, not the Bible, you fuckin' inbred."

"Sweetie," Momo soothed, "that don't make one bit of difference."

"You think if I knew where goddamn Rodney Slash was, I'd be sitting in this dump waiting for you to come fucking kill me?"

"Fair enough," Momo conceded. He plunged the knife in smoothly past the breastbone, through the ribs, and into Rosalind's heart. She jerked in surprise and looked down at the black handle of the blade protruding obscenely from her chest. She tried to reach for it, but the circuits from her brain to her nervous system no longer tallied. Momo knelt there and watched her sip for air that would never make it to her lungs. "There you go," he said, stroking her swollen cheek, talking her into death. "There you go. Die now." She gazed at him helplessly. "That's right. Look at me. Look right at me. The last face you're ever gonna see, you traitorous little cunt. It didn't have to be like this, Rosie. You used to be so delicate. What happened to you? What was you trying to prove?"

Rosalind convulsed once, twice, and the last vestiges of her short life came gurgling out of her. Momo waited to see if something else would happen, something supernatural, like maybe she'd spring back to life and he'd have to kill her again, or he'd see her soul float like a fairy apparition out from her body. When nothing of the sort came about Momo clucked with disappointment, as if the experience wasn't as satisfying as he'd expected.

He extracted the knife from her chest, wiped it clean on her jeans, stood up, and leisurely stretched his arms. "Verbals," he hollered. "Get out here."

Verbals was on the floor of the bedroom with the child, playing little piggies with his pudgy toes. At Momo's beckon, he lifted Jalen into the crib and rustled the toddler's curly hair. "Don't go anywhere," he said, and he went out and joined Momo and Buddy The Face in staring at Rosalind's lifeless body.

Verbals had known Rosalind since they were kids; she was only a year and a half younger than he was, a grade back in school. Buddy had decimated her face with one brutal punch, rendered it unrecognizable, and Verbals couldn't look away from where she used to be.

"What," Momo crowed, "are we to do with this mess?"

"We got that butane in the van," suggested Buddy The Face. "We could light this puppy up, make it look like an accident."

"There's an answer."

"What about the kid?" Verbals asked quietly.

"There's a question." Momo mashed his face around pretending to think it over. "Way I see it, we got to go along with the charade and all, so the kid's gonna have to burn with the house. Don't you think, Buddy?"

Buddy grunted. "Gotta make it look right."

Momo flipped his palms up. "Heard the man. Gotta make it look right. But if you want to put him down in some more humane way first, I'm amenable to that."

Verbals tensed, visibly, and some kind of look must've whisked across his face because Momo cast a dubious eye on him. He scratched under his chin the way a cat would.

"You got a problem with roasting some marshmallows, Verbals? Some moral quandary?"

"Yeah," Verbals said warily, "I reckon I do."

It wasn't often Momo was challenged, especially from within his own ranks, and the proposition exalted him. "Well now," Momo said. "I had no idea you were such a champion of the downtrodden. So do tell, Verbals. I'm curious to hear just what it is that you object to."

To this point Verbals's gaze had been locked on Rosalind. Now he turned and saw that Momo had a hand in his pocket, likely clutching some kind of weapon. Behind him, Buddy The Face stood with a .38 dangling loose by his side. To pacify the situation, Verbals raised his palms out slowly to his sides. "Look, alls I'm saying Momo, is you torch this place, it might stall the police for a little bit, sure, but soon enough they gonna figure out there's no smoke in Rosalind's lungs. They gonna know she was murdered. And they gonna see there's plenty of smoke in the kid's lungs. That's two murders, one of 'em just a baby. Why risk the heat? Ain't no reason for it. I say we throw Rosalind in the van, dump her somewhere she ain't never gonna be found, and nobody'll ever know where she went off to. Maybe something happened to her, sure, or maybe she just up and left. One way or another, it'll confuse 'em, you know. They'll chase their tails for a while till they get something better to do and that's that. They'll forget all about her."

Momo tilted his head and looked at Verbals scrupulously, then wagged a finger at him and glanced back at Buddy. "Look at the big fucking brain on Verbals, huh. Man, what a day. First a lesson from the dying on Shakespeare, and now this. A tutorial on smoke in the lungs. Tell me something, smarty-pants. What are we supposed to do with the freak baby in there, huh? Leave him?"

"Why not?" Verbals said. "Maybe somebody will find him. Maybe they won't. What difference does it make?"

Momo gawked like he couldn't believe what he was hearing, then grabbed his belly and made a demonstration of laughter. "Now that's some sick shit, Verbals. You want to leave it to the fates and see if this baby here straight starves to death in his own crib?"

Verbals shrugged.

"Oh, man. That's fucked up. I like it, though. I do. You like it, Buddy?"

"I don't give a shit."

Momo stepped over to Verbals, leaned in close, and spoke in the dulcet tones people adopt when speaking with babies or halfwits. "Either you think you real slick, or you think I'm a big dodo bird. Which one is it? You think I'm a big dodo bird?"

Verbals feigned ignorance, claiming, "I don't know what you're talk—"

Momo didn't let him finish. In one deft move he had the knife out and the blade extended into the soft flesh below Verbals's Adam's apple.

"Boy, don't play dumb. It won't do you no favors. You think I care if they squeeze Rosie's lungs and smoke don't come puffin' out? Huh?" Verbals didn't reply. Momo twisted the tip of the knife just so and a thin drop of blood trickled down the blade. "The answer is no, I don't care one lil bit. Ain't nobody gonna cry for Rosie, or this baby, 'cept maybe you. You gonna cry for them, Verbals?"

Verbals twisted his head to each side, gentle-like so the knife wouldn't dig deeper.

"This the life you chose, Verbals. I ain't choose it for you. You did. Now, sooner or later you're gonna have to cut your teeth on something nasty. Right now, you're gonna clean this mess up, and you're gonna get rid of that body yourself. Got it."

"Okay," Verbals said, fighting the sudden urge to swallow. "I can do that."

Momo retracted the knife and brushed past him toward the exit. "Hurry it up then," he called back. "I'm getting hungry."

CHAPTER SEVENTEEN
CRIES FROM ALL THE WAY GONE

Ephraim stood at the rim of the irrigation channel, staring down at the wreckage. The ditch was round about five feet deep, eight across. The Lincoln hadn't gone in with much momentum, just tipped over the side of the gulch nose-first and stuck there in the soft dirt at the bottom. Dozens of holes pocked the metal exterior of the car, each of them ringed with silver where the bullets had stripped the black paint upon entry. The left front tire was popped flat. Scattered on the ground beside the opened driver's door was a bunch of money. Ephraim couldn't tell the exact denominations from up top. Once again he raised the binoculars and did a sweep of the country. Seeing no movement, no nothing, he hopped down into the gulch.

All told, the bills added up to four hundred and sixty-five dollars: three hundreds, one fifty, four twenties, and seven fives. He dusted the dirt off them and stuck the wad in his pocket. The car's open door was covered in blood and so were the deflated airbag, the driver's seat, and the steering wheel. There were more bills strewn about the interior, some of them bloody. Ephraim sidestepped around the front of the car to the other side, careful to avoid the hood, which had buckled forward. Shattered glass spread over the ground beneath the windshield.

He fished the work gloves from his back pocket and put them on, then tugged the handle on the passenger door and let it fall open. He reached in and grabbed the interior roof handle, yanked a couple of times to make sure the car would not easily topple, then hoisted himself up into the vehicle. Ephraim got his footing on the crux of the floorboard and scoured all around the interior. The only thing in the glove box was the Lincoln's manual and some loose receipts from where the car had been serviced. Some CDs, a half-empty box of condoms, and a bottle of hand sanitizer were the only contents in the middle console. There was some more loose money in the cab, some of it quite wet with blood. Ephraim collected all the bills and packed them away. He reached across through a gap in the steering wheel and pressed the button to pop the trunk, got down out of the car, and clambered out of the gulch. He looked in the trunk, but it was empty, save for a spare tire and a lug wrench.

Again, he scoped the area with the binoculars and, satisfied he was alone, walked to the back of his truck and opened the rear gate. He reached in, grabbed hold of the tarp, and slid it out. The body thudded onto the ground. Ephraim dragged it over to the ditch and there took hold of the edge of the tarp and unfurled it until Rodney's corpse came flopping out. Ephraim stuffed the tarp back into the bed of the truck and shut the gate, then walked over and looked at Rodney. The dead man's complexion had taken on a gray, wax-like hue. He'd also started to stink.

A sickly feeling bubbled up in Ephraim's guts and he

thought for a moment that he might vomit. It crossed his mind to just get back in the truck and go, just take off and do his best to forget any of this had ever happened. Never speak a word about it to anyone. He could do that. Go back to work. Go back to taking care of Caleb, his father. Store the images of a bleeding man and his whispers of money in the recesses of his mind until one day the whole incident got swept away on the tides of memory. Until it felt like some story he'd heard secondhand, like it had happened to someone he'd known a long time ago.

But what if there was no job soon? The brass had promised the layoffs were coming. And what if Caleb had something really wrong with him? No job meant no insurance. What if his father's health took a turn for the worse? That had to happen sometime, probably sooner than later. And somewhere on those bluffs was a bag full of money, unaccounted for, waiting to be found. Why shouldn't he be the one to find it? All the bad he could do in the situation, he'd already done, and what was it really? Not call the police. Rodney himself had warned him off doing that very thing. His words—*No cops . . . They'll hunt us both down.* And from what Ephraim had witnessed on the news, he had a pretty good idea who *they* were.

Why not wait? he thought. Wait for the car and the body to be found, the ensuing hubbub to die down. *'Cause then you won't be the only one searching, that's why. You will have lost your chance.*

He batted this logic around his brain until the side with three hundred and ninety thousand dollars on it won out, and he gave the body a foot-shove over the ledge of the ditch. Rodney tumbled over, his head thwacking into the driver's side door before landing on the bottom with a muffled crunch of bone, one arm contorted beneath his back, legs twisted sideways. Ephraim went back to the truck and retrieved the Ruger and the .22 he'd taken off Rodney the night before, wiped them down to smear any fingerprints, and tossed them down beside the corpse.

"All right," Ephraim muttered. "How the hell did you get from here to the train tracks?" He again looked across the field to the base of the mountain and the bluffs above, then to the woods behind him. "In some rocks by a cave or in a cave by some rocks. In some woods." He glanced down at the body. "Didn't care to make it simple for me, did ya, buddy? No. You did not."

Ephraim again tried to put himself into Rodney's thinking. You're gut-shot, bleeding out, crashed your car into this here ditch. Not going anywhere fast or easy. It's pitch-black outside; you got a bag of money you're gonna stash somewhere safe, somewhere you'll be able to find it, so you can go and get some help. So you had to have gone toward the woods, right? But then, any caves are likely on the mountain, which is in the opposite direction. So how in the world did you get outta here?

Ephraim studied the ground to see if he could make out where Rodney had climbed out of the gulley, but there was no place where the new grass had been disturbed, save for where Ephraim himself had stepped and where the tarp had been dragged over from the truck.

Ephraim stood there trying to make a decision on what to do next, then said to himself, "How many damn caves can there be?" He got back into the Ranger and drove down along the edge of the canal, tire tracks be damned; he wasn't taking the time to retrace all that nonsense. He followed it all the way to where the pond had been filled in with rubble from the flood. There was a thick copse of oak trees at the base of the mountain.

Ephraim found a space between two of them and pulled the truck far enough in to where it was pretty well concealed. The trees prevented him from opening the doors fully, so Ephraim slotted open the rear window of the cab, slunk out that way, and set off to hunt for hidden treasure.

They divided their duties. Sturges ventured to a prominent Southside neighborhood to round up Norman Hinkle, the small-time drug dealer who still lived at home with his well-to-do parents, in order to question him about the mass overdoses. Hively went the other way, into downtown, where he rang the front buzzer of the nightclub called The Cut. No one answered. He waited for a while, buzzed a few more times, and was about to give it up when a young woman Hively didn't recognize pushed open the door. Her hair was picked out into a curly afro that glistened in the daylight and her face was done up thick with makeup. Her cheeks looked like they'd been dusted with glitter, and her eyelashes looked about as long as her fingers. She was decked out in a black halter that didn't leave much to the imagination and turquoise tights that matched the makeup. The girl raised an arm to shield her eyes against the early-morning sun.

"Yo, we closed," she said lazily. Hively flashed his badge. "Oh." She rolled her eyes. "No wonder you was so persistent. Whatchoo need?"

"You work here?"

"Yeah, I'm the bartender and night manager."

"How old are you?"

"Twenty-two."

Hively asked her to prove it. The girl huffed and smacked her lips, but she brought out her license from a hidden pocket on the tights. He looked it over, saw that she was, in fact, twenty-two, and read her name aloud.

"Maria Woofolk. You're not related to Brianne Woofolk by chance, are you?"

"You know my sister?"

"We came up together in the Terrace."

"No shit, you from the Terrace? And now you a cop?"

"You must be one of her little sisters. I remember a bunch of y'all running around, causing a ruckus."

"Yeah, there's seven of us."

"How's Brianne doing? She all right?"

"You know, she was fittin' to get up out of here soon as she could. Met some dude from North Carolina, moved down there with him. Hardly comes back here."

"Tell her Willis Hively says hello, will ya?"

"Uh-huh, sure."

"Nico around?"

The girl hesitated. "Nico who?"

"The owner. Well," Hively amended, "the real owner. Not Andrew Dobson, whoever that is. Nico Blakes. He here?"

The girl didn't bother pretending further. "Naw, he was here last night." She yawned and covered her mouth. "'Scuse me. Everybody gone now. I'm 'bout to bounce myself soon as I finish closing. If that's okay with you."

"Yeah, just give Nico a message for me. Tell him I'm not gonna stop looking for him until he talks to me about the Sundown Motel. Can you do that, please?"

"The Sundown Motel?"

"That's right. Tell him Rodney doesn't have to die too."

This caught Maria's attention. "Rodney? You mean Rodney Slash?"

"Yeah. Two of his boys got killed last night at that motel. Eric Pippen and Kevon Thompson."

"Damn, they got got, huh? Who did it? Y'all?"

"Wasn't us. You know them?"

"The Spring Street Boys? Yeah, everybody know them. Plus, they were in school with my little sisters."

"You know where they stay?"

"Naw, we ain't, like, tight or nothing. They come 'round the club every once in a blue moon, but that's about it."

"Any of them have kids?"

"I dunno. Probably."

"All right, look, I'm trying to find Rodney Slash before he gets killed too." Hively handed her his business card. Maria took it and flipped it over, examining all sides, concentrated on the words like they were written in hieroglyphics. "You see him, give me a call. The men who attacked his friends are very dangerous. We just want to get him safe."

"Willis Hively," Maria said, referring to the card. She eyed him sharply. "You know what? I *have* heard of you."

"Oh yeah, what'd you hear?"

"Just that you turned out good, you know. Different from the rest."

"Don't believe the hype. Pass the word to Nico, all right? And don't forget to say hey to your sister for me."

"Yeah, okay, *Mister* Hively."

Maria slunk back into the club, and Hively got into his Chevy Malibu. His next stop was the Malcolm Terrace housing projects. The Terrace was over on the East End of town, a bunch of two-story housing blocks with shared courtyards in the middle of them. Neither Eric Pippen, Kevon Thompson, nor Rodney Slash had a listed address, but Slash's mother's last known was in Block D, number 411. Hively had grown up, along with Nico Blakes, in the housing block adjacent to that one, Block J. As he cut across the courtyard he felt the eyes of the place on him, though no one was outside. He ducked a clothesline and rang the bell for apartment 411. It went unanswered. No sounds or movement came from within.

Hively leaned over the air-conditioning unit in the window and through a crack in the blinds peered into the living room. It was dim, no lights on, carpeted. An old couch upholstered in a floral pattern with a caved-in middle sat against the wall. Side tables bracketed the couch; both had matching lamps with frilly shades. Across from that was an entertainment center, two TVs atop it, one an old analog and the other a small flat-screen. Hanging on the wall was a sunny portrait of a family of four—mother, father, and two little boys in their Sunday best. Hively recognized the father in the picture as Sam Slash, an old-time hood who struck fear into just about every path he crossed until one day somebody inserted a bullet straight through his eardrum.

Hively opened the screen and knocked on the door again. Nothing stirred.

"You're wasting your time," a low voice murmured.

Hively let go of the screen and stepped back to look at the door of the neighboring unit. A small figure stood in the shadows behind the mesh window of the screen.

"Don't be gawking over here," the woman snapped. "Just do what you was doing."

Hively faced unit 411, but cut his eyes sideways. "Why am I wasting my time?"

"'Cause there ain't nobody home."

"How do you know?"

"Nobody's come through there in two, three days."

"LaDonna Slash, you mean?"

"LaDonna? Child, LaDonna Slash ain't been seen in two, three *years*. I'd be shocked I ever see her again."

"Her son, Rodney. That who lives here?"

The woman balked at the question. "He in trouble?"

"I'd say so, but not from me. Some men tried to kill him last night, and I'm trying to find him before they finish the job."

A sorrowful noise came through the screen. "Is that what I seen on the news?"

"Yes, ma'am. It was on the news."

"Damn it all. I seen that family get whittled down to nothing over the years. First Sam, then LaDonna resorted to what she resorted to. Then Jeffrey got sent up to Moundsville. Rodney was a sweet little boy, he really was. Quiet. Helps me with my groceries to this day. Damn. He never had a chance."

Hively gave the woman his spiel about wanting to help Rodney, keep him safe, find out what really happened. He asked if she wouldn't mind taking down his number and calling if she saw Slash. The woman said she would and went and got a pen and paper and returned. Hively recited the seven digits, then started to say his name.

The woman interrupted him. "I know who you are. Wouldn't have nothing to say to you if I didn't."

Next, Hively drove over to Spring Street. The road bordered the south end of The Terrace and had long been a main artery for drug trafficking. Most of the houses that lined the street were dilapidated beyond repair or boarded up. The few residents that had stuck it out were old-timers who didn't pose any threat to the crews that posted up on the corners or on the stoops of the abandoned homes. All the trees on the street had been chopped down by the city, ostensibly to make the neighborhood safer by clearing the sightlines and thus curbing the sale of narcotics. It opened up the horizon all right, and gave the dealers the ability to see cops coming from half a mile in any direction. The police hardly bothered patrolling the place anymore.

The street had a slight grade to it and a little ways up it rose to a peak that you couldn't see over. Hively pulled over at the corner where Pippen, Slash, and Thompson were known to operate. Two young men, no more than eighteen, sat on the stoop of the building, staring at him, nonplussed. Hively got out of the car.

"Well hello, Officer," the one with a high flattop said, altering his voice to sound kind of nerdy. His partner didn't move. He just sat there blinking.

"Y'all are new," Hively said. "Nico give you a promotion?"

High Top smirked. "Who?"

"Yeah." Hively nodded. "Y'all know what happened to the boys who worked this spot before you?"

"I know they sought—how do you say it? Other opportunities that didn't work out so well."

His partner found that humorous, snorted a little. Hively said, "Let me see some ID."

"Man, c'mon, what you trying to prove?"

"Me? Nothing." Hively gestured for them to hand it over. They griped plenty, but did as they were asked. Hively looked over both licenses and gave them back. "Paul and JoTae. What do your friends call you?"

"Wouldn't you like to know," JoTae said.

"Yeah, that's why I asked. What about you, Paul? You speak?"

"When it's called for."

Hively got his cards out and handed one to each of them. "Listen, the day will come you and I are gonna need each other."

"Yuh, okay," JoTae said. "When pigs fly up out my ass."

"Just you wait."

Something down the street grabbed the new corner boys' attention. Hively turned to see what it was. Two squad cars came flying past, lights flashing but no sirens. Hively watched the squaddies pass and disappear up over the crest of the hill.

"Y'all know what that's about?" Hively asked.

"It ain't got to do with us, that's all I know," said JoTae.

Hively said, "Tell Nico I stopped by," and started for his car. He got in and sped in the direction of the squad cars. At the crest of the hill he saw down to the bottom where they had parked their cars laterally, blocking the street in front of one of the derelict houses. He pulled up behind them and got out. Two officers stood on the lawn. Between them sat a fat crying baby that screamed every time one of them tried to lift him up. Hively hopped out, walked over, and asked what was going on.

The stouter of the officers answered. "Got an anonymous call that a baby had been abandoned at this location. Arrived here, and this little fella was plopped right here on the lawn."

"You been in yet?"

The officer indicated the other man. "Wendell went in. Door was wide open. Nobody home."

Hively looked down at the baby, then to the apartment building. The upper-floor windows were boarded, but the ones on the first floor and on the porch were not. Something about the child's screams clicked with the scene and the phone call he'd had earlier with the unknown woman. Hively ran toward the building. He bounded up the stairs and inside, called out, and received no response. There were four units, two on each floor. He searched them all. The apartments upstairs were devoid of furnishings; the toilets had even been torn out of the bathrooms. One of the units had a leak in the roof and the entire ceiling and most of the walls were covered in mold. Downstairs was different. In one of the first-floor units, there was a crib and a chest of drawers and a Diaper Genie. The chest had two drawers of women's clothes and another with filled with men's shirts and pants. The closet had piles of musty-smelling laundry on the floor. There was an attached bathroom in working order. The unit's water and electricity were functioning, and there was a stove and a new refrigerator in the kitchen. Jars of baby food stacked in the cabinets.

The main room had no working lights, the only illumination coming from the bulb in the kitchen and a lamp plugged into an extension cord. The windows were draped with bedsheets that had been duct-taped to the sill. The frame for a futon sat against the wall, but there was no pad or mattress on it, which Hively found a little odd. He got out his cell phone, turned on its flashlight, and scoured the room. What he found in the corner confirmed his suspicions. Remnants of a burner phone littered the plywood floor. This was the apartment where Eric Pippen had lived. The child crying on the lawn was his child.

Hively inspected the room for signs of a struggle or a violent altercation. At a glance there was no visible evidence, nothing outside of the smashed phone to raise an alarm, but then his light caught a glint off something lodged in the space between the plywood floor and the bottom of the wall where there were no baseboards. Hively knelt down for a closer look and found that the small glistening object was actually a tooth, an adult bicuspid with a bloody chunk of flesh still attached to the root.

CHAPTER EIGHTEEN
BAD MEN WILL COME

Ephraim started his search for the money at the remnants of the sediment pond, sifted through the loose rocks there, then worked his way along the base of the mountain in a northerly direction, toward the railroad tracks. He didn't stray very far up, figuring Rodney, wounded and in as much pain as he was, wouldn't have been too keen on climbing. He combed the woods for any signs of a cave or rock formation, but minutes stacked into hours, and having made his way deep into the woods without seeing anything of the sort, Ephraim was about to turn around and call it a day.

He came across a fallen pine hanging over a ridge that was least about fifteen feet high. Ephraim leaned over the tree to have a look-see. Beneath where he stood was the mouth of a cavern. He scrambled down the edge of the ridge, came around and peered inside. The height of the entrance was just about as tall as he was, its width probably twice that amount.

Sheet moss clung to the rock edges at the head of the cave and draped down over roots and twigs. Ephraim ducked the moss and stepped into the ancient hole. Immediately he felt the cool drop in temperature. He got out his phone, the display showing it was already past 2:00 p.m., nearly time to pick up Caleb. He tapped on the flashlight button and shined it into the darkness. The cave had some depth to it, fifty feet at least. The floor was uneven, covered in loose rocks in some places, smooth in others. Stalagmites two or three feet tall jutted up from the ground.

Ephraim crept further into the cave, watching his step, panning the light in front of him. The ceiling began to slant and he hunched down. The walls were damp, and he could hear the drip of water coming in from somewhere. He stepped past one of the stalagmites and heard something else. A sharp rattle like that of a maraca came from the floor near his feet. Before he had time to move, another rattle joined the first, and then another. The cave amplified the sound, reverberated it off the walls, making the cacophony seem like it was coming at him from all directions.

Ephraim swung his light down and saw what must have been a dozen snakes, all entwined with each other, their scales shimmering with movement. At the edge of the beam he caught the glint off a pair of fangs launching toward him. Ephraim jumped back, knocking his head against the rock ceiling. The viper, its grotesque jaws staying unhinged, landed near him and, without gathering itself, struck out again. Ephraim hopped sideways to evade the bite and scrambled for the mouth of the cave. He plunged into the daylight and ran well clear of the entryway before bending over to grab his knees and catch his breath.

"Jesus," he panted, watching the ground by the cave to make sure none of the serpents had decided to chase after him. He touched his head where he'd knocked it and felt a large gash, came away with blood on his fingers. "Shit."

It took Ephraim twenty minutes to trek back through the woods to his truck, head throbbing something fierce the whole way. He examined the wound in the Ranger's side mirror. His sandy hair was matted with blood that trailed from the opening at the crown on down behind his left ear. *Could have been worse,* he reckoned. *Coulda knocked myself out and been feasted on by a bunch of god-damn snakes.*

Before he backed the truck out of its hiding spot, Ephraim climbed a little ways up the mountain and peered through the binoculars to make sure the coast was clear in the valley. The high ground provided an unhindered view from the sediment pond down along the valley floor where the Lincoln jutted up from the trench, over the rolling hills, and on up to the high pasture. The facilities and the big house were around the bend of the valley and out of sight, though the top of the grain bin was still visible above the tree line. Across the plain all was calm. Just a bunch of fat cows meandering about.

Ephraim drove back out the way he came, turned onto Greasy Ridge Road, crossed over the train tracks and hooked a right onto State Route 52. Almost immediately upon doing so his phone started to go berserk in his pocket, one buzz after the other, as the messages he'd missed being out of cell range came in all at once. He fished the phone out. Six missed calls from the school and just as many from his father, who'd also sent a bunch of texts. The first message in the queue had come in three hours ago. He listened to it.

Hello, Mr. Rivers. This is Mrs. Brumfield, the principal here at Jarvis Hayes Elementary. This is concerning your son, Caleb. Unfortunately, we've had another incident, and we need you to come pick him up as soon as possible. We're also going to need to discuss our options in what comes next in your son's educational journey. Please call me back as soon as possible.

The other messages from the school were variations on the same theme, albeit with less patience and more urgency as the calls stacked up, the last one saying they could keep Caleb in the office until the end of day if need be, but they'd prefer if Ephraim could pick him up sooner. The calls and texts from Darrell were asking where the hell he was and relaying that the school had been calling the house too.

Addled by the messages, Ephraim nearly didn't notice the line of cars stopped at a police roadblock in front of him. He slammed the brakes and turned the wheels toward the shoulder to avoid colliding with the car at the back of the line. At the squeal of the brakes, the two state troopers conducting the inspections turned their attention to the Ranger, hard scowls creasing their foreheads, but they didn't say anything to Ephraim until it was his turn in pole position.

The smooth-faced trooper, mouth downturned and dumb-looking, took down the truck's license plate number on a clipboard, then came over and indicated for Ephraim to roll down his window. He scanned the interior of the cab before settling his sober glare on Ephraim.

"You trying to go somewhere fast?" the trooper asked.

The sun was perched right over the lapel of his shoulder and Ephraim squinted up to see him. "No, I'm just late to pick up my kid from school. Just got a message that he got in trouble. Sorry, I was distracted."

"You were on your phone?"

"No, just distracted by the situation. Trying to get there on time."

"Uh-huh. Sir, are you aware that your head is bleeding?"

"Yeah," Ephraim lightly touched the cut and winced. "I was hiking over yonder, came on a rattler. Tried to get away from it, slipped on a rock and bumped the old noggin'."

"Looks like it hurts."

"It does smart a little, yeah."

"Rattlesnake, huh?"

"Yeah. Yeah. Big sucker. Like to scared the shit out of me."

"You haven't been drinking, have you?"

"No." Ephraim shook his head. "No."

The trooper laid a stony glare on him. "You almost ran into a car back there. You need to pay better attention to what's going on around you."

Ephraim nodded in agreement. "You been talking to my wife?"

"Where's that you say you were hiking?"

"Uh, out there back of the old strip mine. I like to go up to where they chopped the top of the mountain off. I don't know. I think it's neat I guess."

"You aware that's private property?"

"Really? I thought since they'd abandoned it, it was kinda no-man's-land up there."

"I assume you've seen the sign on the gate that leads up there that says private property, no trespassing."

"I did. I just figured it was old, you know."

"So you can't go back there. You understand? I catch you back there, I'm gonna have to arrest you for trespassing."

"Okay."

"License, please."

Ephraim took his license from his wallet and handed it over.

"You don't live over this way?" the trooper asked, writing the info from the ID down on his clipboard.

"No, I live where it says there, over in Buffalo Township. I work down the road a little ways here at Bismark Carbon."

"So you just come out here to trespass."

"Unknowingly, yeah."

The trooper passed Ephraim his license back. "There was a shootout last night, couple people got killed. Reason to believe those involved came this way afterward. Possibly a high-speed chase. You haven't seen anything strange while you've been over here, have you?"

"No, I haven't seen anything. A shootout you say?"

"Didn't see nothing while you were hiking?"

"Just the snake."

"Okay." The trooper told Ephraim to give them a call if he did see anything out of the ordinary and to watch where he was driving and then waved him forward.

By the time Ephraim got to the school the buses were gone, there were no parents waiting for their children on the lawn, and the parking lot was near empty. He went in and found Caleb sitting with the secretary in the school office.

"What happened?" Ephraim asked his son.

"I dunno," Caleb mumbled weakly. "Some people were making fun of me."

"Okay. What'd you do when that happened?"

Before Caleb could answer, the principal, Mrs. Brumfield, appeared at the door of her office and asked Ephraim to join her inside. She was a gangly woman with a long face and sharp features, both her nose and chin coming to points like gnomons on a sundial. She directed him to one of the visitor's chairs and shut the door. Ephraim apologized for being late. The principal nodded curtly, mouth tight, and inhaled a deep, wheezing breath that made her long nostrils flap open and shut like they were winking at you. She let the air out slow, as if bracing for some unpleasantness, and sat across the desk from Ephraim. She placed her palms softly on the table and proceeded to detail the day's events that culminated in Caleb's expulsion.

"He threw what?" Ephraim asked.

"A hole puncher. A *metal* hole puncher. Luckily it missed the student's head, but not by much. Things could have ended up much worse for everyone involved. After that, Caleb climbed on top of Mrs. Dinwiddle's desk with a long ruler and started yelling things at everyone and swinging the ruler at anyone who tried to get close to him."

Ephraim pictured the scene in his head and sighed miserably. "What was he saying this time?"

"He said that all his classmates would be sorry because bad men were going to come. He said bad men were going to come to the school and kill them all."

Ephraim closed his eyes, squeezed them with his fingers.

"Did something happen to your head, Mr. Rivers?"

"What? Oh, yeah, I'm fine. I banged it right before I came here. That's why I was late."

"It does not look good. Are you sure you're okay?"

"I'm fine. How'd you get him down?"

"From on top of the desk? Once the room was cleared, it took some time, but we were able to coax him off. He cried uncontrollably for quite a while and said how sorry he was."

"He's a good kid."

"I know that, Mr. Rivers. I do. Mrs. Dinwiddle thinks very highly of Caleb. She really does. But you have to understand, I have a whole classroom to consider. A whole school. In a situation like this, I have to make decisions based on what's best for everyone."

"What was it these boys were saying that upset him?"

Mrs. Brumfield clasped her hands together and made a face that was meant to convey sympathy, but really just came off pandering. "I think you'll agree, Mr. Rivers, that no matter what was said to Caleb, and I don't condone any of the language that was used, it's never acceptable to turn to violence, or to brandish any kind of weapon in a classroom. Ever."

"I agree with that."

"From what I understand, the boys were taunting him with chants of 'Crazy Caleb,' and 'Cuckoo Caleb.'"

Ephraim nodded. He started to say something, but found himself suddenly overcome, blinking back tears. He rocked forward with his elbows on his knees and pressed his palms into his eyes in an effort to quell the emotion.

"Fuck," he muttered. "Sorry."

"It's okay. This kind of situation can be very intense. I understand that Caleb has been having a rough time for a little while. Mrs. Dinwiddle told me you've been to—what was it? A doctor or a psychologist to treat him?"

"Yeah. Both."

"I am truly sorry that this is happening to you and Caleb and your family. I really am. But at this time, we feel the school has done everything in its power to help him. In light of today, and the increasing frequency and severity of these incidents, we really have no choice but to expel Caleb at this juncture."

"So he's not a model student, I get that. But you just throw him away?"

"That's not what we're doing." Mrs. Brumfield objected. "Not at all."

"I'm taking him back to the doctor soon to get more tests run. I'm figuring things out."

"That's great. We would love it if you kept us updated with everything. Kept in contact with us. We'd like nothing more than for Caleb to be able to come back to us at some point. When things get back to normal."

Mrs. Brumfield laid out the options available for students in Caleb's situation. If he had a diagnosed medical condition that forced him to miss school, once he was treated, he could theoretically come back next year and repeat the fourth grade. To avoid repeating the grade, they could also apply to another school within the Cain County district. Or a private school, though the expulsion and the reasons for the expulsion would have to be disclosed, so it's possible he wouldn't be admitted. If nothing else worked, they could also homeschool.

"Who's supposed to do that?" Ephraim asked. "Me?"

"There is no easy solution to this, Mr. Rivers. I'm simply laying out the choices you have at your disposal. You could also hire someone to teach him at home. I know a few families that do that."

"How much does something like that cost?"

"It varies. Between a thousand or couple thousand a month, depending on how much time the teacher is needed."

Ephraim chortled. "Okay. So that's out."

On the way home Caleb didn't say much, just that he didn't feel like going to the diner to eat.

"You gotta eat something at home then, okay?" Ephraim said. "If we don't go to Harold's and then you refuse to eat, I'm gonna get very frustrated."

Caleb didn't respond.

"Got it?"

"Yeah, I got it, Dad. Geez."

"Did you eat your lunch today?"

"Some of it. The bell rang before I could finish it all."

"They give you a half hour to eat, bud."

"I know. It's not enough time."

"Okay."

"What? It's not."

"I said okay."

"No, you didn't. You said *okay*."

Ephraim felt himself verging toward anger and bit it back.

"Dad?"

"Yeah."

"I'm sorry."

"I know, bud. It's not your fault."

"Yes, it is."

"Technically it is, but . . ." Ephraim tried to think of the right way to frame his words. "It's not, really. You can't control it, right? For real?"

"No." Caleb started to cry.

"Hey, don't cry. It's not your fault. We've got a lot to figure out. It's not gonna be easy. It's not like your Grandpa can teach you school, and he can't handle you when you get the way you do, you know."

"I know."

"And where I'm workin', I got to sleep most days."

"I'm sorry."

"I know you are. I am too, bud. But we'll figure it out, okay? You just can't give up on me, okay? It's gonna take time, you know. We don't have to work it all out tonight."

"You don't give up on me," Caleb said.

"Hey, look at me. Look at me, Caleb." Ephraim waited for his son to turn his head. "I'll never give up on you. You hear me? Never."

"Okay." Caleb sniffled and wiped his eyes. "What happened to your head?"

"Nothing."

At home, Caleb ate some cereal and went into his room to play video games. Ephraim showered, cleaned the gash on his scalp with peroxide, got some pants on and came out to the living room where he explained to his father about the expulsion. Darrell listened silently, thought it over for a bit, and shook his head.

"Poor kid," he wheezed. Phlegm rattled around in his chest and he coughed.

"That doesn't sound good, Dad."

"No, it doesn't, does it?" Darrell cleared his throat, roughly, for a protracted amount of time. Ephraim patted his father's back and waited for him to finish. Darrell groaned at the taste of bile in his throat. "Ugh. Never get old," he crabbed.

"I'll take it into consideration."

"Bad men will come and kill everybody? What bad men? What's that even mean?"

"Your guess is as good as mine. He hasn't been watching the news, has he?"

"No."

"Maybe he's playing too many video games. I don't know."

"You call the doctor?"

"Yeah, couldn't get through. I'll try back tomorrow. Take him in without an appointment if I have to."

Ephraim yawned. His father eyed him quizzically. "Where were you all day?"

"Picked up a double at work. Told a guy I'd cover for him."

"You look like ass. Got gravestones under your eyes."

"Thanks, Dad, 'preciate it. I'm gonna go catch a few winks right now before I have to go back to work. I told the same guy I'd cover for him tomorrow too. You think you can handle Caleb on your own all day?"

"I'll do my best."

"Thanks, Dad." Ephraim made for the door, then re-membered something and reached in his pocket. "I al-most forgot," he said, pulling out a pair of lottery tickets and handing them over to his father. "Got your numbers for you."

"Oh, when'd you get those?"

"Way in to work, like always. Figure we gotta keep your streak alive. You gotta play to lose."

Darrell took the tickets and examined them to make sure the numbers were correct. "Powerball draws tonight. Up to three-point-seven million or some such. I don't care what you say. This is the night, I can feel it. We're never gonna have to work another day in our lives."

Ephraim smiled wanly, said "Won't hold my breath," and went into his bedroom. Before he lay down he pulled the wad of money from his jeans, took the bills into the bathroom, ran them under hot water in the sink, and set to scrubbing the blood out.

CHAPTER NINETEEN
THE BIG TRUTH

The Honda Passport with dark-tinted windows and false plates was parked beneath a dead street lamp on the far side of the Sundown Courts Motel parking lot. Willis Hively and Clyde Sturges sat next to each other in the back seat where they couldn't be seen through the tinted glass. It had been four hours since they'd removed the squad car surveillance from out front of the motel and a plainclothes officer had parked the Passport with the detectives in back and checked into a room on the second floor under a pseudonym. Since then, two individuals, both men, had rented rooms for the night, gone into them, and hadn't emerged. That'd been about the only action in the place. At one point the owner came out and tore down what remained of the yellow police tape cordoning off areas from the previous night's crime scene.

Hively and Sturges had already pored over every aspect of the case: A BOLO was out for Maurice "Momo" Morrison and Buddy Cleamons, a.k.a. "Buddy The Face," both wanted for questioning in regard to the shootout. To no one's surprise, they hadn't been located. Rosalind Tackett, the mother of the abandoned baby on Spring Street, hadn't been located. The baby was now with Social Services. Hively had not been able to track down Nico Blakes, nor any next of kin for Eric Pippen or Kevon Thompson. The names and addresses the hookers had provided to Officer Mounts during the previous disturbance calls at the Sundown were fakes, so that was yet another dead end. Their other case, the two dozen overdoses, had stalled as well. According to his parents, the small-time dealer Norman Hinkle had gone to Cincinnati to attend a concert.

Earlier in the day they'd brought in Jerry Perky's sister, Juanita, under the pretense of identifying her brother's body. "That's him all right," she'd said, seeming none too broken up about seeing her sibling with half his face blown off. They'd questioned her tactfully, but Juanita played dumb at every turn, claiming she'd never even heard of an organization out of the West End called the Stenders. She swore Jerry was a good brother, a good Christian man, and it was nothing like him to get hisself shot to pieces.

"Who *is* it like?" Sturges asked.

"Who is it like what?"

"To get themselves shot to pieces. Who would be likely to do that?"

"I can sure think of a few, I'll tell you that."

"Give us an example," Hively said.

"Well, I can't think of no names off the top of my head. Lord knows women were always a weakness of Jerry's," Juanita postulated. "Maybe he'd had a romantic rendezvous, was going to get ice or something, and got caught in the middle of the melee. Who can explain the will of the Lord?"

"Certainly not me," replied Hively.

Juanita looked him over head to toe with a marked frown of disdain. "No," she said. "I'd expect not."

All this is to say that now, at a quarter past 11:00 p.m., the detectives found themselves with no real leads and nothing to do except snack on the junk Sturges had packed for the occasion, and bullshit while they waited for hookers to magically appear. Funyuns were Sturges's stakeout food du jour and he crunched on those while he talked.

"So I'm sitting there, I'm watching the game, you know, minding my own business, and she comes down carrying the laundry, making a show of all the hard, back-breaking housework she's doing. And she huffs and puffs, and I hear her go to throw something away, and she huffs and puffs some more and says, 'Do you ever plan on taking this garbage out today?' and I say, 'I don't know, does the garbage *need* taking out?' And she says, 'Would I be asking you to take it out if it didn't?'"

Hively interrupted him. "Stenders haven't made a peep in over a year."

"What?"

"Stenders. They've kept their heads low since that whole mess with Judge Blevins came to light. Him being on the pad for them, offing himself."

"Yeah, I know. I was there. Are you even listening to me?"

"So after being that careful for a whole year, not so much as a parking ticket, why blow it all for this? What was worth bringing the heat?"

"I dunno," said Sturges. "I doubt they expected Rodney Slash would get away from them. If it weren't for that, we may have never even known this happened."

"Maybe."

"Can I finish my story now?"

"By all means, proceed."

Sturges chomped on a Funyun. "Anyway, so I say, 'You didn't ask me to take out the garbage. You asked if I ever planned to take out the garbage. If the garbage is full and you want me to take out the garbage, just ask.'"

"This really isn't about the garbage," said Hively. "You know that, right?"

"Of course it isn't about the garbage. It's about everything she's been pissed at me about for the last twenty-seven years, but I'm not going to pick that scab while the football game is on. It was a good game. Fourth quarter. Anyway—"

"Man, those things stink."

Sturges reached the bag out. "You want some?"

"No, they fuckin' stink."

"What are you, my wife? What do you want me to do? I'd crack a window, but then I'd have to turn the car on and blow our precious cover. Don't worry about it, bag's about cashed." Sturges sniffed one. "I think they smell good."

"That's because the only thing keeping your heart pumping is high-fructose corn syrup."

"Anyways, so she says to me, very condescendingly I might add, 'Can you please take the garbage out?' And I say, 'Sure, I'll take it out here in a little bit.' She says, 'I can't fit one more thing in it.' It's a one-score game by the way. Only like three minutes left or something. So I say, 'If you want it taken out so bad, you've got legs, have at it.'"

"You said that?"

"Yes, I did. So she comes over, gets right in front of the TV and says, 'Listen,' and I'm like, 'You're in the way.'

"'Listen,' she says. 'You need to decide. The rest of your life can go one of two ways. You can either swim with the current, make it easy on yourself, or you can go against the current, and always make every little thing as hard as it can possibly be. But just so you know, I'm the current.'"

"Oh, shit."

"Right? So I thought about it for a little bit. I mean, you know, real consideration, during a time-out, and I said, 'I think I'll fight the current for just a little bit longer.'"

"You said that?"

"Damn right I said that."

"There was only one right answer there, Sturges."

"Oh, I know. But I can't give in to that shit. The rest of my life she'd be Mack-truckin' all over me. A man has to know where he stands."

"So what'd she say?"

"'Have it your way.' Last words she's spoken to me in four days. I actually thought that was pretty good, 'I'm the current.' Well played, you know, but no way I'm giving into that shit."

"So she's the current and you're like the salmon."

"Salmon?"

"Swimming upstream."

"Salmon swim upstream?"

"Yeah, ain't you never been fishing?"

"Then yes. That's me. I'm the goddamn salmon. That's what I'm going to say to her next time."

"You're an idiot."

"Just you wait, pal. You're gonna get a version of that ultimatum one day—just you wait—and we'll see which way you choose to swim."

"Sturges, in my marriage I am the current."

"Uh-huh, okay. Hey, look at this."

The headlights from a truck swept across the parking lot. The vehicle, a dark GMC, bypassed the office and pulled into a spot across by the pool. The truck extinguished its lights, but the motor stayed running, exhaust pluming out from the tailpipe. After a couple minutes, a young girl hopped out. She was dressed in tall stockings, a nothing skirt, and a sweatshirt that had been cut to hang loose off her bony shoulder. She walked to a room on the ground floor that one of the men had checked into, rapped on the door, and was let in. The truck waited until the door was closed behind her, then left the lot.

"That didn't take long," said Sturges.

Hively called the officer staked out in the second-floor room.

"We on?" the officer asked.

Hively gave the affirmative and the detectives got out of the car. Sturges dusted the Funyun crumbs off the shelf of his belly and they walked over to the office. There they met the officer, a beefy young guy named Shrewsberry, and went in.

Merle Frickie looked up from a crossword puzzle, clocked who it was coming through the door, and said, "Aw, hell."

It didn't take much coaxing to get him to hand over a key to room 107 and give his permission to enter.

"Don't let this one out of your sight," Hively told the officer, pointing at Frickie. "Make sure he doesn't call or text anyone. If he wants to stay in business, he'll behave." The partners walked around the courtyard and down the corridor to number 107, slid the card into the reader, and slipped noiselessly into the room. A man lay face-up and buck-naked on the single bed nearest the door. His face was squished with concentration, his fat, hairy body jiggling as the girl, still fully clothed, sat on the edge of the bed with his soft cock in her fist, pumping away, trying to get him going. The man didn't notice the detectives' entry, but she did, blithely saying hello without slowing the task at hand.

The man shot up, panicked at the sight of two strangers standing in the doorway, and promptly fell off the bed. Sturges identified himself and told the man to get up and get dressed so he could go to jail.

"But this—this is my girlfriend," the fat man said. "Tell them—Sarah. Tell them."

Hively asked, "This your boyfriend?"

"My name's Janice," said Janice, a little frisson of delight in her voice.

"That's what I thought."

By this time, a squad car that had been lying in wait down the road had come into the parking lot. Sturges walked the fat man out, Mirandized him, and tucked him into the back seat. Hively looked at the girl. Soft and formless beneath the skimpy outfit. Scabs on her knees, of the type a child might have. Baby hairs clinging to her forehead. She couldn't have been more than five, six years older than his eldest daughter.

"What's your last name, Janice?"

"Fuller."

"How old are you?"

"However old you need me to be," she said coyly. Then, off his stern look, she amended her answer. "Nineteen."

"For real?"

"Yeah, for real."

"Were you here last night, Janice?"

She nodded. "Yeah, been some wild nights 'round here lately."

"I'd say there has. Were you here during the shootout?"

Again she nodded. "Sad what they did to them boys. They was nice, really. Just looking to party, you know."

"Okay. We can do this one of two ways, Janice. We can arrest you and take you to the station, charge you with prostitution, and question you there. Or we can go grab something to eat or get a coffee, whatever you'd like, and you can tell me everything that happened yesterday without anybody else having to know about it."

Janice chewed her lip and pushed her knees together and swayed lightly from side to side. "You put it that way, doesn't sound like I got much choice, does it?"

"That's the best I can do," said Hively.

Janice scrunched her nose up, thought it over. "You know those donuts they got down at the Jolly Pirates? The ones dipped in sugar with jelly in the middle? I've been craving those."

She ordered four of them and a glass of milk, Hively and Sturges each got a coffee, and they sat at a table by the windows that looked out onto the avenue. While she ate, Janice gave her version of the previous night's events.

"You were all in the room when the men came in?" asked Hively.

"Mm-hmm," Janice murmured, biting into a donut. Jelly squirted down her chin. She giggled and wiped it off with her finger and licked the finger clean. Powdered sugar ringed her lips, but that didn't seem to bother her.

"And there were three of you?"

"Uh-huh. One for each of them. But the one guy didn't really want nothing to do with us, so it ended up being more like three on two."

"Which guy was that?"

"Mm. That didn't want none?" Janice stopped eating for a second and looked up to think. "The tall one. I forget his name."

"The one who wasn't in the room when the men came in? The one who went to the vending machines?"

"Yeah, the tall one."

"Who were the other two girls with you?"

"Do I have to tell you?"

Sturges chimed in. "You don't have to tell us anything. But we can arrest you if we have to."

"Ugh," Janice rolled her eyes. "Fine. But they ain't gonna get in trouble, too, are they?"

"No. Scout's honor."

"Funny. It was Brandy and Christina. They're sisters."

"They got last names?"

"I'm sure they do, but they've got about a dozen marriages between them, so they've changed a bunch. I can't keep up. I think the last guy Brandy was married to was named Lennie or something like that. Lennie Waldon, I think it was. I can describe them for you if you'd like."

"Sure."

Janice's description of her two colleagues was very detailed, though not a bit of it, including the names, was true. She even made up a number of tattoos and where they were on their bodies and what they meant. When she started on about how good the fake Christina smelled, the detectives figured out that she was taking them for a ride, but they didn't want her to clam up, so rather than hassle her, they shifted topics.

"Did you recognize any of the men who came in?" asked Hively.

"Just Jerry Perky. He was our boss, y'know. God rest his soul. He wasn't bad to us, Jerry. I think I'll probably miss him." Janice raked a hand through her stringy black hair, leaving a streak of white sugar in its wake. "I didn't recognize none of the other ones. Course it was pretty dark in there, so it was hard telling. Just the TV was on, y'know? No lights or nothing. And I was a little high." Janice's gaze bounced between the two detectives. "Should I have not said that?"

"It's fine," Hively said. "But you weren't incapacitated? You were aware of what was going on?"

"Oh, yeah."

"Did you hear any of them call each other by name?"

"Nuh-uh." Janice took a bite, nearly spilled some more jelly, but caught it on her mouth and moaned with fulfillment. "Oh, that was a good bite."

"Do you know who Momo Morrison is?"

"Momo who?"

"Morrison."

Janice pondered the drop ceiling in the place. "Nope."

"Buddy The Face?"

"Nope."

"His real name is Buddy Cleamons," Sturges offered.

She slurped down the last of her milk. "Still no." She set the empty cup down and scooted it toward them. "Think I can get another glass of that?"

Sturges picked up the cup and took it to the counter. Hively got out his phone, brought up an old mugshot of Momo Morrison and held it out for Janice to see. She looked at it with a placid expression, as if she were viewing landscapes. He swiped it to show her one of Buddy The Face.

"This them?" she asked.

"Yeah," Hively said. "You seen them before?"

"Can't say that I have."

"Look again. These are very dangerous men. We have reason to believe they are the ones who did the killing last night. Do they look like the men who were in that motel room?"

Janice squinted at the mugshots for a good while before saying, "Funny-looking fellers, ain't they?"

"I'd think they'd be hard to miss."

Sturges came back with the refill of milk, put it in front of Janice, and sat back down.

Janice took a gulp, then leaned back in her seat and yawned. "Could be them. Can't really tell. Like I said, it was hard to see."

Sturges said, "Whether they were there or not, I have a hard time believing you've never heard of these two men. They're pretty notorious down on the West End, and they were associates of Jerry Perky."

Janice shrugged. "Nothing I can do about what you do or don't believe. That's up to you."

Hively put his phone away. "It's in your interest to help us here," he said.

"I agree. I want to help you. I don't see a reason for such killing. Hurts my heart the way people treat one another."

"You understand then, the people that did this, they're gonna know we talked to you. That puts you in danger. They're gonna wanna know what you told us."

"Thought you said no one would find out if you didn't arrest me."

"Yeah, well. These things have a way of getting around."

"You don't have to worry about me none," Janice said, winking. "I've seen my share of big bad men. I know how to handle them."

"How's that?" asked Sturges.

"It's easy, really. People tend to think my bulb don't glow too bright, you get what I'm saying, so I let 'em think that. Waste of time trying to prove yourself to people, you ask me. But it lets me get away with things, them thinking that way. What you do, you feed them a pack of lies and one truth. But the one truth has to be a big truth, one that is a no-doubter, one they know is beyond reproach. Unequivocal. Then they think maybe all the lies you tell them are true too. At least, they can't be sure they're not. Even if they suspect something, they second-guess themselves 'cause they know that one thing is totally legit. They get to where they question themselves, can't tell the difference."

"Is that what you're doing with us?"

"No," she said, blinking her eyelids with a put-on innocence. "I would never do that to the police. Y'all ain't dangerous, are you?"

"Are you sure you didn't hear anyone say a name?" Hively asked. "Any name, doesn't have to be Buddy or Momo?"

Janice perked up, like something had come to her. "Slash," she said. "They kept asking them boys"—here Janice modulated her squeaky voice to mimic a man's timbre—"where's Rodney Slash?"

"Slash? Was he the tall one?"

"Yeah, now that you mention it, I think he was."

"And what was the answer?"

"They said they didn't know. I guess that's why they killed them."

"I want you to think about this now," Hively said. "It's important. Did they say anything else, ask those boys anything else, that indicated why they were after them? What they did that was bad enough to get killed over?"

"Mmm," Janice hemmed. "They shooed us out of there pretty quick, but they was asking all of us if we'd seen any money or drugs that the boys had. But we didn't see nothing except what they forked out for, y'know, what we do. Now that you say that though"—Janice reflected for a moment—"I remember now. Yeah, they was asking them over and over where the money was. 'Where's my bag of money?' That's what they said."

"So you think those boys stole some money from them?"

"Sounded like it. Or owed them, I guess, but I don't see why any East End boys would be doing business with that lot. Either way, must've been a lot of dough I reckon, for 'em to have done what they did."

Janice stuffed the last of the donuts into her mouth and chugged down the second milk. "I'm stuffed," she said, rubbing her bare belly. "You take me home now?"

They asked her a couple more questions: How had she and her friends fled the scene? Who had driven her to the motel earlier that evening? Janice provided easy answers that didn't implicate anyone and could have been one hundred percent true or completely fabricated; they couldn't tell. They drove her home to the West End. Janice pointed to a double-wide trailer off Four-Pole Road and said, "That's me."

Before she got out of the car, Sturges asked, "How'd you get into this line of work, Janice?"

"Had a baby," she said. "Needed a job. This was the one I could find paid well enough. You guys got kids?"

"Yeah. Yeah, we both got kids."

"Aren't they just the greatest? My Annabelle is two already. Can't believe it. Time's just whooshin' by."

"They do grow fast."

They watched her go into the house and pulled off. Driving back through the empty streets of Cain City, Sturges turned to Hively. "So which were the lies, do you think? And which one was the big truth?"

"I'd say most all of it was lies, but"—Hively fished out his phone, pulled up a video, hit play, and handed it to Sturges—"take a look at this again."

It was the cell-phone footage of the shootout at the Sundown Courts. Hively waited until the part in the video where Rodney Slash sprints down the second-floor corridor with men from both above and below giving chase.

"What do you see on his back?" asked Hively.

Sturges used his thumb and forefinger to zoom in on the video, and there it was. "A bag of money."

"A bag of money."

CHAPTER TWENTY
ONE WAY TO KILL A COW

When Ephraim got to the change room at work Billy Horseman informed him that the brass had already laid off two people, one from the day shift and another from evenings.

"That's how they're gonna do it, man. Axe one person per shift so they don't fuck up production. You watch. Midnight shift is next."

"Well, we knew it was coming, didn't we?" said Ephraim.

"Knowing something's coming and it actually being here are two different things, friend. I've got thirty-seven damn kids for chrissakes. I need this job."

Ephraim laced his boots. "Thought you had a budding rap career to fall back on."

"Tell you what? I'll throw down a verse for you, and you let me know what you think my chances are of making it."

"I'd rather you not."

"Naw, I'm gonna go write something to bless your ears with, you wait. That is, if they don't fire me 'fore tomorrow. Hey, maybe they'll shitcan Lou Manns, make everybody's quality of life a little better."

Ephraim asked Billy if he had any of those pills for keeping awake. Billy got a bottle out of his locker, tapped one into his palm, and handed it to Ephraim.

"Just one?" Ephraim asked.

"Yeah, that's some primo shit right there. One is all you need."

"What is it?"

"Provigil. Things are like magic. Like that movie where that guy gets real smart for a little while when he takes that pill."

"You take these?"

"Every shift."

"Better give me another one."

"You don't need another one, I'm telling you. That'll do ya until morning."

"Give it to me anyway."

"Okay, but just sayin', you take two of these puppies, you're likely to be awake till next week."

Later, when Ephraim had collected a sample of the carbon and had nothing to do other than sit in the quiet of the station and monitor the furnace temperatures on the computer, he got to thinking about the detritus of his life, the people that populated it. His father, most likely at that moment sleeping in the recliner, TV on, sucking hard for every breath he could get. No way to live, Ephraim thought. He hoped it never came to that for him, a slow decline into infirmity.

Then there was Ashlee, still his wife in name if nothing else, and the many regrets he harbored from that relationship. Somewhere along the line he'd come to view her mental health problems as something he had to endure, instead of an illness that she struggled with every moment of every day, from the inside. He'd been ground down, he knew, by the tumult of her mood swings, the emotional upheaval she left in her wake. But was that excuse enough to stop giving her the support she needed, the love she craved? Because that's what he'd done. He'd walled himself off from her, become cold, and allowed her to indulge in whatever vice she needed to cope, as long as it helped to make his life the least bit more tolerable. And he'd agreed with Ashlee, on the day before she left, that everyone would be better off if she wasn't around. Couldn't forgive himself for that one, even if he believed it.

Ephraim was wired from Billy's pills, and these thoughts and memories came tumbling back on him now, like an invasive species in his brain, one atop the other. Mistakes. Regrets. Failings. Flickering through all of this were images of the previous twenty-four hours. Images of a dying man with whispers of a hidden fortune. Images of blood. He couldn't shake loose from his mind the words Rodney had repeated: *It's your lucky day . . . It's your lucky day.*

And now there was Caleb, his son, seemingly losing *his* mind right before his very eyes. *What luck,* Ephraim thought. He remembered the Facebook group he'd sought out two nights previous, the PANS/PANDAS Awareness Collective, and the question he had posted on its message board about what to ask the pediatrician. There was a corner in the break room where, if you held your phone just right, you could get internet service. Ephraim went in there and moved his phone around until a bar appeared and he logged onto the social network. To his surprise, there were more than thirty responses to his query. Most of them said general practice doctors weren't equipped to diagnose and treat PANS, but they were perfectly capable of administering the myriad of tests needed to determine what could be wrong with Caleb, and he should have those done as soon as possible so that he had results in hand when he got in with a specialist. That could take weeks or months because there were so few of them, and they were usually booked far in advance.

The number of tests the cavalcade of responders suggested was overwhelming. Ephraim had never heard of half the stuff, couldn't pronounce the words if he tried, but he was familiar with a couple of the recommendations. Like Lyme and Strep and Cat Scratch Fever. He retrieved a pen and pad from the office and jotted them all down, as well as the reasons why each test was necessary. All the while his gaze kept being drawn to the bloodstain beneath the light switch on the wall. You wouldn't know it was blood. In the twenty-four hours since he'd scrubbed at it furiously, the stain had dried and faded to a brownish color that resembled a coffee splotch, ringed darker around the circumference.

Ephraim felt a buzz in his pocket, saw that it was a text from Lucia.

Missed you at the diner tonight. Everything okay?

Ephraim thumbed out his response. *Not really. Caleb got expelled from school*

What??? Why? How?

Long story. Tell you about it soon

You okay?

Been better. Missed seeing you

Do you want me to come out there tonight?

I do but not good idea tonight. Not feeling great. Work rough too

What's going on?

Nothing to worry about hopefully. Been thinking a lot about you tho

Good thoughts?

Very

I like that. Will I see you tomorrow?

Definitely. Question for u. If you could go anywhere in the world where would you go?

Why?

Cuz I want to know

The thought bubble dotted up for a while before Lucia's response came through.

Italy.

I'm gonna take you there

Yeah, right.

Watch me. I'm gonna take you on a ride on one of them gondolas. Have some sexy Italian serenade you

Uh huh. Big talk. Don't you gotta work?

Yeah. See you soon

Ephraim slipped the phone into his pocket, ripped the paper with all his notes off the pad, and stuffed it in next to the phone. Walking out of the break room, he looked one more time at the bloodstain on the wall, then flipped the lights off and finished his shift.

The next morning Ephraim called the pediatrician's office, told them what was going on and that he was going to bring Caleb in first thing. The receptionist politely informed him that he'd need to schedule an appointment.

"What I need is for the doctor to see him right now," Ephraim said. "This can't wait."

"Does he have a fever?" the receptionist asked.

"It's not that kind of sick. He's—he was kicked out of school yesterday. Something's wrong with his head. He's not right."

"But outside of his behavior, he doesn't have symptoms of being ill?"

"He's losing his mind. I'd say that's a symptom."

The receptionist, exasperation leaking through her chipperness, said he was free to bring his son to the office, but the doctor had a busy day scheduled, and they might have to wait to be seen for quite a long time.

"Fine," Ephraim said. "We'll sit there as long as we have to."

As it turned out, the wait time wasn't long at all. They arrived at ten, and by half past they were in an examination room. Caleb played some game on Ephraim's phone where a monkey put together puzzles and counted fruits and shit. He put it down when Dr. Fitzsimmons, a plump man with thickly gelled hair, eyebrows that'd been waxed into a high arc, and a Jaguar XJ220 sitting in the lot with vanity plates that read GOLF DOC, entered the room. The doc skimmed the chart in his hands, greeted them with an artificial warmth, and asked what seemed to be the problem.

Ephraim detailed Caleb's recent troubles at school and some of the signs that pointed to more than just behavioral problems. The bedwetting, verbal outbursts, the sudden panic attacks where he could hardly breathe—sometimes over things as simple as him trying to get Caleb to eat or take a shower. The way the blacks of his eyes turned into huge saucers during these spells.

"And I know what everybody says or thinks, that he's doing this stuff for attention or he can control it if he wanted, but I don't believe that, Doc. I just don't. I'm the one with him every day, and I know he wouldn't do this stuff if he could help it. I can see the pain in his eyes, you know what I'm saying? He doesn't want to be doing these things."

The doctor nodded solemnly, said, "Let's have a look," and conducted a brief examination of Caleb, checking his reflexes, listening to his lungs, peering into his ears with an otoscope, then his eyes. He asked Caleb a series of questions to determine how he felt both physically and mentally. Caleb answered in monosyllables—*yes, no, I dunno.* The doctor commented as he went along. "Looks good . . . Sounds good in there . . . Pallor is not great. These dark circles under his eyes are very prominent. Could indicate some kind of allergy . . ." The doctor set his instruments aside. "Do you ever feel sad, Caleb?" he asked.

"I guess. Sometimes."

"Have you felt that way lately?"

Caleb nodded. "Yeah."

"Is there anything in particular that makes you feel sad?"

"I dunno. Lots of stuff, I guess."

"Lots of stuff, huh?" The doctor turned to Ephraim. "I think maybe our next step is to talk to a psychologist."

"Yeah, we did that at the beginning of the year, if you remember."

"Right."

"That's what led you to prescribing the, um, whatchamacallit, the . . . Zoloft."

"Right, I remember."

"Have you ever heard of PANS?" Ephraim asked.

The doctor responded hesitantly. "Yes."

"Well, I've been doing some research, and you know, a lot of the stuff they talk about makes sense. A lot of the symptoms match up." Ephraim pulled a folded piece of paper from his back pocket, spread it out, and proffered it to the doctor. The doctor looked at the lengthy, handwritten list as though it might be infectious.

"What's this?" he asked.

"These are the tests we need to run to see if he has PANS."

The doctor took the paper and read through it. "Look," he said, wincing slightly. "The internet is a great source of information in many cases, but it can also be a bit of a dog whistle. You look up a sore throat and all of a sudden you have cancer."

"Do I have cancer?" asked Caleb.

"No," Ephraim said. "Here, play that game while I talk to the doctor." Ephraim gave Caleb the phone back, waited for him to start playing before addressing the doctor again. "I understand what you're saying, but nothing else has worked, and I want these tests run."

The doctor made a face, half-annoyed, half-patronizing, like he was going to have to explain something very complex to an imbecile. "In the medical community, PANS is something of a—how do I say this?—conundrum. No one has proven definitively that it's a real syndrome. Many think it's likely the result of something else entirely, or a combination of factors that present similar symptoms."

"Like Lyme disease. That's on there," Ephraim said, pointing at the paper. "The Western Blot test. I want that one run too."

"Lyme disease is tricky. Some doctors hand out a Lyme diagnosis like hotcakes, kind of a catchall-type thing. But it's notoriously hard to diagnose, even with the Western Blot test. You get as many false positives as you do real ones, and then you're pumping these patients full of drugs they may not even need. Drugs that can harm your system, especially a young system like Caleb's, in ways that could cause irreparable damage."

"So you're saying you don't believe in these diseases?"

"No, I'm not saying they're not real." The doctor put

a fist to his mouth, cleared his throat. "Excuse me. What I'm saying is, I don't know if these diseases are the cause of a patient's maladies, or if they are the result of another ailment, something we have yet to figure out. As doctors, we don't have all the answers. We're scientists, basically, trying to find the solutions."

"So you're saying because you don't know much about Lyme disease or PANS, you just don't treat them?"

"It's not that I don't treat them. That's not it at all. Lyme disease is a very real thing that can cause various debilitating symptoms. It's that I'm not sure it'd be ethical or responsible of me to treat them with medications that I'm not comfortable will work."

Ephraim, starting to grow impatient now, folded his lips together and nodded his head slowly up and down. "Those tests there, can you run them?"

"Yes, but—"

"Does it cross your ethical line to run them? Does it do any harm to anyone to just see what the results are?"

The doctor scanned the paper in his hand. "This is a lot of tests. HHV-6, IGG. Do you even know what all of these are?"

"That one has to do with the immune system, if I'm not mistaken."

"That's right. Look, I can run these tests for you, but I'm obliged to tell you, because PANS and Lyme are so difficult to diagnose and treat, insurance companies in most states, including our fine state of West Virginia, don't cover the costs for tests, treatment, none of it.

"Obviously, I have no knowledge of your financial situation, but—" The doctor looked down at the list, shaking his head. "I mean, this many tests, it's gonna run you into the thousands, regardless."

"So what then, I should just let my son suffer?"

"That's not what I'm saying. I'm simply alerting you to the fact that these tests will just be the beginning of your expenses. Assuming some of the results come back murky, I imagine you're going to look for a specialist."

"Right."

"I'm not convinced the doctors working in these fields aren't bilking people for all they're worth."

"Because insurance companies don't cover it?"

"Exactly."

"Sounds to me like that's an insurance company problem, not a doctor problem."

"That's true. Look, if you want me to run these tests, I'll run them."

"I do. I very much want you to run them."

"Okay."

"How long will it take to get the results?"

"Depends, some, like"—the doctor went down the list—"influenza, walking pneumonia, cat scratch, strep, parvovirus, the vitamin deficiencies, those could come back soon, today or tomorrow. Pyrroles—that is tested through urine, so it could come back soon too. Everything else will take some time, a week or so."

It took twenty vials to get all the blood they needed out of Caleb. Afterward, in the car, he rested his head against the window and closed his eyes until he felt the car stop. He sat up and saw that they were in the parking lot of the Walmart.

"I thought we were going home," he said.

"I gotta stop in here for something."

"Can I stay in the car?"

"No, c'mon. I got a surprise for you."

"Do I have to?"

Ephraim studied his son in the passenger seat, pale

and puny looking, his eyelids pinked and heavy over glazed pupils. "Won't take a minute," he said. "C'mon."

Ephraim led Caleb to the aisle where they had video games. "Which one did you want on your birthday?"

"What?"

"The game I got you that was the wrong one. Which one did you want?"

"You didn't get me the wrong game. You got me the wrong *version* of the game. You got the one from like five years ago."

"Okay, well. Is the one you want here?"

Caleb scanned the rows of games, raised his arm like a wet noodle and shook his finger at one of them.

"This one here?" Ephraim asked. "*Call To War 7*?"

"Yeah."

Ephraim removed the game from the hook and handed it to Caleb. "You earned it," he said. "You wanna getcha another one?"

"What?"

"Another game. You want another one?"

"Yeah."

"Get you one, then."

Caleb stepped forward and stared, mesmerized. "There's so many to pick from."

"You don't know which one you want?"

"Nu-uh."

"Okay, you stay here and figure it out. I gotta go pick something up. I'll be right back, okay. Don't go nowhere. Stay right here."

"Okay."

Ephraim walked to the other end of the store where they had a jewelry counter. He browsed the glass encasement where they displayed necklaces, bracelets, brooches, and the like. A heavily made-up woman with short bleached hair spiking in all directions approached him. She wore so many pieces of jewelry, she jangled as she walked.

"You looking for something in particular?" the woman asked, a salesman's empty smile pasted to her face.

"I dunno," Ephraim said, gesturing at the contents of the display. "Which one of these would you like?"

The woman looked down with a pretext of deliberation and said, "That all depends on what kind of message you're trying to send." She unlocked the door on the case, slid it open, and extracted a diamond bracelet. "You can't ever go wrong with this piece."

Ephraim picked the bracelet up and saw the price tag of twelve hundred dollars. "This might scare her off a bit."

"I see." The woman took back the bracelet and gave him a little knowing wink. "A newer relationship, is it? How about this?" She brought out a gold locket in the shape of a heart.

When Ephraim got back to the games aisle, he found Caleb puzzling over two different titles in his hands.

"I can't figure out which of these I want."

"Get 'em both," said Ephraim.

"For real?"

"C'mon, before I change my mind."

At the checkout counter, the cashier rang the items up and gave the total. "That'll be six hundred and twenty-seven dollars and forty-eight cents."

Ephraim dug a wad of cash out of his jeans, counted out the bills, and handed them over. The cashier began to tally through them when she stopped abruptly and laid them on the conveyor.

"These bills have some kind of stain on them," she said.

"Yeah, sorry. My buddy, we were playing cards and he accidentally knocked his spit can over, right on the pot, you know. I washed it best I could." The cashier glared at the dirty bills. "It still spends the same," Ephraim assured her.

The cashier collected the money by its edges and finished ringing him up. On the car ride home, Caleb asked, "Where'd you get all that money?"

"I tell you, you can't tell anybody."

"Okay."

"Gotta promise."

"Promise."

"You know how I feel about breaking promises."

"I said I promise."

"Okay," Ephraim grinned over at his son. "I chased a rainbow, found a pot of gold at the end of it."

"Yeah, right. You aren't that lucky."

"Well, nobody's lucky enough to come across some hidden treasure until they do."

"Never mind. Forget I asked."

"Okay, okay," Ephraim said. "I won a big card game at work."

"I thought you said it was stupid to gamble."

"It is."

"Plum stupid you said."

"Yep. Sounds like me."

Caleb cast a suspicious eye on his father.

"What?" asked Ephraim.

"You sure you're my daddy?"

"Last I checked I still held the distinction."

"I dunno," Caleb said. "You sure are acting funny. You sure you're not an alien?"

Ephraim laughed. "Why? Cause I bought you a couple video games?"

"That's one reason. What else did you buy?"

"Nunya."

"That there is another reason you're suspect. You're being all secretive."

"I'm suspect?"

"That's right. You're what Grandpa calls a skinflint. And before today I've never seen anything that proved him wrong. So something ain't normal."

Ephraim, tickled at his son's banter, placed a hand over his heart. "I swear to you on your grandmother's grave, I am not now, nor have I ever been, an alien."

"See, that's exactly what an alien would say."

"You've got me there."

When they got home Caleb darted through the living room, neglecting to even say hello to his grandpa sitting in the recliner.

"Hey, don't run in the house, now," crabbed Darrell.

"Sorry," Caleb cried out cheerfully, having already disappeared down the hallway. Ephraim came into the room. Darrell jabbed an arthritic finger toward the hall. "What's gotten into him?"

"He's just excited. I went back and got him that video game he wanted for his birthday."

"I thought he liked the one he got fine."

"He's had a rough go. I wanted to do something nice for him."

"Something nice? I got him that damned telescope. He ain't looked into it more than once. I've never heard of a kid being rewarded for getting kicked out of school."

"Yeah, well, now you have." Ephraim nodded toward the TV. "What happened here?"

The noon news was on. The same field reporter from the Sundown Courts, Jessica Heller, was now in front of a country road. Behind her was a car that had halfway rolled into a ditch, its front fender and hood crumpled over the right tire. And laid out in the middle of the road was a dead cow. Even from the camera's distance, you could see its thick tongue flopped out, its black marble eyes fixed on nothing, fixed on eternity. A state trooper was standing next to the cow, shepherding traffic around it.

"Damndest thing. Car came around a bend there, ran smack dab into a cow."

"Oh, yeah? Where's that?"

"Yeah." Darrell started to cough. He put a fist to his mouth to ward off a fit. "Out there on Greasy Ridge." Ephraim walked nearer to the TV so he could hear the report over his father's windy talking. "The cell service out there is spotty, you know, so they have to walk down to the closest house, which is the Mercer farm. Hey, weren't you just asking me about that place?"

"Huh? Yeah."

"Yeah. So they tell them they hit a cow. Old Mercer suspects it's one of his cows, of course, wandered off somehow." Darrell took in some air in order to continue. "He goes and checks his property to see how it might have gotten free. Finds a gate blown out, investigates a little further, finds yet another wrecked car right in the middle of his field. Now you'll never guess what they found in *that* car."

CHAPTER TWENTY-ONE
FLIGHT OF THE SCAVENGERS

After a commercial break, the news went back live to the scene of the cow collision. Jessica Heller trotted out Lloyd Mercer for an interview. He was an old man with rusty-looking skin, a face mottled with broken capillaries, and a full head of close-cropped white hair. Best Ephraim could tell, Mercer was near his father's age, though without the frailties of lung disease and arthritis. He still had a little verve to him.

The reporter peppered him with questions, first about his cow getting loose and then about the wrecked vehicle found on his property with a deceased person inside. Mercer didn't have any answers. He didn't know the dead man, had never seen him before. Couldn't rightly describe him. Mostly Mercer just looked vexed at the presence of the steer in the middle of the roadway behind them, eventually yelling to someone off camera, "Can we get that cow out of the road, please? That's no way for him to be just laying out there like that."

"As if his way of killing 'em is so much more humane," Darrell scoffed.

Jessica Heller kept pressing Mercer. "So it's fair to say the gruesome discovery made on your property may have gone unnoticed for quite some time if not for the cow getting loose and being hit by a car?"

"I suppose that's so. It was way down at the far end of our land there." Mercer made a vague sweeping gesture to indicate where he meant.

"So it's possible this is the vehicle police have been searching for, the one involved in the shootout a couple of nights ago at the Sundown Motel?"

"How would I know, Ms. Heller? I believe those are questions for the law."

With that, Mercer begged off. The reporter turned to the camera. "Well, there you have it, folks. A car hits a cow, and an unlikely mystery unfolds."

No mention of the money. The only thing left of the broadcast was the weather forecast. A cold snap coming down from Canada was set to drive the temperatures to an overnight low of thirty degrees.

"Thought you had a shift to work," Darrell said.

"No," Ephraim said. "Billy covered me so I could take Caleb to the doctor."

"You mind if I change the channel, or soap operas your thing now?"

"Go ahead." Ephraim stood from the couch. "I do have some errands to run, though. You mind keeping an eye on Caleb today?"

"What if he has one of his outbursts? What am I supposed to do?"

"Just let him play his game, he should be all right. I'll be back to take him to Harold's for dinner."

"Where you going?"

"Do I ask you about everything you do?"

"Don't have to. I don't do anything."

"You take your meds?"

"Goddammit."

"Take your meds."

Ephraim peeked in on Caleb, who was sitting about an inch away from his TV, hammering at the buttons on his controller. The game was one of those first-person shooter jobs, the soldier's POV running alongside the edge of a building on some war-torn street in some war-torn land. Explosions going off all around him. Screams of agony off camera. Fires billowing from the bombed-out cars. Choppers overhead. Torrents of gunfire coming from the roofs of buildings, tracers coming out every fifth round. Everything more realistic than the stuff they had out when Ephraim was a kid. He didn't bother his son. He snagged his keys, got into his Ranger and backed down the driveway.

There was a high probability the police would erect a checkpoint in that same spot on 52 where he'd been detained the day before. Ephraim didn't want to risk getting stopped again, so he hopped onto the interstate and drove an extra twenty-five minutes to come at it from the back way. Slate Run Road ran along Dock Creek at the base of the mountain opposite of the Mercer farm, and put him out on 52 a quarter of a mile south of the road that led up to the old mining site.

The fence that barred entry to the lane had collapsed long ago and now the chain link lay strewn along the berm. As the trooper had informed him yesterday, there was a *No Trespassing* sign tacked up to a post. The road was beset by woods on both sides and hadn't been maintained for decades. The pavement was cracked and uneven. In some spots, whole chunks of concrete had slipped down the mountain, nowhere to be seen. Ephraim took it slow, following the switchbacks up the face until the road emerged, quite suddenly, onto a flat plateau of rock and sediment. The land up there was devoid of any scrub, no bushes, no trees. Nary a weed in sight. Just skinned earth.

Ephraim pulled the Ranger over, grabbed the binoculars off the passenger seat and, keeping to the edge of the tree line, made his way across the expanse of the plateau. Near the ridge he got down and belly-crawled to the ledge. Laid out below him was a series of tiered plateaus, stacked one atop the other. Beyond that were the valley and the farm. Only the far end of the valley was visible from where he lay. If he wanted to see what was going on by the gulley where the Lincoln had crashed, he'd have to find his way down to the next plateau somehow.

Ephraim trained the binoculars on the main house, saw the dozen or more police and state trooper vehicles parked in the circular drive out front, quite a few people milling about. A great ruck of cows was congregated back near the barns, as far away from the commotion as they could physically get. A wrecker truck came around the corner of the house and slowly made its way down the gravel lane toward the crime scene. Ephraim tracked the truck until it passed the offshoot road he'd gone in on yesterday and went through the busted gate. From there it disappeared below the ridgeline of the lower plateau.

A dog bark echoed across the canyon. Ephraim lowered the field glasses and scouted the area for a route down to the next level. He spotted an old footpath that was used for that very thing, but it was too out in the open, too exposed. He scrambled back to the fringe of the woods. The land was steeper there, but the trees were crowded and he slid on his ass from trunk to trunk until he made it down.

Again he crawled to the edge of the escarpment and peered over. At least twenty police officers were spread out over the valley floor, combing the land for evidence. All of them had plastic booties over their shoes. The wrecker was one of only two vehicles at this end of the valley, the other being an ambulance that was parked in the middle of the field, a good hundred yards from the action of the crime scene. A portly white guy in a white button-down, sleeves rolled up, badge dangling from his neck, gesticulated to the driver of the wrecker. Instructing him, Ephraim assumed, on the course he wanted him to take to reach the Lincoln.

In the gulch, techs in head-to-toe hazmat suits were dusting the upended car for prints. The man who looked to be in charge, a black fella decked out in a snazzy suit and tie, stood on the bank above. Four policemen and a sheriff's deputy surrounded him. He said something to the group and the local officers broke the huddle. They jumped down into the irrigation ditch and, starting near the Lincoln, split off in pairs, walking the trench in opposite directions.

The head honcho then spoke with the sheriff's deputy, pointing out different areas on the ground. A photographer was nearby, snapping pics of the bullet holes in the side panel of the Lincoln. The detective beckoned him over, directed him to take pictures of the places in the field he was indicating. The photog set to it. Ephraim guessed at what it was they were documenting: the different sets of tire tracks.

"Shit," he muttered.

The dog barked again. Ephraim swung the binoculars to where the sound had come from. At the far end of the valley a German Shepard was straining at his leash, leading the officer on the other end along the rim of the irrigation ditch. The dog came to the bottom of the valley fill and tugged its way up the precarious hillside, fervently scouring through the rocks. It made it up the mountain a good ways, enough for Ephraim to worry it was his scent the dog was after, but then the mutt halted abruptly, raised its head and locked its legs, standing completely motionless for a beat. The dog twisted its head, then bounded off in a different direction, down the slope and toward the woods that Ephraim had searched the day before. Toward the cave.

"Shit."

He shifted his sights back on the Lincoln. Two of the hazmats had loaded Rodney Slash onto a gurney. They raised the body out of the canal.

Willis Hively stood over the gurney. Next to him was the on-site tech from the crime lab, a no-nonsense woman in her mid-thirties named Gloria Andrade.

"First impressions?" Hively asked her.

"The gunshot wound to the abdomen is what killed him. Body's been out here in the elements for too long to tell the exact time of death, but it's a safe bet that it wasn't too long after the trauma occurred. Stomach wounds are tricky. You can sometimes last a while, but if you don't get it tended to relatively quickly, reaper's coming."

"What about—?" Hively made a vague gesture toward the body's eyes and mouth. "Was that something someone did to him while he was alive or. . . ?"

Andrade pointed to the sky east of where they stood.

Hively shielded his eyes against the sun and looked that way. Vultures circled high above the treetops on the mountain. "You kidding me? Vultures did that?"

"You see all these tiny scratches around the sockets and where the lips used to be?" Andrade used her gloved hand to indicate where she meant. She peeled the remaining skin around Rodney's mouth back. "The cuts on the gums?"

"Okay, I got it."

"The eyes and the tongue are the most accessible parts of the body for scavengers to get at. They have to wait a bit for the rest of the body to decompose in order to pick it apart easier. Typically, they go for the genitals and the anus next, but in this circumstance, were unable to get that far."

"Said I got it," Hively said, his face in a pucker. "Somebody oughtta shoot those fucking birds."

"They actually play a key function in a healthy ecosystem. Vultures prevent a lot of disease and illness that a rotted carcass can cause if left to a natural deterioration."

"Yeah, well, they come near me I'm shooting them."

Hively watched the techs load the body into the ambulance. After it drove off, he trekked across the field to where the gate was busted out. For the second time, he followed the tire tracks the Lincoln made on foot, all the way down the side of the pasture to where it cut back over the rolling hills and came to its conclusion at the wreck site. From there, he followed where the second pair of tracks, made by a mystery car, peeled off. This car skirted the bank of the irrigation channel and parked in a narrow gap between the trees. Then it backed out, turned around, and took a straight shot back through the mashed gate. All told, this took Hively forty-three minutes. His smartwatch calculated he'd walked a total of 7,340 steps. Or 3.4 miles.

That's where Sturges found him, near the wreckage where the two sets of tracks diverged, staring at the ground as if he were under hypnosis. Sturges snapped his fingers in front of Hively's face.

"Earth to Willis, do you read—over?"

"This doesn't make any sense," Hively mumbled, speaking his thought process aloud. "This second vehicle was very meticulous, right? Makes sure to stay directly in line with Slash's car, takes the exact same course all the way down, then back up and over, all the way to the ditch where Slash's car goes in. From there, for whatever reason, it throws caution to the wind, breaks off course, goes off in a completely different direction, hides itself in the woods, for how long we don't know—a minute, an hour, more. Then it leaves. Why? It would have worked. Look at this track. We would have never known this was more than one car. We wouldn't have even been able to identify the tread. Why would they be so careful all the way up to a point, and then not?"

Sturges shrugged. "Nothing people do makes sense to me, and nothing surprises me. Listen—"

"There's no way this second car was the Stenders chasing him down right after the shootout. They were hauling ass after him, wouldn't have been that careful."

"Unless they somehow lost him, then found out he'd come this way. Followed the bread crumbs until they located him."

"How do they find out Slash comes this way if nobody knows where he went? We didn't find a phone on him. He died right there. How could anyone know?"

Sturges tossed his hands up. "Beats me. How's any of this shit happen?"

Hively gazed across the length of the field to the woods beside the valley fill. "We're missing something."

"I'll tell you what we're missing," said Sturges. "A bag of money."

"Right." Hively jabbed his finger into Sturges's chest. "Right. So say the Stenders find the car. Slash is lying there dead, or fast on his way to dead. They get what they came for, the bag of money. Why then the detour to the woods? That's what's getting me."

"This might have something to do with what I came to tell you in the first place."

"What's that?"

"Guy that runs the K-9 unit just radioed in. Says his mutt picked up something strong going through the woods. The thing's yanked him out across Greasy Ridge Road and is now going strong down the train tracks."

"Which way?"

"North."

"What's over there?"

"Not much. Couple factories I think." Sturges held up his phone. "I can't get a signal to look it up."

The guy operating the wrecker secured the hooks and chains around the undercarriage of the Lincoln, climbed back into the cab, and hit the button to retract the cables. The detectives watched as the truck began to beep and the boom arm on the back gradually lifted the car up out of the gulch.

Sturges said, "Or maybe the farmer found it, couldn't resist."

Hively ignored that and said, "How could that hound be picking up a scent if Rodney got no farther than rolling out of the car?"

Sturges chewed on the question for a minute, squinting at the sky as though it might aid him in finding the answer. "What if there was a second guy?"

"Where? In the car?"

"Maybe. What if there was a fourth guy at the motel, somebody who didn't want to mess with the hookers. Stayed back, waited for his friends to be done?"

"You think somebody stayed in the car for six, eight hours while his friends sat up in the motel getting their rocks off? Naw, that don't sing."

Sturges chafed. "I'm spitballing here. Sometimes you have to muck through all the wrong answers to get to the right ones. Something has to pull all this shit together."

"Don't get pissy on me, baby. You getting hangry? You need some Funyuns?"

"I need something."

"You're right, though," Hively ceded. "We gotta question the damn farmer again."

An ominous metallic groan sounded from beneath the Lincoln, now dangling half out of the ditch. The detectives turned, as did everyone on the scene within earshot. Something crunched. The frame of the car cracked under the pressure from one of the hooks. It dropped a couple feet through the air, caught with a clangorous snap, and hung there doing a one-eighty spin. For a second it looked like it'd hold, but then another hook snapped off the wheel axle and the rest of the chains gave way. The car banged down into the ditch, again, coming to rest in roughly the same position as before.

Every investigator there was stunned silent, the only noise coming from the boom arm of the wrecker, creaking as it bobbed up and down. Sturges broke the spell with a hearty laugh.

"Christ," he whooped. "Only in Cain City."

CHAPTER TWENTY-TWO
THE STINK OF MADNESS

When Ephraim got home, his father was on the porch swing waiting for him. He could tell from Darrell's expression that all was not right with the world.

"What happened?" Ephraim asked.

Darrell stood with the aid of his walker. "Now listen, I didn't do anything."

"I didn't say you did, Dad. I asked you what happened."

Darrell threw up his hands. "Something went glitchy with that video game and I thought he was gonna have a panic attack, started crying and shaking. I tried to help him, but how the hell am I supposed to know what to do with those things?"

"Did you yell at him?"

"I wouldn't say I yelled. I raised my voice."

"Dad, I told you, you can't yell. It only makes him worse."

"Well, shit," Darrell spat. "I can't watch him no more then."

"Dad."

"I was just trying to help him. He's the one went berserk soon as I touched his stuff, screaming at me that I was breaking his Nintendo or whatever the hell. Then he just started wailing like a damned banshee. Knocked over his new telescope. Started throwing fuckin' books at me like ninja stars."

Ephraim closed his eyes. A weight descended on him from above, a gravitational shroud that threatened to sink him into the earth, grind him from existence. How many hours had it been since he slept? Twenty-four? Thirty-six? He couldn't remember. Exhaustion glided temporally over his whole body. He felt an overwhelming urge to lie down right there on the stoop, rest his head on the concrete slab of the porch and never move again, never open his eyes, to go away forever. But then a vision of it came into his mind's eye—Caleb chucking books at his father, Frisbee style—and he couldn't help but to laugh. A deep gut laugh that brought forth tears.

"Glad you think it's funny," Darrell said.

"Like ninja stars?"

"Hell yes, one right after the other. Like a damned pitching machine. *Ffht-Ffht-Ffht*." Darrell demonstrated what he meant, Caleb's rapid hurling technique. "Those corners are pointy too. I'm telling you, you ain't lived till you get hit with a flying Hardy Boys."

"Oh, man. He's got a lot of those."

"Don't I know it. I tried to get out of there, but it's not like I'm fleet of foot. He got me good right in the spine."

The humor of the situation petered out and Ephraim sighed and dabbed the wetness from his eyes. "I'm sorry, Dad."

"I guess it is a little funny, from a certain perspective."

"Where is he?"

"Still in his room."

Ephraim found Caleb lying on the floor in his room, battling it out with a couple of *Star Wars* figures.

"Hey, buddy. You okay?"

"I'm fine," Caleb muttered.

"Heard you had a little dustup with Grandpa?"

"No!" Caleb shrieked, the decibel level going from zero to earsplitting. "He had a little dustup with me!"

"Okay. Okay," Ephraim said. "I'll take a look at your Xbox, okay?"

Ephraim started for the game console on the table across the room. Caleb jumped to his feet to impede his path. "No, just leave. You'll probably make it worse. Then I'll never get to play again. Just leave me alone!"

"If that happens, I'll buy you another one, okay? But if you ever wanna play again, somebody's gotta try and fix it."

Caleb thought about that for a second, saw that there was no other solution, and begrudgingly allowed his father to pass. After the console was sorted, Ephraim told Caleb it was time to go to Harold's for dinner. Caleb protested, saying he wanted to play his game now that it was working again. Ephraim went through all the choices they had for dinner in the house.

"I can make you spaghetti."

"Yuck."

"Chicken noodle soup."

"Ew. That's even worse."

"Peanut butter sandwich."

"Dad."

"What?"

"You know I hate peanut butter."

"Well, buddy. You gotta eat something."

"Not peanut butter. Gross."

"Scrambled eggs."

"Are you joking? Do you want me to puke?"

"Yeah, Caleb, that's it. I want you to puke."

"Sorry."

"Don't be sorry. I just need you to eat. Cause that's it, my man. We don't have any other food, and you gotta eat."

"Cereal."

"You're not eating cereal for every goddamned meal of the day."

"You said it," Caleb said, his eyes going a little wild now. "*You* said I have to eat. I never said I was hungry. I never asked for anything. Why is everybody always so mean to me?"

"I'm not being mean. Grandpa wasn't being mean."

"Yes he was."

"Look man, we're just trying to help you. You need to eat something that's good for you. Not sugar. I guarantee you'll feel better if you eat something good, and the only thing you'll eat is at the diner, so that's where we're going. You can play the game when we get back."

"Ugh, fine."

Darrell was sitting in his chair when they came out. "All fixed?" he asked.

"Yeah, it was an internet connection issue. Had nothing to do with the game or the player." Ephraim nudged his son forward. "Caleb, you have something to say to your Grandpa?"

"Sorry," Caleb murmured.

Darrell feigned deafness. "What was that?"

"He said it, Dad. We're going to Harold's."

Darrell made a grunt of disapproval. "You gotta be kidding me. Kicked out of school, he gets a video game. Throws a tantrum, gets taken out to eat. Boy, I wish you were my daddy. I would have gotten somebody pregnant and gotten a car or something."

"Appreciate the criticism, Dad. Helps a ton."

"Anytime."

* * *

The bell atop the door jingled when they entered. Lucia looked up from where she was wiping down a table and beamed. "Welcome to Harold's." She came straight to their table to take their orders, and as she stood there Ephraim ran a furtive hand up the side of her leg. When he reached the hemline of her skirt, Lucia rapped his knuckles with her pen, though a smile hinted at the corners of her lips.

"I missed you yesterday," she said to Caleb.

"Thanks," he said flatly.

"You want what you always want?" Caleb nodded, and she said, "You got it, sweetie."

When Lucia left to put their order in, Caleb started drawing on the placemat with the crayons she'd given him.

Ephraim got on his phone, brought up the *Cain City Dispatch*'s website. There was a single article posted about the discovery of the Lincoln and the body with it. It had been updated several times and Ephraim read through them, getting the latest information first. Authorities had released the identity of the deceased and linked his death to the multiple homicides two days prior at the Sundown Courts Motel.

There were few other concrete details. The police were searching for three persons of interest in the case, but no mention of motive, no mention of money, missing or otherwise. One odd piece of information they did report was the police's failure to remove the crashed vehicle from the irrigation channel. Ephraim had watched that mishap through his binoculars. The article stated that the police wrecker had been damaged, so the vehicle would not be hauled in until they repaired the wrecker or subcontracted another one to do the job.

There was a video link to an interview with the lead detective on the case, the black man Ephraim had seen through his binoculars. He clicked on the link. The video took a moment to render, then came on loud, and Ephraim quickly lowered the volume.

"What are you watching?" Caleb asked.

"Nothing."

"Can I watch?"

"No." Ephraim clicked off the video and put his phone away. "Whatcha drawing there?"

"A dog."

Ephraim tilted his head to get a better look at the artwork. It could have been a dinosaur. It could have been anything with four legs. "Oh yeah? That's pretty good, bud. That's a good snout. What kind of dog is it?"

"I dunno. A beagle."

"A beagle, huh?"

"It's no good," Caleb said quickly. He started to scribble it out.

"No, it's good. Don't do that." Ephraim grabbed his hand to stop him from ruining the picture. "You still want a dog?"

"I've always wanted a dog, but you said we can't ever get a dog because you're allergic."

"Depends on the dog. Some are worse than others. I get you a dog, you gonna take care of it?"

Caleb looked up from his coloring. "Don't mess with me."

"I'm not. You want a dog, I'll get you a dog. I'll get used to it. Gotta promise to take care of it though. I'm not cleaning up its crap every day, and you know Grandpa's not. What kind you want, a beagle?"

Caleb nodded in disbelief, not quite trusting his ears.

Ephraim said, "I think I can manage that. You got a name picked out?"

"Yeah. Turbo."

"Turbo? Well, we better make it a boy dog then."

Caleb cracked a wide smile that buoyed Ephraim and he thought, if it could be like this, just like this, always, he could make it through this life. And at that instant the image of the police dog sniffing around the rocks at the bottom of the landslide came to him. *That's where it is,* he thought. *Gotta be. Rodney buried it somewhere in those rocks.*

Lucia set an apple juice in front of Caleb, coffee for Ephraim, and told them she was taking a five-minute break, but that she'd be back before their food came up. She walked across to the hallway leading back to the bathrooms, glanced over her shoulder at Ephraim as she went. He told Caleb he had to hit the head and followed her.

A loose brick propped open the exit door at the end of the hallway. Ephraim went out there and found Lucia smoking a cigarette by the dumpsters. The promised cold snap had arrived, the temperature having dropped at least twenty degrees within the hour. Lucia tossed the cig onto the pavement, stamped it out, and tucked her hands into the pockets of her serving apron.

"Hello," she said.

"Hello," he replied, then parroted, "Welcome to Harold's."

"Shut up." She shivered and leaned into him. Ephraim tilted his head, kissed her, and felt all the tension drain from his body. He sank into her, luxuriated in the pillows of her lips. When they broke apart she stepped back and said, "I missed you."

"Oh, me too? Not just Caleb?"

"Yeah, you too. You looked tired."

"Why, thank you. It's been a long couple of days."

"How's Caleb doing?"

"Not great. Took him to the doctor this morning. You should have seen the amount of blood they took out of him. I don't know how he's still walking."

"Do they know what's wrong with him?"

"No, not really. Hopefully these tests will show us something."

"Did the school say he'd be able to come back or what?"

"I dunno. They said maybe when he gets better. I don't know if I even want him going back to that school, you know. He's got the stink of madness on him now. Those kids will never forget all this shit he's pulled."

"I'm sorry."

"Yeah, thanks."

"Is there anything I can do to make your day better?"

"Seeing you makes my day better."

"That's nice."

"Oh, speaking of how nice I am"—Ephraim reached into the pocket of his jeans—"I got something for you." He brought out the small jewelry box. Lucia's expression froze like her brain had glitched. She stared at the object in his hand as though it were coated in battery acid.

"What's that?" she said.

"Open it and see."

"I don't know if I want to."

Ephraim saw then what Lucia was seeing. The box was shaped very much like it might contain a ring. "No, look." He opened it up quickly, revealing the heart-shaped necklace inside. "It's a locket, see. The kind that opens up. Not a—"

"Shoo." Lucia put a hand to her chest, let out a breath. "For a second I thought—"

"No. I mean, I wouldn't—"

"Last night you were talking about taking me to Italy, and then you bring this box out—"

"I mean, I wouldn't do that like this. But if that were something you were interested in—"

"Interested in what? Going to Italy?"

"Yeah, that." Ephraim hesitated. "And the other thing. I didn't think you thought of me that way, but if that were something you were interested in, I'd be amenable to that."

"You would?"

Ephraim couldn't read her. He hadn't expected this conversation, had scarcely thought about the possibility of marriage, but now that the topic had presented itself in accidental form his head had gone delirious, and he felt powerless to stop the words vomiting out of his mouth. "Yeah. I don't know how it'd work, you know. I got my dad living with me, and Caleb's a hot mess. He really likes you though, so I'm sure he'd be okay with it. And my dad, I can't put him in a home, that's just—I promised him I would never do that. But if I'm being honest, he's probably not long for this world—"

"Ephraim."

"Not to mention that I'm technically still married, but I'm sure if I asked Ashlee to—"

"Whoa, Ephraim." Lucia lifted her hands to stop his jabbering, laid them on his chest. "Whoa. You need to slow your roll."

"Yeah. Slow my roll. I can do that."

She took hold of his beard and yanked it lightly. "First of all, I'm flattered."

"Uh-oh."

"No, listen." Lucia paused to figure out the best way to express what she was feeling. "Obviously I'm serious about you, or I wouldn't be doing this. But I think—maybe—we should go on a few more actual dates first."

"Good suggestion. Good suggestion."

"Real dates. Like take me out. You want me for real, you got to earn me."

Ephraim smirked. "I can do that. I've got a solid work ethic. Everybody says so."

"Thank you for the necklace. It's beautiful."

"You're welcome. I just saw it and I wanted you to have it—"

"Shh." She put a finger to his lips. "Put it on me."

"Yes, ma'am."

When Lucia brought the food to the table, Caleb informed her they were going to get a dog.

"Is that so?" Lucia said.

"A beagle. My dad's going to buy it for me."

She raised an eyebrow. "Your father must be in a giving mood these days."

"I know," Caleb said. "I don't know what's gotten into him. Did you get a new necklace?"

Lucia fingered the locket dangling over her breastbone. "You're very observant. I did. A very good friend gave this to me."

"Walmart has some nice stuff," Caleb said, inspecting the gold heart. "Nicer than you'd think." Ephraim covered his face, mortified, and peered up through his fingers at Lucia.

"I guess they do," she said.

"Your friend must be nice." Caleb shot a sly look across the table at his father. "He must be real nice."

"He has his attributes," Lucia said.

Later that night, Ephraim tousled his son's hair as he tucked him into bed, and asked him if he was feeling any better.

"I dunno. Maybe. Dad?"

"Yeah, bud."

"Do you think I'm ever gonna feel better? I mean really better. Like normal. Or is it always gonna be like this?"

"You will get better," Ephraim assured him. If he were being honest, Ephraim would admit that he was racked with worry over this very thing. Would Caleb ever improve? Get back to the clever, happy-go-lucky kid he once was? Or were those days gone for good? Was this just their life now, a snaking descent into the purgatory of mental illness? It was impossible not to think of Ashlee, and wonder if he was fooling himself that Caleb's troubles were anything other than a genetic bad hand. Maladies passed down from generation to generation, picking up momentum through the centuries until they've come home to roost, now, in the body of his son, a boy who'd scarcely lived a decade.

"For sure," Ephraim said, as much to convince himself as Caleb. "And you're gonna be so tough, tougher than anybody else, because you will have conquered this huge, bastard thing. No one will have gone through the trials you have. Suffered what you're suffering. After this, everything else in life is gonna seem like a piece of cake, I'm telling you."

"Dad?"

"Yeah, bud."

"If I die in my sleep and I come to visit you, like you said, before I go to whatever it is that waits for us, do you think you'll know I'm there?"

"I don't know. But that's not something you need to worry about."

"Do you think I would go to visit Mom, too, or no?"

"I don't know. Would you want to visit Mom?"

"I dunno. I mean, you said you would go and visit everybody who is special to you."

"Yeah," Ephraim granted. "That is what I said."

"But how would I know where to go?"

"To find Mom?"

"Uh-huh."

"I don't know, bud. I don't have all the answers. Listen, we don't need to even think about this cause you're not gonna die in your sleep. Okay?"

"How do you know?"

"I just know. You're going to live a long, happy life."

Caleb didn't say anything.

"Kiss tonight?" Ephraim asked.

"Not tonight."

"Okay. Get some sleep."

Ephraim turned out the lights, went out and sat on the couch in the living room, intending to watch TV with his dad, catch the ten o'clock news before work, but sleep took him within a minute and next thing he knew Darrell was shaking him awake.

Ephraim lurched from his slumber, knocking into his father. Darrell stumbled backward, hit against the grandfather clock, and fell over the armrest of the recliner. Luckily he landed softly in the seat, his arms and legs pedaling the air like an overturned pill bug.

"Shit. Sorry, Dad." Ephraim rushed to help his father sit up and get his feet on the floor. "You okay?"

"I'm fine. I'm fine," Darrell said brusquely. He didn't like being fussed over like an invalid and waved Ephraim's concerns away as though they were melodramatic. His oxygen tubes had come out of his nose and he fixed them back. "If you're trying to off me you're gonna have to do better than that."

"Gotcha. So, down the stairs next time?"

"Ha!" Darrell exclaimed. "Now you're talking. Or better yet, just lay me at the bottom of the driveway."

"Oops, I didn't see him."

"Exactly. Make sure you get me with both sets of wheels."

"I see you've been thinking about this."

"Only a little. Don't bother burying me, by the way. I want to be cremated."

"Yeah, you've only mentioned that a couple hundred times." Ephraim plopped back down on the couch. His vision was still fuzzy from sleep and he blinked his eyes clear.

"Have to make sure the information sinks into your thick brain," Darrell said. "And spread my ashes in places that matter. A little bit by your mother's grave. A little bit in the rose garden down at Redding Park. Behind the stone wall."

"Why there?"

"You don't have to know everything. Put the rest of me in the river. I'll flow down the Ohio to the Mississippi and into the Gulf and then out to sea. I'll float around the world."

"Good thing you told me. I was probably just gonna dump you out back and piss on you."

Darrell laughed. "Save a little for that too, if it's something you feel the need to do."

"I'm kidding."

"I know."

"Why is fucking everybody talking about dying today?"

"Probably 'cause they haven't invented a cure for it yet. You getcha a good nap?"

"Must've. I went deep fast."

"I'd say so. Thought you may have crossed over to the other side yourself."

"Not yet. What time is it?"

"Time for you to get to work."

"Shit." Ephraim looked at the hands of the grandfa-ther clock: 10:22. He rubbed his eyes and pushed himself up from the couch. Darrell held a lotto ticket out to him. Ephraim took it. "What's this?"

Darrell bobbed his head around gleefully. "That there is a winner. Got three numbers. You can exchange it for another one."

"And the beat goes on. A whole buck. Congratulations."

"Thank you, son. Big day." Darrell chortled. "Big day. Lady Luck is on my side."

CHAPTER TWENTY-THREE
THE STENDER INQUISITION

By the time Ephraim pulled the Ranger into work the temperature had dipped to below freezing for the first time since winter. He cut through the maintenance shop to avoid having to walk the long way around to the change room. Bo Wayne and Don Sparks were rummaging through the tool chests on the backs of their bikes, making sure they were set with everything they needed for their shift.

"Looky here," Bo Wayne said, elbowing his buddy. "Whatchoo think, you think he's the one they after?"

Don Sparks was bent over, hairy ass-crack exposed, hand-pumping air into one of his tires. He fixed a leery eye on Ephraim and said, "He did thief my bike two nights ago."

Ephraim didn't break stride. "You still bent out of shape cuz I took your baby for a joyride, Sparky?"

"Me? Noooo. But the police are asking all kinds of questions about Tuesday night. Asking if anything strange happened."

That stopped Ephraim walking. He turned around, tried to sound casual. "Fuck you talking about, police?"

"We got some excitement around here tonight, boy," Bo Wayne said. "Police are wanting to know if we saw any-

thing suspicious during our shift. Some kind of murder or
something happened down a ways from here."

Don Sparks swiveled on his haunches, shit-eating glee
smeared across his pufferfish-shaped face. "Specifically,
they asked if we saw anything down there on the south
end of the plant. Down your way."

"No shit?" Ephraim said. "And that was your big scoop
for the cops, huh? I took your bike for a ride?"

"Sure as shit that's the only weird thing I saw Tuesday night."

Ephraim found Billy Horseman sitting in front of his
locker, tucking his crotch into his pants.

"You hear the hubbub?" Billy said.

"Yeah." Ephraim opened his locker and began un-
dressing.

"Everybody's saying they're asking about our end of
the plant. You see anything out of the ordinary Tuesday?"

"Besides you throwing a bullfrog in the furnace,
you mean?"

"Aw, shit," Billy said. "You think I should tell them
about that?"

"No, Billy. I do not think you should tell them
about that."

Billy grinned. "You think I should tell them about
your girlfriend coming to visit you?"

"You better fucking not. You saw us?"

"Course I saw y'all. Relax, I'm just joshin'."

It was a rare occasion when a supervisor visited the
laborer's side of the facilities. Administration had their
own changing quarters that were free of grime and stench.
Ephraim had been in there once. It was like the spa at a fancy hotel, with amenities like soft towels and mini-bottles
of mouthwash, aftershave. They even had a sauna. When

the brass did find reason to set foot in steerage class, a warning call would go up through the whole place. "Supe, supe! Supe's in the house!"

They heard the signal now. Ephraim turned to Billy and spoke in a hushed, hurried tone. "You got any more of those pills you gave me last night?"

"Course."

"I'm gonna need a few more."

"A few. What do I look like to you, a pharmacist?"

The hoots grew closer. "Supe, supe! Supe, supe!"

"Watch this," Billy said. He yanked his pants down, stood up and placed his fists on his hips, Superman-style.

Trent Napier rolled his pudgy ass around the corner and got an eyeful of Billy's bountiful foreskin dangling there like a malformed aardvark. Immediately he shielded his eyes as if he'd been blinded by the sight and made a noise that sounded like regurgitation. Napier composed himself and turned to face the two of them, nose tilted skyward to keep the eye-line leveled above the waist. "You guys hear what's going on about the police being here?"

"The rumors are true then," Billy said seriously. "You and Lou Manns been swappin' kiddie porn."

Ephraim coughed into his fist to suppress a laugh. "Jesus, Billy."

"Sorry," Billy said. "Really, Mr. Napier, I'm sorry. Don't lay me off, please. It's a condition, I swear, like verbal diarrhea or something. Something comes into my brain and I just spit it out. I can't help myself."

Napier, who didn't see humor in much, stayed true to form. "Get dressed and follow me, please. They've been waiting for the two of you."

Napier's distended stomach jutted out at such an obtuse angle that when he walked, it looked as if the belly were leading him and not the other way around. So the belly steered the three of them into the Administration building and into the hallway outside the conference room where they normally conducted their shift meetings. Napier instructed Ephraim to sit and wait. They wanted to talk to Billy first.

Billy arched an eyebrow and pretended to shiver with fear before traipsing into the conference room like he couldn't be less worried. The voices of two men greeted him warmly enough, the doors shut, and the words floating through walls became low, indecipherable vibrations. Napier looked sternly at Ephraim.

"You two haven't done anything stupid, have you?" he asked.

"Define stupid," said Ephraim. Napier frowned at him. "Look, I'm sure Billy's done plenty of stupid stuff. But I don't think it's anything that would warrant the cops coming out here to talk to him, if that's what you're getting at."

"I hope not. I sincerely do. I've convinced the powers that be not to lay off anyone working midnights. It's very difficult to find good workers to fill those spots. But if they think anybody's involved in illegalities, I mean it goes without saying . . ." Napier trailed off.

"Sure, yeah," Ephraim said. "I got you."

Napier gave a somber nod, instructed Ephraim to get to his station as soon as his interview concluded, and repaired back to wherever he'd come from. All kinds of crazy thoughts hurtled through Ephraim's mind. Namely how many years you get for disposing of a body after the fact. The Admin building was one of the few places in the plant that had decent Wi-Fi, but he didn't think it'd be prudent to search out those answers just now, when the web data could easily be traced. He closed his eyes and rehashed everything that'd happened over the last two days, from Rodney Slash showing up and sticking a gun in his face, to the man dying, then needing to clean the station, get rid of the body, search the Mercer farm. *Nobody saw you,* he told himself. *Nobody can prove anything.*

Some fifteen minutes later the door to the conference room swung open and Billy, face ashen with spook, walked out. He glanced at Ephraim with an inscrutable expression and slunk off without saying anything. One of the inquisitors stood in the door. Ephraim recognized him instantly. The black policeman he'd seen running the show at the Mercer farm, the one he'd just watched a clip of on his phone at the diner.

"You Rivers?" he said.

Nobody can prove anything, Ephraim repeated in his mind. He stood. "That's me."

"Come on in."

Every light in the conference room had been turned on. The overhead tubes emitted an ambient buzz. Willis Hively introduced himself and his partner, Clyde Sturges, and invited Ephraim to have a seat, motioning in the general direction of the chair directly across the table from them. Ephraim sat there. A closed laptop and some bottles of water had been placed in the middle of the table and they offered him one. Ephraim declined.

The two detectives kicked off the proceedings by volleying some simple questions: How long he'd worked at Bismark Carbon, where he lived, if he lived alone, where in town he grew up, et cetera. Each had a file in front of them, and after his answers they consulted their own information to see if it matched up. From time to time Sturges jotted a note or something down, like a correction. Ephraim felt as though he were being graded on a pop quiz about his own life.

But Hively and Sturges each spoke with a pleasant, un-hurried tone that lulled Ephraim into a sense of compla-cency. Just as he'd begun to wonder what they'd done to cow Billy, Hively asked, "You know why we're here?" Both detectives abandoned the pretense of paperwork and fixed him with penetrating stares.

"I mean . . . no. There's a rumor going around that you guys were asking about something that happened on the south end of the plant, but yeah, that's all I've heard."

"A man was found murdered on a farm about a mile due south from here," Hively said. The genial tone re-mained, but an acute leap in scrutiny caused Ephraim to shift uneasily in the chair.

Ladies and gentlemen, we've now come to the serious portion of our conversation, he thought.

Sturges said, "You know anything about that?"

"About a murder? No. I saw something on the news about a car hitting a cow and then that, uh . . ." Ephraim wagged his thumb in a southward direction. "That farmer who owned the cow found a crashed car on his property or something. I saw that."

"The Mercer farm, that's where it was. You familiar with it? Off Greasy Ridge Road down there?"

Ephraim scratched at his beard. "Yeah, I mean, I'm aware it exists."

Sturges bore down on him. "You ever go down there for any reason?"

"Down where? To that farm? No."

"Nowhere in that area?"

"Not really."

"Never go hiking down thataway?"

The leap of Ephraim's heart nearly cracked his ster-num. "Oh, well, yeah, I do do that from time to time. I thought you meant . . ." He ran out of words mid-sentence. Beads of sweat rose on the back of his neck and trickled cold down his spine. His mouth went chalky and Ephraim cursed himself for not taking that bottle of water.

"Thought we meant what?" Sturges asked, tilting his head in a perplexed fashion.

"I thought you were still talking about the farm."

"Says here . . ." Sturges thumbed through a couple pages, found what he was looking for. "Says here you were stopped at a roadblock two days ago north on 52. 'Round about 3:00 p.m. You went hiking in the area two days ago?"

"I did, yeah."

"But you didn't see anything out of the ordinary?"

"No. Well, I take that back." Ephraim forced a little chuckle. "I did come across a rattlesnake up there. Thing shot out right at me, liked to scare me half to death."

"That so?"

"Yeah."

"It does say here in the trooper's report, you had a gash on your head."

"Yeah, I fell back trying to get away from it. Hit my head on a damn rock." Ephraim gestured to the injured area on his head.

Sturges cringed. "Ouch. You didn't get a concussion or nothing?"

"No, it wasn't too bad. Just cut me a little."

"Stitches?"

"Naw."

"You know that's private property up there still, right?"

"I didn't, no. Not until that trooper told me. They had a *No Trespassing* sign posted, but I just thought that was from back in the day, you know, when it was being mined."

Sturges asked him a few more questions about his hikes, detail-oriented stuff about how steep the hike was, what the terrain was like, the elevation of the mountain. It was to Ephraim's good fortune that he'd just gone up there, so he could answer these inquiries with some semblance of truth.

Sturges said, "So that mining company cut the top of that mountain off back in the day, didn't they?"

"They did," Ephraim said. "It's kinda cool-looking, actually. The way they do it."

"Yeah. I've seen it from the ground and from the top. Looks like a wedding cake."

"Yeah."

"You ever seen it from the ground?"

"Where they chopped up the mountain? No."

"You able to see down into the valley from up top there?"

"Partly. You can get a view of the far end of it if you get all the way up to the tip-top there, but where they shaped the mountain it cuts off where you can't see directly below."

"That so?" Sturges considered that for a moment. "You mean you can see a ways up to the barns, thataway?"

"Right, yeah." Ephraim cut his eyes over at Hively, who hadn't shifted his posture in any discernible way, or even blinked. He stared at Ephraim, hands flat on the table, unmoving, like a goddamned Sphinx.

Sturges continued. "So you didn't see anything strange in the valley on your hike that day?"

"No. I didn't even make it to the top. Went back down after that rattler, you know, scared the bejesus out of me."

"Gotcha," Sturges said. "Sounds like a cool hike. Shame you won't be able to go back up there."

"Yeah. Gotta find somewhere new to tool around, I reckon. There's plenty of places. I just like that one. Peaceful. Nobody around."

"What kind of car you drive?"

"What kind of—? A Ranger. Ford Ranger."

"That so? You know what kind of tires you got on it?"

"I should know," Ephraim said. "But I don't."

"You remember where you got them from?"

"Down at the Firestone place off 64 is where I usually go. It's been a while. Why?"

"We're just checking. Got some tire prints out there at the Mercer farm we're trying to match up. What kind of tires were those out there, Willis? You remember?"

"One set of tracks was made by a Destination A/T2 tire," Hively answered. "From Firestone."

Sturges's mouth curved into a tight smile that made his chin recede and multiply. "Could be nothing. You don't mind if we take a look at your tires, do ya?"

"No," Ephraim said. "It's out there in the lot if you need to look at it."

"That'd be swell. We just have to go through the paces, you understand. Do our due diligence. Cross off all possibilities until there's only one left."

"Sure."

Ephraim's vision started tunneling and his head went light. Beneath the table he clawed at his knees to steady himself. Sturges grabbed one of the water bottles, cracked it open and took a drink. Without missing a beat, as if this were an invisible baton pass rehearsed to precision, Hively stepped in.

"South end of the plant, that's where you work?"

"Yep," Ephraim nodded. "I operate the two D activators down there."

"And Billy Horseman operates"—Hively checked his notes—"the two D-line bakers."

"That's right."

"And you two are the only people down at that end of the plant at night?"

"Generally speaking, yeah. There might be a rare occasion Napier comes down there, or one of the guys from the maintenance shop comes down."

"But not on Tuesday night into Wednesday morning. You two were you the only ones down there that night?"

"Far as I know." Ephraim looked between the two of them. "Why?"

Hively raised an eyebrow. "You want to know why? I'll show you." Hively opened the laptop and spun it around to where Ephraim could see the monitor. A video was loaded. He tapped "play."

The grainy footage of a security camera popped up on the screen. Wednesday's date in the bottom-left corner, a running time stamp at 1:37 a.m. the only thing moving in the static shot. The angle and the brightness of the immediate foreground indicated the camera was set high on one of the light posts beside the defunct railroad that led through the center of the plant. The image was of the tracks, south-facing, as it ran into the blackness of the woods.

"You were aware of the security cameras situated throughout the plant?" Hively asked.

"Yes," Ephraim said. A lump big as a melon now lodged firmly in the crux of his throat. He swallowed it down, stared intently at the screen. "What am I looking for?"

"Wait for it."

Seven long seconds later the small shape of a person emerged from the darkness of the woods. They hobbled down the middle of the track, clutching at their stomach. At one point they fell to their knees, stayed like that for a bit, then pushed their way back to standing and staggered off beside the track and off camera. Hively cut the video and shut the laptop.

"Do you know who that is?" he asked.

"No," Ephraim said. "I can't tell. It's too far away and it's too dark, too blurry."

"Can you tell where he's going when he walks off the track?"

"No. I mean, I don't know. But that's over by us. Over by where we are."

"That's right," Hively said. "It is. Now, unfortunately for us the only other security cameras in this place are of the main entrance, the parking lot, and this building that we're in now. But that's the funny thing here, Mr. Rivers. Whoever this man is, he never pops up on any other camera. No trace of him. So that leaves us with three possibilities. Either he's vanished into thin air, he's still here at the plant, or somebody's taken him out of here."

Sturges chimed in. "So maybe we should ask you again. Did you see anything, hear anything, or even smell anything out of the ordinary on Tuesday night?"

"No," Ephraim said evenly. "Do you mind telling me what's going on?"

Hively studied him for a protracted moment. "Sure. While we were investigating the murder on the Mercer farm, our police dogs happened to pick up a scent that led all the way from that farm, through the woods"—Hively walked his fingers across the table to illustrate his story—"down the road, onto the tracks, and alllll the way to the south end of Bismark Carbon." Here the detective tapped the table as if to point out a dot on a map. "Now this baffled us at first, because we believed the scene of our crime, at least that part of it that occurred out at the farm, was contained to that area. So it came as something of a shock to find this footage. Do you want to know where the dogs lost the trail?"

The buzz from the overhead lights seemed to all at once grow louder, like somebody was rubbing their wet fingers right beside Ephraim's ears. He stammered, "I mean, if that's something you want to tell me."

"Yeah, I think it's information you should know. Get this. That hound followed that scent right up to your co-worker's door at the Baker Station."

"Really?"

"Really. But that's not all. After that he crossed the way and led us right to your door."

"*Really*?"

"Really. But from there . . ." Hively opened both of his hands wide. "Poof. Gone. Vanished. Now, that seems a little odd, don't you think, that the dog leads us to your two doorsteps, but then nothing? Like the man vanished from the face of the Earth."

"Like he was abducted by aliens from that very spot," Sturges said.

"We had ten guys searching this place high and low all day. Didn't find a thing. Nada. Not a single thing past where the dogs lost that scent. Something about that just doesn't sit right with me. You know what I'm saying?"

"I guess," Ephraim said.

"Yet you and Billy claim nothing unusual took place at all that night."

"Outside of killing a bullfrog," Sturges said.

"Fuck." Ephraim closed his eyes, dropped his head. "That was Billy's idea. He just made me go along with him."

Hively leaned forward. "What are we talking about here?"

Ephraim saw where his words could be mistook and quickly sought to remedy them. "No, no. The bullfrog. Not the guy you're talking about. I don't know anything about that. I'm talking about the frog."

"He made you throw the frog into the furnace?" Sturges asked.

"I didn't touch that frog. Billy, he doesn't take no for an answer easy. I just went along with him to get it over with. It was a boring night. Are you gonna tell our bosses about that? Because they're laying a bunch of people off right now."

"We heard," Hively said.

"Yeah, so, if they get an excuse . . . Look, my son's sick. I take care of my father, whose health is terrible. I can't afford to lose my job right now."

"I'm sorry to hear that."

"Thanks, yeah, so if you could leave out the part about the frog, you know, I'd really appreciate it."

Sturges said, "But that was Billy's doing?"

"Yeah, but like I said, I was there. All they need is an excuse."

"And that was earlier in the night?"

"You mean than the video?" Ephraim asked. "Yeah, that was way earlier."

"But you two were out and about at some points throughout the night?"

Ephraim described how he was in and out of the station a number of times throughout a shift, to take samples of the carbon and monitor the output of the furnaces, make sure nothing got clogged at the mouth of the conveyors, that kind of thing.

"And you saw absolutely nothing during any of those times you were out and about?" Sturges asked.

"Not a thing." Ephraim pretended to think about it a little. "No, I guess I got lucky not to, you know."

"I guess you did."

Sturges said that they'd heard Billy had a bit of a reputation. Some people thought he was funnier than a monkey, while others believed that if anybody were to be involved in illegal activity, or possibly be mixed up with shady types, it'd be him.

"I think that's just sour grapes," Ephraim contended. "If I had to guess, it was Lou Manns told you that. Billy likes to cut up, you know, make jokes at some people's expense. He takes things over the line sometimes, for some of the guys, but in the end, he's just trying to get through the day, like we all are."

"He doesn't cross the line too far for you?" Sturges asked.

"No, well, he doesn't really mess with me like he does some of the guys. He keeps things entertaining at least, I will say that. But I can't see Billy doing anything illegal. He has so many kids for Chrissakes, I don't see how he'd have the time."

Hively put his elbows on the table, turned his palms up. "Look," he said. "This is where we have a problem. Because the man on those train tracks is either a victim of a homicide, or he committed a homicide."

"Or both," said Sturges.

"Now we found a whole puddle of this man's blood where he fell down out there on the tracks, so we're gonna know soon, one way or the other, who he is. Listen to me now." Hively bore his gaze into Ephraim. "The people that we think are involved in this thing. These are bad people. You ever heard the name Momo Morrison?"

"Momo—?"

"Morrison."

"No, I don't think. No."

"What about Buddy Cleamons?"

Ephraim nodded. "Yeah, I know who that is. He was at my high school. Couple years ahead of me."

"When was the last time you saw him?"

"Probably not since then. Since school. Maybe one or two times in a bar or something, years ago. Somebody told me he had some accident, like an animal mauled his head or something. Heard he looks like Darth Vader with his helmet off now."

"He caught his head on fire and lost one of his eyes," Hively said.

"Shit."

"Not at the same time. These were two separate incidents. You ever heard of the Stenders?"

"Sure, yeah. I've heard of them."

"Do you know anyone who is now, or has ever been, in the Stenders?"

Ephraim leaned back in his seat, held out his hands as if to physically repel the question. "Noooo. No way. I steer clear of anything like that. I've heard the stories though, you know."

"What stories?" Sturges prompted.

"I dunno, you know, some of the stuff is like urban legend. How they control all kinds of businesses in the West End. How anybody who messes with them gets disappeared real quick, ends up buried in the woods somewhere. That kind of stuff."

"It ain't no legend," Sturges said.

Hively broke in. "These people we're talking about would just as soon kill you as shake your hand. And if you cross them in any way, forget it. Your old classmate Buddy Cleamons is one of them."

"Can't say I'm shocked. He was always somebody you were best off avoiding."

Hively puffed out some air. "I'd say that holds true to-day more than ever. You said you watch the news from time to time. Did you see the coverage on the shootout at the Sundown Courts the other night?"

Ephraim gulped. "I did catch that, yeah."

"Then you know. These are those people. Not to bela-bor the point, but if you know anything at all about this, whether you're involved or not, I'm talking anything, now is the time to tell us. Before it gets too big. Before it goes too far. This is our chance to help you, or protect you. Whatever we gotta do."

Ephraim's eyes pinballed back and forth between them. "I appreciate that, guys. I do, but I swear to you I don't know anything about any of this." The detectives didn't respond. They just watched him mutely. Ephraim continued. "To be honest with you, I'm pretty freaked out that whoever this was—was out there by us, probably try-ing to get in our stations or whatever."

"But your doors are locked out there, right?" asked Sturges. "Automatically. That's what Billy told us."

"Yeah. Thank goodness."

Hively said, "But you see how this looks a little funny to us, right?"

"What do you mean, funny?"

"Suspicious. You hiking out there by the crime scene the day after all this shit went down. You and Billy being the only people on the south end of the plant. The person in that vid-eo"—Hively pointed at the computer—"had to go somewhere."

"I don't know what to tell you," Ephraim said. "I wish I could help." He and Hively sat there contemplating one another for a long beat, Ephraim doing his best to effect a guileless expression.

"Okay," Hively said finally. "We'll be in touch if we think of anything else. Thank you for your time." He slapped down on both his knees and stood up. "Oh, one more thing. You mind giving us a little tour of the south end of the plant? Show us around, kind of take us through your typical night?"

"I thought you guys had already searched the whole place," said Ephraim.

"We have, but we'd like to get it from the vantage of somebody who knows the lay of the land."

"Sure, if it's okay with Mr. Napier."

"It's okay," Hively assured him. "We've already cleared it."

CHAPTER TWENTY-FOUR
SCORCH THE BONES

Sporting ill-fitting hard hats and protective goggles, the two detectives followed Ephraim through the wind and cold to the south end of the plant. As they drew near, Ephraim saw the yellow police tape cordoning off the area of track where Rodney Slash had fallen to his knees and poured out his blood. He escorted the men to his station and demonstrated the key-card access, but neglected to tell them how the catch on the doorjamb sometimes failed to latch if you didn't shut the door hard enough.

"So nobody could have gotten in?" Hively asked.

"Not without a key card."

"Or someone letting them in."

"Or that. But I'm the only one in here."

Inside Ephraim took them to his workroom, gave a brief tutorial on the process of extracting carbon from coal, and explained what the readings on the computer meant. The detectives explored the rest of the place—hall-way, bathroom, utility closet. Ephraim made sure to enter the breakroom first, flipped on the lights, acted like he was casually standing aside to let them pass. What he was really doing was obstructing the view of the stain on the wall. It looked even lighter now than it had the night before. Hardly noticeable, but he didn't want to advertise it. Hively and Sturges had a short gander at the room and were satisfied.

Ephraim then led them through the duties of his typical shift, took them to the packaging area where the samples were collected, then to the bottom of the furnace where the carbon came out on the conveyor. He described how the operators were tasked with making sure nothing was getting caught up in the grizzly bars, jamming up the works.

"And where'd you guys go to murder the bullfrog?" Hively asked.

Ephraim pointed up at the activator. "Up there."

"Take us."

As the three men trudged up the metal stairs, Hively asked. "If you don't mind me asking, what's wrong with your son?"

"Still trying to figure it out," Ephraim answered. "Had a bunch of tests run on him today. 'Fraid it has something to do with his brain. He's kinda lost control of himself."

"I'm sorry. I hope it all turns out okay."

"Thanks."

They reached the fourth-level landing and Ephraim showed them the door to the hearth, explained how it opened. Hively asked him to open it now.

"We're not supposed to," Ephraim yelled to be heard over the din of the machinery. "It can mess with the temperature of the furnace."

"But you did it the other night?"

"Yeah," Ephraim admitted. "But only for a second. That doesn't affect it too bad really."

"Then open it for a second."

Ephraim did as he was told. As soon as the hatch opened the detectives felt the scorch of the heat sweep over them, the immediate siphon of oxygen. They peered into the lava-like glow of the flames and watched the rabble arms inside guiding the heated carbon through the conveyor.

"How hot is it in there?" Sturges shouted.

"Sixteen hundred degrees, give or take."

"Fahrenheit?"

Ephraim nodded in the affirmative.

"What happened when you threw the bullfrog in?"

Ephraim winced, regretful. "It pretty much just exploded."

"Huh. Anything left of it?"

"Naw, that thing was toast."

Hively stepped up to the hatch, took measure of it with his arms. "You could fit a person into these things."

"I suppose you could, yeah," Ephraim agreed.

"What would happen to them?"

"Well." Ephraim tocked his head back and forth. "If you put it in at the top, the ninth level up there, I reckon by the time they got to the bottom there'd be nothing left of 'em for the most part. But a person is bigger, obviously, so probably some bones might make it through."

"And where would they go?" asked Hively.

"If they don't get caught in those grizzly bars at the bottom, I guess they'd mix in with the carbon that goes into the super sacks."

"What are the chances they'd get caught up?"

Ephraim shrugged. "I'd say pretty good. They'd probably be bigger than the carbon. Shaped different."

"And if they didn't, the super sacks, those were those giant bags we saw in packaging?"

"Yeah."

"Fuck," Hively muttered. He looked at Sturges, then back to Ephraim. "How much carbon is in each one of those bags?"

"Thousand pounds' worth."

This number struck Sturges funny, the sheer size of it.

He let out a hearty laugh that set his whole body to jiggling. When the hilarity petered out, Sturges made the point: "Be a great way to dispose of a body though."

Ephraim didn't know how to respond to that, so he stayed silent.

In the roughly six hours the detectives spent on the grounds of Bismark Carbon, only half of those spent in the elements, a thin layer of soot had settled over their persons. The half-inch cuff of shirtsleeve that protruded from Hively's jacket, once white, was now flecked gray. He tried to brush it off, to no avail. The effort just smeared the coal dust around.

Napier was waiting for them in his office. At hearing what the detectives had in mind, he nearly choked on his spit. "You want to search the super sacks for *what*?"

"Bones," Hively said. "Or rather, remnants of bones."

"You think someone put a human body in one of our hearths?"

"We think it's a possibility."

"You gotta be kidding me." Napier put his hands over his eyes and then dragged them down his fleshy face. He took a deep wheezing breath. "Okay. I'll call the GM. But, so you know, we ship millions of pounds of carbon out of here every day. The stuff that got packaged overnight on Tuesday, it's long gone."

"Where to?"

"Our vendors."

"How many vendors?"

"Hundreds. All over the country."

Hively cinched his mouth tight to quell his mounting frustration. "If there's a bone in one of those sacks, what are the chances we find it?"

Napier made an iffy face. "It's not impossible. But not likely. I'd say it'd be akin to finding a needle in a haystack."

"Great," Hively seethed. "Just fucking great."

By the time they got back to their car it was nearly 1:00 a.m. Hively dove in behind the wheel and sped them around the curves of the state road, bombing up and down the dips. The only noise coming from the windshield wipers Hively turned on when the murky sky started spitting sleet. Sturges held off on broaching any words until they hit the relative safety of the highway. He considered his partner who was leaning forward in the seat, white-knuckling the steering wheel.

"I already know what you are going to say," said Hively, without looking over.

"Oh, yeah? You've joined my wife. The two people in the world who think they can read my mind."

"I'm getting real, real sick of this shit, Clyde. Our whole job, I swear to God, all we do is, we come on the scene after the mess has already been made, look around at the carnage humans do to one another, say, 'Oh, I wonder how this mess got made,' and we bumble around trying to figure something, anything out. We're stewards of crime, that's all we are. We don't stop anything. Maybe we change its shape, divert it for a little while."

"You're getting too deep now, buddy. You've lost me. But I can see that you're a little keyed up."

"What gave me away?"

"What I was going to say was, I can see the anger shimmering off of you like the heat off those furnaces."

Hively threw a vicious look Sturges's way, then focused back on the road. "This one's slipping away already. And it's one of those—it's just going to keep rippling. I can feel it. And now, what? We gotta just sit on our hands and cross our fingers and hope that someone spots a piece of bone in Montana or some far-flung place? That might be Rosalind Tackett in that surveillance footage."

"Yeah, I thought of that."

"Now she's just gone, forever. That little boy will never know what happened to his mother. He may never even have a mother."

Hively squeezed the steering wheel as though he were trying to crush the vinyl, released it and slammed his palm against the top of the column. They rode quietly for a few miles, listening to the rumble of the tires, the swish of the wipers.

"You done throwing a hissy?" Sturges asked. "You need a Snickers?" Hively shot him another look designed to wilt all those it landed on. In their time together Sturges had never seen his partner this discouraged before. Never quite this charged, emotionally. Granted, Hively's de facto operation setting was a high simmer, but this was the first time Sturges had witnessed him boil over. Unfettered, he continued, "Look, there's a lot of loose threads in this case. This mystery person wandering into Bismark Carbon is just one of them. All we need is to tug on the right thread. You'll see. We've got the list of vendors where the carbon went. I'll start calling them in the morning, alerting them to the situation."

Hively shook his head. "I'm done letting them get away with all this shit."

"Who?"

"Everybody. Stenders. People vanishing into thin air. This shit reeks of them."

"Yeah, it does," Sturges agreed. "But none of the guys we just interviewed read Stender to me. Did they to you?"

"No, but what does that really mean? I've sat across from killers who seemed like they'd be the best neighbors on Earth. Who *were* the best neighbors on Earth. Pulled your garbage cans up for you, that sort of thing."

"True," Sturges agreed. "But these were simple guys working a tough job just trying to keep on keeping on. They were scared for their employment, first and foremost. Not scared of going to jail because they just killed a person and disposed of a body."

"That right there. That's what I knew you were gonna say. But those two that work on the south end of the plant, Horseman and Rivers, they looked clammy as hell."

"Sure. Let's book 'em," Sturges said facetiously. "I got news for you, Willis. Police make people nervous."

"Maybe because they have reason to be nervous."

"Maybe. But answer me this. What Stender have you ever sat across from ever showed any fear? They're always cocky as shit because they think they got backing, which, as we've seen in the not-too-distant past, they aren't wrong about. Far as we know, Stenders don't have a hand in any of Bismark's labor unions. Nobody who's ever worked there has ever been linked to them in any way, so."

"First for everything."

Sturges sloughed his shoulders and sighed. "No arguing with platitudes."

Hively couldn't come off it. "They know something. Got to. Look at this." He brought out his phone, navigated to his photos, and handed it to his partner. On the screen was the first in a series of close-up pictures Hively had taken of Ephraim Rivers's tires. "Now scroll back two or three."

Sturges swiped back to a photograph of the tread print in the ground at the Mercer farm.

"Tell me those don't look similar," said Hively.

Sturges hawed. "Sure, it's close. We'll show the techs, but what's it gonna prove? Tens of thousands of trucks probably have those tires around here. And we know his truck didn't leave Bismark the whole night Tuesday. You saw the footage of his car going in and out of the lot just like I did."

"What if he finds the person wandering in, wounded, has an idea what it's all about, calls somebody, and they tell him to get rid of the body? He basically just showed us the method he would have done it with in those furnaces."

"That's a big leap for somebody with no record to speak of. What do you think, that bullfrog was a practice run for a body?"

"No," Hively conceded. "They couldn't have known that person was coming off the tracks."

"Exactly. So all he showed us, in the end, is where his buddy doomed a frog to hell. Besides, it'd be easier to just drag a body through the woods to the river and throw it in."

"That's gotta be three, four hundred yards away."

"Still."

"If that were the case, we'd be equally screwed, just sitting on our hands waiting for a corpse to float up."

"Pretty much," Sturges granted. "You mind me asking why you're taking this so personal?"

Hively chafed. "What are you, my therapist now?"

"They couldn't pay me enough."

"We're just—" Hively grit his teeth, wagged his head. "Fuck, we're missing something."

"We're always missing something. That's why the criminals always have two legs up on us. They get to move first, they get to break the rules. We're reactive. It's the nature of the gig. We have to be diligent and actually prove shit. The deck is stacked in their favor. This is not new information."

"I'd pay you to stop talking right now."

"Tell you what. We find that bag of money, we can split it up, and you'll never have to see me again in your life."

"Yeah, right," Hively said, his tone lifting a little. "You wouldn't know what to do with it, you got you a windfall. Probably blow it all at the dog track."

"No, no, my friend. I know exactly what I would do with my riches. Key West. You ever seen Key West? Beautiful. It's like swimming in bathwater. You can see clear down to the bottom of the ocean. Hundred feet, clear down. I'd stick my toes in the surf every day, lay my fat ass on the sand, and bake. Drink volcanoes until my liver falls out of my asshole."

"That's an unpleasant image."

"Don't disparage my dreams, Willis. You can come visit, you and the family. I'll even put on some clothes when you do, so as not to scare the girls."

"The locals would probably mistake you for a washed-up beluga whale. Spear your ass for dinner."

"There's worse ways to go. Listen . . ." Sturges sat forward to catch Hively's eye. "Not to put too fine a point on it, but we got blood, we got bodies, we got suspects, we got more forensics than we know what to do with. Something will tear the roof off the sucker. Besides, if anybody can solve this thing, it's us. We're the great black-and-white hope of Cain City."

"Don't ever say that aloud to anyone ever again." Hively took the exit for Clifford Avenue.

Sturges sat back and went thoughtful for a moment. "Maybe Horseman or Rivers saw something they weren't sure about. Maybe more than that. Perhaps they were even threatened. One thing's for sure, now they know who's involved, their mouths are sealed tighter than a frog's twat. They ain't saying shit."

"I don't think it's that simple," Hively countered. "Rivers going on hikes up there, that irks me. We need to stay on those two, if no one else."

Sturges threw up his hands. "You ask me, we have bigger fish to fry, i.e., tracking down the perps who actually pulled the trigger on these homicides. But you do you. Far be it for me to get in the way of one of your crackerjack hunches. I know better than that."

"That's right, Clyde. Cause you have a choice. You can either swim with the current or you can swim against it." Hively's mouth split into a thin grin. "And I'm the current."

"Solid callback," Sturges said.

CHAPTER TWENTY-FIVE
THE LOW FROG

Ephraim ran into Billy Horseman in the change room after their shift. Before Ephraim even said a word, Billy was apologizing.

"I told you not to tell them one thing, Billy," Ephraim scolded in a low hiss, so as not to be overheard. "One thing."

"I know. They was freakin' grilling me, man. Acting like I had done something wrong. I had to tell them something to get them off my back. I'm sorry."

"They tell Napier about that goddamn frog, we're gone, Billy. It's no small wonder we still got jobs as it is."

"I know. I'm sorry, E. It just came spillin' out. It comes to it I'll take the fall, all right? Tell them you didn't even know what was going on. I tricked you into coming up there, saying I needed help with something or something."

"Tell me you didn't blurt to them about the weed."

"I'm not stupid," Billy said. Ephraim looked at him deadpan. "Okay, I'm not *that* stupid."

They compared notes on what questions the police put to them. Ephraim omitted the parts of his interrogation that concerned his being in the vicinity of the crime scene the day after it occurred. The scripts between the two interrogations seemed to be largely similar. This eased the knot of anxiety in Ephraim's chest.

"Man, that video they showed us gave me the heebie-jeebies." Billy shivered. "To think a fucking killer strolled right up to our doorstep like that. Right close enough where we could smell its dragon breath. Could have been us on the news right along with that fella they found dead out there."

"Yeah."

"They ask you what kind of tires you got?"

"Yeah, they did. I didn't know."

"You don't know the tires you got on your truck? And you check the box on the census says 'male'."

"What kind of tires do you have?"

"Got me some Nitto Grapplers."

"Well, good for you, Billy. You got those pills for me?"

When Ephraim got home, he found Darrell in the kitchen frying up some eggs. They sat together at the table, Darrell wearing the oxygen tube over his forehead like a headband so he could eat. Caleb was still asleep. Darrell said he'd gotten up at three in the morning to take a leak and saw the light from the TV still on in Caleb's room.

"What the hell is he doing up at three in the morning?" Ephraim said.

"Beats me," Darrell breathed. "I don't know what's going on with that kid. I peeked in there on him. Said he couldn't sleep. I told him to try to get back to bed soon, but what could I do?"

"Nothing I don't guess."

"You want me to go wake him up?"

"No, let him sleep." Ephraim forked the eggs into his mouth, took a drink of juice. "These are good, Dad. Thanks for breakfast."

"Well, I felt bad about what I said last night."

"I don't even remember."

"'Bout how you're coddling Caleb. I shouldn't be butting in like I do. Don't listen to me."

"Don't worry, I don't."

"And I know you been working hard. Too hard, if you ask me. You got to take care of yourself better. When's the last time you got a good night's sleep?"

Ephraim shrugged. "I dunno. It's been a week."

"It's been a year."

"Yeah."

"Look atcha." Darrell reached across and bopped Ephraim lightly beneath the chin to raise his eyes. "Lord, you look 'bout like death thawed you outta the freezer. People are probably gonna start thinking you're my brother instead of my son."

Ephraim snorted a laugh. "I feel about as old as you."

"You say that now." Darrell took a lump of egg down the wrong hole and it got him coughing. A wet, hollow bark that sounded like his lungs had been scraped to bits. He hocked some mucus into his paper napkin.

"Maybe you should go see the doctor, Dad."

"Ach." Darrell waved him off. "What are they gonna do? 'Sides, we got enough to worry about." He sucked in some air to steady his breathing. "Sometimes I think I'm ready for it to just be done."

"Don't start this again, please."

"What? It's true. You'd be better off without me anyway, don't you think?"

"No, I don't think. Who would look after Caleb?"

"Ha! Money you save on my damn medications, you could probably hire someone."

"True." Ephraim feigned mulling this over. "There is your social security checks to consider. How long you think I could get away with cashing them?"

Darrell tapped the side of his head. "Now you're thinking. Best to get in on that before the government takes it away for good."

"Stop it. Oh . . ." Ephraim retrieved his wallet and fished out the fresh lottery ticket he'd purchased on the way in to work, slid it over. Darrell squinted at it to make sure the numbers were right. "They're all there," said Ephraim. "Everybody's birthdays. Your mother's, mine, yours, Mom's, Caleb's, Ashlee's."

"Just makin' sure."

"Have I ever gotten 'em wrong? Maybe you should pick a new number instead of Ashlee's. Unlucky. Probably why you haven't won yet."

"Nope," Darrell said. "You gotta play the same numbers. Thataway, odds gotta increase every time they don't hit. I pick a new number, it's like starting from scratch."

"Ohhhh," Ephraim gibed. "I didn't know this was a mathematical approach you were taking. All we have to do is keep playing those numbers for roughly two thousand more years and they're bound to hit. The forty-fifth generation of Rivers will be in the money. Movin' on up."

"Listen, smartass. I don't play this for me, you know. What am I gonna do with millions of dollars? I can barely walk for Chrissakes. Next year you'll probably be wiping my ass. I play it for you and for him." Darrell gestured in roughly the direction of Caleb's bedroom. "Besides, the universe owes this family one."

This sparked Ephraim laughing. "If only that's how the universe worked, Dad. And so you know, I'm never, ever, not in a *million* years, gonna wipe your ass."

"Oh, just you wait. That's the way it works. Get your ass wiped on the way in, get your ass wiped on the way out. In the middle, you do the wiping. Them's the breaks."

"That's when the pillow comes out in your sleep."

Darrell nibbled his toast. "Just remember where to spread my ashes."

"Hold them out the window while I drive down 64, right?"

"Exactly."

"You're a morbid old fusspot, you know it?"

They talked some more, random things that fathers and sons talk about: The Bengals' chances of fielding a winning team. The amount of antacids Darrell had been consuming to soothe his gut. The time when Ephraim was a child looking out the window at a low fog and Darrell had commented, "Foggy out there." To which Ephraim, in his squeaky toddler voice, replied, "Does it go ribbit, ribbit?" How Darrell had been a spotter on a helicopter clipping low along the Cambodian border, ten days left in his tour, when the VC started winging 50-caliber bullets at them. The Huey diving and zigging through the sky to evade the artillery. Darrell thinking he was a goner. Even had a vision of his family around the Christmas tree, just sitting there sad without him. These were stories they knew by heart, having been told a hundred times over. And these were the ones that stuck, for one reason or another, and turned into family lore.

The discussion inevitably circled back to Caleb, what Ephraim was going to do about him.

"I dunno." Ephraim worked a piece of egg out from between his teeth. "We'll get these tests back and go from there. Probably I'm gonna have to get him into a specialist somewhere. I'll worry about school stuff next week. I don't even have the capacity to think about that right now." He looked at the clock on the microwave. "Speaking of, I picked up another shift. I gotta go."

"You're kidding me."

"No." Ephraim explained about the layoffs. Lied that he was picking up as many shifts as possible just in case.

"You gotta get some rest, son. You're gonna run yourself ragged to where you can't do nothing."

"I know. Hopefully it'll all be settled soon."

"I'm sorry, Ephraim. Maybe it's meant to be, though. You know? Get you out of that plant. Not working nights anymore. That shift work will slowly kill a man. Maybe it'll open up an opportunity somewhere else, you know."

Ephraim stood from the table, rinsed the dishes in the sink. "Tell you what, you see a bunch of opportunities laying around somewhere, you let me know and I'll scoop one up."

"I know, I know," Darrell said grimly. He'd spoken more words that morning than he usually verbalized in an entire day, and that, in combination with the chore of eating, had worn him out, made it hard to draw air, but he had a point to make and he was set on making it. "But things'll work out, you'll see. Hard times come and go. Always gonna be hard times. You just gotta make what you can outta what you got. You stick it out, you'll get your chances," he breathed. "Everybody does. I never recognized mine when they came around. Or maybe I did, but I was just—I don't know what I did."

"You did fine, Pop. You did good." Ephraim placed a hand on his father's shoulder.

"It just goes so fast. I know it doesn't feel like that for you, especially now." Darrell held up his finger, stirred it in a circle. "In the midst of all this, but it does. It goes by like lightning." He reached across his chest and squeezed Ephraim's hand, then patted it. "I'll do anything I can for you, you know that."

"I know you will. We'll be all right." Ephraim leaned down and kissed the top of his father's sun-splotched head, then grabbed the pillbox off the countertop, placed it on the table, and pried open the Friday container. "You can start by taking your medication."

"Ah, hell," Darrell groaned.

"I took out the dick pill, so that's one less you'll have to swallow."

"Shit-fire, son, that's the only one I want."

CHAPTER TWENTY-SIX
NIGHT GLOWS

Ephraim took the long way around to Slate Run, coming out on 52 just south of the road that led up to the mining site. He didn't pass any law along the way. When he reached the top of the mountain and parked his car in the same hidden area as he'd done before it was a quarter past ten. He grabbed his duffel with binoculars and a water bottle from the passenger seat and, keeping behind the tree line, scooted his way down the steep slope to the lower plateau.

A contingent of police officers, dozen or so, milled about down in the valley. One guided that same German shepherd around, sniffing through the rocks at the base of the valley fill and the destroyed sediment pond. Ephraim watched the dog closely, hoping it didn't sniff out the money before he had the chance to find it.

In the field, another of the deputies was making what looked like a plaster cast of the tire marks on the ground. The rest of them were scouring the area for clues. The detectives that had questioned him, Hively and Sturges, were not present. The wrecked car had yet to be removed. Yellow tape stretched across the ditch, cordoned it off on all sides.

Ephraim had prepared for this eventuality, the police being there. Had packed a lunch in the event. He found a setting in the trees that offered a clear view of the valley, put his back against a spruce, and settled in. He watched the officers work for a while. The one accompanying the dog scaled down off the rocky bluff and disappeared once again into the woods at the far edge of the plain, toward the cave. Two additional deputies followed behind the dog.

Ephraim allowed himself to relax then. He stretched his limbs and felt the heft of exhaustion sink into him. This despite the pill Billy had supplied him that morning. It was a pleasant day, the sky a vivid slate of gray, temperature in the mid-fifties. And peaceful up there on the mountain. The soft gale through the tree branches and the occasional raised voice carried up from the valley were the only things to break the quiet. If ever there were a place suited for reflection, this was it.

Ephraim took a drink of water, screwed the cap on, and leaned his head back against the hard bark of the tree. The prospect of sleep tugged at his eyelids like a weighted lure. As he started to fade, something his father had said niggled in the back of his mind. *This universe owes our family one.* Was it possible to hold a thing in the poles of your heart, a thing at once categorically impossible? And yet, the words held the faint aura of certainty. *If ever a thing were true,* Ephraim mused. And on that thought, he closed his eyes and permitted his consciousness to drift, drift, drift away on the mountain winds.

The first, fat drops of rain from the oncoming storm hit his face, stirring his slumber, but they did not wake him. It took a boom of thunder to accomplish that. Ephraim's eyes popped wide and he drew in a shocked gasp of air, as if surfacing from some great depth. It took a moment for his brain to catch up, shake the fuzz, and realize where he was. The downpour commenced. He cast about for the binoculars. Somehow, they'd gotten beneath him. He brushed some sprigs from the lenses and trained them on the valley.

The police were scrambling across the pasture, toward the gravel lane where their cars were parked. They went through the newly repaired gate, shut it behind them, and dashed into their vehicles. They sat there for a while with their lights on and their wipers lurching back and forth, maybe to see if the storm would subside.

"C'mon, you fuckers," Ephraim said. "Leave."

Half an hour later, with the rain giving no hints of letting up, they finally did. It took each vehicle about a seven-point turn on the gravel path to get aimed in the right direction. They bypassed the small offshoot lane Ephraim had come in on, instead caravanning all the way to the main house to get out thataway. Ephraim stayed put for another hour, getting thoroughly drenched and watching to make sure nobody had designs on coming back. It was 4:30 in the afternoon before he figured he was in the clear. Still, he remained cautious.

He drove down the mountain and made a pass of the Mercer house to make sure no more police were lurking about, then flipped a U and came back down to the auxiliary road and turned in. The visibility on the lane was terrible. Ephraim took it slow, not wanting to risk even his low lights. Much as he did two days prior, he got out of the truck, hopped the fence, and trekked to the middle of the field, glassing both ways to make certain he was alone. He figured if Mercer or somebody associated with the farm came that way, he'd claim to be part of some special police unit, give him a fake name, and get the hell out of Dodge. But he didn't think it likely anybody'd come out in this rain.

Ephraim drove his Ranger through the gate and down along the edge of the pasture to that same hidey-hole in the stand of trees. He quickly devoured the sandwich and chips he'd packed, then clambered out the back window of the cab and crossed the range to the valley fill. The rain was still coming down in buckets. He studied the land where the irrigation ditch merged into the sediment pond, trying to imagine how a wounded man would scale the rocks to get out of there, and where, in a pinch, he might stash a big bag of money. Nobody with a bullet in their gut would climb any higher than they had to; of that he was certain. And if Rodney took a direct line from wherever he stowed the bag through the woods and out to the road, as indicated by the path the shepherd had sniffed out, then he could eliminate the east side of the slope.

Ephraim wiped the water from his face. In his mind's eye, he divided the lower west quadrant of the mountain into a rough grid that he planned to search section by section. He had only two hours before the sun was due to set, so he got to it.

Amassed about thirty feet up was a large cluster of boulders that had broken from the lowest shelf of the mountaintop during the landslide. Ephraim started there, pawing around in the sludge, turning over the rocks that were small enough to do so. He found nothing. The hunt continued in this manner for the better part of an hour, his aggravation mounting as the daylight drained from the sky.

The rain stopped and a bitter cold set in, chilling his waterlogged body to the marrow. He began to shiver uncontrollably, and he began to second-guess himself. Feeling an acute sense of urgency now, he followed the route the dogs took into the woods, zigzagging through the trees, looking for any kind of rock formation or anything else that might provide a good place to sock away four hundred thousand dollars. Again, he came up empty.

Darkness began to swallow the forest and visibility decreased. Ephraim backtracked out of the woods. He returned to the valley fill and scurried up the bluff for one last effort for as long as dusk held. Venturing higher and farther east than he'd previously explored, Ephraim turned over rocks and debris, fast as his hands could move, fallen branches and rotted logs. He worked in a fervor. But nothing came. No sign that he was even in the right vicinity. He had just about conceded for the day, and maybe forever, that this might be his last shot at the hidden loot, when he stumbled over a small log. It took a bit of oomph, but he rolled it aside. On the bottom of the log was a dark stain.

Ephraim pulled his phone from his jeans. The device was damp, but his pocket had shielded it from the brunt of the downpour and it still worked. He turned on the flashlight utility and shined it on the log. The stain was unmistakably blood. Dark crimson blood that, by virtue of how the log was situated, hadn't been washed away in the rain. As dusk dissolved into the grainy black of night, Ephraim panned the light over the ground of the immediate area, flipping over every stone he came across, tossing dead branches aside. He found another smear of blood on the underside of a small rock shelf and knew he was finally on the right track.

Ephraim swung his phone around, more frantically now, searching for another sign, another marker. And he found it. Not ten feet from the shelf, the light caught a slip of green, one end stuck beneath a rock, the other flapping softly in the wind. Ephraim was sure that it was money.

Keeping his light fixed on the bill, he scampered up the slope. He was almost to it when his foot slipped on a loose bit of shale that he didn't see and went out from under him. Ephraim pitched forward and as he went to catch himself the phone came down hard on a jagged rock. Its light went dead. He scrambled to his knees, pressed the buttons on the side of the phone. "No," he pleaded. "No, no, no." The screen was ruined, cracked into a thousand tiny shards. The display wouldn't light up, much less the flashlight.

He began crawling all around, blindly feeling for the bill he'd seen. His hand came across something sharp that sliced his palm. "Fuck!" he yelled. He scoured the ground for some time longer, but didn't find anything, only more rocks. He picked one up and slung it as far as he could, then another, and another. He sat there on his knees for a minute, panting and sulking. Then he began to laugh. He laughed deeply and heartily into the abyss. What else could he do?

Ephraim got to his feet and traversed sidelong down the slope. He felt his way through the dark to the woods and his truck, climbed onto the bed and through the back window into the cab. Then he backed it out from the concealment of the trees and into the pasture. There was no moon in the sky, no light by which to navigate. He turned on his running lights and drove slowly across the bumpy remnants from the landslide. He pulled to the base of the valley fill and switched on his brights. They didn't have enough reach to illuminate the area where he'd seen the money, or what he thought was the money. There was no chance. For a good while, Ephraim sat there staring at the mountain, gripping the wheel at a perfect ten and two. *So goddamn close.*

He doused his brights, turned the truck around, and drove up the acclivity toward the gravel lane. He came up over a berm and, much to his shock, was greeted by a lone car that sat idling in front of the gate, no more than a hundred yards away, seemingly waiting for him. Ephraim stomped on the brakes.

"Aw, shit."

He watched the other car, its high beams splayed brightly across the range. For a pregnant moment, the dueling vehicles faced each other like that, as though in a standoff, static cones of light in a sea of darkness. That changed. The other car extinguished its headlamps.

"Shit."

Ephraim threw his pickup into reverse and hit the accelerator. He hurtled backward down the slope of the field, got out of sight from the other car, cut the wheel sideways, and stopped. He doused his lights and cut the engine. The woods directly behind him were roughly fifty yards away. Ephraim put the car into neutral and let it roll back on its own momentum. When he thought he was nearing the edge of the wood, instead of exposing himself with brake lights, he shifted straight into park. The gears groaned in complaint, and the truck jerked to a halt. He rolled down the window, eyed the horizon and listened. The black of the land blended into the trees and was nearly indistinguishable against the night sky. In the distance, he heard the dinging of an open car door, and then the thwack as it shut. A moment later, the silhouette of the vehicle silently crested the knoll and disappeared into the inky nothing beneath it.

Over a maddening stretch of minutes, Ephraim strained to get a bead on his pursuer—or pursuers—but all was quiet, and he saw nothing. Then, from a mere thirty feet away, headlights ignited directly on the driver's side of the Ranger, putting him on full display. Ephraim squinted against the light, hurriedly turned over the ignition, threw the gear into drive, and floored it. For a horrible second the wheels spun in the mud, but the tires gained purchase, and the truck lurched from the divot and shot forward.

The first thing a bullet plinked off his side mirror, splintering the glass. But Ephraim hadn't heard the report from a shot. Then came a bunch of pelts against the Ranger's exterior sheet metal. Then the back window shattered, raining shards of glass into the cab and onto the back of his neck.

Ephraim quickly realized he was being fired upon by guns outfitted with suppressors. He ducked low and sped blindly into the vast pasture. His attackers gave chase. Ephraim made a series of abrupt turns and soon escaped the reach of their headlights.

Again the other party killed their beams, and the whole of the land pitched into blackness. Ephraim let off the gas and coasted through the cool dark. He felt the truck hit a rise, crest some sort of dune, and ramp down. From what he knew of the land, he had a little space to work with, but he didn't know how much, and driving into the pitch-dark disoriented him. It felt as if he were plunging heedlessly through the atmosphere, the knowledge that a collision might, at any moment, be imminent.

He flashed his lights to make sure he wasn't about to drive headfirst into a tree, or the irrigation ditch, or a cow. If he could figure out where he was on the plain, perhaps he could slip past the killers chasing him, find his way to the gravel lane or even the driveway by the main house. Get back onto Greasy Ridge where he had options, where he knew the roads.

But discerning his location in the field wasn't as simple as all that. The only thing within the purview of his headlights was the green swath of pastureland, sliding past him as if he were sailing on a tide. He couldn't hazard keeping the lights aglow for more than a few seconds, so he flipped them off, turned left, and kept roving forward, slowly, cautiously.

In his rearview he caught a glimpse of the other car mimicking his technique, flipping their lights on and off to gauge their surroundings. Every hundred feet or so Ephraim repeated this action, flashing his lights for a few seconds to gain his bearings, then, immediately upon turning them off, changing course. His copycats did the same. It amounted to a slow-motion chase in the dark.

At first, Ephraim thought he was putting a good amount of space between himself and the other party in this charade, but every time their lights flicked on they had somehow crept a little closer—near enough to where Ephraim could track the low rumble of their engine through his open window. He didn't panic as the hunters drew near. He kept rolling forward, gradual-like, so as not to rev his own motor. Every time his pursuers' lights flashed, he veered in the other direction. But then, one of their flashes caught a glint of the Ranger, and the killers threw their lights full-on.

"Fuck!" Ephraim screamed. He accelerated and made a hard left turn, then a right, darting in and out of his pursuers' spotlight. Racing through the dark, Ephraim pulled some quick turns, which seemed to lose them, and once again the other car extinguished its lamps. He didn't want to chance turning his own lights back on until there was a good distance between them. Tearing through the black of night created a multitude of competing sensations—fear, elation, dread, and absolute focus. He gripped the wheel and struggled to make out any kind of marker ahead of him.

The ground rumbled violently beneath the truck's tires; Ephraim realized that he'd gotten turned around and was traversing the landslide area at the base of the mountain, crossing to the far side of the pasture, away from any possible exits. He slowed down to avoid popping a tire and flicked on his beams. To his right was the valley fill. To his left the lowland and the expanse of the farm. And coming directly on him was a large boulder. He veered sharply to the left of it, saw he was near the far side of the range, and switched his lights back off.

The terrain transitioned from rough to smooth as he hit the soft soil of the pasture. Just then a blast of light from behind lit up the Ranger. Ephraim cut the wheel and thrust the pedal to the floor. He sped with abandon into the black void of the field. In the rearview he caught a glimpse of the killers' headlights go dark, then flick on for a split second before blinking out again. They were at least a hundred yards back, pointed away from him. A sudden dip in the land unsettled him and he risked shining his lights. The beams alighted on four cows, their wide eyes filled with fear at the oncoming vehicle. Ephraim swerved to miss them.

Yellow crime-scene tape fluttered before the windshield. Behind the tape, the glint of metal. The tail of the Lincoln sticking out from the gulley. Ephraim slammed the brakes, but it was too late. The truck skidded out of control, busted through the tape, and went airborne over the embankment, smashing headfirst into the far wall of the dike. The airbag deployed, smacking Ephraim in the face and whipping his head back. The Ranger scraped down the gulley wall and came to rest in a position that roughly mirrored the Lincoln's, nose down, its rear end caught on the opposite ledge.

Ephraim pushed against the airbag to deflate it and somehow managed to pull the handle on the door. It fell open. He tumbled out, rolled across the door, and dropped off the side into the ditch. He lay there in the mud, momentarily stunned, the wind knocked out of him. The muted, coal-black sky stretched across his field of vision like someone had pulled the curtain over the world. The panorama of a celestial nothing. The Ranger's tail lights were still glowing, a beacon for his killers, and the roar of the approaching engine spurred him to his feet. Ephraim ran flat out down the length of the ditch toward the valley fill.

Behind him, brakes squealed and car doors opened. Ephraim glanced back and saw, in the mist of headlights, three men walking around to the front of the vehicle. Some kind of van. They stood there on the bank of the gulch, looking down at the two wrecked vehicles side by side, guns with long thin cylinders attached dangling from their hands.

"Search the car. Get the plates and the VIN number," one of them ordered.

"Had to have gone thataway," another said.

Ephraim ran to where the ditch merged with the rubble of the landslide and he clambered up the scree. The men had gotten back into the car and were speeding toward him. He sprinted for the woods without looking back. They caught him in the far reach of their headlights just before he made the tree line. Ephraim heard the muffled shots from the silenced weapons, felt the air move by his ear. He plunged into the thicket and kept running. Bullets exploded into the trees all around him, little spits of bark hitting him in the face. He tripped over a root and fell hard onto the ground. He scrambled for a felled tree nearby and laid flat on his stomach to peer beneath it.

The car pulled to a stop at the edge of the wood. Its high beams illuminated the area of the forest that surrounded him, casting long shadows the trees made against the light. If Ephraim stood they would spot him immediately, cut him down. Two men got out from either side and strolled to the front of the vehicle, no hurry in their steps. The headlights at their backs carved their figures into distorted silhouettes. Halos around their bodies and the long pistols extended in their grips. One of the men was very large, the other quite tiny by comparison.

"Yoo-hoo," the small man sang. "Come out, come out, wherever you are." Ephraim could hear the grin in his voice. The man signaled to his hulking companion, who then moved off to the left, out of sight and into the woods. "C'mon, now. We ain't gonna hurt you . . . much."

Ephraim knew the time to move was now. Staying flat, he wormed fast as he could across the wet ground. He was at the edge of the headlight's ambit when he heard the snap of a twig somewhere close behind him. He didn't wait. He sprung from his knees and broke into a run. There was one spit. It missed its mark, plugging into the trunk of a giant oak at Ephraim's right. Then a hail of bullets, one after the other, besieging him from all sides like a death net.

He ran. Faster than he'd ever run in his life, into the dark void of the forest. Despite an inability to see two inches in front of his face, Ephraim didn't slow. His legs churned so desperately, so swiftly, he felt as though he might take flight. With each frantic step his wet breath plumed out front of him. And just as his eyes began to acclimate to the forest, a giant oak rose up before him. He ran smack into it.

CHAPTER TWENTY-SEVEN
I EAT THE SUN

When Ephraim came to, it took him a moment to grasp where he was, piece together his circumstances and the reason for the acute pain that enveloped his head and body. Ice was crusted on his beard around his mouth and on his lashes. His eyes stung with the cold. The metallic taste of blood was on his tongue. Ephraim sat up stiffly and came face to face with the timber that had gotten the better of him. He brushed the wet leaves off his face and looked around. The air was quiet, clean. He didn't know how long he'd been out, couldn't make out the time on the busted screen of his phone.

The sky had partially cleared, the moon shining through enough that he could avoid running into any more trees. Ephraim sat for a good while and listened to the sounds of the forest. Convinced he was alone, he calculated which direction he thought was north and walked that way. Soon he came to the downed log that hung over the ledge above the cave and knew he was pointed true. He emerged from the woods onto Greasy Ridge Road, walked along the berm until he hit the railroad tracks. No cars passed the whole time he was on the road.

He limped along the railroad ties, the irony not lost on him, this being the same route Rodney Slash had traveled three nights previous. Up ahead, above the treetops, ghost-ly puffs of steam rose from the stacks at Bismark Carbon. A smudge of purple crawling over the horizon heralded the oncoming day. A Saturday, he remembered.

Ephraim got off the tracks near the plant, slinking along the tree line the rest of the way to avoid the security camera fixed on the railroad. He scaled a small bound-ary fence at the south edge of the plant and slunk around the side of the D-line baker station. Before stepping out into the open he made sure no one from the maintenance shop or anybody else was snooping around the area. All was clear.

Ephraim's security access card only granted him entry to specific areas, the baker station not being one of them, so he pounded on the entrance door. When Billy didn't immediately answer, he kept at it.

"Hold your goddamn horses," Billy called from inside. He tentatively cracked the door to peer out and saw that it was Ephraim. Relief registered on his face, and then horror at the sight of his friend. "Fuck you been, dude?" he said, his train of thought taking a second to catch up to his eyes. "Wait, what happened to you?"

"I got in a wreck."

"When, six hours ago?"

"What time is it?"

"Five thirty."

"Shit." Ephraim pushed past Billy into the station and made a beeline for the bathroom. He looked in the small mirror above the sink. His face was dirty, nose swollen, both eyes blacked, and dried blood was matted to his mus-tache. He splashed some water on his face, took a handful of paper towels from the dispenser, and scrubbed at the mud and the blood and the skin.

"You okay, buddy?" Billy hollered through the door. "We got to go tell Napier. He 'bout blew his top when you didn't show and he couldn't get a hold of you. Asking me whether or not we should call the police."

Ephraim dried his face and called back. "Did he?"

"Did he what?"

Ephraim opened the door. Billy stepped back to let him out. "Call the cops."

"Naw," Billy said proudly. "I convinced him it couldn't have nothing to do with that dude came wandering in the other night. Had to be some other explanation. I told him about your son not doing well, said that probably had something to do with it. Hope that's okay."

Ephraim's head throbbed with pain and he wondered if he had a concussion. He squeezed his eyes shut, trying to think.

"It doesn't, does it?" Billy asked.

"Doesn't what?"

"Have something to do with that dude?"

"It might."

"Aw, hell." Billy clasped his hands overtop his head. "What'd you get mixed up in, man? No, wait. I don't want to know."

Ephraim opened his eyes, leveled them on Billy. "I need your truck."

"What? No, you don't. You don't need my truck."

"I wouldn't ask if it wasn't important, Billy."

"I love my truck."

"I know you do. And I'll get it back to you before your shift ends this morning, I swear. I just have something I gotta go do real quick." Ephraim held his palm out to receive the keys. "Won't have a scratch on it, I promise."

"I don't know, E. Maybe it's time we do call the police."

"What do you think's gonna happen to my kid if I go to jail, Billy?"

"Aw, shit. That's not fair."

"Well, it's the fuckin' truth."

Billy shifted back and forth, uncertain. "You didn't kill nobody, did ya?"

"C'mon, Billy."

"All right, all right." Billy reached into his pocket and brought out his key ring, removed the fob for his Silverado, and reluctantly handed it over. Ephraim headed for the door.

"Why do I get the feeling I'm never gonna see her again?" Billy uttered.

"When'd you get so pessimistic?"

"When I was born."

It was 6:15 a.m. when Ephraim parked the Silverado on the lane below Marvel Heights. No lights on in any of the low road's dwellings. He knew his neighbors, knew what they did for a living, figured none of them worked Saturdays and were likely sleeping in. The morning was brisk, a light glow from the sun beginning to spread across the sky. Ephraim crept in between two of the houses, crouched beside a toolshed, and surveilled his own home.

The blue flicker from the TV shone through the living room curtains. His father was probably sleeping in the lounge chair, as he did most nights. Ephraim looked up and down the road. He recognized all the cars. Saw no movement.

He watched his house a bit longer before stepping out from behind the shed and climbing up his neighbor's backyard hill to his street. He walked through the carport to check the rear of the house, make sure nothing was amiss. There wasn't anything. A fawn and its mother were on the hill back there, and when they saw him they scattered into the trees. Ephraim went back around front and let himself in.

The house was still, quiet, save for the low murmur of the television in the next room, the soft tick of the grandfather clock. Ephraim went in there. His father wasn't in the recliner.

"Dad?" he called out. Not too loud. He didn't want to wake Caleb unnecessarily.

"In here," Darrell croaked from the kitchen.

"Up a little early, aren't you?" Ephraim crossed the room and turned the corner to the kitchen. There stood his father, face bloody and beaten, the oxygen tube fashioned into a garrote, biting into his neck. His arm was wrenched behind him by an enormous man with a bare, scarred head, an eyepatch adorned with a skull and crossbones covering his left eye. The man had a gun with a long silencer pressed to his father's temple. Ephraim froze in place, held his hands out from his body.

"Right where you are," Buddy The Face snarled. "You must be Ephraim."

"My family doesn't have anything to do with this," Ephraim said, doing his best to keep his voice from shaking.

"What did you do, Ephraim?" Darrell rasped.

"I fucked up, Dad. I'm sorry. I'm sorry."

Darrell made a pained noise and closed his eyes.

"Where's my son?" Ephraim asked. Buddy The Face grinned cruelly. "Where's my son? Where's Caleb? Caleb?!"

A muffled sob came from the bowels of the house. "Dad?!"

"That him?" said Buddy.

Ephraim spun toward his son's cry. Behind him stood Momo Morrison. He chopped Ephraim in the throat with the butt of his pistol. Ephraim collapsed to his knees, gasping, clawing at his neck. Momo grabbed him by the scruff, yanked his head back and stared into his eyes.

"You're a slippery one, ain't ya?" Momo said. "Well, we got you now." He pistol-whipped Ephraim across the face. Ephraim fell to the ground, rolled over and got to all fours. Blood and bile sluiced from his mouth onto the floor. His vision spiraled. He twisted his head to look at Momo.

"I don't have your money."

"Now, of all the things you could have said to me." Momo frowned. "Buddy."

Next came the unmistakable sound, so fresh in Ephraim's mind from just hours ago, of the spit from a silencer. Ephraim turned in time to see his father's body toppling through the air, an apple-size hole gaping in his chest. Darrell's head cracked against the linoleum, opening up a gash above his brow. A mixed expression of agony and bewilderment on his face as he left this world.

"No," Ephraim blubbered. He reached for his father. "No."

Before he could get there, Buddy The Face took hold of him by the collar and jerked him off the ground like he was nothing, like he was weightless. He set him down hard in a chair. Ephraim immediately tried to stand, but Momo Morrison slugged him in the gut, and he fell back into the seat. Momo reared back to follow with a roundhouse. Ephraim saw it coming, thrust his forehead down into Momo's knuckles. One of them popped out of socket.

Momo made a screwy face and hopped back, wringing his hand out. "Goddamn. He's a stubborn son of a bitch, ain't he?" This was said with a touch of fondness. Ephraim offered a wounded half grin at the small victory, and Buddy literally knocked the smile off his face. Ephraim tongued out a molar.

"Shit," he moaned. A faint scream sounded from somewhere deep in the house, and was quickly cut short. Ephraim attempted to stand, move for the doorway, and instead wobbled into the table and grabbed onto it to keep from falling to the floor. Buddy took hold of his shoulders and sat him back in the chair.

Momo pulled his dislocated ring finger away from the joint and set it back in place. He stepped forward and chucked Ephraim under the chin to get him looking up.

"Before you speak another word, you should know that one way or another, you ain't long for this world. But whatever you say next will determine if your son dies too. You understand me?" Ephraim's eyes fluttered, and Momo said again, "You understand me?"

Ephraim bobbed his head like a delirious parrot.

"Now, you lie to me, I will bring him in here and slit his throat right in front of you. Then I'll go to work on you, kill you inch by inch, piece by piece. You got that?"

Ephraim grunted.

"Speak up."

"Yes."

"You believe me, don't you?"

"Yes."

"Good. You got one chance. Where's my money?"

Ephraim opened his eyes wide, trying to collect his wits and wrap his mouth around the syllables he meant to speak. "I know where it is."

"You lying to me?"

"No."

"You just said you didn't have it."

"I don't," Ephraim tottered sideways and Buddy kept him from falling out of the chair. "I know where it's hidden."

"How?"

"Rodney told me."

Momo narrowed his cunning little eyes. "Begs the question. If Rodney told you where it was, why don't you already have it? Why aren't you swimmin' in a bathtub full of cash?"

"Can't get to it. You'll see."

"It's out there on that farm?"

"Yeah."

"Where?"

The image of Rodney came to Ephraim's mind, sitting on the floor of the station with his legs spread, dying. "It's by these rocks," he said. "In this cave. I couldn't get to where he threw it."

"Fuckin' A," Momo exclaimed. "That kid made it hard on everybody, didn't he?" Momo squatted down to Ephraim's level. "Something don't sit right though. Why'd he tell you where it was hidden?"

"He was hurt bad, came looking for help. Told me he'd give me some of the money. I just had to take him to get it. Told me where it was, kinda. Died before he gave me the exact spot. Took me three goddamn days to find it."

Momo used the barrel of his .32 Smith & Wesson to scratch at his temple. "Wait, so you took his body back out there?"

Ephraim gave another wobbly nod.

Momo laughed raucously. "Man-oh-man, this shit got even crazier than I imagined. You didn't have a clue what you was gettin' yourself involved in, did ya? Thought you'd help yourself to somebody else's property, score you a quick payday, and nobody'd be none the wiser."

"Something like that."

"Shit don't never work that way." Momo's smile waned with a sigh. "Okay, moment-of-truth time. There's more than one cave out there. Which one is it?"

"Couldn't say exact. It's in the woods. I could show you easier than I could tell you."

Momo gazed down at Ephraim approvingly. "You smarter than you look, ain't ya? Huh? Ain't ya?" He tapped the barrel end of his pistol against both sides of Ephraim's face before standing upright and packing it into his waistband. "Okay brainiac, here's how this is gonna go. You take us to our money, I'll kill you quick, one bullet, back of the head, you won't feel a thing. Off you go to paradise. Maybe you'll wake up on a porch swing in the great hereafter with your daddy, who knows. And I'll spare your boy. What's his name?"

"Caleb."

"Caleb gets to grow up. But you try anything funny. Everybody dies. Everybody dies real bad. Got it?"

"Yeah."

Momo smacked his palms together and rubbed them. "Now that's how you barter right there. You use your leverage, I use mine, and the deal gets struck."

"Can I see him?" Ephraim asked. "He's sick. He needs to know some things before I go."

"What kind of sick?"

"There's something wrong with his brain."

Momo tocked his head back and forth. "Mmm, I don't see why not." He hollered back into the house, "Verbals! Get in here right quick!" Then, to Ephraim: "Speaking of your boy being off"—he swirled a finger by his head—"he said some wild shit to us when we came in here. Wouldn't calm down. We had to lock his ass in the bathroom. What was it he said, Buddy?"

"He told us he was gonna murder us."

"Yeah, that was funny. But that wasn't it. He said something else."

"Then he said he eats the sun and he was gonna eat our hearts out of our bodies."

"That's right," Momo howled. "I eat the sun. I love that. I mean he actually caught me off guard there. That's just some crazy-ass shit to say. I might use it myself one day. I eat the sun. Scare people to half to death."

Verbals came hustling into the room. The dead body on the floor stopped him cold. He quickly cloaked whatever the sight provoked in him and asked Momo what was up. Momo laid out the situation and what was to happen next.

"Verbals, you stay here with the boy. If you don't hear from us by"—he looked at the clock on the microwave; it read 6:27—"say, eight a.m. You don't hear from us by eight a.m., I want you to kill him."

"Wait," Ephraim said. "You didn't say nothing about that."

"This is what you call insurance," Momo said. "Make you think twice before you get any clever ideas in that big brain."

"There's no cell service out there," Ephraim protested. "What if we get caught up somehow? It's gonna take us forty minutes just to get out there and get to the cave."

"Then you better make sure we don't get caught up."

"What if the owner of the farm sees us or something?"

"Owner?" Momo scrunched his face in confusion. "You mean the old man they interviewed on Channel 3 the other day? Mercer? Yeah, no, he don't own that farm anymore."

"What do you mean?"

"I mean, somebody owns that farm, I'm sure, but it ain't that old man. He don't own nothing no more."

The implication of this hit Ephraim. He made no further objections. Verbals turned his back and leaned in conspiratorially toward Momo, speaking in his harsh whisper. "He's just a kid."

"We gonna do this again?" Momo asked. "You got a problem, Verbals?"

"No," Verbals said, without hesitation. "Just making sure."

Momo glared at Verbals for the duration of time it takes to make things uncomfortable. "Now you're catching on."

Momo ordered Buddy The Face to fetch the van and bring it around to the carport. Then he and Verbals hoisted Ephraim up from the chair and escorted him to the bathroom. Caleb was sitting on the closed toilet seat, rocking back and forth. Upon seeing the state of his father, he immediately started shaking and crying. Ephraim dropped to his knees, wrapped his arms around his son, and hugged him tight.

"Shh, shh. It's okay, it's okay. You gotta be calm for me, okay? Stay calm for me now. Everything's gonna be all right."

"Dad?"

"Yeah, buddy?"

"Why are these men here? Did you do something bad?"

Ephraim took his son by the shoulders and looked him in the eye. "No, no. Don't worry about them. Just look at me. You remember that buried treasure I told you about?"

Caleb sucked some snot up his nose. "What?"

"Remember I told you I found a pot of gold? You thought I was joking."

"At Walmart?"

"Yeah. See, it's real. I wasn't joking. And I just have to take these men to it, then everything is gonna be okay. Okay?"

"But why did they beat you up?"

"It was just a misunderstanding," Ephraim said. "We got it all figured out now. It's okay, I'm okay."

"Where's Grandpa?"

"They took him somewhere else. He's fine. He's fine. Listen to me now, Caleb. Are you listening?"

"Uh-huh."

"These men are going to take you to Harold's here in a little bit." Ephraim looked back at Verbals and Momo standing in the doorway. "When this is over, you drop him off at Harold's Diner, okay?"

"Sure," Momo said. "Why not?"

Ephraim turned his attention back to Caleb, cupped his son's cheeks in his hands. "You tell our favorite waitress there—"

"You mean—"

Ephraim pressed his finger to Caleb's lips. "Don't say her name," he warned. "Don't say her name. You tell her that we're waiting for some test results from Dr. Fitzsimmons. Okay, you got that?"

"Yeah," Caleb whimpered. The urgency in his father's voice frightened him, frightened him even more than the strange men in the doorway, and tears came streaming down his face.

"I need you to repeat it for me, Caleb. Dr. Fitzsimmons."

"Dr. Fitzsimmons."

"Dr. Fitzsimmons."

"I got it. Dr. Fitzsimmons. We're waiting for tests from Dr. Fitzsimmons."

"Good." Ephraim ran his hands through his son's thick hair. "Good." He kissed the tears on Caleb's cheeks and kissed his head, accidentally smearing blood from his lips all over Caleb's face. "Sorry." He used his shirtsleeve to wipe the mess off and got most of it. "Look at me now, son, look at me. This is important. You'll probably need to see a specialist, okay? You need to tell her that. Tell her when you get the tests back from Dr. Fitzsimmons, you'll probably need to take them to a specialist. Okay?"

"Okay."

"She can sell our house, my truck—" Ephraim hesitated, remembering his truck was nose-down in an irrigation ditch. "Whatever she needs to pay for it, okay? You gotta tell her that."

"What are you talking about, Dad?"

"Just tell her what I'm saying to you."

"Okay."

Ephraim did his best to smile through his busted face and broken teeth. "I love you so much, buddy. I love you so much. You're so brave. You don't even realize how brave you are. You're gonna be okay. Okay? You're gonna be fine."

"Time's a ticking, Ephraim," Momo said drolly.

"I gotta go now, buddy."

Caleb fought back more tears. "No."

"I got to."

"But you're coming back, right?"

Ephraim held his son's face in his hands and kissed him one last time. "I'll never leave you, you understand me? I'll always be with you. You're the best thing that ever happened to me."

"You're the best thing that ever happened to me too," Caleb whispered.

"I love you, son."

CHAPTER TWENTY-EIGHT
THE DEAD ARRANGEMENTS

They wound along State Route 52, past Bismark Carbon, making the left onto Greasy Ridge Road. Momo sat in one of the minivan's second-row captain seats next to Ephraim, a benevolent gaze locked on his prisoner. He waved his Smith & Wesson casually as he talked.

"Buddy drives pretty good for a one-eyed fella, don't he? You ever tried driving with one eye? More than likely you'd veer right off the road, I'm telling ya." Ephraim didn't respond. He glanced at the handle on the sliding door. Momo saw this, stuck the tip of his tongue out through his jagged teeth and clucked. "Nuh-uh-uh. You feeling froggy?"

"Nope."

"Better not be," Momo said. He held the gun up close to his face and shut one eye like he was lining Ephraim up in his sights. "Tell me something. You ever thought about the day you'd die? Picture it in your head?"

"Every day."

"Listen at him," Momo exulted. He lowered the pistol to his lap. "Every day. You got some darkness in you, don'tcha?"

The minivan turned onto the auxiliary lane and crept along the rutted road. The cool early light filtered in through the dense branches of the forest.

"What are you gonna do if the cops come out here?" Ephraim asked. "What happens then?"

"Cops ain't coming out here on a Saturday, I assure you. And if they plan to, we have our ways of knowing, don't you worry."

"You don't have to kill me, you know. I'm as crooked as you in all this. You can just get your money and go. I'll take whatever punishment I have to take from the police. Raise my son up, that's all I want."

Momo frowned, disappointed. "I was waiting for this part. Thought you might not be one to grovel, but guess I was wrong." He looked out the window at the passing landscape. "Sounds nice though, don't it? Perfect world, maybe that could happen. Let you go after we're done with ya. Maybe I could even give you a finder's fee, you going to all this trouble and all. But naw, you gotta die. Just the way it is. Just sound business. Can't risk the loose ends, you understand."

"Well, fuck you then."

Momo cackled with a noxious delight. "The fuckin' nuts on you, man. What'd you think, huh? You think you could just dip your little toe into our world and get out clean? That ain't the way it works, stupid motherfucker."

Ephraim glared through swollen eyes at Momo.

"What, you mad now? Don't blame me. You was dead the moment you went searching for that wrecked car, you just didn't know it yet. You make a decision like that, you set the wheels of fate in motion, ya see. You gonna get what you gonna get. Your kid now, Little Orphan Annie back there, that's a different story. His destiny is in your hands."

Momo grimaced, regretful-like. "I wish y'all had never got caught up in this, I truly do. You seem like you're a good daddy. Your daddy seemed nice enough, too, once he settled down. Disappointed in you there at the end though, wasn't he? I saw the way he looked at you. That's unfortunate. What'd he do for a living?"

"He was a mechanic."

"Yeah?" Momo pursed his lips, nodded. "My daddy wasn't good for nothing or nobody. Couldn't never hold down no job. He was a con man. Grifter type. Not very good at that either, really." Momo squished his face up as though the recollection were painful. "Used to do all kinds of mean things just for fun. Used to wake me up with a butane lighter and an aerosol can, spray it right above my face. I guess that was kinda funny. You know what he told me once? He told me that my face looked like a casserole came out of the oven too early, never fully formed. Half-baked. Said I looked like the bastard child of a human and a Komodo dragon. Made me so mad. I clapped back, said to him, 'It'd be like you to fuck a lizard.' He didn't like that much."

"Like I give a shit what your daddy did to you," Ephraim said.

The minivan emerged from the woods onto the gravel lane at the edge of the field. Momo gazed out over the country. He ran his tongue over his teeth and bobbed his head deliberately up and down, as if he'd arrived at some foreseen conclusion. He cut his eyes toward Ephraim, a murderous look in back of them now. "I bet you never envisioned the day you'd die lookin' like this, did ya?"

"How could I of?"

"Well, maybe you shoulda. Maybe you ought to have thought real careful about everything you ever did or said, and you wouldn't have been sitting here in this position. So you go on and be a good daddy now, one last time, and show me that money."

Verbals watched the seconds tick away on the grandfather clock. The air in the room was thick with dread, tangible, as though it were floating around on the dust. The kid sat on the opposite end of the couch, rocking back and forth incessantly and wringing his hands one over the other. Verbals thought talking might draw him out, or at least get him to sit still.

"How old are you?" he asked.

"Nine," Caleb sniveled.

"That's a good age, nine. Almost double digits. What grade does that put you in?"

"Third." Caleb's eyes brimmed with tears as his face squished tight.

"C'mon, don't cry," Verbals said. "Don't get upset. This will all be over soon."

"Why do you keep looking at the clock?" Caleb asked.

"I like clocks. It's a nice old clock. Can you read that clock?"

Caleb nodded.

"What's it say?"

"Seven twenty-one."

"Hey, that's good. I heard kids these days can't read clocks with hands no more cuz they don't teach them how anymore. You must be smart."

"Not really."

"Third grade," Verbals mused. "I remember being in the third grade. I sat next to a pretty girl with red hair and lots of freckles. Katie McHale. I tried to kiss her once. Know what she did?"

Caleb sniffed. "You tried to kiss a girl in third grade?"

"Might have been fifth grade when I actually tried to kiss her."

"What'd she do?"

"She popped me right in the nose. Bam." Verbals thrust a quick jab out front of him. "No warning, just nailed me. Got me good too. Blood come pouring out. Can you believe that?" The way Verbals talked about it suggested he was quite fond of the memory. Caleb giggled despite the tears. "Oh, that's funny, huh? It might be funny now, but I assure you, it was no laughing matter then. That girl could throw a punch. You can still kind of see where it's crooked." Verbals turned sideways and tilted his head up to accentuate his profile. "See that bump there?"

"Kinda."

"That's Katie McHale. You got any pretty girls in your class?"

"No."

"That's good," Verbals said. "Take my advice, stay away from 'em for as long as you can. Nothing but trouble. Speaking of girls, I was wonderin', where's your mama?"

"Florida."

"Florida? Nice. Nothing but sunshine. You know where?"

Caleb shook his head.

"That's okay. You like school?"

"I got kicked out."

Verbals guffawed. "Kicked out? Of third grade? How's that even happen? What'd you do, stab somebody with a pair of scissors?"

Caleb lifted his shoulders and dropped them. "I dunno. I say a bunch of things I don't mean sometimes. I don't know why I say them."

"Yeah, I get it. School wasn't really my thing either. I liked math, though. I was okay at math. What's your favorite subjects?"

"English," Caleb said. "And Social Studies."

"That's good. You know what you wanna be when you grow up?"

"I dunno. Maybe a writer."

"A writer?" Verbals made an impressed face.

"Or maybe someone who makes video games."

"Well, you seem like a smart kid. I bet you'll be good at either one of those things. You can read clocks, after all."

"Everybody can read clocks."

"That's not what I heard. Listen, when you get back in school, you study hard and stay out of trouble. That's all you gotta do and you'll be good. Sounds easy when you say it. I don't know why I couldn't do it. Anyway, you'll figure it out."

"I don't know if I wanna go back."

"No, no, no, you definitely want to go back, kid. If you take nothing else from this conversation, take that. You go to school for as long as you can, trust me. Don't do what I did. I dropped out of school after tenth grade, and now look. I don't have many options, you know. Not much to choose from. But I wasn't smart like you. I never knew what to do. You got a brain, you gotta use it."

"I did win an essay contest before they kicked me out."

"See? What was your essay about?"

"My grandma."

"Yeah? What about her?"

"How she is my guardian angel in heaven that watches over me. That's what my grandpa says. My dad says nobody really knows what happens when people die."

Verbals flashed to the dead man lying in the kitchen. He leaned back and peeked through the doorway to make sure the kid couldn't catch a glimpse of anything. "Wow, you've got a guardian angel? That's cool. Not everyone gets one of those. You're lucky."

"You believe in them?"

"Sure."

"Do you have one?"

"I don't think so. No one's ever told me if I did."

"So you might, you just don't know?"

"Maybe. If I do, it'd be nice of them to show up from time to time." Verbals looked again at the clock. The number of minutes that had passed distressed him. His leg started bouncing nervously. His phone, along with his gun, lay on the side table. He picked up the phone to make sure there was service. It showed three of four bars. He kept it in his hand so there was no chance of missing the call.

Hively silenced his phone before the first ring was out, before he'd even opened his eyes. He sensed Rachel's absence in the bed beside him, the imbalance of the mattress. The smell of eggs and bacon and something sweet, cinnamon, wafted up from the kitchen. He cracked one eye to check the time on the display and the number on the incoming call: 6:47 a.m. Sturges. He answered it.

"It's fucking Saturday, Clyde."

"Hey, listen, it's not like I missed you so much I was having withdrawal, but when the wheels of justice move, they move. What do you want me to do?"

The detectives had been at the station until the wee hours. Patrol had picked up Norman Hinkle, the small-time dealer out of the South Side, back from his concert in Cincinnati. Despite his low status in the hierarchy of Cain City's drug trade, Hinkle was observant, tapped into the circuitry—the ever-changing players, who was moving what—and he'd down-low assisted the police on a couple of occasions in the past. But as the detectives interrogated him, it became clear that Hinkle knew more about the twenty-three overdoses than he was letting on, and they kept him there until they got it out of him.

"This better be good," Hively said into the phone. "I can smell my breakfast cooking downstairs."

"No shit? What's she cooking? Can you bring me some in when you come to the office?"

"Why am I coming into the office? That where you are now?"

"I never left, my friend. Wasn't tired. Figured I'd catch up on some of that paperwork that's too tedious for you to bother with."

"This your revenge, not letting me sleep more than three hours?"

"Wait for it, sweetheart. It's a good thing I did stay because I happened to check in with the lab a little bit ago, and guess what? Blood results on our mystery man from the tracks came back this morning. You sitting down?"

"I'm in bed, Clyde."

"You sleep naked or in jammies?"

"Who is it?"

"What about Rachel? Naked or jammies? Just trying to get an accurate picture."

"Fucking-A, man."

"All right, all right. Drumroll, please." Sturges paused briefly for suspense. "None other than Rodney Slash himself."

Hively jolted upright. "What? Wait, but how'd he—? If—"

"How'd he get from the farm to Bismark Carbon and back to the farm? This next item on the list might answer your question."

Hively beat his partner to the punch. "Ephraim Rivers."

Sturges continued unabated, as if Hively hadn't already supposed the answer. "The tire molds made from the tracks at the farm, when compared to the pictures you snapped of Rivers's wheels, are a reasonable enough match, five points in common, matching tread, worn down in the same spots, yadda yadda yadda."

"Fuck." Hively was already moving, pulling on the clothes he'd slung over the chair the night before. "We gotta pick him up. He gets off work at seven."

"Remembered that, did ya? That's where it gets interesting, see. I called up to Bismark. Rivers no-showed for his shift last night. Highly unusual, they said. Couldn't get a hold of him."

"We need a search warrant for his house."

"Thought you might say that. I'm putting the finishing touches on the affidavit now. We just need a judge to sign. So see, I actually allowed you an extra hour of sleep. You can thank me for that and all this goddamned paperwork in my eulogy."

Hively said, "I'm not going to Key West for your fucking funeral."

"You can't make the effort for a video message or something?"

"Be there in ten." Hively hung up the phone.

CHAPTER TWENTY-NINE
TROUBLE YOU FOR A MURDER

Ephraim glanced out the window at the valley fill on the mountain, thought he could make out the area where he'd been searching last night. Where somewhere, in amongst the debris, was a bag of money. He leaned forward and pointed through the windshield to a section of woods ahead. "There's a spot in between the trees up there you can hide your car if you care to."

"Look at you being helpful," admired Momo.

"Gotta get this done so you can call your man about my kid, right?"

"Course," Momo said, the corners of his mouth drawing back pitilessly. "Course." He looked across the field. "We had us some fun out here last night, didn't we?"

"Don't know that's how I'd categorize it."

Buddy The Face steered the car in between the trees and cut the engine. There was enough room for the side door of the minivan to slide open and they got out that way. Momo first, then Ephraim and Buddy. The air was dewy and clean and all around them birds were chirping brightly. Momo stretched his arms and said, "Lead on, Sacagawea."

Ephraim guided them deep into the woods, moving at a good clip, so much so that Buddy eventually told him to slow the fuck down.

"We're almost there," Ephraim told the men. He came to the downed tree on the ridge above the cave and side-stepped down the edge of the small bluff. The storm had knocked a good amount of leaves from the trees and they were slippery and made the footing on the slope precarious. Toward the bottom, Buddy The Face fell hard on his ass and slid down the rest of the way.

"Jesus, fuck," he spat. Momo helped the big man to his feet, laughing. Buddy's backside was covered in mud and grass stains. He brushed the stuck leaves off. "Thought you said we was close."

Ephraim nodded toward the cave. "We are. It's in there."

Momo peered into the darkness of the cavity. "Where?"

"In the back there. It's not that deep. Fifty feet or so. Rodney just threw it in blind, I think. Landed in this crevasse I couldn't quite get to."

"Why not?" Buddy asked.

"You'll see," Ephraim said. "You know we were at Westmoreland together. You were a senior when I was a freshman."

"What's that make us, pals?"

"Naw, just weird to think about. You being about to kill me and all."

"You first, bub," Momo said, prodding him forward with the gun.

Ephraim bent beneath the mossy vines hanging down from the upper ledge and stepped inside the dank cave. Momo and Buddy kept a couple paces behind, flanking him on either side. Both had their pistols trained at his back. Ephraim stepped forward cautiously, and they followed. Loose rocks littered the floor of the cave and Buddy turned his ankle on one of them.

"Mother fuck," he yelled. "I can't see shit."

"I used the flashlight on my phone," Ephraim said.

Both captors dug into their pockets, brought out their cells and turned on their flashlights.

"There we go," Momo said. "Now where is it?"

"Right past that stalagmite or whatever over there." Ephraim indicated where he meant. He took a few more steps forward. That's when the first rattle sounded.

"Fuck is that?" Buddy asked. Momo moved in front of Ephraim and shined his light behind the large rock jutting up from the bottom of the cave. As the beam landed on the snakes, they struck up their chorus, and the chasm filled with their vibrating alarm.

"Holy shit," Momo said. "It's a bunch of rattlesnakes."

"That's why I couldn't get to it," Ephraim said. "The bag is in a crater just back of where they're at right there. I was gonna get some chemicals, come back and kill them today."

"You couldn't have told us this before?" Momo asked.

"You told me to show you the money. I'm showing you the money."

Momo glared at Ephraim just then like he was inventing whole new ways of killing a person.

"What are we gonna do?" Buddy asked. Two of the coiled snakes drew their heads back as though preparing to strike. Another rose up and switched rapidly toward Momo. He raised his pistol and fired an errant shot that ricocheted off the walls. The flash from the discharge lit up the cave like a crack of lightning. The viper kept coming. Buddy strode forward and began popping off rounds at the snakes.

Ephraim spotted some loose rocks on a ledge behind Momo. One in particular looked fairly large and had a jagged tip. He leapt for it. Momo registered the movement, but his focus on the serpents delayed his reaction. Ephraim snagged the rock, spun, and before Momo could raise his arms in defense, he brought the barbed end of the rock down hard onto the crown of Momo's head.

Momo's skull gave way beneath the blow. His body went stiff and he wobbled backward into the wall, his jaw hanging, dumbstruck. Blood came sluicing down his face in two thick rivulets.

Buddy The Face was still taking potshots at the snakes, oblivious to what was happening in the periphery of his absent eye. Ephraim lunged across the cave and smacked him in the back of the head with the rock. The impact didn't stagger Buddy; he barely flinched. He touched his head where he'd been struck, as if to make sure what he'd felt was real, and came away with the glisten of blood on his fingertips. He roared a terrible roar and swung his gun toward Ephraim.

At the exact same time, a dazed Momo lifted the .32 and started firing wildly. The cave erupted with flash-bangs of gunfire.

The salvo lasted no more than three seconds. When it was over the three men lay sprawled across the cave floor, one of them dead, another well on his way. The echoes from the gunshots trailed into silence. Into stillness. Even the snakes quit their rattling. Buddy The Face's head crooked unnaturally between the base of the stalagmite and his shoulder. Holes the size of dimes trickled blood from his chest and forehead and, in a twist of irony, from the socket of his one good eye.

Momo Morrison had been shot twice. One bullet punctured a lung. The other plowed through his sternum, severing his spinal cord. He lay flat on his back, disabled from the chest down, struggling to see for the blood running into his eyes. Viscous bile from failing organs surged into his throat, slowly suffocating him. The .32 sat inertly, a mere six inches from his grasp. He flopped his arm over, trying to reach it.

Ephraim crawled across the stony ground to where Momo lay, saw what he was stretching for, and reached across his body to grab the gun. Momo gave up. His arm went limp at his side and he rolled his head over to gaze at Ephraim with what could only be called a malevolent indifference. His mouth puckered open and shut like a fish at feeding time, but there wasn't enough air in his lungs to propel the words he wished to speak forward, and they disintegrated on the blood that burbled upon his lips.

"What's that?" Ephraim asked. "Nothing left to say, you mouthy bitch?"

Ephraim leveled the pistol at Momo's face. Momo pawed at the weapon, but there was no strength in his limbs and Ephraim smacked them away easily. He pressed the gun into Momo's cheek and squeezed the trigger. The hammer clicked. He pulled it twice more, the empty chamber click-clicking in response. Momo's grisly lips twisted into the ghost of a smile, and he choked up a bloody laugh.

Ephraim noticed movement on the ground to their right—tangles of serpent bodies gliding smoothly toward them, their bifurcated tongues flicking out hideously. He chucked the pistol at the closest snake. The gun clattered past the viper; it reared its ugly head and hissed. It was as if a signal had been transmitted, and the chorus of rattles recommenced.

Ephraim clambered off Momo and dragged himself across to the remains of Buddy The Face. He frisked the pockets of his coat and found the keys to the minivan. He groped around on the ground looking for the phone, but it was dark, and he couldn't find it. Ephraim rolled the dead man on his side and checked beneath him. It wasn't there either.

Ephraim dropped the corpse unceremoniously and pushed against it and the stalagmite to get to his feet. Immediately he teetered sideways, catching himself on the rock wall. He used it to steady, and staggered toward the mouth of the cave. From behind him came a loud, aspirated gasp, and then a strangled scream. Ephraim glanced back. One of the rattlesnakes had sunk its fangs into Momo's neck. Another slithered deftly over his chest before ratcheting back and striking his face. Momo let out another feeble moan, and then nothing else.

Ephraim pressed on. As he emerged from the cave, the toe of his shoe caught a root and he stumbled onto all fours. He eased himself onto his knees and then sat back on his heels, tilting his head back to take in the fresh air. The morning sun spilled through the branches of the trees, and gleamed off the dew of the leaves. The taste of copper rose into his throat.

Only now did he brave a look at the wound in his gut. Dark blood gushing from it. Tears pooled in his eyes. He looked away, tried to calm himself, and then looked again. The bullet had plugged into the left side of his torso, gone into the ribs, and hadn't come out the back. Ephraim tried to think what organs were on that side. Liver? Spleen? He couldn't remember. He pressed a hand over his stomach as though it were possible to hold one's life inside of them, to somehow bar its escape, prevent it from leaking out with each beat of the heart.

Air flowed heavily in and out of his nose. His vision skewed out of focus. He attempted to steady his mind, do the calculus on which was closer, the minivan back at the farm, or the Bismark Carbon plant. Figured he was essentially midway between the two points—mile, mile-and-a-half journey in either direction. *I should've kept hunting for a phone,* he thought. *But there's no chance of venturing back into the cave. Doesn't matter—out here's a dead zone for service anyways.*

A car zooming by on Greasy Ridge sounded loud, sounded close, and that made the determination for him. Go for the road. Easier trek, flatter. He could flag a car down if one passed. Or slog it down the tracks to Bismark. They had first aid there, a fire station nearby.

Ephraim willed himself to stand, and then to take one careful step, and then another.

They had to drive all the way to the top of Honeysuckle Lane to get a judge to sign the search and seizure warrant for Ephraim Rivers's residence, his car, and any surrounding property deemed necessary. Since Buffalo Township was in the next county over from Cain, Hively called ahead and alerted the sheriff of that jurisdiction to what they had planned. They rendezvoused at a Shell gas station with two deputies who'd assist in serving the warrant. Everybody introduced themselves, briefly discussed the logistics, and got on down the road.

Hively turned from State Route 75 onto the steep hill that led to Marvel Heights.

"How long you say they've lived here?" Sturges asked.

"Thirty-some odd years."

"Jesus, can you imagine trying to get up and down this hill in winter?"

Hively didn't answer. He'd already clocked the house at the end of the lane. No lights were on and there were no cars sitting out front or in the carport. "Doesn't look like anybody's home."

"It's early. His dad and kid live there, right? Could still be asleep."

Hively parked at the bottom of the driveway and the sheriff's deputies pulled in behind him. The deputies split off and went around to the back of the house to guard against anyone trying to flee, while Hively and Sturges ascended the stairs and pressed the doorbell. When no one answered after a few rings, they announced their presence loudly and stated why they were there.

"I'll try his cell," Sturges offered. He dialed, listened for a couple seconds, and hung up. "Straight to voice mail."

"Try the landline."

Sturges dialed the home number, got a busy signal. Hively opened the screen and tried the doorknob. It was unlocked. The door creaked open.

Sturges grunted. "I don't like it when things are that easy."

Hively hollered into the house, again identifying himself and repeating their reasons for being there. Crickets. He spoke into his walkie. "Anything stirring in back?"

The receiver crackled. "Not a thing, Detective."

"Can you see into any windows or anything?"

"Negative, all the blinds are shut. Hold on . . . There might be one." After a few seconds, the deputy came back over the frequency. "We can see into what looks like a bedroom, possibly the master. No one present."

Hively prepped the deputies. "Be advised. We found the front door open and we are entering the premises. Repeat, we are entering the premises."

The detectives unholstered their sidearms and moved single file through the entryway. Hively broke right into the first open doorway while Sturges proceeded down the small hallway to where there were two doorways directly across from one another. Hively rotated the corner and quickly cleared the living room and the attached dining area.

He caught a glimpse of some photos on the mantelpiece above the fireplace. An older wedding photo of a couple, the man in an army uniform. Another of a young couple, the woman an attractive blonde, and a skinnier Ephraim Rivers with longer hair and less beard. Both of them grinning ear to ear. A third photo was a school picture Hively assumed was Caleb, and the last was one with all three generations of Rivers on a pontoon boat, the kid proudly holding up a bass.

"Clear," Hively said, moving efficiently toward the doorway on the far side of the room. "Got a hallway."

"Clear," Sturges called from the kitchen. He stepped through the second door into the living room. "Willis."

Hively stopped. "Yeah."

"Trouble you for a murder?"

"Who?"

"Looks like the grandfather. Kitchen. Pool of blood under him."

Hively pointed to the picture on the mantel. "This guy?"

Sturges stepped over and looked. "Yeah, that's him."

The two detectives cleared the back hallway, bathroom, and three bedrooms. The only visual evidence back there was smudges of blood on the floor of the bathroom, the edge of the toilet seat, and the rim of the sink.

Sturges called in the cavalry, put out a BOLO on Ephraim, Caleb, and the Ford Ranger. Hively alerted the sheriff's deputies as to what was going on, posted them at the front of the house, and gave them a list of the people who were and were not allowed to enter the crime scene. "Only that list. Everybody goes in and out through the front door. Nobody is permitted to enter in the back or the door off the kitchen."

Inside, Sturges had his phone out and was videoing a walk-through of the house, noting the time they arrived at the residence, and reciting their actions step by step. When he was done, he packed his phone away and found Hively in the kitchen, sifting through the victim's pockets.

"Found a lottery ticket on the coffee table in here," Sturges said. "Wouldn't that be something if it's a winner?"

Hively turned out the last of the pockets, empty like the rest. "Yeah," he said distractedly. He stood and started picking through the dirty dishes in the sink.

"So where the fuck you think Rivers and his kid are?" Sturges asked.

"Nowhere good, I'll tell you that."

"You don't think Rivers would have killed his own dad, do you?"

"I don't know what to think."

Sturges tipped his head slightly and grimaced. "Stenders don't typically leave their bodies behind. Not their MO."

"No," Hively agreed. "They don't." He opened the trash can and peered in. "How many more bodies you think are gonna turn up before this thing's all said and done?"

"Hard to say," Sturges replied. "Been a long time since I've seen something spilled out in so many directions."

"Yeah."

When the techs arrived, Hively cleared out to give them space to work. He stood at the railing of the porch and took in the scenery. It was by no means spectacular—the rooftops of the houses below, the state road at the bottom of the hill, then the woods on the other side, a few scattered double-wides over there. In the distance to the left was a lumberyard. To the right an auto body shop, junked cars scattered all around it. Nevertheless, it was the view Darrell Rivers had probably gazed out on every day of his life, and would never do so again.

An ambulance came silently down 75 and turned up the hill. At the same time, Sturges came hurrying out of the house, phone pressed to his ear. "Yes, sir. We're getting in the car now. You're gonna need to send somebody here to hold this down." Then, after a moment, "I don't know, sir. There's obviously a lot of moving parts to this thing." Sturges cut the call and struck a curious expression.

"What gives?" Hively asked.

"Billy Horseman just called in from Bismark Carbon. You're never gonna believe this."

CHAPTER THIRTY
DELIVERANCE

It took Ephraim ten minutes to make it to the road. He was moving slow. In that time, no more cars had motored by. It was a country road; not many cars traveled it to begin with. Particularly on a Saturday or Sunday. And now he had to make a decision. Wait for a car to come by, for who knows how long, or set off down the tracks for Bismark Carbon. The sky was clear and blue and from where he stood the vaporous clouds rising from the stacks of the plant could be seen above the treetops.

If he could bear the pain, he thought, he could make it. Besides that, something inside told him that to stop was to die, to move was to live. Or at least to fight, to not give in. He shuffled along on the berm of the road, his feet never fully lifting from the ground, both hands clutching at the hole in his stomach. He passed the dark stain in the road where the cow had been struck by the car and killed. Where was that car now, he wondered, when he needed it?

It felt as though all his life was leaking through his fingers—his memories, every pleasure he'd ever experienced, whatever small imprint he'd made on this world, with every pulse, steadily vanishing from his veins. It was as though, if he were unable to replenish this blood that slipped so smoothly from his body, he would be wiped clean from the annals of history. Subtracted from existence. But with that, so too would the petty grievances be gone. The sins vanquished, the relentless toll of living. All the mistakes.

Twice Ephraim went to his knees. Once when he tripped over a chunk of broken pavement that he did not see, another when his legs simply crumpled beneath him. Both times, he wobbled back to his feet and forged ahead. Above him there was a disturbance in the trees, and he looked up to see a large flock of birds depart one of the tall oaks—so many at once they seemed to form a type of avian ceiling across the sky. Then he saw what had agitated the birds. Three vultures glided above the treetops like the heralds of death they were.

"Fuck you. Go away," Ephraim said. The buzzards paid him no mind. One swooped low to get a closer look at the cuisine.

Then his legs seemed to no longer work and he tumbled forward, skinning his hands and forearms on the roadside. As before, Ephraim tried to stand, but this time found that he couldn't. The tracks were not that far away now. He could see the crossing up ahead. He began to crawl, one elbow after the other, but his arms gave out and he plowed face-first into the rough ground.

Ephraim rolled onto his back. A tide of numbness washed over him, taking away the pain. *So this is dying,* he thought. It wasn't like they said it would be. The history of his life didn't unspool in his mind's eye. No long-forgotten memory sparked in the fading synapses of his brain.

He dug his fingers into the soil beneath him, as though he might be able to fasten himself to the physical world, stay a bit longer. But soon his hands lost their strength, and he let go.

The boundaries fell away. Yellow and red and orange leaves floated down from the branches above, danced on the breeze. Overhead, magnificent cumulus clouds sailed across a matte of cerulean sky. The bright sun came out for a wink before slipping back behind the shroud.

This was the place.

The buzzards planed down to land on the grassy knoll between the trees and the roadside, and from there they crept, in that peculiar way they tiptoe atop their talons, ever so careful, toward him. As Ephraim's vision began to winnow in from the edges, a single, vivid thought clung to the slipstream of his consciousness—that maybe he'd get to visit Caleb for a moment, however brief, before he went to wherever the dead go.

An hour and a half prior, Verbals was sitting in the living room and watching the little hand on the grandfather clock strike eight. The Westminster chime sounded, and he checked his phone. Nothing. The conversation with the kid had stalled, so he'd turned the TV on and flipped through the channels until he found a cartoon, *Sponge-Bob SquarePants*. The kid was relaxed now, staring placidly at the screen, even giggling from time to time. Verbals's eyes flicked between the kid and the clock. He waited for fifteen minutes, and then another fifteen, and by 8:30 he could wait no more. He grabbed his gun and stood. The kid saw the gun, the nervy look on Verbals's face, and started to cry.

"Please don't kill me," Caleb begged.

Verbals stood motionless for a beat, like he'd been put in some kind of trance. "Wait here," he said finally.

"For what?"

"Just don't get out of that chair, or else."

"Or else what?"

Verbals held up the gun. "Don't play dumb, kid."

"Okay."

Verbals walked over and yanked the wire to the cordless phone from the wall. "Any other phones in here?"

Caleb shook his head.

Verbals went out of the house. In his absence, Caleb was too terrified to move a muscle. Two minutes later Verbals came back in and said, "Let's go."

He led Caleb out to the carport and ordered him to get into the dark-green Silverado parked there. The kid obeyed, climbed in, and buckled his seat belt. Verbals found a radio station and they drove along 75 listening to a throwback block of eighties music, Phil Collins and Peter Gabriel and the like. Just before they got to the I-64 on-ramp, Verbals turned into the parking lot for Harold's Diner. He pulled to the curb and turned off the radio, left the motor running.

"Listen, kid, I'm sorry about all this. I know you're young, but what I'm about to say to you is very important, and I need you to hear me and do exactly what I tell you."

"Okay," Caleb muttered.

"There are going to be people that come and ask you what I look like, if you heard my name, and they're going to ask the same things about the guys that were with me."

"You mean like policemen?"

"No like about it, that's exactly who we're talking about. Listen to me now, you cannot tell them anything. Not one thing, you understand? Say you don't remember, say you were blindfolded, say I was fat and had long red hair. Say whatever you have to say, okay. Not word one about these tattoos on my neck either, got it?"

"Yeah."

"They might show you pictures and ask you to identify us. You do not identify us. You say no to every picture they put in front of you. Because if you don't, if you tell them what we look like, what names you heard us call each other, anything, and I mean anything, someone will come and kill you. Do you understand me? Don't cry, I'm not trying to make you upset. I'm trying to save your life here, kid. That's just the way it is, okay? Someone will come for you, and I won't be able to stop them. Do you understand?"

Caleb nodded.

"You do what I say and you'll be fine. Stop crying. Crying's not gonna change anything."

Caleb wiped his eyes and held his breath to ward off further tears.

"Okay. What do I look like?"

"I never—" Caleb hiccupped. "I never saw you. I was blindfolded."

"Good. What's my name?"

"You never said."

"What do I sound like?"

"Like everybody sounds. Like normal."

Verbals reached over and tousled Caleb's hair. Caleb shirked from the touch. "You're gonna be all right, kid. Remember what I said. Get through school, watch out for the girls."

Caleb sniffled. "Okay."

"Now get outta here."

Verbals reached across the cab and pushed the door open. Caleb slid down from the truck and stood on the curb as it drove away, its exhaust stinking in his nose. For the rest of his life, every time he caught a whiff of that kind of fume, this moment would come to him.

The bell on the door jingled when he entered the diner. The place was busy with its Saturday-morning rush. Lucia was there, waiting on a table in the corner, her back turned. Another of the waitresses, a stout little woman with a built-in air of dissatisfaction, gave him the customary "Welcome to Harold's" greeting, no enthusiasm behind it.

He and his father's booth was empty. He scooted into the side he always sat in, his back to the entrance, and buried his head in his hands. Twice the bell jingled with the door opening, and with each ring Caleb twisted around expectantly, but neither time was it his father.

The squat waitress came over. "Hello, young man . . . Oh, what's the matter?"

"Nothing," Caleb said, though his eyes were burning and his face was wet and he knew how he must look. "Can Lucia be my waitress?"

"Sure, sweetheart. Is everything okay? Are you here alone?"

"I'm waiting for my dad."

"Okay, is he parking the car?"

Caleb didn't respond. The woman went off to fetch Lucia. Caleb crooked his neck and watched her go. When Lucia finished taking an order, the woman pulled her aside and whispered something in her ear, gesturing toward his booth. Lucia looked over at Caleb with a mixed expression, happy yet puzzled. She walked briskly down the aisle.

"Hey, sweetheart, are you okay?"

Caleb nodded dimly.

"Why are you crying?"

"I'm not."

"Where's your dad?"

Caleb shrugged. "I'm supposed to meet him here."

"Oh, okay." Lucia tamped down her worry, forced a tight smile. "How did you get here?"

"I got dropped off."

"By who, sweetie?"

"I don't know. A man."

"Okay, I'm gonna call your dad, okay?"

"I don't think he has his phone," Caleb said. "Can I have some juice?"

"Sure, baby. I'll get that for you in just one sec."

Lucia headed for the hallway in the back that led to the bathrooms. On her way, a customer flagged her down for a refill of coffee. The bell jingled, and Caleb turned around. It still wasn't his father. It was just some family.

"Welcome to Harold's," someone said.

CHAPTER THIRTY-ONE
DOUBLE THE ANGELS

Hively was speeding so fast down Greasy Ridge they almost missed him.

"Stop the car," Sturges yelled.

"What?"

"Stop the car. That was a damned body in the ditch back there."

Hively slammed on the brakes, threw the Caprice into reverse, and steered it backward until they arrived where Ephraim lay. By the amount of blood pooled around him and the way his mouth hung slack, they thought he was dead for sure, but there were still some shallow breaths moving in and out, and his eyes tracked them as they approached. Sturges immediately tried to raise somebody on the phone and found there was no service.

"Shit. I'm gonna run down to the crossing to see if I can get a signal."

Hively knelt down next to Ephraim. "Can you talk?"

It took Ephraim a moment to work his mouth around a word.

"Yeah," he croaked.

"Who shot you?"

"Mo—Momo."

"Are they still out here?" Hively asked. Ephraim's eyes rolled into his head, and Hively gripped his face and slapped it a little until the eyes came back. "Are the Stenders still here?"

"All dead," Ephraim said.

Sturges came trotting back, out of breath. "Staties are on their way. EMTs won't be here for twenty."

"Twenty?"

"That's what they said."

"We can get him to Kyova Hospital faster." Hively ran over and opened the back door of the Caprice.

"You think it's safe to move him?" Sturges asked.

"We don't have a choice."

Hively bent down and explained to Ephraim what they were about to do, then grabbed hold under his arms. Sturges got him by the legs, and they lifted him up and eased him into the back seat. They folded his legs in and made sure not to shut the door on his feet, then got in the car. Hively turned it around, flipped on the siren, and took off down the road. As they thudded over the rails of the crossing, Ephraim groaned.

Sturges twisted around and looked at him. "Hang in there, Rivers. We're gonna get you some help real fast. Just hang in there."

"Harold's," Ephraim panted.

"What's that?"

"Harold's," Ephraim repeated. "The diner. I have to go there."

"You're not going anywhere except the hospital, pal. If it's your kid you're worried about, you can rest easy, he's fine. We've already had him picked up."

The way Ephraim was lying he could see up through the back window where it curved over. The vultures were sailing directly above the Caprice, as if there were some invisible string tethered between him and them. He was able to take in one deep breath, which he let out nice and slow, and then he closed his eyes.

The hospital room was dim, though the light coming in at the edges of the curtains was quite bright. In a chair next to the bed, a security officer sat playing some game on his phone, the faint electronic sound effects dinging like a slot machine. Quiet except for that.

"Who are you?" said Ephraim, the words coming out thick.

The security officer startled and sat up straight. "Oh, you're awake."

"Seems so."

The man scuttled out of the room, and soon a phalanx of doctors came in to review Ephraim's vitals and evaluate his wound. A large incision stretched from beneath his nipple to down over his ribs and belly. A thick wire was sewn in and holding everything together. The doctors asked him a bunch of banal questions to determine his mental state. They described in medical terms the trauma his body had suffered, and the multitude of procedures they'd had to perform in order to preserve his life: Where they'd dug the bullet out of. How close it'd come to hitting seven different things that would have killed him.

He'd been in an induced coma since he'd arrived to the hospital, some twenty-six hours ago, and came out of it faster than they'd anticipated.

"Where's my son?" Ephraim asked.

All the doctors' heads turned and looked at the oldest man in the room, who'd introduced himself at the start, but whose name had gone in one ear and out the other.

"I'm sorry," one of the doctors hedged. "We don't have that information. The police wanted to be the first people to speak with you, once you were awake. They should have your answers. They're on their way now."

When Hively and Sturges arrived, the doctors filed out. Ephraim inclined his bed and sat up stiffly. The detectives gave their condolences for Ephraim's father, then pulled two chairs over to the bedside.

"Good to see you lucid," Sturges said. "After you zonked out in the car, we had it at five to one you wouldn't make it."

"Yeah, who lost?"

Hively hiked a thumb at his partner. "He owes me a tenner. I'll split the winnings with you."

"Sure. Drop it on the table before you leave," Ephraim said. "Suppose I should thank the two of you for saving my life."

Sturges shrugged. "Tell you the truth, we got lucky to spot you on the side of that road there. Almost mistook you for roadkill."

Ephraim cut past the pleasantries. "You guys charging me with something or what?"

"Not yet," said Hively, nice and blunt. "It took us quite some time to find Momo and Buddy Cleamons in that cave. You're going to need to explain how they came to be there. And I mean every little detail, back to the beginning. Back to when Rodney Slash showed up at Bismark that night. No more lies, got it? You lie to us again, we'll lock you to that bed until you're well enough to be transported to the jail."

Sturges dialed back the rhetoric. "Look, we know you're not affiliated with the Stenders. You've got no record to speak of beyond a drunk and disorderly a few years back. I don't know—maybe you lost yourself there for a minute. It'd be understandable, with such extenuating circumstances. We just need to understand how it all went down, you see."

"Tell you what," Ephraim said. "You bring my son to me right now, and I'll give you the whole thing, from that night on, like you say. Otherwise, I'm not telling you jack shit."

"Relax," said Hively. "We got somebody bringing him here now. The sooner you talk, the sooner you see him."

"Where's he been this whole time?" Ephraim asked.

"We had to keep him in a CPS facility overnight. Protocol in this type of situation. He wanted to stay with your girlfriend—what's her name?"

"Lucia."

"Everything goes well here today, maybe we can arrange for that tonight. With your permission, of course."

"And he's okay?" Ephraim asked.

Hively, understanding what he meant, gave a nod in the affirmative. "They told us there was a little incident last night when they tried to feed him, where he kinda lashed out, but they said he calmed down after that and has been okay since."

Ephraim repositioned himself on the bed, wincing at the soreness throughout his entire body. He breathed and waited for the pain to pass, then settled in and told his tale. For the most part, he stuck to the facts, recounting the events as they had actually transpired, from Rodney showing up and holding him at gunpoint, forcing Ephraim to aid him against his will, to being captured by the Stenders and their demand to take them to the money.

Ephraim only massaged the story in two key areas. He told them Rodney Slash didn't die at Bismark Carbon. That he had been alive until they'd made it to the Mercer farm early that next morning. And knowing he had to account for the presence of his wrecked truck in the irrigation ditch, he lied about when the Stenders had captured him, saying it was not the morning the detectives had found him shot on the side of the road, but the previous night. He concocted an elaborate story about how they'd caught him on his way to work; blocked the road; and, believing he knew where the money was, forced him to take them to it. He described how he was able to get away from the Stenders in the dark of the woods, get to his car, the ensuing chase and crash in the ditch, and his eventual escape to Bismark on foot. How, after he'd talked Billy into lending him his Silverado, he'd planned to pick up his family and skip town. But the Stenders had been waiting for him at the house, where they murdered his father, then dragged him back to the farm to look for the money.

The detectives did their best to trip Ephraim up with the details they knew. Hively asked why he'd followed the Lincoln's tire tracks so deliberately, only to then throw caution to the wind and strike out across the pasture to the woods. Ephraim acquitted himself well, laced enough truth into all his answers to make them plausible.

"Followed the tracks just to find the car. Then when Rodney died, I thought I heard a tractor or something coming our way, didn't want to be seen, so I tore out of there. Hid the truck in the closest place I could find. Nothing came though, so after a while I risked coming on out. Made it back to Greasy Ridge without incident." Ephraim shrugged. "Went and took my son to school."

"Just like that, back to normal?"

"What else was I gonna do?"

"Were you late getting to school?"

Ephraim hemmed, "Ahh, I dunno know about that day. Caleb's hard to get going sometimes, so we've been late quite a bit, but I don't know about that day."

Sturges asked, "So you didn't know what Slash was after when he enlisted you to drive him back to the Mercer farm?"

"Wouldn't say that I enlisted in anything. He had a gun pointed at me the whole time. But no, all he said was he'd forgotten something important and wanted me to take him to it. That was it. I helped lower him into that ditch, and he started to climb into the car but was too hurt to do it. Just kinda keeled over right there on the spot."

"You knew he was dead?" Hively asked.

"I mean, I thought it was a pretty safe assumption."

"Why didn't you call the police right then, soon as he died?"

"I thought about it, but like I told you, he had warned me earlier that if I called the cops, I'd be in danger. Kinda alluded that cops were a part of it somehow, or maybe, you know, with what I know now, if the cops found out, that'd mean the Stenders would find out. I just wanted no part of it. Like I was never there. Then when I saw what'd happened on the news, tell you the truth I was glad I hadn't called you guys."

"Why the bike ride?" said Hively.

"Why the what?"

"The bike ride. The guys in your maintenance shop said you stole one of their bikes around 6:00 a.m. You said Rodney showed up at 1:30 or thereabouts. You were obviously free of him at that time; we saw it on the security footage. Why didn't you call the police then?"

Ephraim claimed that Rodney had his wallet, knew where he lived, saw the picture of his son in there, and threatened to kill Caleb if Ephraim even entertained the idea to rat him out. "He couldn't really walk at that point, so that's how I got him out of there. Biked him to the back of our access road. I was just trying to do what I had to do and get it over and done with, you know."

"Didn't really work out for you in the end, did it, not calling us?" Hively asked.

"No." Ephraim eyed him coolly. "I reckon not. Course, if you guys wouldn't have zeroed in on me, the Stenders may have never come a'knockin', and my dad might still be alive, so maybe I was right not to call you."

"You might be right," Hively admitted. "But after you escaped from them and trekked all that way to Bismark, when you borrowed your buddy's truck. Why not then? I'd think after all that, you'd finally come to your senses, try to get under the law's protection."

Ephraim scoffed. "Man, all I could think about at that point was getting to my family and putting as much distance between us and Cain City as I possibly could. Just drive straight through until I hit an ocean. Far away as I could get."

"But they were waiting for you, you say," Sturges offered. "Beat you to it."

Ephraim nodded gravely. "Wouldn't have mattered none if I called y'all then anyways. Everything still woulda happened the way it did. Coulda been worse."

"Maybe, but we'll never know for certain, will we?" Hively said.

"I reckon not."

The detectives grilled him about the whereabouts of the missing money, skeptical of his claim that he had no clue where it was, or who might have it.

"I couldn't give two shits about that money," Ephraim said.

"Tell us again how it was exactly you ended up in that cave," Sturges said.

Stroke of luck, Ephraim told them. He was leading Momo and Buddy The Face through the woods, stalling the inevitable, when they'd happened upon it. "I was looking for some way out of the whole mess. Thought that cave might give me a fighting chance. Was able to get a hold of that rock. Started swinging, they started shooting." Ephraim shrugged. "Next thing I knew you guys were standing over me."

"Stroke of luck," Hively repeated.

The security officer came in and announced that Caleb had arrived and was waiting to come in. Hively and Sturges stood to leave, said they'd be in touch if they had more questions. Sturges warned Ephraim that the Stenders were a vindictive lot, and while he was pretty sure they would seek their revenge elsewhere—namely, the East End of Cain City—he advised Ephraim to be careful of them in the future.

"Will do," Ephraim assured him.

Before they left, Hively commented offhand, "Oh, I almost forgot. I had a good chat with your girlfriend yesterday."

"Oh, yeah?"

Hively smiled wryly. "Yeah. She's a nice lady. Cares about you. But just so you know, we'll be watching to make sure you don't have any big expenditures that might need explaining. Say, a trip to Italy or something like that."

A wisp of a smile edged onto Ephraim's lips. "Shit," he said. "I don't even have a passport."

The detectives walked down the hospital's corridor and stepped onto the elevator. When the doors shut, Sturges said, "In all that, what do you think was the big truth, and what were the lies?"

"Couldn't tell ya," Hively answered. "Couldn't separate them if I tried."

"Yep. Me neither."

Caleb ran into the room and nearly jumped onto Ephraim, wrapping his arms hard around his father's neck.

"Whoa, easy now," Ephraim said. "It's okay. I'm here. I'm right here."

They embraced for a good while before pulling back and looking at one another. Caleb's complexion was very pale and his eyes were ringed with dark circles. His cheeks were wet with crying. Ephraim bit back his own tears and rubbed his son's face dry.

"You look peaked," Ephraim said. "Have you been eating?"

"A little."

"You gotta eat more than a little, Caleb."

"You're one to talk," Caleb said. "Your face looks like somebody painted it purple with a hammer."

"Well, I got beat up. What's your excuse?"

Caleb looked at his father solemnly. "Are those men going to come back?"

"No, that's all over now." Ephraim clinched his son's head and kissed it. "That's never gonna happen again. I'm so sorry, Caleb. I'm so sorry for everything."

"I'm okay, Dad."

"I know you are," Ephraim said. "I know you are. But listen, I gotta tell you something. It's something real sad, okay?"

"Is Grandpa dead?"

The way Caleb said it, so matter-of-fact, made Ephraim's mouth go dry. "Yes, he is."

Caleb backed out of his father's clinch and looked down at the floor for a long time. At last he said, "Is it your fault?"

"Yes, it is, son. It is my fault. But he didn't die for nothing. Grandpa died so that we could live. So that we could still be together. And now, Caleb—you know how he always said Gramma was up there looking down on us, like a guardian angel?"

Caleb cast a dubious glare on his father. "You said you didn't believe in any of that stuff."

"Well maybe I was wrong. To be honest, I don't see how I could have survived any other way. Maybe I was always wrong. And now Grandpa is with her. You know what that means? Means we've got double the angels up there looking out for us."

"That sounds good," Caleb said.

"You bet it does."

A nurse entered the room carrying a tray with Jell-O, applesauce, and a cup of water. They needed him to take it slow until they were sure he could hold down food. All Ephraim wanted to know was when he could get the damned catheter out of his urethra. The nurse informed him that wouldn't be possible until he could make it to the bathroom on his own power.

"Well," he retorted, "let's give her a go now."

That afternoon Lucia came for a visit, brought takeout from the diner so that Caleb had something he would eat, and stayed until she had to go to work. Ephraim assured her he'd had nothing to do with the whole escapade, that he was just the guy who happened to be in the wrong place at the wrong time, and there was nothing left to fear.

"Maybe we can sell my house," he said to her. "Buy a place of our own."

"That's the pain meds talking," she deflected. But he could tell she liked the idea, or at least that he'd thrown it out there. "You say all the right words, don't you, Ephraim?"

"'Bout half the time."

Later he rang Billy to apologize about the Silverado. Lucia'd told him the police had found the truck's carcass down behind an old warehouse near the river, its insides melted away from where someone set it on fire. Billy didn't pick up, so he left a voice mail. He also called Bismark Carbon to gauge whether or not he might still have a job. The brass was noncommittal. They pawned any serious discussion off to another day, saying only that there were quite a few things that needed to be sorted out, and they wished him well in his recovery.

Caleb refused to leave his father's room, so the hospital accommodated them, rolling in a cot they set up next to the bed. In the evening, the baseball playoffs came on, and Caleb lay next to his father, on his unhurt side, watching the game. It was a back-and-forth affair that went into extras and didn't end until after eleven. The hospital had provided a disposable toothbrush and pocket toothpaste and Caleb took them into the bathroom to get ready for bed.

"Don't use all the toothpaste," Ephraim told him. "That's all we've got."

"They can just give us more," Caleb sassed.

"Just don't use it all, please."

"I won't, Dad. Gosh."

When Caleb was done, he turned the lights out, clambered onto the springy cot and tossed around, trying to get comfortable. The two of them lay there in the darkness of the foreign room, unable to fall asleep. The nurse's station was close by and their shuffling around, their low murmurs, the wet *thwop* of the janitor mopping in the hallway, these sounds were amplified in the quiet.

"Dad?" Caleb said, hushed, as if someone might hear. "Are you awake?"

"Yeah, bud."

"You ever gonna tell me what really happened?"

Ephraim hesitated. "Sure I will. Not tonight though, okay?"

"Okay . . . Dad?"

"Yep."

"Are we still gonna get a dog?"

"You bet we are. Turbo, right?"

"Uh-huh."

"Turbo the beagle. Once I heal up, buddy, we're gonna do a lot of things. Tomorrow I'm gonna call your doctor, and we're gonna get you feeling better, that's number one. That's the first thing. And then you know what I'd love to do? I'd love to go on a hike with you."

"A hike?"

"Yeah. I found this great spot. You wouldn't believe me if I told you."

"Believe what?"

"It's where the rainbow ends."

"Not this again," Caleb said, a note of irritation in his voice. "I know that stuff's not real, Dad. I'm not five years old."

"I swear it, Caleb," Ephraim said. "Just you wait. It's there. You'll see. It's there."

ACKNOWLEDGEMENTS

For many reasons, this book will always hold a special place in my heart. Thank you to my agent, Renée C. Fountain, for being the perfect partner on this mad journey of stringing words together seven at a time. To Steve Feldberg, for going above and beyond as an advocate of these books. Many thanks to Otto Penzler and the folks at MysteriousPress.com. To Shawn Hale, who helped me to understand the ins and outs of factory work, as well as sharing a few workplace anecdotes that made this story all the more rich. Once again, to my first eyes, Kate Martin and Cat O'Connor, I breathe easier knowing you are there to catch me if I fall.

And a special thank you to my family, Chandra, Charlie, Calvin, and Quincy, with all the love in the world.

ABOUT THE AUTHOR

Jonathan Fredrick is the author of the Cain City Novels, which were inspired in-part by his hometown of Huntington, West Virginia. After working in Los Angeles as a writer, filmmaker, and actor for more than fifteen years, Fredrick now resides in Columbus, Ohio, with his wife and three sons.

THE CAIN CITY NOVELS

FROM MYSTERIOUSPRESS.COM
AND OPEN ROAD MEDIA

  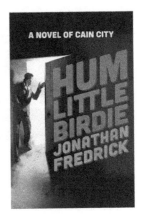

MYSTERIOUSPRESS.COM

THE MYSTERIOUS BOOKSHOP, founded in 1979, is located in Manhattan's Tribeca neighborhood. It is the oldest and largest mystery-specialty bookstore in America.

The shop stocks the finest selection of new mystery hardcovers, paperbacks, and periodicals. It also features a superb collection of signed modern first editions, rare and collectable works, and Sherlock Holmes titles. The bookshop issues a free monthly newsletter highlighting its book clubs, new releases, events, and recently acquired books.

58 Warren Street
info@mysteriousbookshop.com
(212) 587-1011
Monday through Saturday
11:00 a.m. to 7:00 p.m.

FIND OUT MORE AT:

www.mysteriousbookshop.com

FOLLOW US:

@TheMysterious and Facebook.com/MysteriousBookshop

INTEGRATED MEDIA

Find a full list of our authors and
titles at www.openroadmedia.com

FOLLOW US
@OpenRoadMedia